THE HEART OF CHAOS

URSULA SCHEK AND her Sigmarite army have ravaged the Norscan realms in search of her former lover, Kurt Leitzig. But months of raiding have decimated their supplies and Ursula is forced to return to the Empire to restock and seek new allies to aid her in her hunt. Meanwhile, Kurt leads his band of warriors north into the Chaos Wastes, battling to achieve his ultimate goal – ascension to daemonhood and immortality!

Also by Gav Thorpe

A WARHAMMER NOVEL

Slaves to Darkness · Book Three

THE HEART OF CHAOS

GAV THORPE

*Dedicated to the Slave to Darkness that exists within
each of us.*

A BLACK LIBRARY PUBLICATION

First published in Great Britain in 2004 by
BL Publishing,
Games Workshop Ltd.,
Willow Road, Nottingham,
NG7 2WS, UK

10 9 8 7 6 5 4 3 2 1

Cover illustration by Adrian Smith.
Map by Nuala Kennedy.

A CIP record for this book is available from the British Library.

ISBN 1 84416 114 5

Distributed in the US by Simon & Schuster
1230 Avenue of the Americas, New York, NY 10020, US.

Printed and bound in Great Britain by
Bookmarque Ltd, Croydon, Surrey, UK.

See the Black Library on the Internet at
www.blacklibrary.com

Find out more about Games Workshop
and the world of Warhammer at
www.games-workshop.com

THIS IS A DARK age, a bloody age, an age of daemons and of sorcery. It is an age of battle and death, and of the world's ending. Amidst all of the fire, flame and fury it is a time, too, of mighty heroes, of bold deeds and great courage.

AT THE HEART of the Old World sprawls the Empire, the largest and most powerful of the human realms. Known for its engineers, sorcerers, traders and soldiers, it is a land of great mountains, mighty rivers, dark forests and vast cities. And from his throne in Altdorf reigns the Emperor Karl-Franz, sacred descendant of the founder of these lands, Sigmar, and wielder of his magical warhammer.

BUT THESE ARE far from civilised times. Across the length and breadth of the Old World, from the knightly palaces of Bretonnia to ice-bound Kislev in the far north, come rumblings of war. In the towering World's Edge Mountains, the orc tribes are gathering for another assault. Bandits and renegades harry the wild southern lands of the Border Princes. There are rumours of rat-things, the skaven, emerging from the sewers and swamps across the land. And from the northern wildernesses there is the ever-present threat of Chaos, of daemons and beastmen corrupted by the foul powers of the Dark Gods. As the time of battle draws ever near, the Empire needs heroes like never before.

THE HEART OF CHAOS

North of Here Lie The
Dreaded Chaos Wastes.

f Claus

Erengrad.

Here Be Trolls...

Praag.

Middle Mountains.

Kislev

Kislev.

enheim.

Wolfenburg.

Talabheim

The Empire

Altdorf.

Karak Kad

Nuln.

The
Moot.

Sylvania.
Dracken
-hof.

Zhufbar.

Averheim.

Black
Water.

Black Fire Pass.

arak
Norn.

Author's Note

THE EVENTS OF this book took place during a time of great strife and upheaval in the lands known as the Empire. Following the death of Emperor Mandred at the hands of inhuman assassins, the states of the Empire could not elect a new ruler, and war broke out between several Imperial provinces. This continued for several hundred years, and the period in which the following events took place was known as the Time of Three Emperors, when three of the provincial elector counts had declared themselves rightful Emperor – Stirland, Talabecland and the city state of Middenheim. Assailed from outside and divided within, the Empire is all but shattered, the once united states now operating as separate nations. Suspicion and politicking are the rule of the day in the Imperial courts, while the people try to eke out a living amidst the ruins of the former Empire. Anarchy prevails, brigands roam the wilds, vile beastmen

11

stalk the forest roads and the once cosmopolitan people of the Empire have become introverted and parochial. With the rulers of the elector states bickering, towns and villages are left to defend themselves, and the purges of orcs, mutants, skaven and other foul creatures have fallen by the wayside, allowing much of the realm to be overrun. Centuries before the founding of the colleges of magic, all magic is outlawed. Yet the line between divine intervention and sorcery is a matter of perspective, and the populace is terrified by the arcane forces that rule their world and are yet beyond their grasp.

All dates are in the Imperial calendar, dated from the crowning of Sigmar as the first Emperor.

BOOK ONE

CHAPTER ONE
Fatigue
Faeringhold, Norscan coast, Early winter 1711

RUPRECHT TRIED TO blot out the screaming, instead focussing his attention on the crackling of flames. Smoke billowed up in thick clouds from the burning thatch roofs and wooden buildings of the village, the fumes tinged with a stench that he had come to know all too well – burning flesh. In his many years as henchman to the witch hunter Marius van Diesl, he had become used to the smell. The smell of a hot iron on flesh, and of warlocks and witches tied to their stakes.

Seventeen other settlements had fallen to the wrath of the Imperial force in the preceding weeks as they had battled their way along the coast of Norsca. It was a well-practiced drill now. First the ships would bombard the shore, and then, when the Norse were well and truly cowed, troops would land and finish them off with crossbows and spears. After that the buildings were put to the torch, any livestock taken for supplies. It was military efficiency of the highest order.

Today was the first time Ruprecht had become sickened by it. Ursula noticed the distasteful expression crossing his rugged, bearded face.

'They're animals,' she said. 'It's a cull. Nothing more. Give them no more thought than you would a slain wolf or slaughtered ox.'

Ruprecht didn't reply as he turned and looked down at the young woman who was seated on a felled log, scuffing the snow with the heel of her leather boot. Her bronzed hair blowing in the cold Norscan wind reminded him of the flames behind him.

'They could run,' she added, gazing past her burly comrade. 'They have plenty of warning.'

'They stay to protect their homes, their livestock,' Ruprecht said, slumping down beside her and causing the log to shift. 'You cannot blame them for that.'

'No,' said Ursula, her expression hardening further. 'And the people who stay to protect their homes when they see the longships, the men who fight to stop their wives and daughters being raped and murdered, did they receive mercy?'

'You cannot fight darkness with darkness,' Ruprecht said with a sigh.

'What is the matter with you, old bear?' Ursula said, punching him softly on his arm. 'You have woken up with a grumpy head for the last three days.'

'I'm tired,' he said softly. 'Four months we've raided up and down this coast. Four months of fire and blood. I've had a lifetime of it, and now I'm just very tired.'

Ursula laid an arm across his broad shoulders and nestled her cheek into the deep furred collar of his cloak. She could understand his weariness, his reluctance. A year ago she had felt the same, living a hermit's existence in the marshes around Marienburg. She had been devastated by betrayal; her first love had turned his back on her and embraced the Dark Gods. Her life had seemed empty, pointless, and it had taken a sign from the gods themselves to stir her from her self-loathing and misery. Ruprecht had stayed by her through those bad times, and he would stay by her through these trials as well.

'Come on, grumpy bear. Let's find Leerdamme,' she said, standing up.

Ruprecht raised himself slowly, his knees cracking as they straightened. Ursula couldn't stop herself giggling and the tall warrior gave her a mock hurt look.

'I'm not that old,' he protested, but Ursula couldn't fail to notice the more genuine wince that followed. Ruprecht rubbed his hand along his left arm, turning away slightly so that Ursula couldn't see.

'Is it troubling you?' she asked, stepping around and grabbing his left hand. It was made of metal; an intricate machine fashioned by the dwarfs and imbued with rune magic. Ruprecht flexed the fingers, which squeaked slightly.

'You need oiling,' said Ursula.

'All the oil we have left is needed for the lamps,' said Ruprecht, gently pulling his hand away. 'Anyway, it's the cold that hurts, not stiffness. It's like rivers of ice up my veins.'

He looked over the burning village as another roof was engulfed by the blaze and wondered how he could be cold with so much fire to warm him. It was a chill he felt in his soul.

'DO YOU HEAR that?' asked Edouard Leerdamme, his weary face turned towards the hills to the north that overlooked the smoking ruins of the Norse village nestled between the steep hills at the mouth of the fjord. The four months of sailing and fighting had left him haggard, his chin and cheeks bristled with greying stubble. He stood on the shale shore watching boats taking pillaged supplies back to the seven ships moored in the icy waters of the fjord.

'I can't hear anything,' said Ruprecht, seated on a crate beside the ship's captain, his attention focussed on the mechanical hand that was fixed to the stump of his left forearm. 'Do you think it's going to get any colder?'

This time Ruprecht heard it too – a distant percussion, like a drumbeat. Beside him, Ursula stood up, turning to the north as well, her hand unconsciously straying to the hilt of the long sword that hung at her hip. Around them the soldiers, knights and sailors of their small expeditionary force began to gather, glancing at each other for confirmation or exchanging worried glances.

The drumming was definitely getting louder.

'Johannes,' Ursula called to one of the knights as he passed, the armour of the handsome young man slicked with soot from the burning huts that were clustered along the craggy coastline. Hearing her voice, he turned, a look of expectation on his face.

'Yes?' he said.

'Take Boerden and ride up to the hills to see what is happening,' Ursula told him. With a quick nod Johannes turned away, calling for his fellow knight and his squire.

'What do you think it could be?' asked Leerdamme. 'More Norse?'

'It's been three weeks since the last big fight,' said Ruprecht, grunting as he pushed himself to his feet. 'With those damned longships shadowing us all the time, every village along the coast probably knows where we are now. It was only a matter of time before they came in numbers against us.'

'If it is, we'll send them running like the others,' said Ursula, sweeping stray strands of auburn hair back into place under her leather headband. 'It will save us the trouble of hunting them down, at least.'

Ruprecht and Leerdamme exchanged a glance, which Ursula noticed.

'What?' she said with a frown.

'Well,' started Leerdamme and then fell silent, looking to Ruprecht as his eyes avoided Ursula's.

'We're almost out of supplies,' said the burly warrior.

'We'll forage for more,' Ursula said, and turned away but was stopped by Ruprecht's good hand on her shoulder.

'Not just food, but everything,' he said.

'The ships have barely enough shot left for a broadside each,' Leerdamme explained, scratching at his chin in thought. 'We've only a thousand crossbow bolts and less than a hundred lead shot left. The knights are complaining that their horses haven't been freshly shoed in a month. Even day-to-day wear and tear on weapons, armour, even the ships, is getting harder to patch up.'

'So what are you saying?' said Ursula, eyes narrowing. 'That we just give up? We just forget the whole thing, and let these barbarians, these raiders, get back to their lives? Let them carry on burning our towns, slaughtering and enslaving our people? Sacrificing the servants of the Empire to their loathsome gods?'

'If there is a battle today, it will be our last,' said Ruprecht.

'We'll not turn back until I say so,' Ursula said, folding her arms stubbornly across her chest, her hands disappearing into the fur cloak that Johannes had salvaged from the ruins of another village several days earlier.

Leerdamme opened his mouth and then shut it again. He frowned, shook his head and then stomped away, yelling for Verhoen, his Master on the *Graf Suiden*.

Ursula's icy glare followed him as he pushed through the crowd of soldiers forming up under the shouts of the sergeants and knights.

'We'll be sailing back tomorrow, or the day after,' Ruprecht said quietly, massaging his damaged arm with his other hand. 'It'll be proper winter soon, and here in the north, it will be the death of us.'

'We'll find one of their larger settlements, use it to winter here while we build up supplies again,' said Ursula. 'We cannot let the Norse gather their strength.'

'It's winter, for Ulric's sake,' snapped Ruprecht, instantly regretting losing his temper as Ursula turned back to him and he saw the tears welling in her eyes. 'It's winter,' he continued, more softly. 'The Norse will be suffering, don't doubt that. We'll return and gather ourselves for a new venture, and come the spring thaws, we'll be ready to come back. If you insist on staying now, you'll lose the support of the knights, and they'll never come back. Take them home with victories and spoils, and they'll be with you next year. The Norse don't raid in winter, they can't. We lose nothing if we leave, but we risk everything if we stay.'

'I know!' said Ursula with a grimace, her sadness turning to anger. She dropped her voice, suddenly aware of the sailors traipsing back to their ships not far from them. 'What if the knights, now that they have had their jaunt and stretched their horses' legs, don't want to come back?'

'You struck while the iron was hot,' Ruprecht said, stepping beside her and laying a thick arm across her shoulders. He knew that there was something else that worried Ursula, though she had never voiced the fear. When they had left Marienburg, she had brought the magical sword Ulfshard with her, denying it to Count Luiten. On their return Luiten was bound to restate his claim to the heirloom of the counts of Marienburg.

'The iron is almost cold,' he continued. 'We have to return to Marienburg or we'll lose all of the support that we have. The Norse are afraid of us now, and we'll be back to ensure the memory of what happened here stays for a long time. The wolves know that the sheep has grown teeth and bitten back.'

'What about Kurt?' Ursula asked, looking up into the burly man's face. His cheeks were pinched with hunger and cold and his eyelashes tinged with ice. 'Where has he gone?'

'He's probably dead,' Ruprecht said, his voice a low growl. 'If any man deserves to be, he does. Forget about Kurt, he's history.'

The drumming was clearly audible by now, a slow double beat that reverberated from the snow-covered hills nearby. Ursula could see the mounted figures of Johannes and Boerden nearing the summit of the nearest.

'You're right,' she said. 'Even if he isn't dead, he's no threat to me now. He's just another of these barbaric scum.'

URSULA, RUPRECHT, LEERDAMME and several knights were standing close to the smouldering ruins of the village's longhouse, warming themselves against the chill, as Johannes and Boerden appeared at the edge of the village on their cantering steeds. More knights gathered at their approach, and a circle had assembled as the two dismounted, handing their reins to squires who ran forwards from the crowd.

'It's the Norse, for sure,' said Boerden, his lined face grim within the raised visor of his plumed helm. 'A lot of them.'

'They have a war beast,' panted Johannes, stepping close to Ursula. 'A hairy monster with a wooden fort upon its back, sheathed in bronze shields. Their leader rides upon a destrier of midnight black, with flames for eyes.'

There was some chuckling from a few of the knights and murmured comments.

'Shut your yapping,' snapped Boerden, rounding on the knights. 'It's true! There's five hundred warriors, if there's ten, and cavalry and chariots. These are not the old men and boys we've faced the past several weeks. They march at speed and will be here before the end of the watch.'

'They must have taken all the warriors and fallen back before us, sacrificing their homes and families to draw us on,' said Johannes, still breathless. 'Every fighter from a dozen villages is there. Prepare for battle, full battle!'

There was a pause, as the knights stayed to hear more news. Ursula stepped towards them, pulling her sword from its sheath. This was Ulfshard; the ancient elven blade forged thousands of years before, heirloom of the chieftain Marbad who fought alongside Sigmar at Black Fire Pass. In its pommel, a blue gem burned with harsh light, and its blade was wreathed in faint flames. Upon seeing the blade, the knights were stilled, their attention fixed again on Ursula.

'War is upon us once more,' she told them. 'Bring me victory in this one last fight and your duty is done. Slay the wild men this one more time, and our campaign is complete. We shall leave these desolate shores without defeat, and you can return to your lands and homes to gather your strength for the new year, when more glory awaits us. For Sigmar!'

With grunts and cheers echoing the battle cry, the knights drew their swords and held them aloft, the sharpened steel glittering in the cold winter sun. As they dispersed, shouting for their horses, calling to the sergeants and men-at-arms, Leerdamme gave Ursula a polite nod and headed off towards his ship. Boerden and Johannes remained with Ursula and Ruprecht.

'This war beast is larger than a town house,' said Johannes. 'It has great tusks that could disembowel a regiment and feet that'll crush us underfoot by the dozen. We have never fought anything like it before.'

'Will a cannon kill it?' asked Ursula.

'Several cannons, perhaps,' said Boerden, removing his helmet and tousling the sweat out of his thin, greying hair.

'Then we have nothing to fear,' said Ursula, waving her arm towards the greatship and three wolfships down in the fjord. A single rolling salvo from their small fleet was enough to crush any force they had met so far, flattening huts and obliterating longships. Today would be no different, even if they were low on shot.

'Aye, we do have plenty of cannons,' said Boerden with a grin as he looked out over the ships gradually weighing anchor and beginning to move closer in to the shore. His expression changed to one of consternation at the sound of a musket retort echoing off the steep cliffs surrounding the inlet. It was a warning shot.

At the tip of the mainmast on the *Glorious*, furthest out of the fleet to keep watch for enemy at sea, a red pennant was raised – longships were approaching. If it was simply a ship or two, then the wolfship was more than capable of holding its own while the other vessels bombarded the enemy on shore. The pennant dipped and rose indicating two ships. Then dipped again. Three ships. And again. Four ships. Ursula felt disquiet in her stomach as the warning flag dipped and rose seven times. Eight longships in total, and more than enough to swarm over the wolfships and transports. The *Graf Suiden* would be needed, but that would mean abandoning the troops on shore to deal with the horde that was by now only a couple of miles away.

'What will Leerdamme do?' Ursula asked, looking at the knights and Ruprecht.

'He'll protect the fleet, that's all he can do,' said Ruprecht. 'If we lose our ships, we are stranded here and it'll not matter whether we die in battle or from cold and starvation. You can be sure that the Norse will have taken every provision from their homes. There will be nothing to forage, even if we could find our way along the coast by land.'

'There is still time to retreat,' said Boerden, putting his helmet back on.

'Retreat?' snarled Ursula. 'Retreat? We still have more than eight hundred knights and soldiers. We outnumber them, and our ships outgun theirs. Why do you choose to snatch at defeat when victory and glory can still be ours?'

'Ursula's right,' said Johannes with a scowl at Boerden. 'Why, our knights alone could deal with this rabble!'

'Then it's time we joined the others, isn't it, boy?' said Boerden, turning and walking away.

Johannes's shoulders slumped and he turned to Ursula, but she was already striding down the street towards the shore with Ruprecht. With a sigh, he signalled to his squire to bring his mount to him. Putting one foot in the stirrup, he glanced over his shoulder once more, but Ursula was now out of sight behind the smoking ruins of the village.

THE ARMY WAS arrayed for battle a short way north from the smouldering ruins of the village, two hundred crossbowmen, three hundred spearmen and three hundred knights waiting as the advance of the Norse echoed across the hills. Ursula stood facing her army, Ulfshard burning in her hands.

'Once more the warriors of the Dark Gods assail us!' she shouted to her army. 'Once more we must fight to protect those things we hold most dear. If we should fail today, then tomorrow these warriors will be heading to our shores to burn our homes and slaughter our families. We are all that stands between these raiders and our kin, and they look to us to be strong today.'

She raised Ulfshard above her head and they knew what happened next. Kneeling, the army as one bowed their heads in prayer, the knights dismounting to pay homage to Sigmar.

'Almighty Sigmar,' began Ursula. 'Hearken to our praise, hear our gratitude, pay heed to our prayers. Grant us your strength in this battle. Grant us the fortitude to finish what we have begun in your name. Look over us in war and cast your divine protection across us. Let us remember that you watch our deeds and may we stand well in your judgement. In your great wisdom grant us the power to see victory today. For Sigmar!'

The resounding bass beat of the Norse war drum echoed louder and louder over the assembled army as they rose to their feet and the knights mounted their horses. All eyes were turned to the hills ahead, to the north and the bare skyline. Now and then, some glanced nervously over their shoulders out to the fjord, and the ships tacking against the wind to meet the longships approaching from the Sea of Claws.

Atop the crest line a single figure appeared, silhouetted against the pale mountains that lay beyond. He was mounted on a snorting steed that stood twice the height of a man, its mane and tail burning like a dark red flame, its coat almost pure black. The warrior himself was a giant of a man, clad in dark armour with the white fur of a Norscan bear draped across his shoulders, its gilded skull set into a helm that covered his face except for his mouth and chin. In his left hand, he hefted a long single-bladed axe, and in his right a long iron shield pierced with spikes fashioned from bronze-bound bone. He raised his axe above his head and his army moved forward.

Banner after banner appeared on the ridgeline, some tattered, fluttering rags daubed with crude dye in twisted faces and incomprehensible runes. Others were collections of skulls, bones and weapons hanging from thick crosspieces by heavy chains. The warriors spread out around their banners, clashing their axes, swords and hammers against their round wooden shields, waving their weapons in the air and baying to the sky. Amidst the clamour, the heavy beat of the drum could still be heard.

A gap appeared in the line, and from beyond the far side of the hill, a wooden structure rose into view, much like a Norse hill fort; a square palisade made from sharpened logs with gaps cut into them to allow those inside to cast spears and stones onto those below. In front of the tower stood a huge drum, as broad as a man is tall and on wooden platforms on either side, two burly Norse swung large bone-handed hammers, pounding out the incessant beat.

The war beast itself could now be seen, a monstrous mammut from high in the Norscan mountains. Taller even than the wooden tower upon its back, its shadow stretched over the Norse host. Its long shaggy fur was braided with skulls and entwined with chains; the four massive tusks that jutted from its jaw were tipped with iron spikes and hung with more trophies. Bronze shields hung on straps down its enormous flanks, and its ankles were bound with studded rings of silvery metal. Two trunks swayed independently of each other between the tusks, scenting the air and picking at the ground. Its eyes could not be seen, hidden behind pierced half-spheres that jutted out of a bronze cap riveted into its skull. Each metal plate was painted in blood with runes of the Dark Gods.

A nervous murmur spread around Ursula, and horses whinnied and shifted in fear. To the west, along the coast, barbaric horsemen could be seen galloping their mounts around the village, attempting to seize the flank of the defenders. Meanwhile, more gaps parted in the Norse line, allowing heavy chariots of wood and iron to roll forwards, their crews stripped to the waist, angular sigils tattooed across their chests, their beards and hair woven with balls of bronze and gold. Each had a black pennant emblazoned with a golden rune hanging from tall poles on the yokes. The beasts that drew the war machines were mutated abominations, vile crossbreeds of giant wolves and horses. Each had a flowing black mane and hooves, but with canine heads and dagger-like fangs.

Two more figures then appeared beside the warlord. One was clad in rags that blew against the wind, his face covered with a long hood with a single gaping eyehole where no normal man would be able to see. He was hunched, his back twisted almost at a right angle to his legs, but came forward with surprising agility, bells and chimes hung from the hem of his tattered robes clanging and ringing with every contorted step.

The other was encased in a suit of armour chased with gold and gems, his face pierced with rings and studs, his hair cropped to a scalplock that hung down the length of his back. In his hands, he carried an elegantly curved sword, obviously not fashioned by the primitive metalworking skills of the Norse. The two looked to the chieftain mounted on his stamping daemonic mount and each received a nod.

Quiet descended upon the horde. Even the mammut stopped in its advance, its trunks lowered to the ground. The robed man lifted his arms to the sky and began to chant, while the armoured figure ran to the nearest chariot and leapt aboard, gesturing for the crew to urge the machine forwards. Seeing their leader advancing, the other chariot riders whipped their beasts forwards, and the six chariots began to progress down the slope. Behind them, the infantry marched forwards around their banners, the warlord and mummat at their centre.

The Imperial army was arrayed with the knights on the right flank as a single mass, while the regiments of crossbowmen and spearmen were alternated with each other, the long lines of missile troops and the dense blocks of spearmen giving the impression of the battlements on a castle wall

'Crossbowmen, forward!' bellowed Boerden, most senior of the knights and in battle the commander of Ursula's small army. A veteran of half a dozen campaigns, his powerful voice carried over the noise of the approaching Norse easily.

The two hundred crossbowmen paced forwards, moving some seventy yards ahead of the spear line. At Boerden's second command they halted and raised their crossbows to their shoulders. Raising his sword in the air, Boerden stood up in his stirrups and, after a moment's pause, dropped the blade. The order was shouted along the line and the crossbowmen let loose, each regiment of twenty unleashing their bolts a few moments after the band to their left, in a wave of black missiles that arced out towards the slope.

The iron-tipped cloud dropped down steeply into the advancing Norse. Red-shafted quarrels bit into the beasts pulling the chariots, thudded into shields and unprotected bodies, embedded in armour and punched through the horned helmets of the attackers. Nearly half the volley had hit their target, and the Norse were forced to clamber over their dead to continue their advance.

With a wave of his sword, Boerden ordered the crossbowmen back into place, giving ground before the advancing chariots, three of which had been halted, their beasts lying dead in the traces, the blood of the crews dripping from between the crudely nailed planks of their shaft-scarred machines.

In the centre, the spearmen and swordsmen of the knights' armies readied their weapons, drawing swords from scabbards and bracing spears against the ground. A boom behind the army signalled the first firing from the ships, as the Norse longships entered the fjord. Some of the soldiers turned to see what was happening, and were swiftly reprimanded by sergeants and knights. Another solitary roar echoed down the valley; Leerdamme and the other ship's captains were well aware of their lack of shot and were making each count. In the gaps between the intermittent cannon fire, the pop and crackle of handguns could be heard as sharpshooters in the rigging and forecastles took long-range shots at the approaching Norse.

Ursula had no time to spare a thought for the newly erupting sea battle. Her focus was entirely on the approaching barbarians, who were now only a hundred yards away. They broke into a trot, gathering speed slowly. She could feel the ground shake as the mammut broke into a lumbering run.

A swordsman to Ursula's left coughed violently, his blade clattering from his grip as he collapsed to his knees. The man next to him turned, only to drop his sword and shield and clutch his throat as he too fell retching to the ground. Like corn scythed at harvest, a line of several dozen soldiers became similarly afflicted, some running forwards gasping, others toppling into their comrades, who backed away and began pushing and shoving amongst themselves to get away from the inflicted men.

'Sorcery!' snarled Ruprecht, pointing towards the robed figure still on the hill. 'Curses from the Lord of Decay.'

'Shallya protect us,' whispered Ursula, as more and more swordsmen fell victim to the unnatural plague or ran away from their infected countrymen. She ran forwards, Ulfshard blazing in her hand.

'Have faith!' she shouted, grabbing men and urging them back to the line. 'Resist their vile spells!'

Seeing their maiden-champion joining them, many of the swordsmen recovered their nerve, though fully a third of them lay dead or writhing at their feet. Even as the line was redressed and order restored, the first of the Norse were within fifty yards. A forest of short spears appeared in their hands and was launched through the air towards the defenders.

A few of the slowest soldiers were skewered through chest, arm or belly by the heavy shafts, but many raised their shields in time. It was then that the true purpose of the attack became clear, as the swordsmen struggled to remove the weighty spears from their shields, now made too heavy to lift with one arm. Many abandoned their protection and instead stood with two-handed grips on their swords as the Norse swarmed in.

With cries of anger and defiance, the two lines clashed. Norse axes bit into mailed shirts, and Marienburg steel cleaved through leather jerkins and heavy furs. In the sudden press of bodies, Ursula could not see what was happening, but was suddenly joined by the reassuring presence of Ruprecht next to her, his heavy warhammer held over his shoulder.

'No place for a leader, this,' he said, grabbing her by the shoulder and barging his way back out of the press. Ursula did not even attempt to struggle against his hefty strength, and instead allowed herself to be pulled free of the melee that was now erupting all along the Empire line.

'Watch for the beast!' shouted Boerden as the mammut trampled forwards, barely a dozen strides from the fearful spearmen. 'Crossbows!'

The order took a moment to relay, and the volley was ragged and ill-aimed, and many of the shots whistled harmlessly past the beast or ricocheted off its armour plates. No few found a mark, however, and the creature raised its trunks and trumpeted in pain and anger. Lashing with tusks and trunks it gouged a hole in the line of spearmen in front of it, stamping and snapping spear shafts under its weight. The Norse in the tower upon its back threw down javelins into the spearmen, as the creature lurched from side to side, black shafts sticking from its face and legs. The spearmen fought back as best they could, though the thrusts of their spears had little effect on the creature's thick hide.

Its charge ploughed on through the spearmen, leaving dozens crushed and maimed in its wake. Another volley of crossbow bolts struck home, sticking in armour plates and burying iron tips into the softer parts of the beast's flesh. With another deafening trumpet, the mammut stopped suddenly, bending its back legs. Norsemen toppled out of the embrasures in the howdah, plunging to their deaths against the hard ground many yards below.

Out of control, the gigantic beast surged forwards once more, and the spearmen broke and scattered before it as it charged, sweeping left and right with its tusks, scooping men from the ground and flinging them high into the air, crushing them beneath its armoured tread. Barely a dozen yards to Ursula's right, the creature continued its rampage out through the back of her army and into the village, smashing through the ruins of huts and onwards.

Through the gap that had now opened, Boerden led the knights, their horses at a gallop, lances lowered. Like a steel hammer they crashed into the Norse, horses biting and stamping, lances punching through chests and necks, rupturing organs and snapping bones. The sound of the impact of three hundred knights at full charge was like a thunderclap and the Norse were almost physically hurled back by the force of their attack.

The chariots, which had dropped behind the infantry, now counter-charged, draught-beasts snapping with their long fangs, scythed wheels dismembering horses and fallen men, the crew jabbing at the survivors with their long spears. The armoured warrior stood on the yoke of his chariot, slashing left and right with his sword, until a knight's lance caught him high on the shoulder, flinging him under the rumbling wheels of his own chariot.

His battered form rose up from the churned mud behind it, but a moment later a second lance head pierced his side, knocking him from his feet and dragging the knight from his mount. A flailing hoof from the warhorse caught the champion in the side of the head and Ursula could see blood sprayed from the grievous wound, the warrior flung to the ground, his body now still.

Their impetus lost, the knights wheeled around and retreated, preparing for another charge. However, seeing the Norse horsemen who had been making their way around to the rear of the army during the fighting, they set off at a brisk trot to confront this new threat.

A sudden sense of fear gripped Ursula and she turned her attention to the fight between the Norse and swordsmen. In the middle of the fighting was the Norse chief, atop his daemonic mount, hewing in all directions with his long axe, every stroke severing a head or limb. Sword blades glanced harmlessly off his armour, while his riding beast seemed equally impervious to harm, crushing soldiers beneath its bulk and gouging with its long fangs and horns.

Without a thought, Ursula charged forwards once again, hurling herself through the retreating throng. A soldier in front of her was flung backwards, a Norse axe embedded in his skull. As the enemy warrior stooped to pull it free, Ursula slashed out with Ulfshard, the shining blade parting the Norseman from shoulder to ribs with one easy stroke. As he collapsed aside, Ursula thrust through the gap, the tip of her elven blade slicing through the brim of another warrior's helm, splitting his scalp.

Ulfshard was as light as air in her hand, allowing her to easily parry the mace of a barbaric warrior who rushed forwards, and then turn her wrist and flick the glowing blade through his leg, cutting it off above the knee in a splash of steaming blood. A double-handed blow decapitated another Norseman and then Ursula was free, facing off against the chieftain. His beast reared and hissed, pulling back from the light of Ulfshard, and the chieftain fought with the chains of its reins to keep it under control. Stamping its ebon hooves, the creature reared again, howling in pain, and almost of the sword's volition rather than hers, Ursula struck out with Ulfshard.

It was only the merest graze, but the daemonic creature wailed in agony, throwing its rider. The wound erupted into a long gash, peeling away the unnatural skin and flesh, revealing a miasma of energy beneath. The creature's daemonic life-force spilled out like blood, a dark-hued cloud of billowing energy that smelled like charred flesh and decay. As if consumed by a fire, the creature melted away, gobbets of incorporeal flesh bubbling and sizzling on the cold ground.

Ursula heard shouting behind her and saw Ruprecht trying to fight his way through the throng of Norsemen and Empire soldiers, and she realised that in her attack, she had broken through and was isolated. A chuckle focussed her attention quickly though, as the Norse chieftain rose to his feet, using his axe to push himself upright. He was almost twice Ursula's height, and with the weight of his armour, more than three times as broad. The axe was nearly as long as she was tall, and now that she was close, she could see black runes etched into its blade, pulsing with a life of their own.

'The she-bitch,' spat the champion in crude Reik-spiel, standing upright. 'Sutenvulf will be surprised to hear you fall to blade of Jolnir of the Skaerling.'

The name struck a chord in Ursula's mind and for a moment she lost her concentration, letting down her guard.

'Sutenvulf?' she said. 'The southern wolf? Kurt? He's alive?'

'I shall give him your bones as a gift,' Jolnir said with a grin that displayed fang-like teeth and blackened gums. 'Perhaps he will mount them on a spear and parade them when we destroy your lands.'

'Shut up,' Ursula said, her venom-filled voice like a slap in the face to the chosen warrior. Ursula could hear Ruprecht's panicked shouting behind her.

'Even if you kill me, witch, the tide will come,' he said, his voice a bass growl. 'But that is not going to happen.'

With a roar he leapt forward with speed surprising for his considerable size. His axe flew down towards Ursula's head. Ulfshard leapt up to meet the unholy blade, shattering its head into shards that exploded into the Norse warrior's face. As he stepped back, Ursula drove the elven sword into the gap between helmet and breastplate, the tip digging into Jolnir's throat and erupting out of the back of his head. He fell to one side, dragging Ursula's sword arm down.

A moment later, Ruprecht was there, hammer in hand. Ursula looked round at him, and then beyond to where the Norse were breaking and fleeing, out-numbered, their leader dead. She looked Ruprecht in the eye.

'Worried?' she said, pulling Ulfshard free and lifting it up in front of the tall Talabheimer.

'Why ever would I be?' he said with a scowl. He looked out towards the fjord, and she followed his gaze. Two longships were nearing the shore, the *Graf Suiden* alongside. 'Enough of this, there's still more fighting to be done'.

CHAPTER TWO
A New Glory
Faeringhold, Norscan coast, Early winter 1711

THE EARLY DAWN light dappled off the Sea of Claws, the ships of the invaders from the Empire now nothing more than dark spots in the distance. Kurt Sutenvulf, dispossessed lord of the Fjaergard, watched them disappear into the gloom with a scowl. Though he was almost naked, clad only in heavy boots, loincloth and fur cloak, the biting wind had no effect on his inhuman flesh. The same could not be said for Jakob, who stood shivering just behind his master, his heavy cloak wrapped tightly around his wiry frame, his teeth chattering. Frost had formed on his scraggly beard, and he cursed quietly to himself that he had been forced to come out into the elements before the weak northern sun had had a chance to warm the ground. Though the half-Norse shaman had grown up in these inhospitable climes, he had never got used to the winter cold.

With them were Gird and Undar, completing the chosen warrior's cabal of trusted companions. Gird was half-asleep, leaning on the pole of the banner he carried for Kurt, its crosspiece hung with the bones of Gird's own brother. Undar was dressed in a long suit of mail, the bitter wind tugging at his black cloak, his long raven hair pulled back by a silver circlet fashioned in the shape of a dragon. A heavy mace hung from his belt, amongst numerous daggers and small axes.

Kurt turned his attention to the now empty ruins that had been Faeringhold. Smoke still rose fitfully from a few of the collapsed buildings, and from the cliff top they could see the mounds of bodies that had been piled on the shore. The wreckage of two long-ships had been washed up amongst them, and Kurt remembered the awesome sight of the Imperial great-ship cutting between the two of them, risking running aground, and unleashing a rolling broadside down each flank. The much smaller Norse vessels had both been sunk with that single salvo, the survivors picked off by marksmen as they swam for shore, or cut down by vengeful soldiers as they dragged themselves out of the surf.

'Jolnir was an idiot,' Kurt said, turning to the others, his scowl twisting the swirling patterns etched into the flesh of his face.

'Perhaps he would have succeeded if you had not let him go alone,' said Undar. Gird and Jakob both visibly shrank back from Kurt, expecting an outburst prompted by Undar's questioning tone. Only Undar, another Chosen and the equal of Kurt's fighting prowess, ever dared to question their leader.

'That wasn't the point,' Kurt said. 'Killing Ursula and the others would have achieved nothing. Now we have lost eight ships and five hundred men, not to mention the mammut. It was wasteful.'

They walked in silence along the cliff top, and at a word from Kurt, Gird waved the banner three times, indicating to the army that waited further back from the hill top that it was all clear. Made up of those who had sided with Kurt rather than Jolnir, they now numbered barely a thousand warriors. For two days they had hidden in the forests many miles from Faeringhold, sending out scouts to watch for when Ursula's army had left. Now they traipsed across the hills towards Faeringhold, heads low, their despondency like a cloud hanging over them.

'We might have carried the day,' argued Undar, who was only barely less headstrong than Jolnir had been. 'Our warriors with Jolnir and Fengris would have overwhelmed them.'

'And then what?' asked Jakob, walking beside Kurt to use the chosen warrior's considerable bulk to shield himself from the wind. 'The ships sail away, and Faeringhold would still lie in ruins. And what of us? Perhaps a shattered, spent force.'

Undar grabbed the shaman by his cloak, nearly yanking him off the ground.

'Little weasel,' the champion said, dragging Jakob close. 'You would avoid battle with any excuse. You're just buying time, hoping that our venture never succeeds.'

'It's not true,' said Jakob, squirming in Undar's grip, twisting his head to look pleadingly at Kurt, his true master. The Sutenvulf gave him a hard glare.

'He is a weasel, but he is right,' said Kurt, laying his hand on Undar's arm. The other Chosen looked at Kurt for a moment, and then released his grip on the shaman, who stumbled and nearly fell. 'It will take an army the like of which you have never seen, nor has existed in the lifetime of your father, to attack the Empire.'

They were now stood where Jolnir's army had paused before attacking, looking over the desolate settlement. There were obviously no survivors, even Gorl of the Many Poxes had been ridden down as he tried to flee when Jolnir had fallen and the knights had returned to pursue the broken Norsemen.

'Search the ruins and the bodies, take what we can,' he said to the others, motioning for Gird and Undar to take the message to the others. As they walked off, Kurt stopped for a moment with Jakob beside him.

'There will be a reckoning,' the Chosen said, resting his meaty hand on the pommel of his old sword, the only evidence that remained of his days as a knight of the Osterknacht. 'This is bigger than Ursula now. Those knights followed her, those soldiers were paid. Someone in the Empire thought it a great endeavour to finance this expedition. I don't care who it was. The sheep do not attack the wolf, it is unnatural. These sheep need teaching again, and I will be the teacher.'

'And so what will you do next?' asked Jakob. 'How will you get such an army?'

'That is why I keep you around,' said Kurt, starting off down the slope. 'Tell me a way that would give me such power.'

Jakob thought for a moment, and then stopped suddenly, staring at the corpse of a Norse warrior lying in the frozen mud of the hillside.

'What is it?' asked Kurt looking at the body. It was then he noticed the hands had been chopped off. It was a grave insult among many Norse tribes, for how could a warrior wield sword and shield in the afterlife if his spirit had no hands?

'It seems the Sigmarite bitch didn't ignore everything I taught you when we first met,' Jakob said. 'She listened enough to learn how to hurt us the most.'

'There is an old saying in the Empire,' said Kurt, looking up from the body. "Know thine enemy". She knows plenty about the Norse, but I know more about the Empire. They are divided, weak. The east is weakest of all, ravaged by orcs in the south. In the spring, when the rivers are in full flood, it is hard for them to move armies upriver, and the roads through the forests are long and winding. We shall mass an army and strike through Kislev. From there, to the Ostermark. Ostland will not aid them, afraid of Reikland and Middenland taking their lands while they are occupied elsewhere. If an oafish orc brute can take the Runefang of Wissenland, then why can't an ex-Osterknacht knight wield the sword of the Count of Ostermark?'

THREE DAYS HAD passed since the destruction of Faeringhold and the loss of Bjordin and his allies. Campfires burned brightly amongst the charred ruins of the village, each of the tribes that had gathered under Kurt's banner keeping to their own company.

There was no singing, no feasting, no drinking. A sombre mood had descended on everyone, and on Kurt the most.

There was dissent, and not just from Undar, but from other chieftains, even those who were not as gifted by the gods as Kurt. He could easily slay them in challenge and take their warriors as his own, but there had to be another way. There were some who muttered that the Sutenmjar, the southern pup, was a bad omen, and was not sent by the gods at all but had merely usurped power. Even his extraordinary voyage to distant Nehekhara and his battle against the Tomb Kings of that land no longer inspired them. The fact that he had thrown all of the plunder from the expedition into the sea had not won many hearts either, he realised. He had to show them that his way was the true way, that this was the intent of the gods.

He needed a sign.

Jakob was quiet as Kurt explained his worries, the pair of them sitting with bowls of thin stew around a small fire in the burned timbers that had once been the long hall of the Faering chieftain. When Kurt had finished, Jakob sat for a while in thought, slurping his stew with a wooden spoon, gobbets of boiled horse-meat dribbling into his beard.

'Well?' said Kurt, growing impatient as he swilled down the last of the stew in one long gulp. 'Perform a ritual, talk to the gods, summon a messenger for me.'

'I cannot do these things,' replied Jakob slowly. 'You know that I do not have that kind of power. The gods do not exist to answer to the calls of men. They bestow their gifts on those that please them, and their curses on those that displease them.'

'Surely the ruination of the Empire is pleasing to the gods?' said Kurt, casting his bowl aside and standing up. He paced to and fro with long strides, looking up at the cloudy skies. 'I cannot win. Without their help, I have no army, and with no army they will not help.'

'There is another way to prove yourself,' said Jakob quietly, almost reluctant to offer the suggestion.

'Another way to prove myself?' said Kurt, stopping his pacing and turning to the shaman. 'Like the ritual in Tungask?'

'No,' chuckled Jakob. 'Not at all like that. That was merely an initiation, to let the gods see you for a short while. You did well and they granted you favours, but your exploits bore them now, and like their people, perhaps they have lost faith in your abilities.'

'So what must I do?' asked Kurt, his voice almost pleading. 'How do I attract their gaze again?'

'You must stand before them, and challenge them in person,' said Jakob, gazing into his bowl.

Kurt laughed deeply, but then his good humour passed and he kicked out in a fit of temper, scattering broken, charred wood.

'And how does one do that?' he said, stooping over Jakob, his flittering shadow from the campfires bathing the shaman in darkness. 'Grow wings and fly up to them?'

'There is a way, a path that many have trod, yet few have returned,' Jakob said, ignoring Kurt's scorn. 'In the north, at the very north of the world, the gods can be found, it is said.'

'It is said?' scoffed Kurt. 'Said by whom? Old wives?'

Jakob said nothing, and stood up. Kurt grabbed his arm and spun him around as the shaman took a step away.

'You are serious?' the Chosen asked. 'This place is real?'

'In the north, such questions are irrelevant, as you will see,' said Jakob. 'The realm of the gods is a place of dreams. And a place of nightmares.'

'And if I dare the realm of the gods?' said Kurt, releasing his hold. 'Will they see me again? What will I earn?'

The shaman grinned, showing the blackened stumps of his teeth.

'Immortality,' Jakob said.

GIRD WOKE SUDDENLY, sensing movement close by. He wrapped his fingers around the hilt of the sword beneath the pack he used as a pillow and opened his eyes. Against the light of the twin moons he could see a large shape moving towards him.

He relaxed as he heard Kurt's whisper.

'Stay your hand,' the Chosen told him, crouching down next to Gird. 'Get your things together, we're leaving.'

'Leaving?' he asked, and then noticed that Kurt had his small pack slung across his back. 'Where?'

'North,' said Kurt, standing up again. Gird could see Undar, Jakob and a few others outside the remnants of the hut that he had taken shelter in, the dying embers of the many fires casting a glow behind them. They were similarly dressed for travelling.

'What's north?' he asked, sitting up and sheathing his sword. 'Why so quiet?'

He heard Undar's deep chuckle.

'The gods,' answered Kurt, stretching out a hand to help Gird to his feet. 'We're going to pick a fight with the gods.'

Gird's grip loosened and he slumped back onto his backside, and Undar's laugh grew louder.

'Pick a...' said Gird, and then looked past Kurt to the others. He stood up, his expression one of annoyance. 'I'm in no mood for jokes. Go away and let me get some sleep.'

'No joke,' said Kurt, striding to the ruined back of the hut where his skeletal banner was propped up against a half-charred log that was once a roof beam. He grasped the standard and thrust it towards Gird, the bones clattering against the wooden stuff, swaying on their rusted metal joints. 'We've got food for you, just grab your spare boots and hunting gear.'

Gird took the grisly icon without thinking, his brow creased with confusion.

'I still don't understand,' he said, looking to the others again. 'One of you tell me what's going on.'

'Just as the Sutenvulf says,' Bayor told him. Once chieftain of the Fjorlingas, Bayor's men had disobeyed his wishes and joined Jolnir's army. Now he was entirely at the mercy of Kurt's whim and not to be trusted to have any reasoned opinion, so Gird turned to Bjordrin, who was also stood with the group.

Bjordrin had known Kurt ever since the battle at Tungask and had travelled to Nehekhara with him, and was well known amongst the Norse for having a wise head on his broad shoulders. 'What mad idea is this?'

'Stop asking questions,' Kurt told him, shoving Gird forward with a hand between his shoulders. 'Get ready now, or I'll leave you behind.'

'What makes you think I want to come with you?' asked Gird, stepping out of Kurt's reach.

'Who would turn down a chance at immortality?' the Chosen asked, and then smiled as realisation dawned in Gird's eyes. He face grew stern again. 'Besides, I didn't say I'd leave you behind with breath in your body.'

'You really mean it?' Gird asked, as he handed the standard to Bjordrin and began to rifle through his scattered belongings, taking what he needed and placing it into a small sack. 'We're going to the Gate of the Gods?'

'What else is worth going north for?' said Kurt, stepping outside into the dim firelight. The runes carved into his skin seemed to glow with their own energy, and his eyes were bright in the darkness. Gird had never felt the breath of the gods, the invisible winds of power that blew across the world, but he could feel the aura of energy that radiated from Kurt at that moment.

'Why the secrecy?' asked Gird as he slung his sack over his shoulder and stepped through the scattered ash and wood splinters covering the cold ground.

'Too much trouble to take an army,' explained Kurt as the six of them walked quietly towards the outskirts of the village, heading inland.

'Anyway, who wants to share?' added Undar as he looked over his shoulder at Gird. 'The less of us, the more glory for each.'

'And more power,' said Jakob quietly to himself, as he followed in the darkness, unheard by the others.

FOR SEVEN DAYS they had headed north, climbing higher and higher into the mountains, searching for a pass. They had been slowed as the vicious wind and snows had closed in, and now on the seventh day they were high up a ridge, the air thin in their lungs, the snow falling fitfully around them,

Kurt stopped in his stride, knee-deep in a snowdrift, causing Bjordrin to almost stumble into him, half-blinded as he was by the swing blizzard.

Bjordrin began to ask what was wrong, but Kurt waved a hand for him to stay silent. The chosen warrior listened carefully, attuning himself to the howling of the wind. His instincts had been right; it was not only the wind that howled, there was another sound, a high-pitched wail that seemed to be coming from above.

Drawing his sword, Kurt stepped back and looked up, the others readying their weapons behind him and following his gaze. Above them, an icy cliff face stretched into the snow and out of sight. There was no sign of how far up it reached. For the last five days they had been steadily climbing along the ridgeline, eking out the supplies they had gathered before they had left and supplementing them with hunting in the foothills.

'No point standing here freezing,' said Bjordrin, sheathing his sword.

Kurt hesitated for a moment longer before nodding and pressing on, the unnatural howling silent now.

The cold affected him and Undar little, but he knew the others were freezing, even wrapped up in their layers of untreated furs, taken from the bodies of the dead deer and wolves they had slain on their way up to the mountain pass. They did not even know where the path they were following would lead them, if it led anywhere at all.

That was Kurt's worst fear. He could slay any creature or warrior they met, and certainly the others were more than capable in a fight, but there was nothing he could do against the elements or the terrain. It was just as possible that they were slowly winding their way back and forth around the same mountain, having had no reference on the sun for the last three days, its guiding light hidden behind the thick snow clouds. Ahead could be a wide precipice, forcing them to turn back, or perhaps the causeway they were following would simply narrow and disappear altogether.

And yet there was no point turning back, all they could do was press onwards, and hope that perhaps the next time they felt a downward slope underfoot they would have passed the shoulder of the mountain and were heading into a valley beyond, out of the wind and snow. After that there would be another mountain, and another, and another, for a hundred leagues at least. Beyond the Norscan mountains lay the wastes, and at the centre the realm of the gods. Kurt's heart sank and he turned to Bjordrin behind him, looking for some encouragement.

'What legends do the Fjaergard have about the Gate of the Gods?' Kurt asked, falling back a couple of steps to walk alongside Bjordrin.

The Norseman was hunched over, his beard and eye-lashes coated with snow, the hood of his cloak pulled tightly around his face to ward off the worst of the blizzard. Kurt remembered when he had been sun-blistered and red only a few months ago, as their longship had lain becalmed off the coast of Araby, tortured by the incessant southern sun. This man had become like a brother to him, even more so since his real brother, Hrolfgar, had been slain defending Fjaer-gardhold from Ursula's first attack. It was a while before Bjordrin replied, and Kurt thought perhaps he had not been heard, but then Bjordrin spoke up, voice raised above the noise of the snowstorm.

'We have few stories about the realm of the gods,' he said. 'What we know was learned from others who live further north than us. The wastes are dangerous, a place of battle where the champions of the gods challenge each other to prove their worth. We in the south look to a single chosen warrior like you for our protection, but in the north there are said to be whole tribes gifted by the gods.'

Bjordrin paused for breath, wiping the ice from his face with a gloved hand before continuing.

'As we get closer to the gods, their power over the land grows,' he said. 'The ground shows their touch, and the beasts of the wilds are marked by their attentions. They are feral, bloodthirsty creatures. As for the realm of the gods itself, few can ever say, for none return who are not changed. Some legends say that the Gate of the Gods can be reached in a single day of walking, others that a man might travel for hundred years, not aging, and yet never find it. Some are unable to cope with the gifts bestowed upon them, or are cursed by the gods for their impudence. They are driven mad, or their bodies torn apart by the power of the gods flowing into them. Great champions who emerge are said to take part of their gods' might, becoming impervious to mortal weapons, or who can fly upon the breath of the gods and wield sorcery greater than the best of our shamans.'

'But what do they do with this power?' Kurt asked.

'They fight of course!' Bjordrin replied with a short laugh. 'Once the gaze of the gods is upon you, it does not turn away. If we reach our goal, it is not the end, it is the beginning. We will be gifted and we will be expected to use those gifts for the greater glory of the gods that bestowed them. They do not give their favours lightly.'

'We will be the victors,' Kurt said, stumbling as he slipped in a particularly deep snowdrift.

'Does it matter?' asked Bjordrin as he helped Kurt haul himself up. 'All we can do is try. The gods will challenge us, as will others, and if we prevail then it is up to them to decide if we are worthy of their attention.'

'So why did you come?' asked Kurt, clearing a path through the snow with sweeps of his arms. 'Why risk such horrors? You know my reasons.'

'What else is there to do?' asked Bjordrin, and bitterness entered his voice. 'My home is destroyed, my family slain. I have nothing but what I carry on my back. What better reason does a man need to see his gods, and perhaps prove to them that he will not be broken by the fate they have laid down for him.'

Kurt did not reply, but forged on through the snow. On occasion he thought that he heard the distant howling again. As darkness fell, they sought shelter in a large snowdrift, digging several small ice caves to shield them from the wind. Feeding upon raw meat and drinking melted snow, Kurt nestled in his small burrow, but sleep would not come. He could sense something close by, and it was not long before his ears heard a deep snuffling noise from outside.

Rising quietly, he dragged himself to the opening of his ice cave and looked out. Glancing to his left, he saw that Undar was also still awake, and with him was Gird. There was something prowling around in the night gloom, that was certain, and the two emerged warily into the falling snow.

A noise to Kurt's right snapped his head round, but he could see nothing in the swirling snow and darkness. Pacing forward a little way, treading carefully to avoid losing his footing on the treacherous ledge they had chosen for their campsite, he ventured further into the darkness.

A shout from Undar had Kurt turning and running back to the campsite. As the others came into view, he saw Gird lying on the ground, clutching his side, while Undar had his back to Kurt.

Beyond him stood a beast roughly the size of a bear, standing on its rear legs. It had long fur that was bald in patches, revealing thick grey scales. A snake-like tail whipped back and forth, sending flurries of snow into the air. As it dropped to all fours, Kurt could see that its front legs looked more like a man's arms, the fur thinner, revealing leathery skin beneath.

Opening a fanged maw, it howled, a plaintive sound to Kurt's ears. Undar leapt forward with his mace raised and the creature jumped to meet him, smashing a hand-like paw across the warrior's front, knocking him off his feet. As Undar struggled to rise, the monster backed away, tensing to spring forward again.

As Kurt got closer, he could see the creature's face more clearly. It had the muzzle of a bear, but the eyes were strangely human. The beast regarded him with a basic intelligence, and Kurt thought he saw something close to desperation in those eyes. It opened its mouth again, the creature's thick tongue lolling out, growling and snorting.

Undar stepped forward again, but Kurt laid a hand on his arm.

'Wait,' Kurt told the warrior. 'See to Gird.'

Undar turned his head and looked at Kurt for a moment, before stepping back, keeping the beast in view. He backed off towards Gird's still form, his mace held ready. Kurt stood his ground, and he and the creature stared at each other. Movement and sound caused the creature to flinch, and Kurt turned his head slowly to see Jakob emerging from his little ice hole. The shaman stopped when he laid eyes on the beast, eyes fixed on it.

'Fetch some meat,' Kurt said, but Jakob did not respond. He kept his voice low but firm. 'Jakob, fetch some meat.'

Jakob snapped out of his mesmerised state and looked at Kurt. As comprehension dawned, he ducked back into the small ice cave and came back a moment later clutching strips of deer flesh in his fist.

The creature snorted again, its attention now fixed on Jakob, and took a pace forward, its strange paw-hand sinking only a small way into the snow.

Jakob walked warily towards Kurt, eyes fixed on the beast, and handed the meat strips to the chosen warrior. The creature's eyes followed Kurt as he took a couple of steps away from Jakob and took one of the fatty pieces of meat in one hand. He tossed it to within a few feet of the creature, and it pounced forwards, grasping the deer flesh in one hand and scooping it into its maw. Chewing ferociously, it continued forward, sniffing the air. Kurt threw another chunk of meat out to it, which was similarly grabbed quickly.

The creature was now just in front of Kurt. It sat on its haunches and held out one paw, its gaze fixed on Kurt's eyes agreeing the unspoken truce. Kurt nodded and placed the rest of the meat in its upturned palm. It wolfed down the food gratefully, bloody saliva dripping across the snow and its dark fur. Kurt stood there and watched, hearing a groan behind him as Gird regained his senses.

Having finished eating, the creature gave another moaning growl, and Kurt could see real emotion in its eyes, perhaps something like frustration. It whined and pawed at the snow, looking up at Kurt.

'By the gods,' he heard Jakob whisper. Glancing round he saw the shaman looking closely at the marks in the snow. Only then did Kurt realise that the furrows in the snow were in the shape of two Norse runes.

'What do they say?' he asked the shaman, having only learned to speak the tongue. Jakob only knew them from long nights spent secretly observing the shaman of his original tribe.

'Stormraven,' Jakob said, and the creature bobbed its head heavily, as if trying to nod. 'It says Stormraven, one of the tribes that lives further east of here.'

The creature made a half-moan, half-cough. It repeated this several times, and Jakob leaned forward and listened carefully.

'Hursk?' he said, and the creature waggled its head and made the noise again. 'Lort? Gord? Orst?'

At this last suggestion, the brutish thing raised itself to its back legs, and beat at its chest with its fists.

'You understand us?' Kurt said, turning his attention back to the creature and its large head nodded again as it dropped back to all fours, a stuttering growl emanating from its throat. 'I am Sutenvulf, and this is my shaman Jakob. We are heading north, seeking the Gate of the Gods.'

At mention of the legendary place Orst whined and pawed at his face, and then shook his head vigorously from side to side. He paced back and forth a couple of times in agitation.

'Have you seen it?' asked Kurt, stepping forward as Orst tried to back away. 'Have you been there? Could you lead us there?'

The misshapen tribesman gave a long moan and hung his head, his shoulders slumping heavily.

Tilting his head to one side, Orst gave Kurt a long, hard stare. After a while he straightened and nodded. Kurt stepped forward and slapped a hand on to the creature's broad shoulder.

'Good!' said Kurt with a grin. He turned and faced the others, who were standing behind Jakob. 'Now we have a guide, I think the gods have granted Orst Stormraven a second chance at glory.'

Orst arched back his neck and roared into the sky.

CHAPTER THREE
Unwelcome Return
Marienburg, Winter 1711

GREY WINTER SUNLIGHT dappled off the murky waters of the Reik estuary as Leerdamme called for the sail to be shorted, the *Graf Suiden* drifting into the Marienburg harbour under its topsails. Lighters coasted back and forth between the ships anchored out in the harbour, while smaller merchant vessels were moored up alongside the city's many wharfs, stevedores and teamsters swarming around them, loading and unloading their cargoes. Ships from further up the Reik traded between Marienburg and Altdorf, while others sailed to the south to ports in Bretonnia, Tilea and Estalia. Some came from even further afield, to places that were half legend, such as Cathay and Ind, carrying rich cargoes such as silk, spices and ivory. Most that set sail for these distant lands never returned.

The city itself sprawled around the harbour, a haphazard conglomeration of roofs and garrets that bore an awkward similarity to the sails of a fleet of ships, their snow-covered slopes rising at odd angles to each other. Three tall masts stretched above the other buildings, flags at their heads fluttering limply in the slight breeze. These came from the roof of the ancient library, itself built from the hulls of three old ships.

'That doesn't bode well,' said Ruprecht, as he and Ursula stood on the foredeck looking at the city.

To starboard, less than three hundred yards away, another greatship was getting under way. There were soldiers on deck and its gun ports were open, and it was clear to see officers on the deck, some of them looking at the *Graf Suiden* and pointing. From its main masthead flew the flag of the Marienburg navy, recently formed by Count Luiten. Leerdamme had noticed it too and joined the pair.

'There's trouble brewing,' he said, crossing his arms. 'A warship keeping an eye on us, and soldiers waiting on the quays.'

What he said was true. The soldiers' blue and yellow uniforms were clearly visible as they stood in line along dockside. A crowd of locals had gathered, perhaps drawn by the soldiers' presence or maybe just to get a look at the *Graf Suiden* and its famous captain. Behind them, the Marienburg man of war had now placed itself between their ship and the rest of the small fleet that had accompanied them. Her gun ports were still open, but as yet her guns had not been run out.

'It's Luiten, no doubt,' said Ursula. 'That's no welcoming committee. I think he means to take Ulfshard.'

'I agree that'd be a bad thing,' said Leerdamme. 'Still, nothing we can do yet. We'll have to play this by ear.'

They turned at the sound of metal-shod feet on the wooden planks behind them, to see Boerden, Johannes and two other knights, Reynus and Karl-Huth, climbing the steps to join them.

'What have you got us into now?' said Boerden, his expression stern.

'We can't let Luiten take Ulfshard,' said Johannes, seeing the looks that Ursula was directing over the prow. 'We need to get Ursula out of the city.'

'I know I defied the count when I stood up for you to lead an expedition to Norsca, but I'll not draw my sword against his soldiers,' said Boerden. 'I'd caution against doing anything rash. Count Luiten is not an unreasonable man, I'm sure some arrangement can be made. We've got the whole winter to decide what to do.'

'No,' said Ursula with a scowl. 'I'll not risk Ulfshard in the hands of a puffed up merchant. Help me or not, but I'm not parting with Marbad's sword, not while I have breath in my body.'

'Ursula is right, we gave blood for Ulfshard to be returned to the Empire,' said Johannes. 'I doubt that Luiten would do anything other than use it to consolidate his position. This gift could be so much more. We have to take it east, perhaps to Talabheim.'

'Well, I second that,' said Ruprecht, flexing the fingers of his artificial hand. 'Marienburg, Middenheim and Altdorf are too dangerous for something as important as Ulfshard.'

'Look, I'll not stand in your way, but I can't have any part of this,' said Karl-Huth, walking away. Boerden stayed for a moment longer before joining him. Reynus gave them a dark look.

'This borders on treason,' the knight said. 'If you try to escape and fail, you'll give Luiten every excuse he needs to have you thrown in prison, and confiscate the sword. Listen to Boerden, don't do anything rash.'

The four of them exchanged looks as Reynus departed. The voice of Verhoen, the ship's master, could be heard calling for the last sails to be taken in and the anchor let out. As the ship slowed, Leerdamme slapped his hand against the rail in agitation, looking out towards the dock.

'Well, we can't do anything here, so let's get the boat swung out and head ashore,' the captain said, turning to face the others. 'You can take your chances when you get there.'

THE REGULAR STROKES of the oarsmen soothed Ruprecht's nerves as their boat scudded across the choppy waters towards one of Marienburg's many jetties. The twenty sailors rowed to the stroke called out by the bullish bosun, Kieter van der Stree. Leerdamme sat in the sternsheets next to Ursula, with Boerden, Johannes and Ruprecht in front of them. As they closed in on the jetty, Ruprecht could see some twenty soldiers, carrying long halberds, their breastplates polished to parade ground brightness. With them stood Chancellor Gorstend, a small, thin man dressed in riding boots and breeches, his blue cloak wrapped around his body to ward off the light sleet that had begun falling a short time before.

Two of the sailors leapt onto the planking of the jetty as the boat drew alongside, carrying tethers to tie up the boat. Leerdamme stepped out next and extended a hand down to help Ursula clamber out of the boat, followed swiftly by Johannes. Ruprecht and Boerden took their place behind Ursula as the sailors lined up on either side of them, and Gorstend walked forward, no hint of feeling in his expression.

He stopped just in front of Ursula and glanced down to where he hand rested on the blue gem embedded in the hilt of Ulfshard. He matched her stare with his own cold gaze.

'Fraulein Schenk…' he began, but Ursula cut him off.

'No,' she said, with a quick shake of the head. 'He can't have it.'

'The sword rightfully belongs to Count Luiten,' Gorstend stated, showing no sign of surprise or annoyance. If he believed that Ursula would just hand Ulfshard over, then he wouldn't have needed the soldiers. 'He is Elector Count of Marienburg, wearer of the crown of Marbad, and therefore true claimant to the sword of Marbad.'

'I gave him that crown!' snarled Ursula and at this Gorstend flinched for the first time. 'Order your soldiers forward. Take the sword from me.'

'Please, reconsider,' Gorstend said, regaining his composure. 'There is no reason for this to end unpleasantly. Count Luiten has been very understanding and generous so far, do not force him to be unreasonable.'

'If he was here himself, I would do the same,' said Ursula, her fist whipping round, connecting solidly with Gorstend's jaw, knocking him to the ground.

Around her the soldiers rushed forwards, and Ruprecht leapt to meet them, the quayside ringing with metal on metal as he slammed his silver fist into the helmet of the nearest Marienburger. Johannes was beside him and delivered a very un-knightly kick to the groin of another soldier, whilst Ursula ducked to one side as two others dropped their halberds and lunged forward to grab her. Gorstend was rolled up in a foetal ball on the ground as the soldiers swarmed around him.

'Right lads, let's show these bastards a real fight!' roared Leerdamme, launching himself towards the Marienburgers, throwing punches left and right. Behind him, his sailors charged forward, relishing the chance to get one up on their land-based counterparts, in a rivalry as old as warships themselves.

In the middle of the scrum, Ursula grabbed a hand reaching for Ulfshard, sinking her teeth into it and eliciting a scream from the soldier it belonged to. Ruprecht was using the handle of his hammer in an attempt to avoid seriously injuring the soldiers, who were after all only doing their job. He felt a brief pang of sympathy as he drove the thick wooden shaft into the chin of one man, snapping his head back and throwing him into the path of one of his comrades.

Although Johannes was a knight of Talabecland, he had spent four years selling his services to the highest bidder and spent much time in the company of other mercenaries, learning from them some of the dirtiest street fighting tricks in the Old World. With low punches and kicks, eye gouges and elbows in the eyes of his adversaries, he managed to keep the press of foes at bay. Most of their wild blows glanced off his armour, and more than one Marienburger found himself sitting on the ground clasping a broken hand.

Ursula felt an arm wrap around her waist and she struck back with the point of her elbow, feeling it connect with a bristled jawbone.

'It's me, you mad woman,' she heard Ruprecht mutter close in her ear, as the burly Talabheimer dragged her free of the throng. Releasing his grip, he felled a soldier with a stiff right hand, creating a gap that he widened with a shoulder barge.

Glancing over his shoulder, Johannes saw Ursula and Ruprecht making their escape and turned to run after them. A hand grabbed his ankle and he tripped and spun, kicking out. The soldier loomed over him, the point of his halberd directed at the fallen knight's chest. Boerden appeared to the soldier's left and drove his fist into the man's chin, knocking him unconscious with one powerful blow.

'You changed your mind?' gasped Johannes as he stumbled to his feet and tried to catch his breath.

'No,' said Boerden with a grin. 'Do you see a drawn sword? Now, get out of here!'

With the old knight's laughter in his ears, Johannes pushed free, via a kick that buckled another soldier at the knees, and he was soon sprinting down a cobbled street, following the large form of Ruprecht as he shouldered his way through the throng rushing to the docks to have look at the commotion being caused.

RUPRECHT HAD ALWAYS thought that people were never actually dragged into alleys except in badly written plays, but realised his error as he grabbed hold of Johannes's arm, yanking him off the main street into a refuse-strewn gap between two warehouses as the young man ran past.

'Down here!' the large man hissed, wincing at the cliché even as he said it.

'What's the matter?' Johannes asked, seeing Ruprecht's sour expression.

'Another illusion shattered,' he replied, then waved away Johannes's inquiring look. 'It doesn't matter.'

'Where's Ursula?' said Johannes, glancing down the alley.

'Watering pixies,' replied Ruprecht, standing directly in front of the knight.

'Watering?' said Johannes, then his eyes widened. 'Oh…'

'Any idea where we are?' asked Ruprecht, changing the subject quickly. 'I think we headed west from the docks.'

'I'm not sure, but it certainly looks like one of the less affluent areas,' said Johannes, waving a hand to encompass the mouldy cabbage leaves and dead rats strewn along the alley.

'There you are, Johannes,' said Ursula, walking back up the alley and tying a knot in the laces of her leggings. 'What kept you?'

'An inquisitive watchman,' Johannes replied, avoiding her gaze. 'Best to leave it at that.'

'Any idea where we are?' she said, peeking past Ruprecht into the road beyond.

'I already asked him,' said Ruprecht. 'I think we're lost.'

'Good,' said Ursula. 'If we don't even know where we are, then there's more chance that Luiten's men don't either.'

'That doesn't make sense,' protested Ruprecht. 'There could be a watch house just around the corner.'

'Actually, there is a sort of logic to it,' argued Johannes with a creased brow. 'If they think we're heading somewhere in particular, they'll block off the roads.'

'Either way, it doesn't matter,' said Ruprecht, scratching at his beard. 'I think you can be pretty sure we're not going to get out of the city. The gates'll be guarded for certain.'

'We need someone who knows the city to help us,' suggested Johannes. He paused, looked down at his foot and curled his lip in disgust. 'I hope that once belonged to a dog.'

'Can you pay attention for a moment, at least,' snapped Ursula, slapping her palm against Johannes's chest plate. 'I think I know where we can go.'

'You do?' said Ruprecht, taken aback. 'Where?'

'We've been there before,' said Ursula with a wink. 'All we have to do is find the Haggard Fox.'

'Who?' said Johannes. 'Who's the Haggard Fox? He sounds like a criminal.'

'It's a where, not a who,' Ruprecht explained. 'Although, you are right in a way. It's a tavern, but it's also a safe house for Ranald worshippers.'

'Ah, a thieves' den,' Johannes nodded in understanding. 'So how do we get there?'

'I don't know, but getting there's the easy bit,' said Ursula, nodding with her head for them to start walking down the alley. 'Convincing them to help us, that's going to be the hard part.'

THE THREE OF them watched from the darkened doorway of a guildhouse as the watchman crossed the street and took his long tinder pole to an oil lamp on the far corner of the square. As the flame caught, another part of the wide, open space was bathed in the soft yellow glow that had been creeping across the city as evening had come and the night watch had started their rounds. In the light of the lamp, Ruprecht could see more clearly the building on the opposite side of the square. A bas-relief of a warhammer trailing twin comet tails was clearly visible over the double doors of the building.

'You didn't just come here to get your bearings, did you,' he said accusingly, glancing at Ursula.

'A bit of prayer in times of need never goes astray,' she replied sombrely, but her expression brightened. 'Besides, we're about to consort with roguish followers of Ranald, and I would feel better if I had the chance to spend a little bit of time with Sigmar first. You know, explain what's happening. But I do know the way to the Haggard Fox from here, as well, so I wasn't lying.'

Ruprecht frowned, concerned by her light tone. Ursula was in an uncharacteristically good mood, and had been ever since their escape from Luiten's soldiers. Perhaps it was just relief, he decided.

The watchman had moved away out of sight, and they waited a moment longer to be sure. The square was empty, paved with small bricks, an impressive statue of some distant count on a pedestal at its centre. He was mounted on a warhorse, holding aloft his Runefang, the swords that were the symbol of each elector count. Such symbols had become meaningless over the years of bickering and outright infighting between the provinces of the Empire. It was the reason that Luiten was so keen to claim Ulfshard; he would be able to use it as a potent sign that the gods favoured him. It was a ploy that may work, but Ruprecht now doubted it was enough to unite the warring states again. Even Ursula seemed to have decided that was beyond the power of Ulfshard, and was merely content to raise another army to hunt down Kurt.

'Come on,' whispered Ursula, breaking Ruprecht's reverie as she stood up and stalked cautiously out into the square.

The three them ghosted from shadow to shadow as much as they could, walking briskly through the puddles of light that surrounded the street lanterns. On reaching the doors to the Temple of Sigmar, Ruprecht cast another glance around the square while Ursula tried the handle. With a creak the door opened and they slipped through, Johannes closing it behind them as quietly as they could.

''Tis an odd hour to visit the home of our Lord Sigmar, is it not?' boomed a voice from the far end of the open temple.

A rotund priest was kneeling on the floor, bucket and scrubbing brush beside him, between the two long rows of benches that led up the floor towards the statue of Sigmar himself. It was carved from dark marble, in a design that Ursula had seen many times before – Sigmar standing tall and proud, his bearded face raised to the sky, right hand outstretched clasping his hammer Ghal-maraz, the Skull-splitter. The hammer itself was made from solid gold, or at least was heavily gilded, and it glittered in the light of the large candles that stood in sconces along the walls. The floor itself was a vast mosaic, and as they walked forwards, they saw that the scenes depicted the life of the Empire's founder.

First they crossed a scene depicting his birth in a rough wooden hut, his father beside him, his crown marking him out as a great chieftain of the ancient Unberogen tribe. The next saw a teenage Sigmar battling a gigantic orc warlord with an axe the size of a man, King Kurgan of the dwarfs behind the young man. The next showed the grateful king gifting Ghal-maraz to Sigmar, and here it was also picked out with solid gold tiles.

As they walked on, the priest pushed himself to his feet with much huffing and puffing, and stood regarding them suspiciously. Ruprecht's strides took him across scenes of Sigmar's other confrontations and victories, and finally they stood upon a huge picture that stretched the width of the large temple. The united tribes of men and the army of King Kurgan battled against an endless army of orcs, the twin mountains to each side symbolic of Black Fire Pass.

'I ask again, what brings you here after dark?' the priest said.

'What other reason would a pious person need to come into a temple,' Ursula replied, her tone frosty. 'We're here to pray of course.'

'Prayer sessions are conducted between the hours of eight and ten in the pre-noon, and four and six in the afternoon,' the priest said stiffly.

'What is your name?' Ursula asked, stepping right in front of the priest and staring him in the eye.

'I am Brother Elbrecht,' he said, stepping back.

'And have you ever prayed to Sigmar outside of this temple?' Ursula said, pacing after him. 'On a battle-field perhaps?'

At this the priest stopped his retreat and straightened up, puffing out his chest.

'Though my portly frame may suggest otherwise these days, I was once a Knight of Sigmar's Blood,' Elbrecht said proudly. 'I have wielded the lance and the hammer against the foe!'

'Then you will understand why, after many battles and travels, I would like to give thanks to Sigmar for looking over me,' Ursula said. 'Your past does you great credit, Brother Elbrecht.'

Taken aback by Ursula's forthright tone the priest stood there wordlessly for a few moments. His gaze then strayed to the sword hanging from Ursula's belt, and his eyes widened as he saw the glimmering pommel stone.

'That's Ulfshard!' he exclaimed, raising a hand to cover his mouth in astonishment. 'The whole city has been awash with rumours that it had been stolen! Everyone knows it, there's a thousand crowns reward for its return.'

Ruprecht stepped forward quickly and slapped a large hand onto the priest's shoulder.

'Let's you and me go and discuss theology somewhere quiet, eh?' Ruprecht said, pulling the man to one side. 'We can give my friend a little time to herself, while we discuss the finer points of Sigmar's divinity.'

Ruprecht bundled the priest across the tiled floor, heading for an archway beyond the statue of Sigmar. As he thrust Elbrecht into the chamber beyond, cast a glance over his shoulder to see Ursula on one knee, Ulfshard on the ground in front of her.

URSULA COULD FEEL the warmth coming from the magical fire that burned within the blue pommel stone of Marbad's blade, and closed her eyes. She focussed her thoughts on the sword in front of her, picturing it in her mind. She could hear her heart pounding in her chest, slow and rhythmic.

She did not speak. She did not have to. Mere words no longer conveyed her prayers to Sigmar. Instead she just contemplated the blade that was in her possession, her soul filled with gratitude.

Opening her eyes, she looked up at the gigantic statue towering above her. The shining hammer looked as bright as the sun, and she focussed her attention on it. The light brightened and brightened, and she resisted shielding her eyes against the glare. The hammer was now a blazing sword, wreathed in dark flame. Sigmar no longer stood there, and instead the weapon was wielded by a massive shadow, with great bat-like wings that spread around her, seeming to enclose her in a cave of darkness. Two burning red eyes gazed at her malevolently. Ursula felt no fear, as the warmth of Ulfshard heated her palms.

'Are you alright?' Johannes's voice broke her trance-like state, and for a moment she felt dizzy.

Coming to her senses, she saw the knight standing beside her, his expression one of deep concern. She realised she was holding Ulfshard by its blade; blood was trickling from her hands and dripping down the sword onto the tiles. Looking down, she saw that she was kneeling on the picture of Sigmar himself, her blood spattering his stern bearded face.

'Yes, yes, I'm alright,' she said. 'Where's Ruprecht? We should leave.'

'I think his theology discussion got a bit heated,' replied Johannes. 'There seemed to be a bit of bumping around and the sound of furniture being broken.'

It was at that moment that Ruprecht appeared from the archway he had disappeared into, rubbing a hand on his chin.

'He wasn't lying, he's certainly a tough one inside all that blubber,' he said with a scowl. 'Luckily he decided to hit the chair over my head rather than somewhere soft.'

'What did you do to him?' Ursula said with an accusing tone.

'Relax. I just gagged him and tied him up,' Ruprecht assured her. 'His assistants will find him in the morning and he can tell everyone how he almost caught the infamous Ulfshard thieves.'

Ursula nodded in acceptance. She realised she still held Ulfshard and carefully changed her grip to the hilt. Spying a table with an embroidered cloth on which was set a few gold and silver talismans, she used the altar cloth to wipe her blood from the blade. This done, she sheathed the elven sword.

'How are your hands?' asked Johannes, striding forward and grasping Ursula's hands, turning them palms up. There was no mark on them and he let go his hold and stepped back in shock.

'How is that possible?' he said, glancing at the floor to confirm what he had seen, and sure enough droplets of blood were still splashed across the image of Sigmar.

'We'll explain later,' said Ruprecht, laying a reassuring arm across Johannes's shoulders. 'Ursula and Sigmar have, well, what you might call a special arrangement. Again.'

This last word was spoken softly, and Ursula met Ruprecht's admonishing stare with a blank expression, and then shrugged softly and nodded. Banging and muffled shouting from the bound Elbrecht caught their attention, and Ursula nodded towards the door as a signal to leave.

THE HAGGARD FOX looked the same as it had half a year earlier, except that the stuffed animal hanging over the door looked even more bedraggled, if that was at all possible. A drunken sailor staggered down the street ahead of the trio, reeling from side to side before collapsing against the wall of a shop a little further along. Ruprecht went in first, glancing up to confirm that the secret symbol of Ranald was still carved into the underside of the lintel. The small circle with a vertical line through it could still be faintly seen. Ruprecht gave a wink to Ursula and they stepped inside.

They hung their cloaks and small packs on the row of hooks along one wall of the entrance hall, and Ruprecht looked pointedly at Johannes.

'Some odd things may happen here but they're trustworthy enough,' Ruprecht said. 'Don't say anything out of turn.'

Johannes's expression of indignity wordlessly pleaded his innocence of any such crime, but Ruprecht continued to give him a warning stare.

'On my honour,' Johannes said, placing his hand over his heart.

With a grunt, Ruprecht opened the door into the common room and they followed him inside. There were few patrons around the room: a couple of swarthy Tileans sat at one of the tables by the roaring fire, and a few sailors lounged in a drunken stupor by the thick-paned windows. From a back room, the guesthouse's patron appeared, a tall, broad man with a golden eye patch and a pearl-studded band holding his dark hair back.

'I see that times have been good to you, Ruud,' Ursula said, crossing the room and giving the surprised man a hug,

Stepping back from her embrace, he looked at her, then Johannes, before turning his gaze to Ruprecht. A broad smile split Ruud's face.

'Ah, the beautiful wanderer returns, with her bear in tow I see,' he said, stepping forward and shaking Ruprecht's hand vigorously. He turned to Johannes and offered his hand. 'And who is your new companion?'

'This is Johannes,' Ursula said, and the knight took the proffered hand and gave it a perfunctory shake before letting go. 'He's a good man, a friend of ours.'

'A good man?' laughed Ruud Goeyen. 'Well, he's the only one in Marienburg! Come my friends, there is food in the kitchen. Follow me.'

They trailed after him as he crossed the room and led them through a low door at the far end. Turning left, he led them down a short flight of stairs. As they filed past into a bare cellar, he closed the door behind them. Taking a long key from his pocket, he locked the door. Turning back to them, Ruud's face was a picture of anger.

'What do you think you're doing, coming here?' he snarled. 'The watch have already been here looking for you!'

'They have?' Ursula said, dismayed. 'What did you tell them?'

'The truth,' Ruud replied, his expression softening slightly. 'That I hadn't seen you and hoped not to. You have to go. Now.'

'There is nowhere else to go,' Ursula said, taking Rudd's hand in hers. 'You have to help us.'

'Look, you're a nice enough lass, and you pay your bills, but no means no,' Rudd said firmly, pulling his hand away. 'I can't risk it. Look, I might lose business if it gets around that you were even here, never mind smuggling you out of the city. You're far too hot for me to handle, and if I get caught with you, well that's the end of it. The count's throwing around accusations of treason left, right and centre.'

'Who said anything about smuggling us from the city?' said Ruprecht.

'What else would you be after?' Rudd replied, his annoyance clear from the tone of his voice. 'Or were you thinking of just walking out of here with the count's sword?'

'It's not the count's sword!' snapped Ursula.

'I don't care who it belongs to, it's more bad news than I'm used to, and I don't want it here,' Ruud said, crossing his arms stubbornly.

'Excuse me,' said Johannes, raising a finger.

'What?' said Ruud and Ruprecht in unison.

'The crow that flies by night is seldom seen,' Johannes said.

'What?' Ruprecht repeated.

'Why didn't you say so?' said Ruud, his anger turning to a smile. 'While doves that flutter in the sun are often caught.'

'What are you two talking about?' Ursula asked, but Johannes and Ruud were now concerned with each other and nothing else.

'Waifs make pennies by begging,' said Ruud, tilting his head one side.

'Kings are no happier in their grave,' countered Johannes, his expression serious.

'What are they talking about?' Ursula asked again, and Ruprecht took her by the arm and dragged her to one side.

'It's some kind of thiefspeak,' he whispered. 'Best not to interrupt, I think Johannes is negotiating. There's more to our young knight than we knew. I know a few phrases, but he's an expert. I must remember to ask him about that later.'

'Yes, you should,' Ursula agreed, darting a suspicious look at Johannes.

'Milking cows is for maids,' Ruud was now arguing angrily. 'Swinging swords is for soldiers.'

'Alright, alright,' said Johannes, grinning and holding up his hands in mock surrender. He banged his fist against his chestplate. 'The executioner does not swing his axe for good subjects.'

Ruud nodded and they both spat into their left palms and shook hands. Johannes began pulling the buckles on his armour, taking off his greaves and vambraces.

'Could you help me with this, I'm supposed to have a squire to do this sort of thing,' he said, looking at Ruprecht.

The big man sighed and walked over to stand behind the knight, unbuckling the straps on the armoured skirt protecting his lower back.

'You've traded your armour for our escape?' Ursula said. 'That's too much; I couldn't ask you to do that. What is a knight without his armour?'

'A common squire who stole armour from his master when he ran away from one too many beatings?' suggested Johannes.

'Oh…' Ursula said, the word drowned out by a clatter and a yell as the shocked Ruprecht dropped a shoulder plate on his foot.

CHAPTER FOUR
Battle
The Chaos Wastes

THE SKY WAS swollen, almost bruised, and hung heavily over the land, though Kurt was sure that it was not long past midday. Time had become meaningless lately, as each day had merged into the next in a never-ending cycle of sleeping and toil. A snowfield unbroken by any peak or valley stretched out to the dark horizon, a stark contrast to the glowering clouds overhead. Here and there a small upthrust of rock pierced the flat plain of ice, but that was all. For many days Kurt and his followers had traversed this wasted land without sight of life, intelligent or otherwise.

Their journey through the mountains had been arduous, but guided by Orst they had made good time. The twisted, bestial warrior had led them away from the few settlements that could be found in the depths of the inhospitable peaks, but still they had twice chanced upon Norse warbands, both also heading north. Kurt and his men had slain many of them, including their leaders, and the survivors had sworn allegiance to Kurt in return for him sparing their lives. Thus his warband was now some twenty strong, and he was confident that any foe, beast or otherwise, would think twice about attacking the well-armed party.

That did not help with the task ahead though, as they stood on a plateau of dark exposed rock, looking out over the wastes. Kurt knew there was life here, that there were tribes that lived this far north; he just wasn't sure how they survived in such an unforgiving landscape. There was no fertile land to till, no rivers to fish, no woods to hunt, but the people of the north must eat and drink, he consoled himself.

Orst snuffled impatiently and lumbered along the cliff edge to the right. Seeing the others following him, he settled into his loping stride, leading them towards a way down onto the plains beneath. Kurt walked beside Undar and Jakob, the others following behind.

'Can you feel how strong the breath of the gods blows?' said Jakob, walking along with a thick, twisted branch as a staff to aid him. 'It burns my veins.'

'I can feel it too,' said Undar, taking a deep breath as if to inhale the magical energy that poured around them from the north. 'I can feel it in my bones and in my blood. We should be wary of anyone we meet, for if they have been born and raised with this power around them, there is no saying how powerful they might be.'

'I'm not afraid,' said Kurt, turning his head to look at Undar. 'We are truly in the lands of the gods now. If we do not fight under their gaze here, then nowhere will they see our endeavours. I can feel their power, and it is there for us all, whether we were born in these barren lands or not. It is they who will decide who triumphs and who fails.'

'I admire your confidence,' replied Undar with a grin. 'If it was the gods who crossed out paths together, then I thank them.'

Jakob merely grunted and slowed his pace, waiting for the others to pass him by. When the rest of the warband were some way ahead, he stopped and pulled a pouch from his belt. Inside, his runestones clattered heavily. Opening the pouch he pulled one out. Once it had been the size of his thumbnail, and he could have held them all in one hand. Now it was a pebble the size of an eyeball, and it almost throbbed with power as he held it on his upraised palm. He could see blood-red veins on its surface, and striations of gold and silver that he had never noticed before.

With another glance to make sure he was unobserved by the others, he sat down, cross-legged, and placed the runestone in front of him on the hard rock. Closing his eyes, he held his hands a finger's breadth above the stone and breathed in, calming his mind, Focussing his thoughts, he began a mumbled chant, one that he had first heard many years ago as he had lain hidden at the back of the old shaman's tent, silently mouthing the words he overheard. Now the enchantment was simple, and it took him barely a few minutes to absorb the power of the runestone into himself, feeling its burning energy coursing through his body, almost painful in its potency.

Opening his eyes, he saw that the stone was perhaps half the size it had been. With a smile, he placed the stone back in the pouch and pulled out another. Yes, the breath of the gods blew strongly, and Jakob knew just how to use it.

ORST HAD LED them to a winding gulley, and as they made their way down the narrow defile, Kurt noticed the man-beast sniffing the air suspiciously. He seemed agitated, and often paused, cocking his head to one side and listening. Orst's tension began to seep into the thoughts of the others, and the quiet chatter that had echoed from the walls of the thin canyon had ceased. Kurt caught the scrape of a sword being loosened in its scabbard, a nervous cough from Bjordrin, the off-key whistling that Gird had become prone to when he was anxious.

Nearing the bottom of the descent, the defile widened, and at its centre stood a great monolith, easily three times the height of a man, and wider than Kurt's outstretched arms. Like a guardian it stood at the opening of the defile onto the plains beyond. From its base to its roughly hewn tip, it was carved in large runes, worn to scratches by many years exposed to the elements. On a great iron ring, driven into the stone at head height, a horned skull was hung, painted with flaking red dye. It had three eyes, and the crack in one temple was obviously from a blow of some kind.

'A warning?' Kurt asked, turning to Bjordrin who was following directly behind him. 'A territory marker?'

'A grave,' said Jakob, pushing past and hurrying forward to look at the monument. He craned his neck to look at its tip. 'The runes are faint, and strangely drawn, but I recognise some of it. Here is found the skull of, I'm not sure what the next word is, perhaps it means something like blood, perhaps heart. Yes, it is Blood-drinker, Vandel Blood-drinker. Here he fell, axe in hand, Kharneth's name upon his lips. May his soul be granted the eternal fight, for he battles on with the armies of the gods. Blessed is this skull, and curses of the Lord of Skulls on those who would defile it. There is more, about who he fought and killed, the great gifts bestowed upon him by Kharneth, the skulls he harvested for his god, and so on.'

'And would you erect such a marker for my grave?' asked Kurt, looking at Bjordrin.

'Not yet, Sutenvulf,' Bjordrin replied with a shrug. 'Perhaps when you have achieved something, you might be worth it.'

'I took you to the lands of the ancient kings and back, and I'm not worthy of such a monument?' said Kurt, genuinely incredulous.

'Not when you have now promised to lead us to the Gate of the Gods,' said Undar, looking at the imposing monolith. 'Perhaps when we've got a bit closer, you might deserve one.'

'I don't like it here,' said Gird. 'This place has an ill feeling about it.'

'Everywhere has an ill feeling about it, according to you,' replied Bjordrin. 'No wonder you whimper in your sleep.'

'I don't!' argued Gird, his outburst rattling the skeleton upon the banner pole he carried.

They fell silent as they heard a noise echoing along the canyon walls from ahead – the distinctive sound of metal on metal. Kurt pulled his sword free, and stepped to the left, circling around the monolith. The others fanned out around him to the left and right, readying their own weapons.

At the mouth of the defile, barely visible against the dark sky, a group of warriors stood, axes, maces and swords in hand. Each was clad in full armour, enamelled with red and painted with black runes, and at the front their leader held a massive hound on a chain, its fur a deep bronze colour. In his right hand he held a single-headed axe, a skull split from chin to brow adorning the shaft and blade.

He raised the axe, and his warriors stepped forward alongside him, some two dozen in all. He then lowered the axe until it was pointing at Kurt, the challenge obvious. As he strode forwards, Kurt raised his sword and then returned the gesture, accepting the challenge, in a ritual that had been undertaken in these lands ever since man had first recognised the power of the gods.

With a shout, the enemy champion released the chain and the hound ran towards Kurt, its slavering jaws gaping wide, filled with finger-long fangs. Grossly swollen muscles bunched and released under its thin skin as it bounded forward. With a moaning howl, Orst lumbered out from Kurt's right and the hound, scenting the bestial warrior, turned it its run. In a storm of claws and fangs, the two leaped at each other, gouging at fur and ripping flesh.

Kurt had no time to watch the display of raw savagery being acted out, as the rival champion and his followers rushed forwards with wordless bellows ringing from their helms. Kurt stopped his advance and took up a wide-legged stance, sword in both hands, learned over many years on the training ground of the Osterknacht. One of the enemy warriors, faceless behind his helmet, heavy chains clanging against his breastplate, hurled himself directly at Kurt, a short sword in each hand.

Kurt parried the first blow easily enough, and swayed backwards as the tip of the enemy's second sword swung past a few inches in front of his face. As he prepared to riposte, Kurt was struck by the sheer speed of the foe's assault, the warrior filled with a manic energy as he thrust forwards with a sword again. Blow after blow rang against Kurt's blade and he found himself giving ground, forced back pace after pace. The sounds of fighting had erupted around him, but he could not even spare a glance to see how his comrades fared, the lightning blows by his enemy requiring all of his attention.

Another red-clad warrior appeared to Kurt's right and he ducked beneath a screaming axe blade, thrusting forwards, the point of his sword clanging off the newcomer's armour. Neither seemed to slow in their assault, invigorated as they were by the power of the Blood God. Realising that he could not defend forever against such a remorseless attack, Kurt delved down into himself, drawing in the energy that flowed around and through him.

His sword erupted into flames as he unleashed the magic of the gods, the blade shearing through the axe head of one of his foes, spattering him and Kurt with droplets of molten iron. Ignoring the scalding metal splashed across his chest, Kurt lunged forward, smashing the tip of his burning blade through the chest of the warrior with the destroyed axe. A blade from the other fighter bit into Kurt's shoulder and he gave a yell, more of anger than pain.

Wrenching his sword free in a spurt of arterial blood, Kurt swung his sword overhead and brought it down towards the helm of the surviving foe. The two swords raised to block the attack shattered under the impact of the magical blade, and Kurt cleaved down with all of his strength. The blow split the warrior's head in two and carved down into his chest, almost bisecting him.

There was no pause for respite though, as the remains of the warrior fell at Kurt's feet, bubbling thick, dark blood onto the snow-covered ground. A glance to the right showed that Orst had despatched the hound and was snapping and snarling at two enemies with long spears, who thrust and prodded at his body, already streaming with blood from dozens of cuts and punctures.

A warning shout from the left spun Kurt around, in time to see the champion of Kharneth leaping over the headless body of one of Kurt's men, running full tilt at Kurt himself. Kurt had no time to brace himself, such was the speed of the other champion's sprint, and the two of them collided heavily, the wind smashed from Kurt's lungs as the red-armoured warrior drove his shoulder into Kurt's body. The two rolled on the ground, Kurt slamming his forehead against the armoured face of the enemy, his foe pounding at Kurt's head with the pommel of his axe.

With a kick, Kurt pushed himself to his feet, tearing himself free from the grasp of his enemy. Axe in hand, the other champion launched himself up from the ground; by this time Kurt was ready, sidestepping the charge and swinging his sword at the exposed back of his foe as he swept past. The blade bit into the armour of the champion, hurling him across the ground in a cloud of ice and dirt. The warrior pushed himself to his feet, retrieved his axe from where he had dropped it, and charged again.

This time Kurt met force with force, dipping his body and putting all of his considerable weight behind his outstretched sword. The impetus of the champion's onslaught carried him onto the blade, the sword punching through the armour of his helm into his nose before erupting out of the back of his head in a fountain of gore. The man collapsed, hanging by his head from Kurt's blade. With a roll of his shoulder, Kurt ripped the sword out of the top of the champion's head, thick, oozing ichor hissing on its supernaturally hot blade.

Kurt turned away to view the rest of the fight, but spun back as he heard the sound of a metallic laugh behind him. His helm ruined, the champion stood up, axe still in hand. Through the torn metal, Kurt could clearly see the man's face, ravaged and bloody, strands of muscle and fat hanging down from the ragged wound.

'Mother of the gods,' Kurt whispered to himself as the champion took up a fighting stance, and gave an ironic salute with his axe.

An explosion of light to Kurt's right attracted the attention of both. There stood Jakob, back against the monolith. A few yards from him, three smoking suits of armour lay on the ground as purple lighting played from the shaman's fingertips in a storm of crackling energy. Jakob's expression was one of terror as the energy pulsed from his hands, the charred corpses bucking and trembling as the lightning poured into them. With a shuddering gasp, Jakob collapsed to his knees as the energies dissipated.

Kurt reacted more quickly, swinging his sword in a rising arc, its tip connecting with the enemy champion in his groin. Lifted off the ground by the force of the blow, the champion was hurled backwards again, one leg spinning off to the left. Kurt stalked forwards, sword ready, but this time the champion did not move. Standing over the body, Kurt plunged his sword down through the armoured chest, just to make sure.

Undar was swinging left and right with his huge mace, keeping two warriors at bay, the corpses of three more lying mangled nearby. Bjordrin stepped over the body of another, blood streaming from a long cut down his left arm, and drove his sword into the back of one of the fighters facing Undar. As the other turned his head at this fresh attack, Undar's mace struck him in the chest, crushing his armour and sending blood, splinters of bone and shards of metal exploding outwards, the jagged remnants hurled across the ice-layered ground.

Some ten of Kurt's men were down, most of them likely dead by the grievous wounds hacked across their bodies and heads. Two more of the Kharneth worshippers stood back to back, hemmed in by Gird and three others. One of the armoured warriors leaped forward and Gird swung the banner around like a staff, connecting heavily with the warrior's head and spinning him to the ground. The other, realising his back was unprotected, glanced back and forth at the closing circle of foes, and then with a roar, took a double-handed grip on his axe and waded forward, disembowelling one of Kurt's men and sending the others scurrying back out of reach.

As the stalemate continued, Kurt strode over, sparing a glance for Jakob who was now stood leaning against the monument, one hand clasped to his face as blood streamed from his nose. Gird stood aside as Kurt approached, and the enemy fighter charged through the gap towards Kurt. Two steps to the left and a back-hand strike sent the warrior's head sailing into the air, streaming blood like a comet trail.

'See who's dead, and who can walk,' ordered Kurt, stepping over the headless body, with a look at Gird and the others. 'Any that can't walk, send them to the gods with honour.'

Gird nodded and hurried off while Kurt stood next to the still form of the surviving foe, who was shaking his head groggily as he sat up, looking for the sword that had been knocked from his grasp by the impact of Gird's blow with the banner.

'Get up,' said Kurt, resting his hands on the pommel of his blazing sword, its tip melting into the snow at Kurt's feet.

The warrior stood, and with a snarl, threw a punch at Kurt, which he caught easily on his right forearm, turning the blow aside. In the same movement, Kurt leaned forward and caught a grip on the warrior's throat, between his heavy breastplate and full helm. Lifting the man a few inches off the ground, Kurt looked at the wild, fury-filled eyes that stared at him from the helm's visor.

'What is your name?' Kurt asked. The man kicked and struggled against Kurt's iron grip until Kurt drove his sword into the ground and with his free left hand, smashed a fist into the side of the man's head. 'What is your name?'

'Vlamdir, beloved of Khargha,' the man replied. 'I will not surrender. Kharga would feast upon my soul and shit out my honour for such weakness.'

'How long have you waited in ambush here?' Kurt said, looking over his shoulder at the monument. 'Why here?'

Vlamdir remained silent for a moment until, Kurt raised his fist again.

'Every spring we come to the great cliff, to the stone of Vandel,' the warrior said. 'Here we fight for Kharga until he eats the sun and sends us back to our fires and wives.'

'And how long until Kharga eats the sun?' Kurt asked.

'It will not be many days now,' said Vlamdir, raising a hand to point at the glowering skies. 'Even now, he opens his mouth wide. His hunger has come early. The battles have not fed him this year. The blood for his cup has not flowed long enough. The skulls for his belly have been few.'

'And if you refuse to surrender, I will have to kill you,' Kurt said, lowering the man to the ground but maintaining his grip. 'You are a fierce warrior, and

Kharga obviously favours you. Would it not be better to swear your oath to me so that perhaps you can feed him more skulls?'

The man did not reply, and Kurt could see the man's eyes looking at him and then over Kurt's shoulder at the monolith. After a long while in thought, Vlamdir nodded. Releasing his grip, Kurt straightened, towering over the warrior who he now realised was quite short, even for a man not as blessed by the gods as himself. The top of his head barely reached to Kurt's chest.

'You will honour Kharga with me?' he said, removing his helm to reveal a young face, scarred with lines across his forehead, along each cheek and down his chin, in a rune that resembled a crude skull. His eyes were large and bright blue, in contrast to the thick mane of black hair that was roughly tied back at the back of his head.

'I have never heard of Kharga before, but I will honour him with the other gods,' said Kurt, extending a hand. Vlamdir gripped the hand and grinned with a flash of white teeth that contrasted with his weathered, olive skin.

'Kharga truly works in strange ways,' said Vlamdir. 'I woke this morning from a dream. A dream of blood. I saw my own body, pierced through with a hundred spears, afloat in a lake of crimson. I feared that today would be my last when I saw that there were warriors at the stone of Vandel. Perhaps Kharga has spared me for another purpose.'

'Perhaps he has,' agreed Kurt with a nod, plucking his sword from the ground and crouching to wiped the bloodied blade in the snow. 'I find it best not to worry about the gods' intentions too much. Experience has taught me that their eyes see further than those of mortal men, that dark times may get better and that good times are often only the beginning of sorrow.'

'Don't I know it,' he heard Jakob from behind, and turned to see the shaman, leaning upon his staff as if he were a hundred years old. His lip and chin were bloodstained and his eyes sunken and dark. He looked up into the sky, kissed his fist and raised it in front of his face in a gesture of appeasement. 'The minds of the gods are indeed beyond us, for who would give such power to those who cannot control it? I am sure they are amused by my folly.'

'Perhaps you just need some practice,' suggested Kurt, garnering a laugh from Vlamdir.

'It is indeed folly to wield the powers of Akhench in lands dedicated to Kharga,' the red-armoured warrior said. 'Anyone would know that.'

'Yes anyone would know that,' echoed Kurt with a vicious grin as Jakob closed his eyes and shook his head mournfully.

GIRD AND THE rest of the warband gathered the dead, from Kurt's warriors and their foes, and placed them and their weapons in a great heap around the monolith of Vandel. Those who had been too badly wounded to continue, but who could still hold their swords or axes, had their throats slit by Jakob, as he mumbled lamentations to the gods. Their bodies were added to the pyre. Those who had discarded their weapons were left for scavengers while the bodies of the honoured dead had been burned in a great flame that climbed up the pillar of stone and into the heavens.

With this duty done, they left the grave of Vandel, Vlamdir telling Kurt that no other warband was in the area, his former leader being the last to concede that the fighting season was over early. Vlamdir led Kurt and the others out of the gulley and turned eastwards, towards a cave not far distant where his former band had made camp for the last few months. Here, he told them, were horses and food for everyone. He laughed heartily as Kurt explained his goal of reaching the Gate of the Gods.

'You were going to walk there?' the incredulous tribesman said, walking between Kurt and Undar, dwarfed by the two chosen warriors. 'You are brave or foolish, or both. And what did you plan to eat?'

'We would hunt, as we would anywhere else,' said Undar, his face creased in a scowl. 'Do we look like farmers?'

'Then you would have gone very hungry indeed,' said Vlamdir.

'Oh, and so what do you eat, the air itself?' said Undar.

'We eat the great elk that roam these lands,' Vlamdir told them. 'But there are many miles between you and the hunting grounds. As Kharga opens his mouth to swallow the sun, they go eastward, and we follow. Hunt in the dark, fight in the light, that is the way of the Kurgan.'

'Is that your tribe, the Kurgan?' asked Kurt. 'Where do the Kurgan live?'

'You are Norse, yes?' said Vlamdir. 'From the south?'

'Well,' said Kurt, unsure how to answer. 'I am from the south, and the Norse are my people now.'

'But the Norse are not your tribe, are they?' said Vlamdir. He carried his helm under his arm as he walked, and for the first time, Kurt noticed thin strands of bronze wire woven into his hair. In fact, he realised, there were even tiny slivers of bronze imbedded into the scars cut into his flesh.

'No, my tribe is, was, the Fjaergard,' Kurt replied.

'And my tribe were the Haktars,' explained Vlamdir. 'When the darkness of Kharga's maw is lifted, we leave the tribe and fight with the other tribes. When the light of the sun is swallowed again, we return to our tribes, to hunt. Eastwards, far across the ice sea, the Kurgan can be found. This is the horseland. Men do not walk here.'

'Nothing wrong with walking,' Undar said, slapping his thigh. 'Makes your legs good and strong.'

'So does riding,' said Kurt, who had spent many long hours in the saddle when he had been a knight of Ostermark. 'It seems you will have to learn to ride, Undar, as will everyone else who has never sat in a saddle.'

'Never met a beast I could not master,' Undar said proudly. Kurt and Vlamdir exchanged a knowing look and the Kurgan had to fake a cough to hide his smirk, Undar looking at them suspiciously.

'It's just riding a horse, how hard can it be?' Undar demanded.

'I'm sure you will be fine,' said Kurt, looking northwards as dark clouds boiled on the horizon.

Out there, in the growing gloom, lay the Gate of the Gods. Somewhere, many leagues distant, Kurt's destiny awaited him. As he thought of the long journey that was about to begin, his heart was light and he felt confident. Surely his encounter with the enemy warband, and claiming their steeds and food with his victory, was sign that the gods still approved of his quest?

CHAPTER FIVE
Purpose
The Talabec, South of the Howling Hills, Late winter 1712

SODDEN WITH SEWER water they had finally made their escape into the marshes around Marienburg and had met one of Ruud's associates who had taken them to a boat moored on the Reik a few miles from the city. From there the boat had headed upstream along the Reik, covering the slow miles during the day, taking cautious refuge by nights at the guarded mooring points along the river.

Travel by river was safer than the roads through the deep forests, but was by no means uneventful. Beastmen often stalked the banks, in the deepest stretches where the river patrols did not venture often. River pirates would also ply their own murderous trade on the mighty river, some of them on ships large enough to be seaworthy, capable of taking their ill-gotten loot out of the Empire to be sold in the bazaars of Copher and the markets of Bordeleaux.

Ten days into their journey and they had sighted Altdorf, once the greatest city in the west, capital of the Reikland princes. Its massive walls rose out of the farms and meadows reclaimed from the all-covering forest, the towers of the count's keep atop the central mount. Ursula had been keen not to linger long in Altdorf, fearing that if her presence were known, and more particularly that of the magical sword in her possession, then escaping from Marienburg would have been for nothing.

They stayed one night in the wharfs at Altdorf before moving along in the morning, taking the easterly route up the Talabec. They had no plan except to get as far from the grasping hands of Luiten as was feasibly possible, and that meant heading south and east. The boat they were on, a merchantman owned by a cousin of Ruud's, was bound for Talabheim, and Ruprecht and Johannes were looking forward to seeing the city of their birth again.

JOHANNES WAS AWOKEN by a shuddering scream. Flinging back his blankets, he leapt up, his head crashing against the planking of the decking above. Cursing, he pulled his sword from the scabbard hanging from the hook at one end of the cot. He glanced at his boots and then changed his mind, padding half naked out through the door onto the stairwell beyond. Taking them two at a time, he raced up to the deck of the long barge. As he emerged into the cool night air his skin prickled at the chill. The sky was cloudy and dark, the moons having set many hours ago. The boat's single sail creaked noisily in the wind, the canvas flapping loudly against the mast, startling Johannes.

A thumping behind him heralded the arrival of Ruprecht, half hopping up the steps, pulling on his left boot as he came, his hammer awkwardly held under one arm.

'Never go anywhere without your boots,' the large man admonished him with a glance at Johannes's bare feet. 'You never know where you might end up.'

The scream sounded again, from forward and they dashed towards the source of the noise, running along the narrow space between the side of the boat and the piles of boxes and sacks on the centre of the deck, which made up the barge's legitimate cargo.

They came to the small superstructure at the fore that was the wheelhouse and upper cabins, where Ursula's bed was hung. A man, one of the ship's crew, came stumbling out of the open door, clasping his hands to his face. In the glow of the prow lantern they could see blood on his white shirt, pouring down through his hands. The bargeman collapsed to his knees on the deck and shrieked again, the same high-pitched scream they had heard earlier.

'What is it?' Johannes asked as he stopped beside the wounded man.

'Leave him,' snapped Ruprecht, hefting his hammer in his right hand and advancing into the dark cabin.

A faint blue glow emanated from the doorway into the room to the right. Ursula's room. Johannes pushed past Ruprecht as the larger man paused at the doorway, and instinctively ducked as movement hurtled towards him out of the gloom.

'Ursula?' he managed to say before Ruprecht grabbed him by the shoulder and hauled him back.

In the middle of the room, Ursula stood with Ulfshard in her hands, her auburn hair hanging in long curls down her naked body. Her eyes were wide open, staring at something in the ceiling. She leapt backwards on the balls of her feet as if she were being attacked and swept out with Marbad's sword, the blade trailing blue fire in the air.

'Ursula?' Johannes said again.

'Shut up, boy,' hissed Ruprecht, crouching down and leaning forward to get a view of the roof of the cabin. There was nothing there.

'What's she saying?' Johannes asked, noticing that Ursula's lips were moving constantly, as she whispered to herself.

With a shriek, Ursula was hurled back against the bulkhead behind her, Ulfshard toppling from her hands onto the deck. It glowed fitfully for a moment longer and then dimmed. Ruprecht stepped forward, but Johannes was quicker, jumping past and crouching down beside the dazed woman as she half-lay against the wall, legs crumpled beneath her. Ruprecht appeared next to him with a blanket and draped it across Ursula's naked form.

'Is she alright?' Johannes asked, looking with concern at the stunned girl. Her lips were still whispering, so low that Johannes could not hear what she was saying even though he was right next to her.

With a gasp of air, Ursula snapped her head back, banging it against the wall, and her eyes seemed to focus. Johannes smiled with relief, but his smile faded as he saw that Ursula's attention was fixed on Ruprecht. She stood up, the blanket slipping to the floor, and Johannes averted his gaze, blushing as he stared at the planking of the deck underfoot. He could hear the sound of more people clustering outside, bare feet slapping on the deck, boots clumping on wood, the hiss of torches. Turning, he saw Meisten Kempter, owner and captain of the boat. He had a pistol in his hand, the match glowing. Beside him stood Hunda, his younger brother by many years, a belaying pin in his meaty fist.

'What is going on?' the captain demanded, raising the pistol in a shaking hand.

'Wolves and hounds,' Johannes heard Ursula say behind him. He was torn between turning around and keeping the angry crewmen in sight. He settled for positioning himself in front of the door, side on to both, his sword arm closest to the sailors.

'Wait a moment,' he said, holding up his other hand in front of the Kempters. 'Wait.'

'What did you say?' Ruprecht said, his voice low and soft. 'What about wolves and hounds?'

Ursula stepped across the room and picked up Ulfshard, its pommel stone burning softly. She crossed back to her hanging cot and sheathed the magical blade, before pulling a smock from the pile of clothes in a chest underneath the bed. Pulling it over her head, she turned around and swept her hair out of her face.

'I had a dream,' she said, a trickle of sweat running down her nose and forming as a drip at the tip. 'I saw a great pack of hounds, devil hounds, sweeping down upon me.'

'She's bewitched,' said Hunda, dropping the belaying pin and making a protective sign in front of his chest with his thumbs intertwined. 'Shoot her, Meisten.'

'If you pull that trigger, you'll know what three feet of cold steel feels like,' hissed Johannes, glaring at the captain. 'If it's the last thing I do, I swear it.'

The captain's hand wavered even more and after a moment he dropped his arm to the side. Two more of the crew pushed in behind Hunda, one with a cudgel, the other with a sword in his hand.

'It's not natural,' Meisten said. 'She's bewitched. One of my men with his nose cut off, strange lights, shrieking and dreams about hounds. That's witchery, for sure.'

'Tell me about the dream,' Ruprecht was saying, his hands on Ursula's shoulders. 'What about the hounds?'

'Devil hounds, with fire for eyes and bronze fangs,' Ursula said. 'They came from the snow, from the north. A great pack of them, covering the lands in one great tide of evil.'

'What did the hounds do?' Ruprecht pressed. 'What happened?'

'There was one, their leader, a hound larger than a man, with a tongue of flame,' Ursula said, and she shuddered at the recollection. She remembered the terror she had felt as the beast had loomed over her, its massive jaws opened wide, its hot breath on her face. 'I was all alone, and I cried out for help. I tried to fight it, but it was so very strong. It knocked me down. But then the wolves came, the wolves helped me.'

'What wolves?' asked Ruprecht. 'Where did the wolves come from?'

'She's babbling, for sure,' said Meisten and was about to say more when Johannes silenced him with a wave of his sword tip.

'A great host of them swept up from behind me,' explained Ursula, eyes fixed on Ruprecht's face. 'Great wolves with white and black fur, and claws of burnished steel. The wolves attacked the hounds, and it was savage. They came from the city of wolves, to help me against the daemon hounds.'

'The city of the white wolf, Middenheim?' said Johannes. 'Was this a sign. Are we supposed to go to Middenheim for something?'

'What's this about signs?' demanded Meisten. 'We're on the Reik, going to Talabheim. There's not even a river at Middenheim, and even if there was, we're not going there. In fact, you're not going anywhere. I want you off my boat, for sure.'

'Now wait a minute...' began Johannes.

'It's alright,' said Ursula stepping out of Ruprecht's grip and pacing forward. The sailors clustered in the doorway elbowed each other as they tried to shuffle back.

'Get back, witch,' said Hunda, snatching up his belaying pin again. 'Get back, or we'll burn you.'

'Burn me?' snarled Ursula, her face suddenly contorted with rage, 'Burn me? They tried to burn me once before, didn't they? But he came, didn't he? Swept me away on his charger like the noble knight we all thought he was. Perhaps I should have burned, but I didn't, and you aren't going to be the ones who do it!'

'Ursula, calm down,' said Ruprecht, and Ursula sagged at the sound of his voice. The burly Talabheimer stood next to her and cradled her head against his chest. 'Calm down.'

'She's not a witch,' said Johannes, almost choking on the word. 'There's not an ounce of evil in her. It's the gods, it's they who send her these dreams. She speaks with Sigmar, he shows her things, warns her of things.'

'Oh, yes, it's the gods, of course,' said Hunda.

'Shut up, Hunda,' said Meisten, pulling the match from his pistol and dropping it to the floor. He crushed it beneath his boot and looked at his young brother. 'I believe them.'

'You believe them?' said Hunda with an incredulous shake of his shaven head.

'You never knew your Aunt Gilda,' Meisten said with sadness in his voice. 'She died two years before you were born. They said she heard the voices of daemons, but she always claimed it was the voices of the gods. They burned her, tore down her house, murdered her little kid. Only five he was, five summers old. The spawn of devils they said he was, on account of Gilda being unwed and such.'

'What of it?' asked Hunda.

'She used to sit me on her knee, by the fire, ever since I was old enough to understand,' Meisten explained, his voice cracked with emotion. 'I thought they were stories, just stories, until our ma explained them later, when they had taken Gilda away. She had the sight, you see, the dreamsight. She told me her dreams. Some of them scared me, for sure, scared me for nights afterwards. But others were beautiful, so beautiful, for sure.'

'That doesn't stop this wench being a witch,' Hunda argued, gesturing towards Ursula with the metal club in his hand.

Johannes bristled at Hunda's insulting tone, but before he could say anything, the barge captain was speaking again.

'Know what ma said as they took her away?' said Meisten, now his eyes brimming with tears. 'As the priests dragged her away, and she never said no word, nor kicked nor struggled? Ma looks down at me, for I was all of ten summers, for sure, and what did she say? She told me it wasn't right, them taking Aunt Gilda.' At this point he looked at Johannes and gave a sad smile. 'Ma said that she didn't have an ounce of evil in her, them exact same words, for sure. Said there weren't many in the world like that, and I'd been lucky to have known one of them.'

Hunda opened his mouth, and then closed it again. His brow furrowed in thought, and his hand dropped heavily to his side.

'Ma said that, did she?' Hunda asked. Meisten nodded, using a fingertip to clear the moisture from his eyes.

Ursula turned to them, and her face was set. She looked at Meisten Kempter calmly.

'You have to help us get to Middenheim,' she said, her voice quiet. 'Please.'

'Actually, I don't,' said Meisten.

'You have to help them, after what ma said,' protested Hunda, but Meisten waved him to silence.

'Shut up, Hunda,' the captain said, before turning to Ursula. 'You see, you don't want to go to Middenheim, you want to go to Wolfenburg, for sure.'

'What?' exclaimed Johannes. 'But Middenheim is the city of the wolf!'

'The city of the white wolf, for sure,' said Meisten with a sly smile. 'But the lass's wolves were white and black, yes? Colour's very important in dreams, you know, my aunt taught me that.'

'Yes, they were white, with black stripes across their haunches and shoulders,' Ursula said with a nod.

'The colours of Ostland,' said Ruprecht, looking at Meisten with surprise and admiration. 'Wolfenburg is the capital of Ostland, and the state colours are black and white. The black and white city of the wolf.'

'For sure,' said Meisten, with a grin. 'For sure.'

SOUTH AND EAST they travelled down the great River Talabec, sacred river of Taal himself. They had left behind them the disturbing memories of glorious Altdorf now half in ruins, the scars of the city's long stand against the orc warlord Gorbad Ironclaw still torn into her high walls and armoured towers. The wide river carried them past the Howling Hills, a bleak land of barren mounts and treacherous fens, and onwards they wound their way through the great dark forests that swathed the Empire.

As their journey continued, Ursula succumbed to a silent melancholy. She would more often than not sit alone at the prow of the barge, where the sailors did not have to give her a wide berth, staring to the north-east. Out there lay the forests of Hochland, and in the dim distance the white-tipped peaks of the Middle Mountains. Beyond lay Kislev, the snow-shrouded realm where she and Kurt had fled from the witch hunter Marius van Diesl. North still, on the borders of Kislev and the hostile lands of the Troll Country lay the burned ruins of Tungask, where Kurt had finally turned from the light. There she had lost him. Now, even further north, lay Norsca, his new home, where even now she knew that he was gathering his army. Her dream was clear to her. The hounds of the north were the Norse; the great beast that led them was Kurt. It was Ursula who had unwittingly unleashed the evil within him, and now Sigmar looked to her to right that wrong.

Johannes tried to lighten her mood whenever he could, though she never spoke of her troubling thoughts. Ruprecht brooded more and more, and the atmosphere on the barge was often tense. The crew trusted them little, and if not been for their loyalty to their captain, would have long ago thrown them overboard, or worse. Despite his brother's faith, Hunda was still wary of Ursula in particular, and would often leave the deck if she came out of her cabin.

Ursula's solitary depression saddened Johannes terribly, and often Ruprecht would catch him looking wistfully towards the prow where she sat, far away in thought. When asked, the young man would blush and hurry away with no answer. To Ruprecht it was clear; Johannes was lovesick. Ruprecht had neither the

heart nor the tact to tell Johannes that his feelings
were unrequited, and in truth Ruprecht harboured the
secret hope that perhaps Ursula would actually notice
the lad's affections and at least be brought out of her
silent contemplation.

Even with Ruprecht, the only man she truly trusted,
Ursula was often distant and curt. Though she did not
know it, her burly friend often sat outside her cabin in
the chill nights, listening to her mumbling in her
sleep, and he was always there first when she awoke
from the terrifying dreams of the great hound that
chased her through the night.

After many more days of sailing, Johannes started to
become more excited again, and Ruprecht shared his
enthusiasm, for even as the Middle Mountains grew
closer to the north, so too their travels took them
closer to Talabheim, the city of their birth. Here they
ran into many more craft on the water, plying their
trade between the capital of Talabecland and the settlements further down the river.

In the villages and towns they moored in, the smithies
were constantly busy. Barges laden with weapons and
swords, large bundles of bow stakes and bales of bow-
strings, heaved their way upstream, supplying the armies
of the Ottilia. It had been nearly four centuries since the
Ottilia of the day had declared herself Empress in defiance of the claim by the Prince of Altdorf, the duly
elected Emperor of the time. Four hundred years of
rivalry, first between Talabecland and Stirland, then with
Middenland, then the Reikland and Stirland again.

Back and forth across the decades alliances had been
made and broken, armies sent to war with those who

had once been neighbours, all the while the farms were overrun by the creatures of the woods and bandits preyed upon those who could not defend themselves. Four hundred years of division had left its scars upon the land, as they passed the ghostly ruins of towns that had fallen to the forest-dwellers, now consumed again by the dark-boled trees.

As Ursula looked upon the ruins of a mill built next to a pool fed by the Talabec, she thought scornfully about her own ambitions only a year before. It had seemed so simple, to deliver Ulfshard to the Count of Marienburg to aid his claim to the throne. Even when Count Luiten had revealed himself to be as self-serving and greedy as the rest of the nobles, Ursula had still harboured a secret hope. She had thought that perhaps her war against the Norsemen, her valiant fight against the barbarians who preyed upon the coast of the Empire, would somehow catch the imagination of the great and the powerful.

Now she realised that faith was a scarce commodity, and next to gold and steel, was judged worthless by many. Her hopes that the Empire might be united within her lifetime were dashed, and now all that concerned her was seeing at least the scattered remnants of the one great nation survive to the end of her life.

At Wolfenburg, perhaps she would find an ally; perhaps she might once again set a flame to the fuse that was the Empire's anger. This time she was more realistic in her intentions, though. She was no leader of armies, she was no general. She could fight well enough, and wielding Ulfshard she knew she was a match for most foes, but war was not fought alone by brave men and women. War was fought with supplies and weapons, with thousands of men, paid for by their masters. She had none of these things, but perhaps, Sigmar willing, she would find them in Wolfenburg.

And so she bent her every thought to what she would do when she got there. She would risk her life if she declared that she heard the will of Sigmar, as she had done in the town of Badenhof when she had been put on trial for witchcraft. The thought of death no longer scared her, but the thought that she might fail was terrifying. The hound that stalked her through her dreams had begun to hunt her waking thoughts too. She could hear its heavy panting just behind her; feel the heat from its fiery tongue upon the back of her neck. She wanted to run away from it, to hide, but she knew there was no real hiding place. She had to face the beast, and whether it was alone or with an army would depend on what she found in Wolfenburg.

On the thirtieth day since they had been ushered through the dank sewers of Marienburg by Ruud Goeyen and handed into the care of Meisten Kempter, they caught sight of Talabheim. In the distance to starboard, a great line of hills rose out of the forests, a continuous dark line at their crest. As they approached closer, Ursula could see a wall atop the nearly even slopes, large towers positioned every few hundred paces.

'That is the wall of Talabheim,' Johannes said proudly as he stood next to Ursula and looked at the place of his birth. 'It is the rim of a great bowl, more than half a day's travel from one side to the other. It takes five thousand men to man the wall at full strength.'

'Have to admit it's good to see it again,' said Ruprecht, walking up and leaning against the wall of the forward cabins just behind the pair. 'I was born there, and it still impresses me.'

'The Eye of the Forest it's called,' Johannes said to Ursula with a smile. 'A place of refuge from the dark forests, a sanctuary from the beasts that inhabit the shadowy places of the world.'

'Talabheim must be massive,' said Ursula, shielding her eyes against the morning sun. 'I can see why the Ottila feels safe to claim the throne of Emperor.'

'Indeed it would be a foolish army that besieges Talabheim, though some have tried,' said Johannes. 'Middenheimers may claim that they live in the most impregnable fortress of the Empire, but I am sure there are those who would rather scale a mile-high rock than storm the great wall of Talabheim.'

'The city itself is not so large,' Ruprecht said, pushing himself upright. 'Much of the land inside the wall is farmland, and Talabheim itself sits at the centre.'

'Oh,' said Ursula. 'So it isn't that big, then?'

'Well, certainly big enough,' said Johannes, mildly affronted at the unintentional slight on the city of his birth. 'Maybe Marienburg and Altdorf are larger, but not by much.'

The sailed onwards for several more miles as the sun rose to its zenith, before they came across a break in the crater wall. Tall, narrow buildings clustered along the banks of the Talabec, long wharfs jutting into the river, and stretched up street after street along the hillside to the curtain wall itself. Barges and fishing boats were laid up on the shore and moored to the jetties, and a pall of smoke hung over the settlement.

'This is where I was brought up,' Ruprecht told them as the crew busied themselves across the deck taking in the sail. 'Talagaad, gateway to the Eye of the Forest! All the trade between Talabheim, Altdorf and Kislev passes through here, one way or the other.'

'It looks very... busy,' said Ursula.

'I was born in Talabheim itself,' Johannes said, standing with one foot on the bulwark of the barge. 'I was squired to a knight of the Ottila's court.'

'Yes, and then you stole his armour and ran off,' Ruprecht added, earning himself a scowl from Johannes.

'I made my own way in the world, unlike the spoilt brats who fight each other with wooden swords for the amusement of the knights,' Johannes said, frowning. 'I certainly had you fooled, old bear.'

'Yes, you certainly played the part of the dashing young knight very well,' said Ursula, not turning around.

'Really?' said Johannes, his anger forgotten. He puffed up his chest and gave Ruprecht a smug look. 'I suppose I looked very stylish in my armour, charging across the field of battle.'

'You looked even better when you fell on your arse,' muttered Ruprecht, but Johannes did not hear. The young would-be knight sauntered over and stood next to Ursula.

'If we stay here a few days, I can show you some of the best taverns in Talabecland,' he suggested. 'All very hospitable and clean, of course.'

'No,' Ursula said, not really listening, lost once more in her own thoughts. 'We have to get to Wolfenburg.'

'Well, we're two-thirds of the way there, surely a few days…' Johannes trailed off as he saw the faraway look in Ursula's eye. 'Well, have a think about it at least.'

Shoulders sagging, Johannes turned away, avoiding Ruprecht's gaze, and slouched off towards the main deck. Ruprecht watched him go, his heart heavy. The lad's got persistence, he thought, but perhaps it would be better if he stayed here and found himself a good lass, rather than following Ursula around like a puppy into the gods only knew what kind of trouble. He was young, he would get over it. He looked up to suggest this to Ursula, but she was gone. She was sitting in her usual place on the prow, staring out to the north.

It took a day to unload their cargo, with Hunda bellowing obscenities at the stevedores the whole time, while Meisten headed into Talagaad to seek fresh wares to take on to Wolfenburg. As he saw it, he was going there anyway, there was no point missing an opportunity. He returned late in the evening, clutching a sheaf of papers, his permits to travel onwards. Of late, Ostland and Talabecland had been on good terms and trading was picking up, and the prospect of war with Stirland was growing again so the Ottila had commanded the armouries to be filled once more in preparation, should hostilities actually erupt. This had garnered Meisten a contract to go to Wolfenburg to collect tanned leather for saddles and belts, a nice round trip of thirty days, wind permitting, which would net him a tidy profit.

As night fell, the fishing boats were pushed out and crewed, drifting quietly into the dark. Lanterns on either side of the river were lit, illuminating the ferry landings that were still busy with passengers well into the night. Not wishing to pay a night mooring fee, Meisten had the crew row the barge a little way upriver, and as they swung to and fro on the anchor, the sounds of Talagaad bubbled over the river to them: outbursts of riotous singing from riverside taverns; the regular chiming of a bell in the distance sounding out each hour; dogs barking and shouted arguments between unhappy neighbours.

With these familiar noises in his ears, Ruprecht slept soundly that night, the first time in many years. He dreamed of his childhood and his contented snoring kept Johannes awake in the next room as the young man fretted about Ursula and her growing coldness.

THE NEXT MORNING, Johannes looked tired and weary. As the crew set the sail he suddenly dashed back down to his berth and then re-emerged a moment later carrying a wineskin he had procured from Talagaad the day before. He had vehemently claimed that he had paid for it, too vehemently for Ruprecht's liking but he had held his tongue. As the sun broke over the wall of Talabheim, Johannes leaned over the side of the boat and pulled the stopper from the wineskin, pouring out the deep red contents into the lapping waves.

'What are you doing?' Ursula called from the other side of the deck. 'Has it gone sour?'

'Not at all,' said Johannes with a smile. 'Libations for Taal, the finest quality wine I could afford. Never hurts to keep the gods happy.'

He leaned over the side, precariously balanced on the bulwark, and then dipped the empty wineskin into the water, filling it to the top. Stoppering the skin, he waved it at Ursula.

'And what's that for?' she asked.

'This is the Talabec, sacred river of great Taal,' Johannes said, crossing over to stand next to her. He gave the wineskin a shake. 'Holy water! You never know, it might come in useful.'

For much of the time the wind was foul and the crew were forced to take in the sail and row upstream. Heavy clouds gathered overhead and the first of the spring rains began, turning the river into a riot of splashes. On the eighth day they had turned off the Talabec onto a narrow tributary that rushed down from the Middle Mountains. Their headway was even slower along this stretch as the crew pulled against the strong current of the flooded river. On the seventeenth day, they sighted Hoarsonburg, a port just thirty miles from Wolfenburg.

Meisten wished them well, and even insisted on paying them for their help, thought they had done little except get in the way of the regular crew. He had a tear in his eye as he embraced Ursula, who gave him a perfunctory nod in return and then turned away without saying a word. Ruprecht was more profuse in his thanks, knowing that without the captain's belief in

Ursula, they would still be stuck in the forests five hundred miles away. Their present situation was much more preferable. At worst they could walk to Wolfenburg in two days, at best they would be able to hitch a ride with one of the many merchants travelling along the road.

Ursula had neither hope nor fear of what lay ahead, as they walked up the steep streets of Hoarsonburg towards the centre of the town. Whatever happened next, for good or ill, would be in the lap of the gods. She knew how to get an army now.

CHAPTER SIX
Power
Realm of Chaos

TIME HAD NOT only ceased to have meaning, it had ceased to pass. The sun never rose or set, the wind never blew, the stars never came out. The sky was simply a constant, eternal miasma of shifting colours, without form, rhythm or substance. The winds of power that blew from the north were like a hurricane to Kurt. The air felt like a furnace, an ever-present blasting energy that suffused his whole being.

Direction had become almost meaningless, with no stars or sun as a guide. But Kurt could feel the power around him, could feel it strengthening nearly with every step. There was only north, towards the Gate of the Gods and his destiny. For so long he had headed north, been drawn there by the paths he had taken.

When he had fled with Ursula from Badenhof, it was to the north they had headed. When Ursula had betrayed him at Tungask, it was to Norsca that he had gone. Only his ill-fated expedition to Araby had taken him south, far to the south, and the ironic fact that his wife and child had been slain while he was away was not lost on him, though he saw no humour in it. Now he was heading north again, to challenge the gods themselves to grant him the power to avenge himself on those who had destroyed his family.

Now Kurt found himself in a realm of half-worlds, a dreamscape of shifting realities. Distance was altered, curved. On occasion he would spy a distant structure, but they would never appear any closer. Shapes on the periphery of his vision would cause him to turn his head, but there would be nothing to see. The ground itself changed underfoot, one minute being a snow-covered tundra, while another step would see him sinking into dank bog, or walking through sand.

Shapes appeared in the skies, like floating castles, grinning faces and skulls with eyes that dripped blood. They were never quite there, and if one focussed on them they would disappear like cloud-shapes, but always there was movement all around. They would see distant figures but never met another soul. They came across a towering keep of bone and ice, and could hear a great bell tolling from within. There was no gate nor windows, and no creature to be seen. As soon as they passed and looked back it was gone.

The magical winds brought fell voices and strange sounds. Often Kurt would think his heart hammering in his chest, only to realise it was a distant drumbeat carried to his ears. Marching feet echoed around them as they walked, accompanied by half-glimpsed dread legions passing through them. Rank after rank of twisted entities strode past, following banners of skulls, accompanied by the blaring of brazen horns, but if one were to reach out to touch them, they were no longer there.

Cackling laughter plagued Kurt for a long time, accompanied by incessant whispering of half-heard words, most of them meaningless, but now and then he thought he heard his name mentioned. The flap of great leathery wings would beat in the sky above and they would stop with weapons drawn, searching the roiling mass of the heavens for some beast.

Slowly, but with increasing power, the breath of the gods had begun to take its toll. Bjordrin's skin became flaky and then as it fell away in great clumps, glistening silver scales were revealed beneath. Gird could barely carry Kurt's standard, his fingers on both hands having gradually fused into crude, dark-skinned claws, while his back twisted and hunched as a tail grew from his spine. Each new discovery was greeted as a gift from the gods; proof positive that the Powers of the North were indeed aware of them now.

When Undar's armour split apart, burst open by his bulging muscles threaded with veins like ropes, they stopped and thanked the gods for their power. The shaman led their prayers, cavorting back and forth gabbling in a tongue none of the others understood. Orst, who had been to these lands before, suffered badly. His eyes had dimmed and his behaviour showed almost no sign of intelligence. Bony spines now erupted from his fur-covered body and his neck had elongated, while extra eyes had sprouted from his forehead, a disturbing pale blue with no pupils.

Kurt fought hard against the breath of change, though he could feel it working within his own body, splitting and tearing, knitting and reshaping his bones and flesh. He found that if he concentrated hard, exerted his will on the forces ravaging his form, he could control the mutation, even shape it. He had not learned this trick before a vast, curved horn had extruded from his skull, seemingly made of marble. His hair fell out, and small knuckle-like nodules dotted his scalp. Under the skin of his back he could feel something writhing and moving, as his flesh warped and eddied like liquid under the constant barrage of magical energy.

Jakob perhaps suffered most, his hand now fused to the staff that he had carried, fingers of wood entwined with the shaft, while leafy branches grew out of his arm and shoulder. He had lost an eye, covered over with a scabrous mass of pulsating flesh that beat like a second heart. His other eye was now like a sphere of pure gold, though he claimed he could see perfectly well. His teeth protruded over his lips from bleeding gums, carving grooves into his flesh. It was impossible to say when it happened, but at some point the runestones that he had once carried at his belt had moved and fused to his flesh, seven glowing fist-sized rocks. Stars circled at their core, and when Kurt looked into them, he thought he could see distant lands: towns of the Empire, the sparkling domes of Araby, the dark jungles of the Southlands.

Ever northwards they continued, the Realm of Chaos exacting its influence on their bodies and minds. Over an untold time they had met and fought other warbands, and men had died and men had joined Kurt's service, but he no longer knew nor cared about them. Existence – for there was no true life here, no hunger, no thirst, no sleep – had become a never-ending battle. It was a battle against the challenges of the gods, who poured forth their power to turn him back from his quest. It was a battle against other champions, half-remembered men in armour or furs, with writhing tentacles and faces like beasts, who fell to Kurt's flaming sword. Whenever he unleashed his power now, fireballs erupted from the blade, and the ground itself burned at his feet.

And still the voices were always there, goading and taunting him, urging him on, whispering promises and threats from somewhere inside his head, until he was not sure whether the voices belonged to others or they were his own thoughts. Sometimes they said such beautiful things, conjuring images of silver-watered streams pouring through luscious forests. Other times they described places of nightmare, where walls of burned flesh caged men in pits filled with twin-tailed snakes.

The waking dreams never ceased now, and Kurt often walked with his eyes screwed shut, trying to blank out the voices, not looking at the scenes around him. When he relented he would find himself walking through a town, or down a rocky hillside, or wading through crimson pools of blood. Wailing faces appeared in up-thrusts of quivering rock, and fanged maws opened up beside him, gnashing together like mantraps.

At times he was a child again, in the warm redness of the womb, listening to his mother's heart, or a child of a few years old toddling excitedly across the gardens of his father's manor house. Many times he thought he had been sleeping, as he awoke with his heart pounding, plagued by images of his father, mother and sister burning at the stakes.

With these memories came greater resolve. Kurt dragged himself onwards, back from the brink of madness he had teetered along. Soon one scene was all that he could see – van Diesl and three burning figures, who cried out to him with ghostly voices to avenge them. Anger grew with the memory, and anger turned to cold hatred. Fire and death would engulf the Empire as the Empire had engulfed Kurt's life with fire and death. From his birth-family to his wife and child, the flames had consumed them all. Now he would bring the fire of the gods to the south, and raze the Empire to ashes, and choke their corpulent leaders on the smoke.

The promise pleased the gods and he could feel their approval wash over him in waves of golden strokes, invigorating him, hardening his flesh, strengthening and building him. He felt buoyed up by their energy and at times would break in to a run, to reach them all the quicker, though in this land such things as distance and time could not so easily be defined.

They spoke little to each other, each man following his own path, enduring his own challenges. Bayor had long since disappeared without trace, thought Kurt suspected that his mangled, misshapen body lived on somewhere behind them along with the other unfortunates who had succumbed to the breath of the gods.

It was with some surprise then, that Kurt heard a voice that was not inside his head. The first human voice he had heard in a whole day, or perhaps a hundred days, he could not be sure. Looking around, as if seeing through a fog, he saw Vlamdir. The short warrior's armour had fused into his skin, a shifting, metallic layer of muscle and sinew, pierced with rivets and hung with the same chains that he always worn. His face was almost unrecognisable, the skin peeled away and hanging in folds to reveal tendons and white fat, thin blue veins tracing a maze across his flesh, his eyeballs bulging in their sockets.

'Did you say something?' Kurt said, surprised at the sound of his own voice. For a moment he had to think hard, working out whether he had really spoken at all, or whether he had just imagined that he had.

'We are being hunted,' Vlamdir said, and he pointed out to the left, and then to the right.

Canine shapes could be seen loping alongside the warband, dark shadows that drifted in and out of sight. Vistas of snarling trees that seemed to fade into existence masked them, and they skulked behind rocks that were not truly there. For a while they were beside them, sometimes closer, sometimes just a reddish shadow in the distance. Other times they were being tracked from behind, and as Kurt walked on he would often glance over his shoulder, certain that he heard a panting breath or distant howl. Now and then they seemed to be leading the party onwards, as Kurt stumbled across shallow paw marks larger than his hand, which dissolved away as he bent to look at them. The stench of blood hung heavy in the air.

'What are they?' Kurt asked Vlamdir, perhaps straight after the Kurgan had spoken, although to Kurt it felt like several days had passed since they had first sighted their stalkers.

'They are the hounds of blood, the hunters of Kharga,' Vlamdir replied. 'Once they have caught the scent of their prey they will hunt them anywhere, across seas, mountains and forests, to the ends of the earth.'

'Why do they not attack?' Kurt said, glancing left and right as he caught flickers of movement at the edge of his vision.

'I do not know,' admitted Vlamdir. 'Perhaps they are seeking only one of us, and are waiting for him to fall behind.'

They walked on in silence as a great shadow fell over them. Above, a great skull-shaped rock floated in the skies, an impossibly angled tower atop like a clawed crown. Flocks of winged creatures, little more than specks from this distance, poured from the gateway and battlements, circling like vultures overhead. Kurt blinked and the image was gone, an after-shadow remaining for a few moments before melting away.

A bestial howl tore the air and they all stopped, looking in different directions. The howl reverberated again, coming from all places and none, and a moment later they were surrounded by eight hounds, which paced back and forth, throwing their heads back and howling, growling and pawing the ground.

Each was almost as large as a horse, furless except for a heavy black mane. Their skin was leathery and crimson, taut muscles rippling beneath. Their heads were long, jaws filled with dagger-long teeth. Each had pure white eyes that glowed with inner fire, and wore a great spiked collar of brass. Snakelike tails lashed to and fro in the thick air. They growled and snapped as the warband drew their weapons, closing in towards each other, facing outwards.

Slowly, the hounds of blood advanced, their footprints burning briefly on the ground, leaving a trail of molten snow and burned grass. The air shimmered around them, giving glimpses through into the daemon world from which they were spawned – a clashing swirl of colours and darkness, streaming together and coalescing into vaguely recognisable shapes, faces forming from the magical mist, and scenes of people going about their lives.

The beasts circled cautiously, getting closer and closer. Kurt adjusted his grip on his sword, realising how damp his palms were. To his left he heard Bjordrin spit and mutter something under his breath. He could hear the laboured panting of Orst to his right.

One of the hounds stopped directly in front of Kurt and stood there. The others joined it, circling just a few yards away, their blank eyes staring at the group of warriors. When all eight were standing in a line, they raised their heads and howled, a deafening noise that sounded inside the skull as well as in the ears. The nightmarish noise echoed with the sound of death rattles and tortured screams, of whetstones on blades and the clash of metal on metal and the crackling of flames. It was a howl of battle and death.

One by one, each finished howling and sat back on its haunches, looking at Kurt. Silence descended, broken only by the heavy breathing of the hounds and the odd whisper from the men behind Kurt. He was aware of his heart beating in his chest, and odd double-thump against his ribcage, unnatural in its speed and power.

Kurt stepped forwards, flaming sword in hand, and the hounds simply waited. Slow step by slow step, Kurt walked towards them, sheathing his sword and stretching out his hand. He could hear them sniffing the air, their gaping nostrils expanding even more. Eventually he was standing right in front of them, close enough to touch the muzzle of the nearest. He heard relieved laughter from his followers, but barely registered it. In the eyes of the hound he could see reflections of himself, in blood-red monochrome.

Turning to the north, Kurt began walking again, this time flanked by the hounds, four to his left and four to his right. Now he was certain that the gods wished him to succeed.

ONWARDS AND NORTHWARDS they travelled, faces ever turned into the harsh winds of power that emanated from the Gate of the Gods. The closer their eternal march took them, the stranger the lands became. Warped and twisted creatures fluttered in and out of existence around them, taunting them with cackling laughter, telling them to turn back. Lascivious apparitions appeared before them, begging them to stay and indulge in all manner of pleasures of flesh and soul. After much walking, they crested a ridge to look out at the realm beyond and be greeted by a sea of roiling mists that ebbed and flowed around their feet, revealing glimpses of distant places and times.

Kurt saw his mother as a young woman, being courted by his father in the grove around their family home. The birth of his sister, bloodied and screaming as his father paced nervously along the corridors outside. Strangers, in long robes and wide-brimmed hats, sat in a circle and chanted as incense burned around them, the sound of a gong reverberating in the background.

As they walked through the flow of unreality, clouds gathered overhead, a roiling mass of colours that boiled against one another, while shadow-shapes flitted on wings of silver and gold. The ground seethed under their feet, flinging them to their knees and backs, as titanic forces shifted beneath them, spires of metal and bone crashing up around them in spiralling patterns, until they towered high into the skies and melted away once more. Explosions of energy detonated across the heavens, sending showers of blood and offal raining down onto them, coating them in a patina of gore.

Onwards through the nightmare madness they pushed, Kurt ever at the fore with his hounds leading the way. One by one they succumbed once more, some wandering into the mists, drawn by bobbing lights, others falling to the ground, their bodies a pulsing mess of flesh as uncontrollable energies seethed through them, distorting and breaking, twisting their frames into unrecognisable conglomerations of flailing limbs, mewling mouths and foaming orifices.

Kurt could hear nursery rhymes from his childhood, sung by cackling, evil voices. They begged him to come with them and play, half-shades that coiled around his legs. The daemon-hounds snapped and snarled at these creatures, chasing them away and then returning to their master. They hacked their way through a forest of trees that grew clawed hands and grasped at them, while roots tripped them and tried to drag them into the sucking mud. Four-winged birds fluttered from the treetops, nesting in leaves of spiked gold, swooping down in great flocks to tear at their faces and arms as they swung swords to keep them at bay.

The storm broke with clashes of thunder that echoed with deep laughter, and flashes of green and purple lightning that burned into the eyes leaving white after-images. A hot wind blew up around them, a cyclone of power that battered at their flesh and tore at mutated skin. Men were sent tumbling by daemons that rode on the currents of the wind, their clawed hands snatching at weapons and shields, their whipping tails lashing across thighs and arms.

Jakob could see the centre of the vortex a short way ahead, and Kurt was walking straight into it, arms by his side. The whirlwind of power enveloped the chosen warrior and the beasts that walked beside him, obscuring him from view. The shaman felt something was wrong, more wrong than anything they had yet encountered. With his golden eye he could see a great gaping rip in the land and the sky, a tear in the fabric of everything, and Kurt was stepping into it. With a yell, Jakob rushed forwards.

It was too late. As the winds died down and the mystical tornado subsided, the gash upon reality had sealed. The hounds stood there, bolt still, staring at the spot where Kurt had been. They snarled at each other and then turned away, loping off at speed. Jakob stopped still, shocked to the core.

Kurt was gone.

KURT COULD NEITHER see nor hear nor feel, his body awash with power and sensation that overloaded his senses. Torment after torment was visited upon Kurt's mind. He could hear the voices more clearly now, questioning him, doubting him.

You still love her.

'I do not,' Kurt snarled between gritted teeth. 'She destroyed my family.'

You are not strong enough.

'I will prove you wrong. I am strong enough!'

Why do you care for her still?

'I do not care for her. I will kill her and destroy the land she loves.'

You killed your father.

'The witch hunter killed my father, and he is now dead. I will destroy the temples of his god and burn the false priests that sent him.'

You abandoned your son.

'My son was murdered!'

You are frail and mortal.

'I shall become immortal, and by the will of the gods I shall bring destruction upon those who would fight against them.'

The gods do not care about you.

'It is not for the gods to care.'

We will eat your soul.

'My soul does not belong to you, it is sworn to the gods, with fire and blood. The gods would not give up such a prize.'

Your enemies are strong, they will defeat you.

'Glory is not in the victory, but in the fighting. I will fight for the gods and if they grant me victory, I will be blessed.'

You are no wolf, you are the southern pup. You do not belong here.

'All men belong to the gods, no matter where they are born. They have guided my hand and I have repaid them with my life.'

You dare to question the gods. They do not even see you.

'I will make them see me! I shall stand before them and declare myself to them!'

You are all alone.

Kurt did not reply, suddenly sensing that the voices had gone. His hounds were not by his side, and he was struck by the sudden silence. Turning around he saw that was indeed alone, his warband nowhere to be seen. The storm had passed, and he found himself standing on green grass. Around him the fogs swirled and parted, revealing a large house built in the style of the east Empire, with square garrets jutting from the many roofs and two great chimney stacks at either end. The image shimmered for a moment and then solidified.

As he watched, he saw a pale-skinned woman opening the wide doors that led into the ballroom, wearing a yellow dress. It was his mother, singing in the beautiful voice he had not heard for so many long years. He was back at his father's estate, which had been burned to the ground a lifetime ago. Kurt nearly collapsed, stunned by the realisation of where he was.

He was home.

CHAPTER SEVEN
Unexpected Welcome
Wolfenburg, Early spring 1712

THE PEAKS OF the Middle Mountains were shrouded in low, dark clouds, threatening a spring storm. Magnus Simeon looked at them with an antipathy bordering on hatred. He disliked rain intensely, and clouds just as much. Perhaps it had been brought about by the long years in a leaky loft above his old master's house, damp and cold in the night, musty in the day, making it difficult to study. Clouds also made it difficult to see the stars, and when one earned payment as an astrologer, clouds could prove troublesome. He could remember the words of his old master as clear as a crystal ball, as Magnus had sat there with his books open, the strange diagrams and symbols meaningless.

'You have a talent that other men will be afraid of,' the white-haired tutor had said. 'I saw it in you, but you must endeavour to ensure that no other does.'

'Why so, master?' the young Magnus had asked.

'Men fear what they do not understand, and what they cannot see with their own eyes,' the master had told him. 'They will call you warlock and sorcerer, and they will try to kill you. You must hide your talents, with the astrolabe and the compass. You must obscure your skills with the pestle and mortar, alembic and lens. Astrology, they trust. Alchemy, they trust. Magic, they fear.'

And so now it was, twenty years later, that Magnus was court astrologer to Count Vapold of Ostermark, living in this tower crammed with its books and its telescopes and its charts. Of course, the real texts lay hidden in secret drawers and behind false covers, the true references of his work.

There was a knock at the door, interrupting his sour contemplation of the rain clouds that the wind was bringing ever nearer. He glanced around the room, instinctively looking for anything out of place, a tell-tale sign of his true nature. As ever, there was none.

'Enter, my lord,' Magnus intoned in his bass voice, turning back to the window.

The man who stepped through the door was tall and slim, his dark hair and pointed nose giving him a lean, hungry look. He had a high forehead and arched eyebrows, a feature that was exaggerated by his long hair swept back with silver pins.

'You sent word for me,' Count Vapold said, closing the door behind him.

'She will arrive soon, my lord,' Magnus said, turning around and folding his arms. 'Within the hour, I would say.'

'Ha!' said Vapold with a dismissive wave. 'Your charts and readings are not so accurate as to predict the hour of her coming.'

'You are correct, my lord,' said Magnus. He turned half back to the window and pointed. 'However, a rider from the west gate hurries through the streets at this very moment, and unless my assumption is wrong, he brings news that she has been seen approaching the city.'

'So that is why you insist on living in the highest part of my castle, is it?' said Vapold with a lopsided smile. 'So that you can spy on all the comings and goings of my city?'

'Of course, my lord,' Magnus said, returning the smile. 'A man may stare at the heavens for a lifetime and not gain wisdom, and yet spend an hour gazing upon the streets and learn much.'

'Must you always be so pompous, Magnus?' Vapold asked, idly picking a stoppered bottle from one of the cluttered desks and shaking it. He peered at it with a raised eyebrow as the agitation caused the liquid inside to turn from green to blue.

'A professional necessity, my lord,' Magnus laughed. He had a genuine affection for the count, who had proven to be both witty and circumspect in equal measure during the five years of Magnus's current employ. 'If one does not make one's pronouncements with suitable gravitas and veracity, then any bloody fool could do it.'

Vapold laughed and placed the bottle back on the table and bent down to look at the scattered scraps of parchment. He picked one up to examine it more closely.

'You are delaying, my lord,' said Magnus, striding across the circular room and proffering a hand to take the parchment. 'It is a trait I have found to exist only in those who do not need to keep appointments and pay no heed to keeping their guests waiting. Why are you nervous?'

'The girl, Magnus, the girl!' the count replied, handing over the paper. 'Ever since your proclamation three months ago, I've been all astir. Is she really everything you and my agents say she is?'

'We shall see soon enough, my lord,' Magnus said after a moment's thought. In his heart he was not sure whether he wanted her to be or not. He glanced out of the window as he heard a shout from the castle gate. 'Rest assured, I will be with you, as will the High Wild-father, and a contingent of your guards. You should go and prepare, your messenger will be coming up shortly.'

'Yes, of course,' said Vapold, and yet still hesitated for a moment. With a nod to himself, the count turned and walked towards the door. He stopped again, one hand on the great brass handle at its centre. 'A visionary they called her.'

'A very apt description, my lord, by all accounts,' Magnus said. 'I shall see you in the audience chamber shortly.'

Vapold did not reply as he opened the door and stepped out, closing it gently behind him. Magnus waited for a few moments, reassuring himself that the count was not about to come back in. He then grabbed up a deep pile of papers from a particular desk and dumped them onto another table. Running his hand over the grain of the exposed wood, he located the crack he was looking for and inserted a long nail. With a snick, the hidden catch was sprung and the secret drawer within the desk slid open on its well-oiled runners.

Inside was a picture of the girl, blindly sketched by Magnus himself as he had entered a meditative trance. The count had asked whether she was everything he had been told. That she carried the ancient sword of Marbad was now confirmed, and scattered reports of the last several years all attested to her strange behaviour and vehement faith in Sigmar. More importantly, Magnus had now seen, with his own dreamsight, her trip into the distant snows. Yes, the gods might have touched her, but Magnus was far more interested in what she could tell him of the sorceries of the northmen.

WOLFENBURG SQUATTED ACROSS a large hill, overshadowed by the enormous presence of the Middle Mountains. There was a ramshackle accumulation of houses outside of the city wall. Like an infant town stretching up the skirts of its mother, tottering upper storeys piled upon each other, climbing towards the battlements that towered above them.

Squared towers every hundred yards, cut with deep embrasures from which the muzzles of cannons stuck out like uneven teeth, punctuated the wall itself. Hoardings covered with slate protected the battlements, and outcroppings of brick suspended on heavy beams loomed out over the buildings below, their floors pierced to allow defenders to pour oil, lime or arrows onto an attacker below.

Beyond that could be seen the keep, the castle of the count himself. Standing atop the highest point of the hill, its curtain wall was painted black, an imposing shadow that dominated the cityscape. White flags with black eagles, each big enough to cover a house, fluttered from eight tall poles, and from the central tower the count's personal standard flew over all.

The western gate stood proud of the wall, flanked by two enormous barbicans almost twice as high as the wall itself. A company of soldiers stood guard at the huge oak gates, a hundred men armed with spears and shields who flanked the road leading into the imposing gatehouse.

Ursula could feel their stares as she, Ruprecht and Johannes walked through, surrounded by farm carts, coaches and ponies laden with bales. None of them spoke as they passed into the shadow of the gatehouse. Ursula had not spoken of what she planned to do once they had arrived, and Johannes and Ruprecht had not asked, both regarding ignorance as bliss in that regard.

Through the gatehouse, having passed under four sets of heavy iron portcullis, they came out onto the main street, which wound around the hill in a clockwise direction. As they pushed their way through the morning crowds, ignoring the shouts of hawkers and beggars alike, Ruprecht notice the distinctive layout of the city. None of the streets passed all the way from one circle of the spiral to another, meaning that any attacker would either have to break through the buildings themselves or fight their way along the entire circuit.

The road under their feet was cobbled, a brick gutter at each side, and the buildings were mostly two and three storeys high, brick at the bottom and wooden on the upper storeys, many roofed with black and white tiles. Shop fronts lined the streets displaying all manner of wares, from baskets to pets.

Ruprecht watched Ursula closely. She was focussed straight ahead, barely glancing when a particularly loud shout from a baker or farrier tried to attract their attention. He was also very aware of the looks they were getting from the other people in the street. He could hear whispered conversations, and caught several people openly staring at his artificial hand. He had forgotten what a sight they were: a woman dressed and armed as a warrior, and a great bearded man with an iron hand and a warhammer. They had spent so little time in the cities of the Empire in recent years, he had never given a second thought to their outlandish appearance. He ignored the crowd's curiosity, but was more perturbed when, on turning to speak to Johannes, he caught a glance of a small group of soldiers following them up the street. He nodded to them and Johannes looked back and raised an eyebrow.

'Could be nothing,' Johannes said. 'Perhaps they're the guard for the citadel.'

'It never hurts to be cautious,' Ruprecht replied. 'We're a long way from Marienburg, but we're not far from Badenhof. Who knows what tales have spread around these parts?'

They quickened their pace until they were alongside Ursula, the crowds were thinning now, about halfway up the main street, as the shops petered out and gave way to houses and guild buildings.

'There are soldiers following us,' said Johannes, laying a hand on Ursula's arm.

'I know,' she replied. 'They broke ranks and came after us when we left the gate. I thought you had already noticed.'

'Perhaps we should find somewhere to hide,' suggested Ruprecht.

'Why?' Ursula asked, finally looking at him. 'Is there anything to be afraid of?'

'I just like to be careful,' Ruprecht said with a heavy shrug. 'I don't know what you think you're going to do, but I'm sure getting arrested isn't part of the plan.'

'If they were going to arrest us, they would have done it at the gate,' Ursula replied, and Ruprecht couldn't fault her logic. 'I think we're going exactly where they want us to go. I was sure that they were looking at us specifically when we passed them.'

'And just where are we going?' asked Johannes, with another nervous glance over his shoulder. The soldiers were still some way back, keeping to the same pace.

'To the keep of course,' Ursula answered. 'Where else would we be going?'

Neither Johannes nor Ursula heard Ruprecht swearing under his breath.

MAGNUS SMOOTHED THE creases in his robes, sighing inwardly at their gaudy design. Count Vapold had insisted that if he were going to have a court astrologer, Magnus was required to wear suitable vestments. Magnus had pictured something austere, even severe. Instead, he had been given this horror of a shapeless sack, decorated with star and moon design, in yellow on blue. They were no more vestments than a jester's costume, he thought.

Vapold was sitting on his throne, fidgeting with the hem of his black doublet. It suited him well, the black and white slashed sleeves matching his dark hair and pale skin, the white hose picked out with gold thread adding a nice touch of wealth to his appearance. Magnus resolved to find out who tailored for the king, and to make arrangements for the same person to address some of the shortcomings of his own attire.

Where Magnus was standing to the count's left, High Wildfather Talbrin stood to his right. Even he managed to look regal and important, despite the theoretical difficulties of his robes of office. His green smock hung to just above the knees, intricately worked with yellow thread in designs that reflected a forest theme. Leaves of different shapes intertwined with deer and bears, and down each arm, a bubbling brook teeming with fish. The priest of Taal was certainly showing his age though; his white beard neatly trimmed at waist length failed to hide the heavy lines in his ancient face. It had never struck Magnus before, but now he looked at the Wildfather, he noticed a certain tree-ness about him, a bark-like cragginess to his features. His thinning white hair escaped in wisps from the circlet of golden oak leaves around his head, and his eyes were almost white with cataracts.

There were a few others loitering about the place. Hemden Keffel, the highest-ranking priest of Sigmar stood close to the doors, talking to the city treasurer, the hatchet-faced Engrim Stor. Captain Felsturm, head of the count's guard, stood with a modest contingent of twelve men behind the throne, their highly polished breastplates dazzling in the light of the sun streaming in from the high windows of the audience chamber.

Magnus resisted the urge to tap his foot or hum while he waited. Several minutes had already passed since he had hurried down from his high tower, following an agitated pageboy who had brought the message that the count required his advisor. He gave an audible sigh of relief as there was a loud knocking on the double doors, earning himself a warning glance from Vapold.

The doors swung open and the herald bowed as he entered, his feathered hat nearly draping on the ground, but not quite. Then the girl followed him in, and Magnus started to pay more attention. She was dressed in leather trousers tucked into short boots, and wore a sheepskin jerkin laced at the front. Her hair was tied back in a simple plait, the colour of molten bronze. As she entered, Magnus's other senses twitched, those instincts that his old master had taught him to hone.

There at her belt was the sword, the elven blade Ulfshard. Magnus could feel the magic within it from here, at the far end of the long hall. Perhaps, if circumstances permitted, he would be able to spend some time studying the sword, to divine the secrets of its forging. The girl herself walked with confidence, staring straight at the count. It was not just her posture that exuded strength. Magnus could detect the corona of power that surrounded her. Some of it was from the sword no doubt, but there was an edge to it, a strange aftertaste to Magnus's hidden sense, that the warlock recognised immediately.

His master had taught him that magical energy flowed in different ways, and that with study, the practitioner of the Other Arts, as he referred to the use of magic, could discern their flavours. This was very familiar to Magnus; he tasted it every time that Talbrin was in the same room. But he had never met someone with such a strong aura before, and as the girl approached, Magnus had to concentrate to keep his focus. Not even in a temple on a high day had he felt this type of power with such potency.

The girl exuded a shield of raw faith.

The others had followed her in, but Magnus paid them little attention, he was focussed entirely on the girl. He didn't even really hear what Vapold was saying, as the count made a very formal speech of welcome and introduction. The allure of the girl was far more than her physical beauty, to one such as Magnus. As she bent to one knee in front of the count, instead of curtseying, Magnus noted subconsciously, a wave of energy swept out from the girl. It was almost intoxicating to the warlock, and he suppressed a shudder. Yes, he thought, this girl is everything they say she is. And a lot more besides.

'MY LORD, I come before you with a request,' said Ursula, straightening, her hand unconsciously resting on the glowing hiltstone of Ulfshard.

'I am happy to hear it,' said Vapold, leaning forward with one elbow on his knee, his chin in his hand.

'I request that you assemble an army, for a march to the north, to wage war on the barbarians,' Ursula said.

Vapold said nothing, his smile seemingly slightly more fixed than it had been before. Ursula did not mind, she had expected worse. Derision and laughter had been her greatest fear, disbelief the next. Shock she was quite comfortable with. With a deliberate blink, the count straightened up.

'An army, you say?' he said, with a glance towards the astrologer to his left.

'Yes, my lord,' replied Ursula. 'I believe that the Empire is in peril, and beg you to cut short this threat with force of arms.'

'To the north?' said Magnus. 'And why would the count wish to do such a reckless thing? What is this threat that you speak of?'

Ursula took a deep breath, and glanced around the room.

'Perhaps my lord might care to have his servants bring refreshments,' she suggested. 'This could take a long time.'

'THAT WAS YOUR plan?' said Ruprecht, pacing back and forth across the antechamber they had been taken to while the count deliberated with his advisors. 'Tell them everything?'

'It is quite a tale,' said Johannes, seated on a long velvet-trimmed couch, a goblet of wine in one hand.

Outside, a bell tolled the late hour. For nearly the whole day, Ursula had spoken, almost uninterrupted by questions. She had told them of how she had met and fallen in love with Kurt, and of Kurt's history with Marius van Diesl. She had told them about her visions, and the sham trial that van Diesl had been forced to preside over. She had continued on through their amazed expressions as she told them of the attack from the rat-like mutants and Kurt's timely arrival. Without wavering, without any show of emotion, she related their flight northwards and the taint that had grown inside Kurt, fuelled by the half-Norse Jakob.

As calmly as if she had been describing the weather, Ursula had spoken of the carnage in Tungask: the burning of the houses, the slaughter of the knights of the Osterknacht. Only when she talked of Kurt did her voice tremble slightly, of his transformation into an unnatural creature of the dark gods. She ignored the count's exclamations as she described the grievous wounds Kurt suffered without effect and the final encounter between him and the witch hunter, as his sword had burst into flames and engulfed van Diesl as the flames had engulfed his own corrupted family. Ruprecht had shuffled uncomfortably under the attention of the nobles as Ursula described his aiding of her escape from Kurt and their journey south to Marien-burg.

She had fallen silent for a moment and then pressed on with the story of the Arabyan enchantress Jasmina el Al, who had masqueraded as the Lady Hal-ste and led them on the fateful expedition to the dwarf hold of Karak Norn to retrieve Ulfshard. Her voice had grown passionate again as she had spoken of the sorceress's true intent to claim daemonic power for herself, and the events in the court of Count Luiten that had led to Ursula taking up Ulfshard herself.

With no sign of passion, she described the attacks on the Norse villages, the executions and burning. As she finished, describing the final battle and the words of the Norse leader concerning Kurt Sutenvulf, she had looked to the count and asked again for an army to fight this warlord of the north.

Now it had been an hour, perhaps more, since the count had asked them to retire while they discussed her story. Ursula sat on a high-backed chair near the door, Ulfshard across her lap, and had said nothing since. At Ruprecht's question, she turned her head and smiled at him.

'What else would I tell them?' she asked. 'If the truth does not prove my providence, than nothing does.'

'You're putting a lot of faith in him,' warned Ruprecht. 'Did you not learn anything about how nobles think when you were dealing with Luiten? What if he tries to take Ulfshard from you, for himself? What about that?'

'He won't,' said Ursula.

'How can you be so sure?' said Ruprecht, sitting down next to Johannes. 'They're all of the same breed.'

'The city of the black and white wolf,' Ursula said, her eyes taking on the now familiar distant look. 'Sigmar led me here for help.'

URSULA WAS DOZING when the door opened, but she became instantly awake. Ruprecht's snores still drifted over from where he was lain on the floor, half a goblet of wine balanced on his chest, head propped up on an embroidered cushion. Johannes was asleep too, head lolling over the arm of the couch.

It was the astrologer who stepped through and smiled at Ursula. He seemed distracted for a moment and then gathered himself. He looked at Ruprecht and Johannes and shook his head. Without a word, he gestured for Ursula to precede him back through the door, and closed it quietly behind him as they walked back into the audience chamber.

Vapold was seated on his throne, in conversation with a broad-shouldered man in plate armour. The knight wore a long purple cloak with a yellow trim, and he carried a purple and yellow plumed helmet under his arm. The colours were familiar to Ursula, but she couldn't place them. As she approached, the knight turned, the expression on his age-lined face one of suspicion.

'There's someone who wishes very much to speak to you,' Vapold said, waving an arm towards the knight. 'May I introduce Lord Bayard, new Commander of the Osterknacht?'

CHAPTER EIGHT
Sundered
Realm of Chaos

ACTINIC FLARES OF energy criss-crossed the roiling skies, forking down in bolts of purple and orange lightning. The clouds themselves formed half-faces, screaming wordlessly at the hapless mortals below. Malignant eyes, filled with malicious intelligence, glowed within the dark haze.

The ground itself seethed with the power of the magical storm, its shape flowing like a river, undulating and cracking apart, reforming into new and strange structures. Great rib-like towers tore through the tortured earth, glowing with unearthly runes. Pools of burning oil bubbled to the surface, belching noxious fumes that stank of rotted flesh.

As the earth opened up, it revealed a layer of corpses, some fresh, others little more than ragged bones. The cadavers seemed to writhe with unlife as the ground shifted and changed, playing out an obscene dance in death. Bodies tumbled over skeletons, heads lolling to some maddening, unheard rhythm while limbs twitched and flailed in erratic patterns, gripping long-decayed weapons and shields.

A terrible moaning could be heard from the clouds above, a bass lamentation that trembled the ground and caused the air to shake with its strength. Behind its deep tones a chorus of high-pitched wailing joined in on occasion, a strident, ear-splitting cacophony of daemonic voices.

Jakob felt himself battered from side to side by the arcane forces unleashed by the Realm of Chaos. The breath of the gods lifted him up into the air on unseen wings, violently spinning and turning him, his ragged clothes spiralling from his body as he plummeted back to the ground, which opened up beneath him like a slobbering maw, enveloping him in caresses of fleshy folds.

Orst howled and whined, swaying back and forth insanely, gnashing his fangs and clawing at the ground. As the ground rippled like a stone-disturbed puddle, the champion-beast reared to his hind legs, beating his chest with his fists, his eyes blazing. His claws ripped great chunks from his fur and thick hide, his pelt stained with thick ichor from the self-inflicted wounds.

Vlamdir was curled into a foetal ball, pounding his head against the rocky ground. His armour burned and smouldered within his flesh, bringing with it the stench of charring human fat. Beside the devoted of Kharga stood Bjordrin, his silvered skin mirroring the torment that was tearing across the earth and sky, his beard fusing into writhing bundles of wiry threads that waved and knotted themselves with a life of their own.

All about was Chaos unleashed, the full fury of the realm of the gods given vent. Through the blinding flashes of energy, another world could be seen in momentary glimpses. Great armies of daemonic creatures marched against each other, their dark, living banners held above the dark hosts. Immense creatures with bestial faces and wings of fire and shadow swept to and fro in the skies, lashing at each other with burning, screaming blades.

The harsh blare of horns could be heard in the distance, accompanied by rapid, lunatic drumming that followed no even beat. The screams of immortal creatures and the deafening bellows of the gods' servants mingled into a meaningless dissonance.

Pulling himself from the slavering hole into which he had fallen, Jakob looked around for Kurt, desperately seeking a sign that his master was close, perhaps obscured or slightly shifted, but nearby nonetheless. There was nothing, no tell-tale mark within the swirling magical energies.

As the magical storm broke, there was still no sign of Kurt. Above them the sky calmed to its normal shifting waves of translucent colour. Jakob could feel nothing of the Chosen, no lingering presence nearby that he had become so accustomed to. It was then that he realised just how familiar he had become to following Kurt, and now that reassuring presence, that palpable incarnation of the gods' will, had gone. There was a new emptiness inside Jakob that ate at his soul.

* * *

WITH THE ABATEMENT of the storm came a new danger. Shapes gathered in the distance, dark shadowy things that could not be seen when directly looked upon.

'Stay close,' said Undar, a heavy axe in each hand.

'Where is Kurt?' asked Bjordrin, looking around. 'We need him!'

'He is gone,' said Jakob with a disconsolate shake of his head.

'Gone?' said Gird, still holding on to the shaking banner pole decorated with the bones of his brother. 'Gone where?'

'He is gone,' said Jakob, still not quite able to believe what he had seen, or what he thought he had seen.

'The storm took him,' said Vlamdir, picking himself up. 'I saw it. It swept him away.'

'Then the gods have taken him?' suggested Gird. 'Perhaps he is with them now.'

'Here they come,' warned Undar, silencing the others.

In a dark wave, the daemonic pack swept towards them, the earth and air warping and shifting around them. Through the breach caused by the terrible storm, seven of the creatures had broken through. They were pus-slicked, rotted things formed from the whims of Nurgle, god of decay, patron of the diseased and dying.

They stalked forwards on malnourished legs, their limbs thin and wasted, their joints swollen with cankerous fluid. Each had a bloated gut, reminiscent of a corpse swollen with gas, tears in their unnatural flesh spilling entrails and sickly gore.

They were cyclopean, famished faces pinched around a single staring, yellowing orb, their heads rising to a single broken and cracked horn. In their hands they held jagged knives and cleavers, like obscene butchers. As they approached closer, Jakob could see their lips moving constantly and the sky was filled with an eternal murmuring, a disturbing whisper of regular rhythm. It was the sound of the plaguebearers counting, tallying the diseases and poxes of the world.

The air around the tallymen swarmed with black, fat flies, buzzing in a dark cloud. Their red and black bodies batted against each other and the grey-green skin of the daemons, their droning rising and falling in volume to the count of the plaguebearers.

'Their touch means death,' warned Vlamdir, gripping his axe tightly. He gagged as he looked at the approaching visions of mortification. 'We can't fight them!'

'We can!' roared Undar, lifting his axes above his head.

'I'm with Vlamdir,' said Gird, backing away from the approaching monstrosities.

'What about Kurt?' said Bjordrin, unsheathing his sword. The stench from the daemons of Nurgle was overpowering, filling his mouth and nostrils like a noxious soup. 'We can't leave him.'

Orst growled in agreement.

Jakob had recovered his senses now, and looked upon the plaguebearers with his golden eye. He could see the miasma of power at the heart of each of them, the kernel of magical energy that allowed them to stay in the realm of mortals. Here in the north such power faded slowly, and was not easily destroyed.

'We cannot fight them,' Jakob called to the others. 'Our weapons are useless against them.'

'I would rather die than retreat,' replied Undar.

The plaguebearers were close now, sniffing the air, grinning to each other in the manner that a skull grins in death.

'Then you will die,' said Jakob.

'You can banish them!' said Vlamdir, moving to stand beside the shaman. 'Command them to return to the realm of the gods!'

Jakob started backing away from the creatures.

'I did not summon them,' the shaman said. 'I cannot send them back.'

'Use your magic to destroy them, then!' said Bjordrin.

'It is too dangerous,' Jakob pleaded. 'The power of the gods is too strong!'

'Risk it!' snarled Bjordrin, pointing his sword at the shaman. 'If not, I'll kill you myself. If our weapons are useless, your magic is the only defence we have.'

Jakob saw the others staring at him expectantly. A glance at the plaguebearers showed them to be less than a dozen yards away now. With a sense of foreboding, Jakob opened himself up to the energy swirling around him.

As the magic poured into Jakob his runestones began to glow more strongly, and with wet noises they detached from his flesh and began to circle him, bobbing up and down erratically. Little forks of energy played between them as Jakob drew in the power he needed and began to chart, calling upon Tzeentch, master of magic.

With a pained shout, Jakob released the energy inside him. The runestones were sucked back into his body, knocking him from his feet as an undulating wave of power burst from his staff towards the plague-bearers. Shifting from yellow to orange to red, the swelling beam of magic erupted around the daemons, engulfing them in its miasma of ruddy light.

The plaguebearers writhed with agony, their bony limbs snapping, their skin peeling away to reveal the magical core within, each a small galaxy of putrescent filth swirling around a glowing centre. Like pus leaking from a lanced boil the creatures of Nurgle began to melt away, pustules and blisters erupting across their incorporeal flesh and exploding with filth. Within a few heartbeats all that remained were oozing puddles of ichor, gently bubbling and steaming.

JAKOB'S HEAD SPUN, his stomach fluttered and nausea swept over him. The spell had robbed him of his energy and he fell to his back, his spine arching as the magical winds flowed into the vacuum within his soul. Black sweat gathered on his pallid flesh as his good eye fluttered open and closed. His breathing became a feverish panting and his mind slipped away into a dark recess of his self.

The shaman found himself away from his pain-ravaged body, floating in a clear night sky. He was free from all mortal bonds and he wondered for a moment whether he had died. He dismissed the thought and looked around.

The ground below was dark but covered with thousands of tiny pinpricks of light, as if the stars were reflected in a great, still lake. He found that he could move himself around with a mere thought and lowered himself hesitantly towards the ground, inching downwards. As his confidence grew, he began to accelerate.

There was no sensation of falling other than the lights on the ground getting closer and closer. There was no howling of wind, no feeling of falling, no rush of air against his bodiless form. Jakob laughed.

The feeling was of total freedom.

As he neared the ground he slowed his descent and could see that the flickering pinpricks were in fact torches, thousands upon thousands of guttering flames held aloft. Swooping over the lights he saw that it was a massive army, heading southwards through the night. The warriors were dressed in all different styles and manners, and he recognised the furs of the Norse alongside the leather and horsehair of the Kurgan.

The army stretched out as far as he could see, a great tide of northmen heading in a single direction: south. South towards the Empire, south towards the lands of those who had so brazenly opposed the will of the gods. It was with a start that he realised that it was not night at all, but some monstrous shadow had engulfed the sun, blocking its light. Darkness had truly descended upon the world. To Jakob it was clear what he had to do.

WITH A GROAN Jakob awoke. For a few moments he was not sure of this, though, for the Chaos Wastes, the writhing sky and uncertain ground, felt less real than his encounter with the army. His face was wet with sweat and he wiped it with the cuff of his furs and sat up. The others were gathered close by, deep in argument. Jakob pushed himself to his feet, his breathing laboured and listened to what was being said.

'Of course we can't just wait here forever,' Bjordrin was saying. 'The gods have taken him from us, and he may never return.'

Orst growled and clawed at the ground.

'All the more reason to press on,' argued the malformed Undar, his chest, shoulders and arms, blistered with inhuman muscle, heaved in and out as he spoke. 'I will lead us to the Gate of the Gods. I am just as worthy!'

'But what about the hounds?' argued Vlamdir. 'They came to the Sutenvulf, not to you. I think the gods have made their choice.'

'And the daemons?' said Gird. 'There are fell creatures abroad in these lands, and we can't fight them off forever.'

'Kurt was one man!' Undar said. 'I am just as worthy a leader.'

'So what do you propose we do?' asked Gird, cradling the shaft of the banner pole like it was a babe, no longer able to grip it in his clawed hands. 'Jakob! What do you think?'

The shaman did not answer, but instead stared into the sky.

'Hi! Jakob!' Undar called and finally the shaman turned to them. He hobbled over, gazing at them with his golden eye.

'Bjordrin is right, he is with the gods now,' Jakob said slowly, the words slurred. 'If he returns, he will not return here.'

'So we go back?' said Undar. 'We just turn back and head south?'

'Yes,' said Jakob, stepping close to the enormous warrior, gazing up with the metallic orb of his eye. 'We return to our lands and wait for a sign.'

'What sign?' said Gird. 'What if they never send him back?'

'It is by the will of the gods that he is gone, and not for us to guess,' said Jakob. 'We go back, and we prepare.'

'Prepare for what?' asked Bjordrin.

'The war to come,' said Jakob with a smile. 'Blood and death, Kurt vowed. In blood and death he will return. When he does, he will need an army. We go forth and prepare the way for him.'

'And what will this sign be?' Undar demanded. 'How will we know he has returned?'

Jakob laughed, a cruel sound that caused even Undar to recoil in fear.

'You will know,' cackled Jakob. 'The whole world will know.'

CHAPTER NINE
Wolfenburg. Early 1712

URSULA'S FIRST REACTION was to run, but she held her ground and instead directed a venomous glare at Count Vapold. He held up his hands as if to ward away the accusation. She could feel the presence of Magnus close behind her.

'Purely coincidence,' the count said. He hesitated before continuing. 'Lord Bayard is here on entirely different matters. However, he may be able to verify some of the details of your... exploits.'

The knight was looking at her with an odd expression, partly of disbelief and partly of awe, or perhaps it was fear. Ursula now noticed that his cloak was travel stained, his boots muddied.

'You really are Fraulein Schenk?' Bayard said. 'The accomplice of Kurt Leitzig?'

'She is,' said Magnus, stepping forward. 'Our information is quite detailed.'

'Then perhaps it is you who can provide verification for me,' said the knight-commander.

'It is very late, and both of you have been travelling,' said Vapold, rising from his throne and walking forward to stand between them. 'I suggest that we all get some rest, and perhaps tomorrow, with clearer heads, we can provide answers to each other's questions.'

'I must check on the boy before I retire,' said Bayard.

'Of course,' said Magnus, stepping away from Ursula, towards the main doors. 'He and your men are being cared for in the north tower. If you follow me, I will have you taken to them.'

Bayard nodded and the two of them turned and walked down the length of the audience chamber, Ursula and Vapold watching them in silence. As they left, Magnus closing the door with a last look at Ursula, Ursula turned to the count.

'Boy?' she said. 'What boy?'

'Tomorrow, Ursula, tomorrow,' Vapold replied. 'You should rouse your friends, while I send for someone to show you to the chambers I have had prepared for you.'

'How did you know I would be coming?' Ursula asked.

'Tomorrow,' Vapold said again. 'Tomorrow we will have answers, tonight you should sleep.'

MAGNUS COULD NOT sleep. His body was tingling, infused by the power emanated by the girl. He lay in his bed, eyes closed, and he could feel her presence, the wash of energy that had swept over him. Much of the power was wasted on her, seeping away and dissipating, but the core of it, the raw faith that suffused her soul, was potent. So very potent.

The last time Magnus had felt anything like this had been the first time his old master had taken him to a tavern and made him drink so much wine that he could barely stand. The room spun slowly around Magnus, and his stomach fluttered lightly. His old master had never prepared him for this. The drinking session had been very important to the old master, a lesson in humanity and control. Drunk to the point of insensibility, Magnus had been instructed to use a conjuration, a mere cantrip that he had learned within a few days of his apprenticeship. It had gone horribly wrong though, as his addled mind and mouth had fumbled the incantation, and had inadvertently set fire to a chair in the master's study. The next day Magnus, feeling sick and sorry as a hound, was quick to agree that one who practised the arts must do so with absolute concentration and power at all times. He had never drunk since.

Was this how it felt all the time, he thought, in the north, the source of the power? How did the barbaric sorcerers that dwelled there control such amounts of energy? It was impossible for Magnus to imagine the sheer potential of harnessing such vast waves of magic.

And yet the girl managed it, untrained as she was. She had been somehow touched by her experiences and yet had survived. The girl, Magnus thought, as sleep still failed to envelop him; she could perhaps provide the key.

AFTER BREAKFAST, AT which Ruprecht, Ursula and Johannes had eaten alone, served by a young kitchen boy, a page appeared and requested Ursula's presence in the audience chamber once more. She insisted that Ruprecht and Johannes accompany her. The large hall was once more almost empty: only Vapold, Magnus and Bayard were present, sat around one end of a long table that had been placed in front of the count's throne. Between them were bowls of fruits, plates of cold meat cuts, crumbling white cheese and starchy bread, with pitchers of wine, and Vapold was using a knife to cut slices from an apple, his feet up on the table.

'I did ask just for you,' the count said, standing and pulling out a chair for Ursula. She did not sit.

'They stay, or I leave,' she replied, crossing her arms.

Vapold paused and glanced at Magnus and Bayard, who raised no objections. Stepping back, he waved all three to sit down before resuming his place at the head of the table.

'So, where do we start?' the count asked, looking around the table. 'It appears that events have caught up with us, perhaps, and they may be connected or not.'

'What events?' asked Johannes.

'I want to know what happened with Leitzig,' said Bayard, leaning forward with his elbows on the table, a half-full goblet held in his hands. He was out of his armour, dressed in a plain black doublet and purple breeches. 'Our recent misfortunes are of no concern to these people.'

'I disagree,' said Vapold quickly. 'Ursula wishes me to gather an army to combat the growing menace in the north, but the news that you bring may well influence my decision.'

'What news?' asked Ursula, exasperated at their coyness. 'Just tell me what's happening.'

Bayard and Vapold looked at each other for a long moment, before Bayard conceded, nodding slightly and looking away.

'Count Emmereind of Ostermark is dead,' said Vapold with a sigh.

'Murdered,' added Bayard quickly. 'Baron Steinhardt has seized the count's palace, and is even now petitioning the other nobles to recognise his claim to be count.'

'Then why are you here?' asked Johannes. 'Surely your place is in Bechafen, fighting against Steinhardt?'

'We fought, but the Osterknacht is not the force that it was,' replied Bayard, giving Ursula a dark look. 'That is the fault of Leitzig. Nearly half the order chased you into Kislev, and many did not return. Seeing this, Steinhardt has spent these past few years gathering support and hiring mercenaries in the south. He has even offered haven to soldiers from Solland and Wissenland, survivors from the fighting against the Ironclaw.'

Bayard's expression had grown pained, the lines in his face deepened, and he took a sip of his wine.

'We tried to hold the palace, but it was in vain,' the knight continued. 'Those of us that survived decided to withdraw, and my plan was to escape with the count and his younger brother, Hensel. We managed to reach Hensel, but Steinhardt got to Count Emmereind before us. We thought perhaps he would hold him to ransom, but instead had him killed. I panicked, I admit, and we fled with Hensel. He is the true heir to the Ostermark Runefang, and he had to be kept safe.'

'That is disturbing news, I agree,' said Ursula, looking at Vapold. 'But what concern is it of yours?'

'My concerns are twofold,' the count replied, tossing his apple core onto the table. 'Emmereind was my cousin, distantly by my great aunt, but he is still family. I have a duty to protect Hensel as well. I'm sure you can understand that.'

'And the other?' said Ruprecht, reaching across the table to grab a wine pitcher.

'As Count of Ostland, any dramatic change in power must be my concern,' said Vapold, taking his feet off the table and straightening in his chair. 'Especially when it is one of my neighbours, virtually on my own doorstep no less. Instability in Ostermark is not good for Ostland. Who can say where Steinhardt's ambitions end? Perhaps this is just the first step in a plan to contend for the throne of the Emperor.'

'If Steinhardt can seize power in Bechafen, what message does it send to the nobles who owe fealty to Wolfenburg?' said Magnus, looking directly at Ursula. The astrologer seemed depressed. 'I regret, very deeply, that I have advised the count to reject your petition for an army to be raised for your cause. We must look to the defence of Wolfenburg, both from our own, but also against Steinhardt, especially now that Hensel is held here.'

'I concur,' said Bayard. 'The Osterknacht will be setting forth to Ostermark again, though the count has kindly offered us haven here. We will attempt to raise resistance against Steinhardt, and see Hensel back on the throne of Bechafen. We will be leaving within the next day or two, and if we can gather support, I have asked the count to provide some of his own troops to further back our claim for the true count.'

'This is madness!' snapped Ursula, standing up and sweeping her hand across the table, scattering bowls and goblets. 'If Kurt comes back with an army of northmen, what does it matter who sits in Bechafen or Wolfenburg? While we war against each other, he grows stronger. He will come, and we will be unready. We must strike now while his strength is still growing.'

'Ursula is right,' declared Johannes. 'While the death of your cousin is saddening, surely Kurt is a more pressing threat than some distant scheme of Steinhardt?'

'And where would you go?' said Bayard quietly. 'We went north before, and now we are undone. You cannot fight the northmen in their own lands. A defence against Steinhardt is a defence against any attack. Whilst Ostermark is divided, Ostland is vulnerable. If we can regain the throne for Hensel, the two states can stand together against this threat. The two are not exclusive.'

Ursula opened her mouth to speak again but Vapold raised his hand to silence her.

'My decision is made,' the count said. 'For now. Lord Bayard and his men will return soon, and perhaps his cause will be supported, or perhaps I will reconsider my position. I will not be rushed into making a rash choice.'

* * *

URSULA WATCHED MISERABLY as the knights of the Osterknacht filed out of Vapold's castle, mounted on their warhorses, their banners fluttering in the wind at the head of the thin column. The clatter of their hooves echoed eerily back up from the quiet, pre-dawn streets. Heavy clouds were gathered overhead in the pre-dawn light, and the atmosphere of the city was sombre. Ruprecht and Johannes stood on the rampart with her, a little distant from the count and his advisors a little further along the wall. It had been three days since Vapold's pronouncement, and he had refused to meet with Ursula since. In turn, she had said little to her two companions and had instead spent most of her time in the temple of Sigmar.

'Perhaps they will return soon,' said Johannes, wrapping his cloak more tightly around himself, standing close to Ursula.

'Perhaps they won't return at all,' said Ruprecht, his expression gloomy.

Ursula said nothing, as the first drops of rain began to patter off the stonework around her and moisten her hair. She watched the knights intently as they wound their way down the road, disappearing from sight behind a large building.

The astrologer, Magnus, walked along the wall towards them, a heavy cloak and hood protecting him from the rain. He stopped a little way from the group, looking distastefully up towards the clouds.

'What do your observations tell you?' asked Johannes, turning to Magnus. 'Are the omens good?'

Magnus did not reply for a moment, his glance hovering on Ursula for a while.

'My readings are unclear on the matter,' he said, looking at Johannes. 'There are many potential fates that await us, I cannot yet divine the path that we have chosen. The future is… uncertain.'

'Is that a good thing or a bad thing?' said Johannes. 'I mean, surely it isn't coincidence that has led us here at this time.'

'The will of the gods is involved and not easily discerned by mere mortals such as us,' said Magnus, pulling his hood further forward, hiding his face. 'I too believe that there is a purpose to us being brought together, in this place, at this time. It is too soon to say whether it is for good or ill.'

'Then we wait,' said Ursula, causing them all to turn and look at her.

'Wait for what?' said Ruprecht.

'Another sign,' Ursula replied, still gazing out over the city. 'It is not as if I have any choice in the matter.'

Magnus coughed nervously, and Ursula turned her cold stare to him.

'Yes, I have heard of the count's edict,' she said.

'Edict?' said Johannes. 'What edict?'

'We are to remain as guests of the count, indefinitely,' said Ursula.

'For your own protection,' added Magnus, though his voice betrayed his lack of sincerity.

'We have the run of the city but may not leave Wolfenburg,' said Ursula, breaking her stare and looking at Johannes and Ruprecht. 'I suspect it is not just our safety that concerns the count.'

There was an odd gurgling noise and Ruprecht looked down at his stomach, embarrassed.

'I think we should avail ourselves of Count Vapold's hospitality and get some breakfast,' he said with a rueful look, glad to change the subject.

'The proverbial gilded cage,' said Johannes, stroking his chin in thought. 'I suppose there are worse things that could happen.'

Ursula turned away without speaking, walking briskly along the parapet. There were indeed much worse things that could happen, she thought. She offered a prayer to Sigmar that they did not come to pass.

THE DAYS WENT by and then a week, and another. Ursula became ever more fretful, and when not at the shrine of Sigmar, would often be found standing on the castle walls looking to the north, day and night. At night the hounds of the north invaded her dreams again and again, despoiling the land and rending her flesh with slavering mouths and vicious fangs. She would wake, sweating, and see the faint blue glow of the hilt-gem of Ulfshard in the darkness. She would walk out into the cold night air, constantly looking to the north, waiting.

Ruprecht and Johannes busied themselves about the city, learning its layout, its people. Johannes, by circumspect means, made contact with other devotees of Ranald, in case they needed to leave the city without attention as they had in Marienburg. Ruprecht learned what he could of Count Vapold, and what he heard left him with some hope. It became obvious that not only did he have his own interests at heart, but also that of his lands and people.

In a time when the nobles warred and politicked amongst themselves, and the poor folk paid with high taxes, disease and their lost ones falling in battle, Vapold seemed to have steered a path of relative stability for Wolfenburg during his rein. He was still unmarried, and the unspoken promise of a wedding to the royal family of Ostland kept many of the other noble houses loyal, both within the province and outside.

His army was well maintained, trained and disciplined, but unlike some of the other counts, they operated solely within the well-defined borders of Vapold's realm, foregoing the usual excursions and forays into neighbouring territory that seemed so popular with the contenders for the Emperor's throne.

Ursula's apparent calmness worried Ruprecht. In appearance alone, she seemed resigned to the long wait, and yet he knew that inside she was in turmoil, frustrated by the lack of activity. On the few occasions that he had spoken to her she had seemed distant. It was obvious that she was very tired, her sleep broken every night, but there was more than just fatigue. Her mind was elsewhere constantly, and quite often she would simply fall silent in the middle of a conversation or meal, her eyes filled with a faraway look.

The astrologer concerned him also. The man seemed to spend an unusually frequent amount of time in Ursula's company, sometimes asking her questions about her past, particularly Ulfshard and her experiences in the north, other times simply hovering nearby. On occasion Ruprecht thought that he saw a longing in Magnus's eye; an almost lustful look. He began to pay more attention to the stargazer.

Johannes had noticed the attention the astrologer was bestowing on Ursula too, and had become somewhat even more irritating than normal with his attempts to get her to notice him. Ruprecht had caught the young man on more than one occasion, glaring at Magnus, toying with the hilt of his sword. Johannes would then notice Ruprecht looking at him and leave, half angry, half embarrassed.

For four weeks there was no news from the east, either good or bad. Ruprecht began to feel some of Ursula's frustration himself. Routine turned to boredom, and he found himself increasingly losing his temper over small matters: Johannes's drunken snoring, Ursula's apparent indifference, the count's guards following him through the streets, Magnus's unwarranted fixation with Ursula. Things came to a head one evening as he sat down with Johannes and Ursula for their meal.

'A pox on the count!' Ruprecht snarled suddenly, throwing his knife onto his plate with a clatter. 'He has no right to keep us here.'

'Better than being stuck in a cell,' said Johannes, tearing a chunk of bread from a loaf. He waved it in the air as he spoke. 'I mean, it's not damp, we have proper beds. Besides, what else are we supposed to do? Go where? Do what?'

'I don't know,' said Ruprecht, slumping in his chair. 'It just doesn't feel right, sitting here on our arses while Kurt is doing gods knows what. We should be preparing, planning to do something.'

'You've too much time on your hands,' said Johannes, biting at the bread. 'Perhaps you should find something to distract yourself, you know, a hobby or perhaps a job in the city. One of the courtiers, Lady Hauen, is teaching me to dance, you know.'

'Yes, what I really need to do is waste my time with some court strumpet,' said Ruprecht.

'It's just dancing lessons, that's all,' said Johannes with a glance at Ursula, who was toying with the meat on her plate but not eating. She was paying neither of them any attention. 'I mean, I know you might have heard things, but it's nothing more than dancing.'

'I'm sure she's fine with that arrangement, for now,' said Ruprecht. 'But mark my words, she'll want something in return sooner or later, and a young man like you, well we can guess can't we?'

Johannes stood up sharply, knocking his chair over.

'She's married!' he said, his face reddening. 'What do you take me for?'

'Be quiet, the pair of you,' said Ursula, silencing them both. There was no venom in her voice, no hint of emotion at all. 'I have to talk to Magnus, I had a new dream last night.'

'Well, you can tell us first,' said Ruprecht.

'We can help,' said Johannes, righting his chair and sitting down again, his anger disappearing.

'The great hound ate the sun,' she said. 'The world was drenched in a shower of blood from the dark skies and flames erupted from the hound's eyes. He was looking at me, he knew who I was, what I was doing.'

'Hmm, that's a tricky one,' said Ruprecht, picking up his knife and cutting a slice of cheese from the round sat on a silver plate in front of Ursula. 'Seems like pretty much normal omen stuff to me. Skies of blood, darkness, flames.'

'I'm with Ruprecht,' said Johannes. 'I don't see there's any reason to see Magnus. He's an astrologer, anyway, what does he know about dreams?'

'He divines the future, sees into the mists of what is yet to be,' said Ursula. 'He doesn't just draw star charts and horoscopes, I've seen him read the entrails of a goat and use the elder stones too.'

Ruprecht felt a stab of suspicion, but kept his face passive. In his years with Marius van Diesl, hunting down those who practised the occult and forbidden, many times had such seemingly acceptable practices been used to mask darker purposes. He would keep his suspicions to himself for now, there was no point stirring up trouble. However, it would do no harm to investigate a little more closely.

'Perhaps you should consult Magnus,' Ruprecht said. 'I'll come with you.'

'So will I,' Johannes added hurriedly.

They finished their meal in silence, Ruprecht trying not to brood, Ursula reverting to her customary silence, and Johannes catching the mood of the other two, keeping quiet for a change. When they were done, Ursula led the way through the castle, along galleries of portraits of the past counts of Ostland, along flagged corridors and up stone steps into the highest reaches of the keep. Neither Ruprecht nor Johannes had been to this part of the castle before. She took them to a small wooden door at the top of a flight of rickety steps, and knocked loudly. There was sounds of movement inside, papers being shuffled, a chair scraping.

'Enter,' Magnus's voice came through the door and Ursula opened the door and stepped through, the other two close behind.

Magnus stood by the window, his back turned to them, arms crossed. He was dressed in a plain, scholarly robe of grey, his more ostentatious robes of office carelessly flung over the back of a low couch that was set along one wall of the room. Ruprecht looked at the tall bookshelves, teetering with tomes and scrolls, and took in the assorted paraphernalia scattered across the various desks and tables of the astrologer's workplace. A small cot was hidden in the corner with a side table next to it on which stood a large candle, the only light in the room. It was chill, with no fireplace to provide warmth and a cold draught spilling through the cracked panes of the window.

'How may I be of assistance?' said Magnus turning around, his smile slightly obsequious.

'The dream has changed,' said Ursula. Magnus signalled for them to seat themselves on the various chairs around the room and leaned back against the windowsill.

'Has it, indeed?' the astrologer said, his eyes full of inquiry. He crossed the room to one of the tables and sat down behind it, picking up a quill and piece of parchment. He poured a little water from a small jar onto an inkplate and dipped the quill into it. He sat there, poised. 'Describe it to me.'

Ursula sat in thought for a moment, brow wrinkled in thought, trying to recollect the details of the dream.

'It starts in darkness,' she began. 'There is no light, no moon, no stars, nothing. I am standing on a blasted waste, the wind howling around me. I am naked and cold. I feel something watching me, and turn. The sun burns in the sky, but doesn't shed any light, and looks like a great eye staring at me. I hear the baying of the hounds, and can feel them all around me, watching, but I can't see them. The great hound appears, incredibly large, on the horizon. It opens its jaw and barks deafeningly. With a leap, it bounds into the sky and its jaws close about the sun. It's just as dark as before, but now the hound's eyes blaze with fire.'

Magnus held up his right hand to stop her as he wrote hurriedly on the parchment, occasionally refreshing the nib of the quill with fresh ink.

'What colour were the flames?' he asked, not looking up.

'Red, orange, yellow, just like ordinary fire,' Ursula said, Magnus nodding, as if this meant something to him. He finished writing and then looked up, giving Ursula a nod to continue.

'It's pitch black, but I know there are no clouds,' Ursula said, sitting immobile in the chair, her gaze distant as she recalled the dream. 'I feel something dropping on me and hold out my hand. It's blood, droplets of blood, falling from the empty sky. It starts to cascade down, drenching me in crimson. The hound lolls out its tongue and laps at the falling blood, looking at me.'

She finished and the only noise was the scratching of Magnus's quill.

'And that's everything?' he said, sitting back and running an eye over his notes. 'No other details you may have forgotten?'

'That's everything I can remember,' she said.

Magnus nodded once more, stroking his chin as he read his notes once more. Without saying anything he stood and crossed to one of the shelves. He ran his finger along the spines of the books and then stopped, pulling out the volume. Bringing it back to the desk he sat down again and opened it, flicking quickly through the pages.

'Gerimiah Ondeecht's *Book of Portents and Visions,*' he muttered in explanation as he glanced up and saw them looking curiously at the book. 'It's a little out of date in some of its beliefs and I am working on a more contemporary piece, but it will suffice for this. Ah, here it is.'

He said nothing for a while as he read. Ursula sat patiently, while Ruprecht's gaze wandered around the room, looking for any tell-tale signs of wrongdoing. Johannes toyed with an astrolabe on the desk next to him, absent-mindedly spinning the little planets around on their orbits.

'Yes, it's as I suspected,' Magnus said suddenly, closing the book with a thud. 'It is a prophecy of warning. Did you feel afraid?'

Ursula shook her head.

'Hmm, that is slightly unusual,' Magnus continued, pursing his lips. 'But not unheard of.'

'What is it warning against?' said Johannes. Magnus looked at him as if noticing the young man for the first time. The scholar frowned in irritation.

'Well, that would be the real question, young man,' the astrologer said. 'That is what we must try to discern, is it not? I suspect that it has a more specific meaning than just a general portent for danger. After all, you've been having those for a while now. No, it must be something particular that it is drawing your attention to.'

'Perhaps we shouldn't stay here any longer,' suggested Ruprecht, half hopeful. 'Perhaps it means that we need to be doing something.'

'I don't think so,' Magnus countered, looking back to Ursula and so not seeing Ruprecht sag slightly in his chair. 'You felt no fear, no apprehension, no sense of urgency?'

'Nothing,' she said. 'I was very calm.'

'Are we sure the hound is Kurt?' Johannes asked. Magnus gave him a withering look and Ruprecht sighed heavily. 'Well, it is just an assumption, perhaps the hound is someone, or something, else.'

'It's Kurt,' Ursula said heavily. 'I'm not sure how I know, but I know.'

'I was just asking.' Johannes shrugged in acquiescence.

'You can't be suggesting that we just sit here and keep waiting,' growled Ruprecht. 'I know that it's folly to second-guess the gods, but there must be something we can do.'

'We can prepare,' said Ursula, her expression grim. 'We will talk to Captain Felsturm, teach him everything we know about the northmen, how they fight, how they can be beaten. If it is the will of Sigmar that we wait for the hounds to come to us, then that is what we shall do, but we do not have to be unready.'

'I have many questions too,' said Magnus, and Ruprecht's eyes narrowed for a moment, unnoticed by the astrologer. 'I too would know of the ways of the northmen, the better to read the portents of their coming.'

'War is coming,' said Ursula. 'Whether the count wishes it or not, this war cannot be ignored. My future and Kurt's are one and the same, I am sure of that. If the count does not wish me to leave, then he must prepare for that war to come to him.'

'We'll be ready,' said Johannes, banging a fist against the table. 'If they come, we will teach them not to forget their fear of the maiden of Sigmar.'

Ursula smiled, though her eyes were hard as flint. Looking at her, Ruprecht felt an unnatural quiver of apprehension. For the first time since he had met her, he suddenly felt afraid. Afraid of what the future might bring, and afraid of what her part in it would be. Afraid for her, but afraid of her in equal measure.

NINE DAYS HAD passed, during which Ursula, Ruprecht and Johannes spent much time with Captain Felsturm and his officers, telling them about their experiences fighting against the northmen. They told them of the Norse shieldwall, which protected the warriors as they advanced. They related stories of how the barbarians often used short throwing spears, usually from horseback, heavy enough that their weight would drag down a shield raised against them, exposing the soldier to attacks from the Norseman's sword or axe.

They warned of the dire perils of the shamans and the vile sorceries they could conjure. For these discussions, Magnus would be present, as would the ranking priests of the city. Ursula learned prayers that would ward away evil magic, and Magnus would marvel at the way her aura would blaze as she spoke them. When she made the sign of Sigmar, the symbol of the twin-tailed comet that had heralded his birth, her raised hand was like an incandescent ball of energy to Magnus's secret sight.

All the while, the ranks of the army of Ostland swelled, as the call went out for able-bodied men to defend their homes, though whether against Ostermark or an even direr foe was never specified. All the common folk knew was that war was brewing once more, and if they did not wish to stand and be counted in the fight, they would suffer nonetheless. Many were those who were persuaded to take the count's shilling in return for reporting to the castle once a week for weapons training. The courtyard echoed through every day with barked orders, the clatter of wooden practice swords and halberds and the bark of handguns being fired. Ruprecht joined them in their fire drill, and though he had difficulty at first loading his arquebus with his artificial hand, he soon became fairly proficient.

Johannes spent time with the knights of Wolfenburg, having procured a horse and armour as a gift from the count, although the count was as yet unaware of his generosity. The young would-be knight would be seen from dawn until midday on the tilting fields, practising with his lance. On rare occasions,

Ursula would visit, in between her lengthy discussions with the priests, and Johannes would show off his riding skills for her. Ursula would clap dutifully as Johannes's horse would double-step past her, or prance on its hind legs, but there was no enthusiasm in her support, as if she were merely remembering it.

All the while, Ruprecht kept a close eye on Magnus, listening carefully as the astrologer would quiz Ursula for hours at a time, asking intricate details about symbols and runes she had seen, of the language she had half-learned from Jakob, and the sorceries the northmen had employed against her. All the while he would sit with his parchment and quill, writing notes, drawing diagrams, sometimes copying text from another of his books as further reference. Ruprecht resolved that he would try and have a closer look at the scholar's works, though he suspected Magnus was too cunning to leave anything incriminating where it could be easily found. Often Ruprecht would admonish himself for being paranoid, as the priests and other advisors were more than comfortable with Magnus's research.

And yet he still had a nagging doubt. Not only had the long years with Marius taught Ruprecht to be wary, but also more recent experiences with the sorceress Jasmina el Al had reminded him that often the greatest foe was the one who was closest, the enemy within.

For nine days this continued, the castle growing ever more full with men and materiel for the coming battles. Bow staves and arrows soon filled the storerooms, and the smithies worked from dusk till dawn beating armour, forging blades and casting shot. From the guildhouse of the alchemists out near the city wall, barrels of more and more blackpowder began to be moved up to the castle in small covered wagons, each protected by an escort of twenty men. Whetstones scraped, hammers banged and small lads ran to and fro constantly. It was quite easy to get caught up in all the activity, and Ruprecht had to remind himself frequently that this was not readying for a battle against Kurt and whatever horde he had gathered, but instead was likely to march to war against another state of the Empire.

Ursula seemed to have put this from her mind, though when Ruprecht had raised it with her, she had simply said that whether it was by way of Bechafen or by more direct means, this army would face the northmen. Rather than becoming disheartened every day seemed to strengthen her resolve.

And as dusk began to fall on the ninth day since the warning dreams had come to her, Ursula was once more on the battlements of Wolfenburg keep, staring to the north.

A great cry went up from the east gate and a bell began to toll. As she paced along the wall to see what the commotion was about, she saw Count Vapold appear in the courtyard below, flanked by Captain Felsturm and two sergeants-at-arms. He strode quickly up the steps and met her by the outside of the wall.

From their high vantage point they could see out across the city, beyond the outer wall to the road winding between the dark eaves of the Ostland forests. There a long ribbon of flickering light came towards them along the road, a parade of torches and lanterns that stretched for nearly half a mile. The flames glittered off gilded armour, and illuminated tattered banners of purple and white and purple and yellow.

The Osterknacht had returned.

CHAPTER TEN
True Beginning
Realm of Chaos

IT MIGHT HAVE been only a heartbeat or a whole lifetime that Kurt had stood and looked at the house and the woman, who appeared to be his mother. Entranced, he watched her walking through the garden. It seemed almost real, but on the edge of his vision, disappearing as soon as he turned his head, he would have sworn that he saw other landscapes: dark and empty wastes, mountainous valleys and great rivers of fire.

The smell was real enough, the mix of jasmine and roses that his mother had always attended to herself, ever since he had been a boy. Even now she stooped and, with a practiced twist of her fingers, snapped a dying bloom from a rose bush.

His mother turned and looked straight in his direction, but did not seem to see him. Kurt wanted to say

something, to call out, but could not. He did not know
what to say. She turned away and began to walk back
towards the house. Suddenly snapped free from his
trance, Kurt stepped forward, at first taking a couple of
paces and then breaking into a run as he followed her.

He tripped and sprawled across the ground. Instead
of landing on the grass, he found himself on grey rock,
dust smeared across his face. He looked up and the
house was gone, the garden had vanished. He was on
a high plateau, looking out over a desert torn with
flaming cracks and dark crevasses. Kurt felt feverish,
his vision kept blurring and there was a constant
buzzing in his ears.

You are all alone.

Kurt looked around, but still the voice came from
thin air.

You could be with them again. You could save them.

'How?' he said, turning back and forth, angry.

You know how.

'They are dead, the dead cannot come back,' snarled
Kurt. 'You offer false promises.'

They do not have to die. You know what you must do.

'It was fifteen years ago,' said Kurt. 'I cannot save
them.'

You could be with them again. You could save them.

'I don't know how,' Kurt said, feeling tired. He
slumped to the ground, head in his hands.

You are no champion.

Kurt looked up at the sky, a roiling mass of blackness
tinged with dark blues and purples.

'I am chosen,' he said, desperation clawing at his
heart. 'You chose me.'

The gods chose poorly. You are not a champion.

'I am, I will prove it!' said Kurt with a surge of anger. He had not come so far to fail now. He stood, ready to face whatever challenge the gods set him next.

You know what you must do.

'How can I save them?' he asked. 'It has been fifteen years since they were murdered.'

You know what you must do.

'Kill Marius?' Kurt said, voicing the thought that had been lingering at the back of his mind. 'Marius is already dead.'

You know what you must do.

'How can I kill Marius?' he asked. 'History has passed, you cannot go back.'

In this place there is no future, there is no past, there is only now.

'But how can I go back?' Kurt said, his desperation returning. His head spun with dizziness, his lungs filled with acrid air. 'It is many months travel from the north.'

In this place there is here. All places are one. Everywhere is but a step away.

Kurt tried to fight through the fatigue, to concentrate on what the voice was telling him. A thought occurred to him suddenly and he laughed bitterly.

'I know you, I know what you are trying to do,' he said. 'It's a trick! If I kill Marius, then he would have never have murdered my family. My whole life would have changed. I might not have gone to the north, I might never have become chosen. This is a test of my faith!'

You have always been chosen. You have always been one of ours. You will always be one of ours.

'No, it's a trick,' said Kurt, laughing manically. 'It's not true. I can't save them, and if I try it's proof that I am not loyal to you. I can see it now!'

You know what you must do.

'Stop saying that!' said Kurt. Like a small child, he stuck his fingers in his ears, trying to ignore the voice, but it was inside his head.

You know what you must do.

Kurt began to caper around in circles, singing to himself, hands clamped over his ears, his eyes screwed shut. Dust clouds rose around him as his feet scraped over the rock.

'I'm not listening!' he screamed. 'It's a lie. You're tricking me.'

You saw her, you know that you can save her. You have the power.

Kurt stopped his childish dance, head cocked to one side.

'I have the power?' he said. He began to laugh again. 'I have the power. I have the power!'

You know what you must do.

Kurt's laughter subsided to a chuckle.

'I have the power,' he whispered. 'In this place, where there is no time, where all places are one.'

He looked back into the roiling sky and grinned.

'I understand!' he yelled. 'I know how it works now! The power of the gods is here. I can use it! I can do whatever I want with it. The power of the gods, it's my power now.'

Dizziness swept over Kurt again, and he staggered and fell to his knees. Pain throbbed in his head and chest. Gritting his teeth, feeling sick, he forced himself to his feet once more. He could feel the breath of the gods around him. It was like hammers beating at his ribs, like a furnace inside his skull.

'Take me to Marius!' he declared, flinging his arms into the air dramatically.

Nothing happened.

Kurt waited a while, trying to think. The power was his to command, he could feel it, crushing down on him. Perhaps he was inside the gate itself, he did not know. He wondered for a moment how Jakob and the others were faring.

'Voice?' he said, suddenly aware that he had not heard it for a long while. His thoughts drifted again, and he clenched his fists as he tried to concentrate. 'Voice? How do I use the power?'

You know what you must do.

Of course he did! As if his mind were a man wading through thick mud, the memories came back to him, the sensations of his body returned. He realised he was lying down on the rock. Perhaps he had passed out.

'I have to focus!' he shouted, and then was unsure why he had said it aloud.

Closing his eyes, he tried to blank out the swirling thoughts inside his head, the white-hot touch of the breath of the gods that seared at his soul. He calmed himself, breathing deeply, listening to his own roaring heart, counting the beats. Slowly, but with gathering speed, he began to push his mind out of his body, encompassing the magical storm that surrounded him. He knew how to do this. Take the energy into himself, shape it, command it.

The power imploded into Kurt with thunderous force. Like a river through a broken dam, it poured into him, gushing into his body and mind. The world turned around him, spinning outside his head, while his blood boiled and his bones began to melt. He felt the forces warping and twisting him. His back began to split, and he felt his face burning, steaming away into the air. A second face tried to push out of his chest mewling like a newborn pup, its single white eye glaring at him.

This was not how it was supposed to be, Kurt realised. The power was too much. He couldn't control it. As the doubt flared in his mind, something bristled on his back, a frond of fingers pushing out from his spine.

Control, I must control it, thought Kurt. He pictured his body. Tall, lean, dark-haired, roughly handsome. He focussed on it, and his body began to shift again, the appendages that sprawled from his stomach receding, the eyeballs that had blistered open in the palms of his hands disappearing. With a shout that was torn from his throat, Kurt exerted his will over the power of the gods and made it his own.

He collapsed.

THERE WAS LUSH grass under his body when he awoke, and Kurt realised that he was naked. Sitting up, he saw a green meadow spread around him, a cloudless blue sky above. There were trees not far away, the familiar, normal trees of the Empire. Kurt chuckled to himself. Looking around, he spied a rough stone building a few hundred yards away, amongst the trees, surrounded by a low wall. He began to walk towards it.

As before, the landscape was not wholly real, and he wondered if perhaps it was some fever-driven dream. Perhaps he was just lying in the harsh north, on the brink of death, and this was not happening at all. Flickers of deep valleys filled with fire and roads paved with skulls hovered on the edge of his vision.

There is no history or future here. All places are here. Kurt laughed again at his own doubts.

As he approached he saw a group of people standing outside, about twenty of them. They were laughing and clapping, their backs turned to him. The women wore long gowns and had flowers wreathed in their hair. The men stood in smart suits of doublets and hose. He stood behind a tree and watched them. As they parted, he caught sight of a man and a woman, standing at the centre of the group.

The woman was pretty, although by no means beautiful. She had a garland of flowers around her neck and wore a loose white robe that revealed an ample bosom. She was smiling at the man next to her, one arm around his waist, the other holding back the fronds of her long blonde hair. She laughed and leant forward to kiss the man.

It was Marius.

Though much younger than when Kurt had last met him, the witch hunter was unmistakeable. Gaunt, raven-haired, with sharp eyes and a wry smile, he held his new bride close. For a long while, Kurt stood and watched, his eyes never leaving van Diesl. The wedding party began to drift away, in twos and threes, until only Marius, his wife and the priest were left. With a nod, the priest turned away and walked back into the shrine. The happy couple stood there for a moment longer, looking at each other. With a laugh, the woman nodded her head towards the woods. Marius shrugged and laughed, and hand in hand the pair walked out of the gate and turned into the forest.

Kurt followed them at a distance, catching glimpses of them as they walked between the trees. It was idyllic, he realised. A perfect day. With the thought, anger welled up inside him like blood from an old wound.

It should have been his perfect day. With Ursula, or with someone else. Marius had taken that from him. He had slaughtered his family and made him a fugitive, a young boy running for his life across the wilds of the Empire. Even when he thought he was safe, Kurt had been plagued by Marius van Diesl. When he had met Ursula, tending a shrine to Sigmar not unlike the one they had just left, he thought that his life was finally complete.

The witch hunter had destroyed that as well. He had followed Kurt to Ostermark, had come to the town where he had lived. He had taken Ursula from him. Even as he watched the two of them lay down in a bare patch between the boles of two trees, caressing each other lovingly, hatred burned inside Kurt.

That could have been Ursula and him, gently undressing each other, about to consummate their love for each other. They would have raised children, fine and strong boys and girls, and life would have been good.

But Marius had ruined any chance of that. The accursed witch hunter had dogged Kurt throughout his life. Not content with making him and Ursula fugitives, he had turned Kurt's beloved against him, turned her into a serpent in his midst. With his twisted words, he had made Ursula his puppet, and led her to betray Kurt. In that one vile act, Kurt's life had been shattered.

Kurt clenched his fists, his anger like a fire inside his chest, his breath coming fast and shallow, as he watched the two clumsily fumbling with each other, young and unsure. Even in the north, when Marius had already died by Kurt's blade, the witch hunter's curse had continued to follow him, sending Ursula forth on her hate-filled raids and attacks, leading to the death of Kurt's wife and son.

Yes, it would all end here. Kurt would have his revenge against this monster, this most vile of men who had ruthlessly crushed any hope Kurt may have had for happiness.

Marius must have seen or heard something because he sat up, staring into the woods. Kurt stepped out and the witch hunter's eyes widened. His wife, whose name Kurt had never known, sat up and grasped her discarded dress, holding it across her bare chest.

As Kurt stalked forwards, fingers flexing, Marius stood, his mouth opening and closing wordlessly. The woman sprang to her feet beside her husband, clinging to his arm.

'Vengeance will be mine,' snarled Kurt as he advanced.

Marius stood immobile as Kurt closed. When Kurt was only a few paces away, the woman shrieked and rushed forward, snatching a fallen branch from the ground. Kurt raised an arm as she swung it at him, the wood splintering and breaking against his forearm. With his other hand, Kurt grabbed the newlywed around the throat. Holding her to one side, he looked toward van Diesl.

He was running away, sprinting between the trees. Kurt stood there for a moment, surprised, unsure what to do. The woman struggled in his grip for a moment until he squeezed tighter and she began to choke. Lifting her easily with his inhuman strength, Kurt began to follow the fleeing Marius.

Kurt moved rapidly with each stride, the bride dangling like a doll in his grip, as with each pace he moved himself through the slightly unreal landscape. While Marius was panting, his face reddened, Kurt covered several yards with every stride, using the power that ebbed and flowed within him to slide effortlessly along the edge of reality. He could catch Marius at any moment, he realised. A simple flex of his mind and he would be beside the running man. And yet the chase in itself was enjoyable. He could feel the fear that lay like clouds in the wake of Marius.

They burst from the tree-line, and Kurt was halted as if he had walked into a wall. He tried to step forward again, but found his way barred. Looking down, he saw the low wall of the shrine in front of his feet. Beyond the wall, Marius stood, his back against the shrine, breathing heavily, looking aghast at Kurt.

'Come back here, coward,' Kurt said, lifting up the unconscious woman in front of him. 'I have your woman. If you want her to live, then come here.'

'You cannot cross sacred ground, can you?' Marius shouted back. 'Hellspawn, I'll see you burn for this.'

'She dies by my hand if you do not come out,' warned Kurt. Marius did not move, and a flicker of doubt entered Kurt's mind. Perhaps he would sacrifice his wife to save his own life. Even as the thought occurred to him, Kurt felt a shimmering of power around him, and for the briefest of moments the woods and shrine flickered away.

'You will kill us both,' said Marius. 'I am no fool!'

'You have my oath that I will spare her, in return for your life,' Kurt said, lowering the woman so that her feet were on the ground. 'I just want you.'

'You think I would trust you?' said Marius. 'You are in league with evil forces, and your oath is without worth!'

'If you do not come out, she will certainly die,' said Kurt. 'Would you stand there and watch her burn?'

Kurt extended some of his power, which had become second nature to him. The sigils carved into his flesh began to glow with energy and his skin flickered with flame. The woman started awake as her flesh began to singe, and she tried to scream, but Kurt's grip was too tight.

'It is still not too late,' said Kurt. 'You will die anyway, van Diesl, so you may as well save her. I just want you.'

The flames across Kurt's body began to grow in intensity and the woman's struggles increased until she was flailing wildly, her hair alight, her skin blistering and peeling away. Kurt stared at Marius and saw tears rolling down the man's cheeks.

'Save your sadness,' Kurt spat. 'Where were the tears for my family?'

The woman's struggles began to ebb as the stench of her charring flesh filled the air. At that moment, the priest emerged from the shrine, timidly looking around the edge of the door. His mouth dropped open.

'B-Baron Leitzig?' the priest said. Kurt now recognised him, from the depth of his memories. He was Brother Fauchleden, who kept the shrine not far from the lands owned by Kurt's father. A terrible thought began to form in Kurt's mind, and as it did so, the scene began to shimmer and twist away from his control, replaced for a split second by the view of the rocky plateau.

'No,' said Kurt, shaking his head.

'Baron Leitzig?' said Marius, his tear-streaked face twisted in fury. He melted away for a moment, and dizziness struck Kurt. His legs began to buckle underneath him. 'Now I know the name of the man that I will hunt down 'til my dying breath!'

'No, it doesn't…' began Kurt, but it was too late. The image shimmered and then faded as Kurt fell to his knees. He felt dust and rocks against his skin, and the sky swam overhead. 'No, it's not meant to happen this way.'

The crushing magical energy around Kurt was squeezing the life from him, and with one last effort he tried to stand, but fell to one side, unconscious once more.

WHEN HE AWOKE, Kurt was covered in a sheen of sweat, yet his body felt chill. The fevered dreams of his confrontation with Marius still lingered, half-remembered, at the back of his mind. A rank smell filled his nostrils and with a groan, Kurt turned his head. Lying next to him, her pretty face untouched but the rest of her body a charred mess, lay the remains of van Diesl's wife.

Kurt sat up and fought back the sickness rising in his throat. He reached out a hand and the burned corpse seemed just out of reach. Perhaps it was just a waking dream, he thought, and yet the smell was so distinct, so real. Leaning over he stretched further to touch the body, to reassure himself that it was real, and yet still it remained just beyond his fingertips.

You have done what needed to be done. You have always been ours.

'No, it wasn't meant to happen like that,' Kurt said, standing up. 'I will go back and kill Marius.'

The gate to heaven awaits you. If you leave now, you will not return.

'The gate?' said Kurt, swaying with fatigue. 'I don't see any gate.'

It was then that Kurt noticed that the ground had shifted and warped again. He was on a flat plain, which stretched out forever. There was no distance, no horizon. Just a barren landscape of dust and rock. The sky was gone. There was no blackness, no colour, nothing. Just an emptiness that made the land curve back around in on itself. Kurt felt nauseous looking at it.

He could feel something looming behind him and turned slowly. There, perhaps just an arm's length away and yet at the same time incredibly distant, stood the gate. It was an immense structure, an incomplete annulus that towered above him, leaning at an odd angle, which changed each time Kurt moved his eyes. Its surfaces, of which there seemed more than there should have been, were carved with intricate, geographic designs. Some looked like pictures of faces picked out in impossibly-sided polygons, others reminded Kurt of maps, or perhaps more accurately sea charts.

It was broken and cracked in many places, and shards and chunks of its structure lay scattered around it. As he looked towards it, the breath of the gods was a hurricane, and Kurt could feel it tearing at his flesh. This was where the gods resided, where their power came from. Perhaps he had always been here. Perhaps he wasn't even here now. It was impossible to say.

All thoughts of Marius were forgotten. Here was the gate. He was the goal he had been searching for, seeking it for an eternity. Here lay immortality. Here could be found everlasting power. He would be the reward for his suffering, the means of his revenge against those who had tried to kill him, who had despoiled his life.

Walking forwards was painful. Every step into the hurricane of power that howled around Kurt send slivers of agony raging through his body and mind. Every fibre of his being, every vein, every hair, every smallest part of him was infused with sensation. Kurt fixed his stare on the gate and held it in his mind even as it felt like his eyes were melting and his body disassembling.

Every slow step, every stride that Kurt forced himself to take, took him closer and closer to the gate. He could not count them, and at times felt like he was walking backwards. He had no sensation of his body any more. He was a drifting cloud of motes, blasted by the howling magical winds. He was powerless to resist the mystical current that poured from here across the whole world.

He gazed at the centre of the twisted circular structure, at a point of nothingness that floated in the air. Or perhaps it was everything else that floated around that single point. That was where it came from. That was where the gods lived, that impossibly large pinprick of otherworldness.

Kurt realised he was within the gate now, bodiless, soulless. There was nothing else left but him. He stretched out a hand he no longer possessed, as if to grasp the realm of the gods between his fingers.

As he touched it, Kurt Leitzig was no more.

BOOK TWO

CHAPTER ONE
War
Ostland, Summer 1712

THE SKY WAS cloudless and the sun nearing noon, but there was still a chill in the air as Ursula reined in her horse at the crest of the latest hill, guiding it off the road. Trying not to be too conspicuous, five Osterknacht directed their steeds off the road a short distance away, keeping a wary eye on their charge. Ruprecht reined in beside Ursula, darting the knights a distasteful glare before following her gaze, back towards the west.

For mile after mile the army of Ostland marched, a snaking column following the road that cut through the thick forests. Over ten thousand soldiers followed Vapold, from all across his realm. Only a few hundred men had been left to guard Wolfenburg as the count had set forth, few compared to the might of the host on the road, but enough to defend the city against all but a full army.

Eastwards they marched, towards the Talabec. Vapold, under advice from Lord Bayard, hoped to meet the army of Steinhardt as it crossed the river. There were few fording points and even fewer bridges, and as soon as the Osterknacht had returned with the news that Steinhardt had been recognised as count by the cowed nobility of Ostermark, Vapold had despatched riders to patrol the borders to watch for any foe.

Agents across the river sent back scattered reports. Steinhardt had moved the capital to Mordheim in the south, the ancestral home of his family, and even now was strengthening its defences. Meanwhile, his army of mercenaries and dispossessed southerners remained in Bechafen, in the north, less than two weeks' marching from Wolfenburg. Emissaries from the new count had ridden to Wolfenburg with a simple message: Vapold was to hand over the false heir, Hensel, and the traitors of the Osterknacht, as the letter had named them. The demand had incorporated no specific threat, but was accompanied by a written promise from the Ottila of Talabecland to allow Steinhardt to cross his borders with an armed force. It was then obvious that Ostermark had allied itself, however temporarily, with Talabheim. As soon as the heralds had returned to their master with Vapold's curses still ringing in their ears, news began to come back to the count and his court, of the army of Ostermark gathering.

Ruprecht, for no reason other than the count had not sent him away, had sat in on some of the councils of war that he had held with Lord Bayard and Captain

Felsturm. The plan was simple but effective. They would hold the river against Steinhardt's army, and if that proved untenable or the Ostermarkers crossed before Vapold could reach the river, they would retreat to Wolfenburg and hold the capital. Ruprecht hoped that Steinhardt was bluffing, perhaps showing off his force to quell any thoughts of opposing him before his control was absolute. The boy and Osterknacht were no threat to his position, though Ruprecht knew that wars had been fought over even pettier reasons.

'You don't seem worried,' said Ruprecht, looking at Ursula. A regiment of swordsmen marched past, their black-and-white-painted shields strapped to their backs, their fluttering banner emblazoned with a silver eagle device.

'Why should I be worried?' Ursula asked.

'If Kurt amasses an army of any true size, he can overwhelm Wolfenburg with hardly a fight,' Ruprecht said.

'Kurt and I will meet, but it isn't necessarily at Wolfenburg,' she replied, not averting her gaze. 'If I am not there, perhaps Wolfenburg is safe.'

'You're assuming a lot,' said Ruprecht. 'Even if you're not there, Wolfenburg will make a natural target for any invaders. Kurt is from the east, he knows these lands.'

'And he also has no reason to believe that it will be defended by anything less than its full strength,' said Ursula, turning to look at Ruprecht. Her eyes were hard, like chips of stone. 'Besides, the count has made his choice, and it is not my duty to watch over his people.'

'Oh yes?' said Ruprecht, disturbed by the zealous glare in Ursula's gaze. 'What is your duty?'

'To find Kurt and kill him,' Ursula replied with the same grim smile that had so worried Ruprecht before. 'Sigmar wills me to stop him, nothing else. His other servants must look to their own defence.'

'You used to care about the Empire,' said Ruprecht, kicking his heels into the flanks of his horse and urging it back on to the road. 'You wanted to save it.'

'If the Empire is truly worth saving, it will save itself,' Ursula called after him.

Ruprecht glanced back to see her watching the army as it marched past, the same look of satisfaction on her face. She had her army, he realised. It was just that the army didn't know it was hers yet. With a rueful shake of his head, Ruprecht rode away.

WITH WOLFENBURG TEN leagues behind, the army stopped for the night, a complicated process in its own right. Pickets had to be sent out, woodsmen chopped down trees for the cooking fires and to clear space for the hundreds of tents, those tents had to be erected and the fires started. In all it took several hours for the camp to be made, by which time night had fallen and Mannslieb, the white moon, was high in the air.

Johannes sat with some of the other knights, under the awning of their tent. They were Vapold's men, and he had come to know some of them while he had been training at Wolfenburg, re-learning the skills he had honed whilst he had masqueraded as a freelance. The night was not too chill, and he had stripped off his armour and sat in a simple woollen smock. This had caused some amusement amongst his new comrades, who wore embroidered doublets and silken hose, but there had only been so much that Johannes was able to safely liberate from the count before they left.

He sat gazing across the camp, towards the tall marquee where Vapold was staying, along with members of his court. And Ursula. He wanted to go and speak to her, but even more than ever, she was ignoring him. It told himself it was unintentional, that she was simply preoccupied with other matters. He simply didn't have the heart after a long day's riding to be rebutted again. Perhaps tomorrow he'd talk to her.

'So you've known her a long while then?' said Gastren, a middle-aged knight with thinning hair that he plastered over his scalp with pungent oil in the hopes of hiding his encroaching baldness.

'Hmm, who's that?' asked Johannes, turning his attention to his new companion.

'Ursula, the maiden of Sigmar,' Gastren explained. Johannes suppressed a smile at hearing the title used by someone else. He had meant it half in jest when he had first coined the term, but now it seemed fitting.

'I've known her for nearly two years, by my reckoning,' Johannes said.

'Looks a feisty enough lass, you know,' Gastren said, scratching at his armpit. 'Odd hair, mind, but a nice face.'

'She used to be,' said Johannes, trying not to sound too wistful. 'I think she has a higher purpose at the moment. Feisty doesn't come into it, really.'

'I know what you mean,' added Fakje-Stohl, a lean-looking knight who had long moustaches that hung below his chin, though full beards were currently the favoured fashion for facial hair about the court. 'Strutting around with that sword of hers, she cuts a fine figure.'

'Strutting?' said Johannes trying to keep his temper in check.

'Well, you know, I expect she waves it around well enough, you know, giving speeches and such,' explained Gastren. 'There's worse for a soldier to follow. They're not too bright, you know, and a pretty lass like that telling them Sigmar's with them might give them a bit more backbone, you know.'

'Waves it around?' Johannes was lost for words for a moment.

'What, you don't want to tell me that she actually tries to fight?' laughed Fakje-Stohl. 'I mean, I've heard the fanciful stories, about killing Norse and such, but everyone's heard them, haven't they?'

Johannes cast his mind back to the battles along the Norscan coast. He could picture Ursula clearly, Ulfshard flaming in her hands, beheading and gutting the northmen with clean, quick strokes. She had confided in him, back when she confided anything at all, that it was mostly the sword, but that hadn't made it any less impressive for Johannes to watch.

'If we're lucky, those stories will be all you know,' said Johannes. 'When she draws that sword, the blade of Marbad remember, you know that there's serious fighting to be done.'

The other two exchanged amused glances, but Johannes allowed it to pass. If Ursula was right, and

Johannes feared that she was, then perhaps they would all come to look to the maiden of Sigmar for far more than just inspiration.

THE SOUND OF voices outside disturbed Magnus as he read, and he looked up from his small book. He recognised the deep tones of the big Talabheimer, Ruprecht, talking to the guard posted outside his tent. He slipped the grimoire under the blankets of his bed and lay back, closing his eyes. Magnus did not know much about the burly man, but what he had heard worried him. He had served with a witch hunter, one of the Grand Theogonist's Templars of Sigmar. Lately Magnus had felt himself being scrutinised by Ruprecht more than he cared for, and was irritated at the intrusion.

'Just let him in!' Magnus snapped as he caught the general topic of the increasingly heated discussion.

As Ruprecht ducked through the tent flap, Magnus opened his eyes and sat up, as if rousing himself from quiet repose. Ruprecht stood there uncertainly until Magnus nodded towards one of the chairs set on the rugs covering the bare earth, and the tall man sat down, perched uncomfortably on the edge of the small chair.

'I am sorry to intrude,' Ruprecht began, stroking at his artificial hand nervously.

'Do not give it a second thought,' Magnus said, intrigued by Ruprecht's unusual demeanour. 'You are after advice?'

Ruprecht nodded and glanced away for a few heartbeats, before returning his gaze to Magnus, his eyes now steady.

'I am very worried about Ursula,' he said.

'She is very capable, you know this,' replied Magnus, swinging his legs off his cot and leaning forward. He reached for the pitcher of water on the low table and poured some into a goblet. 'What is your concern, and how do you think I might help?'

'I can't put my finger on an exact cause,' Ruprecht said, flicking his glance around the tent. 'Something is wrong, something about the visions and dreams is having a bad effect on her.'

'In what way?' said Magnus, delicately sipping the water. 'One with her gifts often has their perception of the world and others altered.'

'That's just it,' said Ruprecht with a nod. 'It's like she doesn't see anything else any more. She's, I don't know, removed from the rest of us. Her mind is somewhere else most of the time. She's becoming heartless, almost inhuman. It can't be good for her.'

'Well, I agree, to some extent,' said Magnus, placing his goblet carefully back on the table. 'Her belief is extraordinary, and that stems from her visions. Is it not understandable that she is very focussed? It is true, is it not, that she is being guided by the gods, and that is a heavy burden to bear sometimes. Perhaps it is for her own sake that she has removed herself from us. Perhaps because she realises that what she must do, the gifts she has, mark her out as different from us.'

'But she's forgotten why,' said Ruprecht, his iron hand clenching and unclenching as he spoke. 'She's forgotten the ends and is thinking only about the means. She's becoming obsessed.'

'What would you have me do?' asked Magnus, suppressing a sigh.

'Nothing much,' said Ruprecht. 'Just talk to her, or try to. She seems comfortable with you. Perhaps you can get her to open up more than I can.'

'I will see what I can do,' Magnus said with a thin smile. 'Do not give up on her yet, she is a remarkable young lady.'

'Oh that I know,' said Ruprecht with a grin, standing up. 'Thank you.'

Ruprecht stooped to leave and stopped and turned back, as if a thought had just occurred to him.

'It must be difficult for you,' he said. 'I mean, the count dragging you out on the march like this. I'm sure that the services of an astrologer are going to be somewhat limited for the moment.'

So this is it, thought Magnus. This was the real question. All that nonsense about Ursula was just a sham, really he was hear to find out what Magnus was up to.

'Although my post is court astrologer, I have other uses,' Magnus said with a fake sigh of resignation. 'I am a man learned in other fields, and the count seeks my advice on many matters.'

'Well, I am sure he will find it useful,' said Ruprecht with one last fleeting look around the tent. 'Good night.'

Magnus sat there for a long while after Ruprecht had left, considering what had just happened. The Talabheimer was certainly suspicious of Magnus, though he knew he was innocent of any wrongdoing. He wanted some fresh air and was about to leave when he heard the distinctive pattering of rain on the canvas of the tent. With a sour sigh to himself, he sat back down on the bed and pulled his book from beneath the covers.

FOR TWO MORE days they camped, awaiting the returning of the scouting parties. Though Steinhardt had permission to cross Talabecland, Vapold was confident that any attack would come across the more northerly stretches of the border. For a start, it was a more direct route from Bechafen, where most of the new count's forces had been billeted. Secondly, despite the co-operation of the Talabheim ruler, Steinhardt knew not to approach too closely to the capital with an army, for fear of provoking a response from his erstwhile allies. This still left a hundred miles or more of the Talabec to keep watch on.

Ursula was keen for the men to say prayers each morning, and passed among the regiments, exhorting the soldiers to look to Sigmar to protect them and guide their sword arms in the coming battle. As she passed, the soldiers' confidence grew, and her presence filled them with hope.

Magnus watched her with fascination as she walked amongst the soldiers and knights. When she left, there was an afterglow of energy, a residual cloud of faith left in her wake. Spirits were buoyed along her route, the courage of the men swelled. He had never seen anything of its like, and followed her at a distance as she tirelessly moved from regiment to regiment, her hand upon the hilt of Ulfshard.

Though it was impossible for her to see every man in the army, the effect she had was like ripples in a pool, radiating out from those touched by her presence. The other priests of Sigmar acted like conductors, generating a small amount of energy themselves, but more importantly serving as conduits for Ursula's energy to permeate through the army.

Though he did not have Magnus's secret sight, Count Vapold had also observed the difference in his fighting men. As midday neared on the second day, he found Magnus some way from the centre of the camp, following in the wake of Ursula. The warlock had barely noticed the count's approach, even though he was mounted on his warhorse. As a shadow fell over him, he glanced up to see Vapold, resplendent in his full suit of armour, a black cloak hung from his shoulders, a white tabard over his breastplate emblazoned with a stylised blue griffon flanked by two swordsmen, his personal coat of arms. At his belt hung the Runefang of Ostland, heirloom of the rulers of the realm since the time of Sigmar, the first Emperor. Tied to his saddlebags were a quiver and a compact, recurved hunting bow, which had originally been made for his grandfather. Magnus could sense the aura of power that surrounded both, and had seen first hand the mighty Dragon Bow being loosed, even though it was only at a wooden target. The arrows, tipped with shards of dragon horn it was claimed, had punched clean through the thick oak, empowered by the enchantment of the bow.

'It's quite amazing, isn't it?' the count said, staring at the figure of Ursula as she disappeared into a throng of bowmen, who were now jostling with each other to get close to her.

'Remarkable, my lord' agreed Magnus. 'It is plain to see that she is no ordinary girl.'

'Not at all!' laughed Vapold. His face then grew serious and he leaned across from his horse, his voice low. 'We mustn't let the men get too carried away though. This is my army, after all. All of this worry about the renegade knight and an army of northmen, it could start to distract the soldiers.'

'The men are loyal to you, my lord,' said Magnus, though he could understand the count's concern. 'However, I believe she is much more useful as an ally than an enemy.'

'Of course,' said Vapold. 'Of course. No, I wasn't thinking about anything drastic, not at all. We just need to make sure we keep an eye on the men, that sort of thing. When this sorry business with Steinhardt is over, we must make sure she doesn't have too much contact with them. Useful, as I said, but let's not get carried away.'

'No, my lord,' said Magnus with a polite bow.

Vapold grinned again.

'Well, if Steinhardt doesn't have second thoughts when he sees this ugly lot, they'll certainly be up for the fight,' the count said.

'It is my fervent hope that actual battle will not be necessary, my lord,' said Magnus, meaning every word of it.

'I agree, Magnus, I agree,' said Vapold with a wink. 'Still, does an army good to get stirred up once in a while, doesn't it? Remind them what they're getting all my money for.'

'Against an army of refugees and mercenaries, I am sure they will carry the field, my lord,' said Magnus, unable to share his master's enthusiasm for the conflict. There was something about noble blood that made a man forget that war was a horrid affair. Perhaps it was all those tapestries and paintings of glorious charges and brave last stands that they had hanging in their houses and castles, Magnus mused.

As NIGHT BEGAN to fall at the end of the second day, one of the groups of scouts had returned. The news they brought with them did not bode well. Once more overlooked, Ruprecht stood quietly in the count's tent as the scout's sergeant explained to the court what they had seen. The count, Bayard and Felsturm sat in canvas chairs beside a table spread with a cloth map of Ostland and the Middle Mountains. Others, mostly officers but also the ever-present astrologer, crowded into the tent, leaving a small circle for the war council. Over the heads of the murmuring throng, Ruprecht could see Ursula at the other side of the tent, also listening intently. He gave her a wave, but she did not notice.

'Crossed already, you say?' said Lord Bayard. 'That is not good at all.'

'Yes, my lord,' the sergeant replied. His badge of office, a black and white sash over his dull brown and grey leggings and jerkin, was mud-stained and hung limply across his chest. 'They are slightly to the south of us, perhaps a day's march, near Ludenkort. We counted perhaps six thousand men, roughly half of that knights and other cavalry. I think they have more men on the way; they were setting up camp a few miles from the river.'

'Then we strike as soon as we can,' said Captain Felsturm. 'We must attack while we have the numbers.'

'Our plan was to contest a river crossing,' Vapold reminded the captain. 'If that is not possible, our first thought must be the defence of Wolfenburg.'

'That is true,' said Bayard, stroking his chin. He leaned forward and looked at the map. 'Ludenkort is quite forested, some farmland, but not much. There's not much room for cavalry to work.'

'Meaning?' said Vapold.

'Meaning that we might not want to engage them there,' explained Bayard.

'Spoken like a true knight,' said Felsturm, sourly. 'Half of Count Steinhardt's army is mounted.'

'Mostly mounted infantry,' said the scout sergeant. 'Gunners for the most part.'

'We have no idea of the number of reinforcements he's waiting for,' said Bayard. 'If it's several thousand, and they arrive before we do, or even worse during the battle, it won't be good for us.'

'For all we know it could be a few hundred,' countered Felsturm.

Vapold sat in thought, looking at the map and glancing at his two advisors. A movement in the crowd attracted his attention and he looked up to see Ursula pushing her way to the front.

'Yes?' the count asked.

'I agree with Captain Felsturm,' Ursula said.

Vapold raised one eyebrow.

'I never asked,' said the count, looking back at the map.

'If you retreat now, you surrender the initiative,' Ursula said.

Vapold sat back and rested his hands in his lap in a pose of studied patience.

'I would rather have a good solid wall or two between me and the enemy,' the count argued. 'Steinhardt would be a fool to attack Wolfenburg.'

'He will return with a larger army,' Ursula said. 'You must make a show of strength, demonstrate that you will not be bullied. Attack him in the open field. Sigmar grants strength to those who are forthright, and will ensure us victory.'

Vapold saw the look in Ursula's eyes, the fervent conviction that she was right. Felsturm was nodding vigorously in agreement, and Bayard scratched his chin in thought.

'Is it not time that Count Vapold of Ostland, commander of one of the finest armies in the Empire, shows his true mettle?' asked Ursula. 'Your people look to you for courage and strength. Show that courage; exercise that strength. It is what Sigmar would have done. He did not simply sit and wait for the orcs to come to him. He took the fight to them. He drove them from his lands. Would you allow this army to roam your state unhindered? Would you have your villages and farms looted, the wealth of your people claimed by this usurper?'

Ursula's words struck home like bolts, piercing Vapold's pride. He felt a wave of righteousness swelling up inside him.

'You're right!' he declared, standing up and slamming his fist onto the map table. 'Steinhardt has gone too far. First he has spilled the blood of my family, and now he threatens me, in my own lands! Ready the troops, we march at first light. We'll send his rag-tag army scurrying back over the Talabec with their tails between their legs like whipped curs!'

There was a ragged cheer from the assembled soldiers. Ruprecht watched Ursula turn and leave without a further word. She had her knowing, disturbing smile on her lips. Whatever she was planning, things seemed to be going her way for the moment.

JOHANNES HAD SET out at first light with the other cavalry, riding ahead of the rest of the army to find out if Steinhardt was still at Ludenkort. They were split into small groups, some flanking the road, wary of enemy scouts, the rest following along the muddy turnpike that led to the small town. Johannes rode with Fakje-Stohl, Gastren and a short, wiry knight called Fredericks. Their mood was light, though as they had entered the forest their banter had faded and they had become more watchful.

The sky was cloudy, but the summer heat was beginning to permeate through the forest canopy as the rode between the sprawling boles of the trees, shafts of sunlight occasionally piercing the leaves in golden rays, The mulch of last year's leaves still lay underfoot, padding the steps of their horses, and only the odd distant bird call disturbed the quiet. Ahead, the flitting shape of a deer disappeared into the undergrowth, and Fakje-Stohl sighed.

'I wish I was out riding on the hunt,' the knight said, removing a gauntlet and stroking his moustaches, 'instead of riding to battle.'

'Steinhardt has to be taught a lesson, you know,' said Gastren. 'I was there last night, when the count made his proclamation. He said we needed to teach that bastard usurper a lesson.'

'That's all well in theory, but it'll not seem so fine when the shot and bolts are whistling past your head,' muttered Fredericks.

'Aye, it's hard for a knight to be left alone these days, you know,' said Gastren with a laugh. 'Anyone would think those damned crossbowmen and gunners didn't like being run down on a lance!'

'Pah!' snorted Fredericks. 'This black powder is no joke. I blame the dwarfs. Trust a dwarf, who would no sooner ride a steed than kiss an orc, to devise black powder. What happened to a good, honest charge with wood and steel, eh?'

'It's their short legs,' said Johannes, who had spent several weeks at Karak Norn on the ill-fated expedition to reclaim Ulfshard, and so considered himself more of an expert than most on the subject of dwarfs. 'They do have small ponies, but they prefer to ride around in carts, or walk everywhere.'

'What's that?' said Fakje-Stohl.

'Why dwarfs don't have cavalry,' Johannes said. 'Their legs are too short for them to ride comfortably. Wicked powerful cannons though.'

'Aye, it's not just the dwarfs with the big guns,' said Fredericks, hawking and spitting. 'I heard from a merchant that in the Reik, in Nuln in fact, they've forged culverins big enough to fire shot the size of a man's head.'

'Well, they obviously didn't help too much against the Ironclaw, you know,' said Gastren. 'Still, let's worry about the Prince of Altdorf another day. Plenty of fighting to be done right here without going looking for it.'

They rode on in silence for another mile, keeping a watchful eye on the road just in sight to their left, scanning the trees around them for any sign of the enemy. Johannes's back began to ache. It had been many months since he had last spent a whole day in the saddle, not since they had returned to Marienburg from Karak Norn in fact, he realised. He ignored the soreness at the base of his spine, and instead focussed his attention on the winding tracks that criss-crossed between the trunks of the trees. There were small game trails, barely visible in the ferns and brush, and wider tracks, perhaps from wolves or bears.

The thought reminded him that there were more than just enemy soldiers out in the woods. Out in the deep forest of Ostland, as elsewhere in the Empire, dread foes lay in wait beyond the patrols of the count's soldiers. Foul beastmen lurked in the darkest havens of the woods, ready to come forth on their raids to pillage and murder, ambush convoys and raze small villages. Other mutants and twisted creatures also found safety in the dense forests, waylaying lone groups of travellers. There were goblins too, the gods alone knew how many. He had heard some rumours that there were thousands of them, scattered all across the Empire, from Ostland to Averland.

North of where they were, two days' hard riding, was the Forest of Shadows. Shrouded in dark tales, almost as infamous as the Drakwald that surrounded Middenheim, the Forest of Shadows was home to beastmen and goblins, and also innumerable bandits and worshippers of the Dark Gods. From hidden fastnesses in the woods, they would rampage out on occasion, sometimes few in number, other times under the leadership of a great warrior, numbering in their hundreds. If Kurt did come south with an army, those foes might well further bolster whatever forces Kurt had mustered in the north, some out of loyalty to the same twisted gods he worshipped, others merely for the spoils of victory.

A movement to Johannes's right caught his attention. Even as he swung his horse around to investigate, he heard a hissing noise and a cry from Gastren. Looking over his shoulder, he saw an arrow piercing the older knight's arm.

'Ware!' cried Fredericks, wheeling his horse to the left. 'Ambush!'

Another arrow whistled past Johannes as he dragged on the reins and kicked his heels into his horse's flanks, searching the trees for the hidden foe. More arrows slashed the air nearby, one glancing off Johannes's helmet, stunning him for a moment.

'This way!' Fredericks shouted, drawing his sword and pointing to the left.

Fredericks kicked his horse into a gallop and the other three followed, unsheathing their swords. Ahead of them, in a small thicket of brush, Johannes could now see two men crouched amongst the leaves. Seeing the knights charge towards them they turned and began to run.

'I'll get you, you bastards,' shouted Gastren, driving his horse on strongly, surging ahead of Fredericks, low branches whipping at his face and arms. 'Come here!'

'Wait!' warned Johannes with a sudden sense of foreboding, pulling his steed up as Gastren thundered after the fleeing archers. Fredericks raced after him, shouting as well. They were about fifty yards ahead now, passing into a shallow, bush-shrouded dell.

'What is it?' asked Fakje-Stohl, reining in beside Johannes.

There was no need for Johannes to answer as the other two knights rode into the archers' trap. Arrows flew at them from all directions, some bouncing harmlessly off their armour, others punching through the plate steel, piercing their flesh. Fredericks fell first, sliding sideways from his slowing horse, his back studded with three shafts. Gastren tried to turn but was going too fast, and his horse lost its footing, sending up clods of earth and rotting leaves as its hooves carved furrows in the ground. Off balance, the knight tottered for a second before two arrows slammed into his chest, almost simultaneously, knocking him backwards, one leg still stuck in the stirrups as he did an ungainly cartwheel off his horse.

Johannes watched in horror as the enemy loosed more arrows into the stricken knight, half a dozen or more sticking out of his head and torso and he collapsed into the mud. Glancing left and right, wary of more foes, Fakje-Stohl turned his horse and began to ride back towards the road. With one last look at the men emerging from the bushes, cautiously trying to grab the harnesses of the fallen knights' horses, Johannes turned and followed. To do anything else was to invite a similar fate for himself.

IT WAS WITH heavy hearts that the army made camp that night, the glow from the campfires of Steinhardt's host glimmering on the horizon. Throughout the day, the Ostermark scouts had waylaid and ambushed the outriders of Vapold's force, until the count had moved up his own archers and gunners to clear the way, slowing the advance and buying the enemy more time for their reinforcements to arrive.

Their losses were not that significant, a little more than a hundred men had been killed in the brief clashes, but the effect on the army's morale had been significant. From the confident host of the morning, they had been reduced to a weary, edgy force. Brother Hordicant, most senior of the three priests of Morr accompanying the army, lamented that thirty bodies had not been recovered and had therefore not been dedicated to his god. This boded ill, he warned.

In the distance, the lights of Ludenkort shone dimly from the hilltop where the town was sited, while in the fields and woods around the town, campfires burned like stars in the firmament. Steinhardt's army had been swelled since the scouts' earlier estimates, though perhaps by only a thousand more men. Vapold still held the advantage of numbers, though his foe were better positioned, on higher ground and with the tree-line at their back to cover their retreat.

It was the count's hope to deal a single shattering blow to the enemy. Urged on by Bayard, who still retained the hope that Steinhardt himself might be slain or caught and Hensel restored as the true count, Vapold would break the usurper's army upon the field and as they fled, crush them against the Talabec which cut through the forests ten miles further to the south east. With one blow, the threat from Ostermark could be quashed.

Captain Felsturm was also confident, sharing the opinion that an army of sellswords and dispossessed would have little stomach once battle had been joined. He ordered the woodsmen and carpenters to fell trees and begin construction of a gallows, in order to remind the enemy of the fate that awaited those who would war upon their own. The sound of hammers and saws echoed through the night as the men laboured by torch and lantern light.

Johannes could not sleep, a mixture of tension about the coming battle and unspent energy from his encounter early in the day kept him pacing back forth through the camp as the moons rose and fell again. Fredericks's and Gastren's bodies were two of those that had not been found, and he wondered if he could have recovered them. He sought out Ruprecht, who was sat dozing by a guttering fire outside one of the large barrack tents, and shared his fears.

'It sounds like you did the right thing,' the burly warrior assured him, the dull yellow light of the flames glinting off his left hand. 'Better two bodies lost than three bodies found.'

'I tried to warn them,' Johannes said, staring into the fire. 'I guess they didn't hear me.'

'Or didn't want to,' said Ruprecht. 'You know what knights are like, always ready to charge off at the slightest provocation. I hope they show a bit more restraint tomorrow.'

'Do you really think that Steinhardt will fight?' asked Johannes. 'Even with the hill to hold, he must realise that he is outmatched.'

'I wouldn't expect anything rational from a man who murders a youth to steal his crown,' said Ruprecht. 'Besides, blood has already been spilt, it's not like Vapold is just going to let him walk away now, is it?'

'I suppose you're right,' said Johannes, standing. 'I'll let you get some sleep.'

Ruprecht watched the young man walk off into the gloom. Around him the snores and farts of the soldiers sounded in the night, against the backdrop of the work on the gallows. Another figure appeared out of the night, swathed in a heavy robe. As he approached, Ruprecht saw that it was Magnus. The astrologer looked as if he were about to walk straight past and then stopped and turned towards Ruprecht.

'Have you seen Ursula?' Magnus asked.

'Not since dusk,' Ruprecht replied with a shake of the head. 'Why?'

'No particular reason,' Magnus said, though Ruprecht was unconvinced. 'Nobody has seen her since we made camp.'

'Nobody?' said Ruprecht. 'That is odd.'

'Yes, it is not like our maiden of Sigmar to be inconspicuous,' Magnus said, gazing up at the sky. He pointed and Ruprecht looked up to see a clear night, the stars just about visible over the glow of the campfires.

'You see that circle of five stars, with a line of three to the right?' Magnus said, and Ruprecht nodded. Two of the stars in the line had a reddish tinge to them. 'That is the warrior, his shield and sword. There are others that make up his head and legs, but it's too light to see them. Anyway, you see how his sword is bloodstained? It is a good omen.'

'For us, or for Steinhardt?' asked Ruprecht. 'It can't be a good omen for both.'

'The sword points to the north,' Magnus said, crossing his arms. 'Perhaps it is not for us at all.'

Ruprecht did not reply, but sat watching the blood-red stars as Magnus walked off. As the fire crackled, ash rising into the night air, his head lolled against his chest and he slept fitfully.

LUDENKORT WAS BUILT upon one of a pair of hills known locally, for a reason lost to antiquity, as the Twin Goats. The northernmost hill on which Ludenkort was stood was known as the Little Goat and the other, where could be found the ruins of an ancient elven watchtower, was the Big Goat, half a mile to the south. The forest grew up the eastern slopes of the Big Goat, all the way back to the Talabec, while for several miles to the south and west were open fields, dotted with the occasional barn or farmhouse.

With the sun reaching midmorning, the two armies deployed for battle. Led by the drums and trumpets of their musicians, the soldiers of Ostland and Ostermark filed out in their orders of battle. Steinhardt retained his position on the hills and had two cannons protected by handgunners sited just outside Ludenkort itself. His cavalry were split into two wings, one on each flank, just visible behind the twin hills, in reserve. Spearmen, bowmen and swordsmen stood almost shoulder-to-shoulder in a dense mass along the slopes of the Big Goat, another cannon behind them.

Vapold's army stretched out in a long line, the three hundred surviving knights of the Osterknacht to the far left, opposite Ludenkort, the cavalry of the count to the right, south of Steinhardt's defensive position. At the front of the line, the handgunners lit their matches and the archers strung their bows. With grunts and curses, the crossbowmen set their weapons, loading the stocky, deadly quarrels and hefting their pieces to their shoulders to march forwards. In all, Vapold had some two thousand missile troops, and his plan was to reduce Steinhardt's men with their fire before charging in with the knights and following up with the infantry. Unfortunately, he had no cannons of his own. The need to move swiftly had been too great to allow for the slow carriages and shot wagons of his artillery. With no counter-battery fire, his army would have to run the gauntlet of the enemy guns before they were in range.

Perhaps half a mile apart, the two armies faced each other, individual regiments redressing their ranks or changing position in the lines as last minute adjustments were made. Banners flapped in the growing wind, the black and white of Ostland against the purple and yellow of Ostermark. There were even a few picked out in the grey and red of Wissenland, the green of Stirland and the brilliant white of Solland, now a desolated, ravaged land. The banners and totems of the mercenary companies were staggered throughout the enemy line, each flanked by other troops. Steinhardt had realised not to place too much faith in the sellswords and had therefore spread them throughout his army. If they were to run, there would be more steadfast troops to hold the line.

The battle opened as puffs of smoke billowed out from the two hilltops and a moment later the bark of cannons echoed over the muddy fields. Cannonballs screamed though the air, dark blurs of movement, and ploughed into the ground, short of the Ostland line. A jeering roar rose up from the ranks of soldiers and they waved their weapons in the air in mockery of the enemy's efforts.

As the cannon crews reloaded their guns, trumpets sounded from the Ostland army and the archers, gunners and crossbowmen began to advance, opening up gaps in the line. When they were some fifty yards ahead, they closed their ranks, concentrating near the hill on which Steinhardt's personal banner fluttered at the crest. The sword- and spear-armed soldiers marched forwards behind them, shields ready, weapons glinting in the bright light of the summer sun. The knights remained where they were, their horses prancing and pawing the ground in anticipation.

More smoke erupted from Ludenkort as Steinhardt's gunners opened fire, the crackle of their muskets barely audible over the tramping feet and drum beats of the advancing Ostland soldiers. They were obviously ill-trained, firing far too early for their volley to have any effect, most of their bullets spent before they reached the Ostland line. Here and there a crossbowman fell, but no more than a handful in total.

Vapold rode forward, accompanied by Captain Felsturm, between two halberdier regiments. Sitting astride his horse behind a unit of archers, he drew the Dragon Bow from his saddlebags and handed its gold-embroidered cover to his captain. Pulling out an arrow, he fitted it to the string and took aim. The sharpened, polished dragon horn of the arrow tip shone in the sunlight. With a smooth action, Vapold pulled back the string of the bow and loosed the arrow. The keening flight of its passage took it arcing across the gap between the armies, finding its mark in the knot of officers standing at the crest of the hill around Steinhardt's standard. The banner toppled and fell as the man holding it collapsed, the dragon arrow through his chest, its tip punched out of the back of his breastplate. There was confusion as the other men around him scrambled to stop the banner from falling, and yet avoided making themselves the next target by picking up the banner. More laughs and cheers erupted along the Ostland line as Vapold held the Dragon Bow above his head and with a flick of the reins caused his horse to rear up and kick with its forelegs. Felsturm shook his head at the extravagant display.

'The next one is for that bastard Steinhardt,' the count said through his fixed smile as his horse settled on the ground.

The Ostermark cannons fired again as Vapold's army continued its advance, this time the shots smashing through the archers and handgunners to the right, flinging bodies and limbs into the air, scattering mud and blood as they bounced and spun through their ranks. Arrows and crossbow bolts began to rain across the blue sky in dark clouds, and more men fell to each volley. The shouts of the sergeants and captains kept the Ostlanders moving forwards, closing the range for their own attack. Shooting uphill, as they were, they would have to get closer before they could fire. When they were just three hundred yards apart, jagged gaps in their line from the enemy fire, the Ostlanders stopped and prepared to loose their first salvo, awaiting the order.

A murmuring cheer began to the left, growing in volume and rippling along the line. Craning his neck to see what was happening, Vapold spied a lone rider galloping out from the left flank, heading diagonally across the open space between the two armies. Seeing the long, red hair of the rider flapping in a pony tail, he realised it was Ursula.

'What in Taal's name is she doing?' cursed Felsturm. Vapold simply shook his head and looked on, stunned.

With the shot and arrows of the Ostermarkers flying overhead, Ursula galloped the length of the Ostland line, staring towards the hill on which Steinhardt stood. She turned as she reached the end and headed back to the centre, stopping just in front of Vapold.

'Come with me,' she called out, and turned her horse towards the foe.

'What?' Vapold said with a disbelieving laugh.

'Follow me,' Ursula said. 'Trust me. Trust Sigmar!'

Vapold sat motionless for a moment, and then looked at Felsturm. The captain merely shrugged, abstaining from voicing any opinion.

'Where are you going?' Vapold shouted to Ursula as arrows and quarrels sung through the air around her.

'Over there!' she cried back, pointing towards the hill occupied by the Ostermarkers.

Silently, Vapold handed the Dragon Bow to Felsturm and nudged his horse into a walk. The archers parted for him to pass, as Ursula waited patiently. The volleys from the enemy had slowed, and then stopped as the two of them rode out into the open ground between the two armies. A hush had descended on the battlefield as the soldiers of both forces watched their strange behaviour.

Unmolested by the enemy, they crossed the gap and began to ride up the hill. Ursula stopped some fifty yards short of the enemy at one end of their line and Vapold reined in beside her. He could see the gaping looks of curiosity on the faces of the opposing soldiers stretching out to his right, and further up behind them, the urgent conference of nobles commanding the army.

'Wait here,' Ursula told the count, turning her horse along the line.

Her horse pacing slowly, deliberately, Ursula rode along the line, staring into the faces of the enemy. Few could meet her gaze. The unnatural quiet lasted for several minutes as Ursula walked her horse up the line and back to the centre. She sat there, waiting, as Vapold's heart hammered in his chest. One wrong move and they would both be dead within half a minute.

'Do you wish to parley?' came a distant shout from the officers at the top of the hill.

'Parley?' Ursula shouted back. 'Not with you!'

She reached down and grabbed the hilt of Ulfshard. Pulling the sword free, she held it aloft, its blade wreathed with blue flame. There were gasps and mutterings from all over the hill.

'Men of the Empire!' she shouted. 'You have heard of me. I am the one they call the maid of Sigmar. I come before you, not to fight, but to speak to you. Heed my words well! Men of the Empire, descendants of almighty Sigmar, I beg you to look into your hearts. Would you raise your weapons against me? Would you bring death to your fellow men while dire creatures and fell enemies gather in our lands?'

Ursula pointed her sword towards the knot of figures at the brow of the hill.

'Your leaders have brought you here to wage war upon your own countrymen,' she continued. 'It is your blood that will be spilt, your homes destroyed, to further their ambitions. You brave men, the lifeblood of our lands, must die while the nobles tax your families and greedy merchants rob your purses.'

She paused again, her eyes unwavering from Count Steinhardt, who stood in a circle of his fellow nobles looking back at her.

'You leaders of the Empire!' she called out. 'You who are entrusted to protect our lands. It is not your right to bring death and famine upon us. It is your sacred duty to uphold that which was created by Sigmar himself. He looks down upon us and weeps at what we have become. A great and terrible foe gathers in the north, unseen by you while you look enviously at the lands of your neighbours. You muster your armies, you draw your blades, not to defend this realm of ours, but to despoil it! I beseech you to hearken to the word of Sigmar. Waste not the blood of your subjects in this self-defeating war.

'I call upon you all, men of the Empire, brave warriors of Sigmar, to fight the true foe. Wet your blades in the blood of the northmen. Raise your shields against the warriors of the Dark Gods. With faith and steel, we can yet avert the coming disaster. A storm is about to break upon us, and divided, we shall be scattered and broken. United, fighting as one under the glorious gaze of Sigmar himself, we shall prevail. Look to your hearts and your sword arm, and do what is right!'

Ursula turned her horse and rode back past Vapold, looking over at him as she passed.

'It is up to you now,' she said, her face stern, her eyes glittering and hard. 'Do what is right.'

As THE PARLEY continued, the armies uneasily poised across the battlefield from each other, Ruprecht saw Ursula again. She had disappeared back into the forest for several hours after her performance, but was now sitting on her horse towards the rear of the army, looking intently out towards the tent that had been erected for the truce. He walked over and stood beside her.

'So you do care after all,' Ruprecht said, and she turned and looked down at him. Ursula's lips formed an enigmatic, chilling smile.

'Now I have two armies,' she said.

CHAPTER TWO
The Gathering
Northern Steppes, Summer 1712

THE BROTH WAS thick and hot, and Jakob wolfed it down hungrily, the bowl balanced awkwardly on his lap, a deep spoon in his good hand. Seated next to him, Vlamdir ate at a more sedate pace, the exposed muscles of his face expanding and contracting as he chewed. They were sitting on thick woollen rugs inside the tent of Asdubar Hunn, chieftain of the Mendhir, and the old warrior watched them with a mixture of fear and distaste. The walls of the tent, stitched-together elk skins, rippled as the north wind blew across the open steppes, howling outside.

Finishing his soup, Jakob laid his bowl to one side and looked at Asdubar, his golden eye glinting in the light from the small fire pit at the tent's centre. Asdubar returned his gaze coolly. It was clear from their appearance that the pair was marked by the gods, and the chieftain had welcomed them to his tribe accordingly. His hospitality had been flawless, but he had the feeling that food and shelter were not the only things the two men were after.

Messengers had brought news of their coming to him from the Vangirs, and it had not been the first time he had heard their names mentioned. For months, since the beginning of summer, they had been travelling the steppes, moving from tribe to tribe. Some said that they brought the blessings of the gods with them. Others claimed they were raising an army. Some rumours even claimed that they were messengers from the north of the world. Asdubar had dismissed such claims, but now that he looked at them, the shaman's fused hand and staff, the shifting metallic skin of his companion, the chieftain knew that the touch of the gods lay heavily upon them.

'War is coming,' said Jakob, his voice little more than a harsh whisper. 'A great war, a war for the gods! We have come to you, so that the Mendhir might be counted amongst our numbers.'

'War against whom?' Asdubar asked, gesturing for one of his council, the stocky Gengris, to fetch the stoppered jugs of fermented milk that were stored in the corner of the tent. As the jug was passed around the circle of twelve men, each taking a deep gulp of the potent brew, Jakob's normal eye remain fixed on the chieftain.

'Does it matter?' he asked. 'The gods call, men answer. That is the only truth you should need to know.'

'And yet I ask again, war against whom?' said Asdubar. 'I have heard of you. I have heard that you send men to the west, to the Pass of Kings high in the mountains. It is a long journey for us, and the summer is almost over. We should be preparing for the coming winter, not looking for war.'

'In the south, the winters are less harsh,' said Jakob, accepting the jug of spirits from Vlamdir, who sat silently beside him, his staring eyes looking at the others in the tent. 'There are crops to take, cattle to steal, sheep to slaughter. Come with us, and winter will not be your concern.'

'And who leads this army?' said Asdubar, with a glance towards his companions.

'The Sutenvulf,' said Vlamdir, speaking for the first time since they had sat down. 'The greatest warrior of our times, chosen of the gods.'

'And where is he now?' asked Sudai, the chieftain's nephew who sat opposite Vlamdir. He stroked a hand through his long, oiled black hair, a sneer on his face. 'We have heard your fanciful tales, that he sits with the gods.'

'He does,' said Jakob quietly. 'But he will return, and those who are his followers will reap the rewards of his friendship.'

'And those who refuse to follow?' said Asdubar. 'We will become his enemies?'

Jakob shook his head and looked at the ground for a moment.

'We do not come with threats, but with promises,' he said, not looking up. 'The eyes of the gods will be upon you, as they have been upon us. Their gifts will be bountiful for those who would ally themselves with the Sutenvulf. Join with us, join with him, and your glory shall be sung until the grandchildren of your grandchildren can hear them.'

'Wage war in the name of the gods, and perhaps you too might be granted the immortality of our master,' said Vlamdir.

'And if we refuse?' asked Sudai. 'What then?'

'We will leave and we will go to meet the great one,' said Vlamdir.

Jakob looked up and his golden eye blazed with power.

'The eyes of the gods are upon you, Asdubar Hunn,' the shaman wheezed. 'You have until tomorrow morning to make your choice. Choose wisely, for the favour of the gods will be power and riches, but their displeasure shall see you howling with grief, your tribe split asunder and your children weeping over the bones of their parents.'

Jakob stood, using his staff-hand to lever himself to his feet. The others stood in deference to the shaman, Asdubar standing last.

'Do not let foolish notions cloud your judgement,' Jakob warned. 'The day of our deliverance is close by, I have seen it in the skies and I have heard it on the winds. The gods call to you, will you listen?'

'I will think on the matter,' Asdubar said, stepping aside and waving his guests towards the flap of the tent. 'By morning you shall know my answer.'

Jakob smiled and nodded, before hobbling across the scattered rugs, his stooped, twisted body moving awkwardly.

As he stepped out into the cool evening air, Jakob breathed deeply. There were thirty or more other tents, each containing at least one and probably two warriors. They were not many, the Mendhir, but every warrior who fought for the army was welcome. For many months he and Vlamdir had travelled the steppes, first to the east, and now heading westwards, back towards Kislev and the Old World. Sometimes whole tribes had heeded the call. Other times only a single warrior, or nobody at all had believed Jakob's prophecy of the return of Sutenvulf and the great invasion that was to come.

Undar and Bjordrin had travelled back to Norsca, to rally the tribes there. Theirs was both an easier and harder task. Many of the chieftains would already know of Kurt and his exploits by now. Some would be willing to strike back against the southerner who had raided their homes and attacked their kin. Others would probably scoff, remembering how Kurt had retreated before the advance of the Empire forces, marshalling his followers.

It mattered not to Jakob. As he stood there, listening to the wind, feeling the breath of the gods around him, he smiled to himself. He knew what true power was now. He could set his spirit free, soaring from his body to glide over the lands, seeking out the scattered tribes in this vast wilderness. The secret of fire was his to command with a few simple words. He did not even need to tap into the power of his runestones except for the most difficult rituals.

And he also knew the price to pay for such power. Though the gods had granted him these abilities, Jakob was well aware that it was for their purpose and not his. Kurt had been chosen, and in turn Jakob had been chosen. The gods did not give their gifts lightly and Jakob was no fool. To spurn the task the gods had handed to him was to insult them, and an affront that he was not likely to survive.

He had everything that he had dreamed of, those many years ago when first he had seen the young knight, Kurt Leitzig. He had seen the aura of the youth, the mark of the gods upon him. He had supported the young man, protected and guided him. He had risked his life to help him escape from his foes, and had drawn upon terrifying entities and dangerous powers to help Kurt defeat his foes. Now such things were easy for him to achieve, and other knew it. Once the runt, the outcast, the bastard half-Kislevite who no one would have deigned to spit at, now he was a great shaman and all were wary of him.

The road had been long, and painful. It was not yet finished, but Jakob was content. He was content with the knowledge that he could wander these lands and none would raise a hand against him, out of respect for his prowess and fear of his anger. This was the power that he had always dreamed of.

THE NIGHT SPIRALLED away from Jakob as he lay under the thick blanket of his bedroll, protected by the small tent he shared with Vlamdir. He no longer slept as ordinary men slept, but instead found rest in lying down and allowing his spirit to break free of its mortal bonds. While his fatigued, twisted carcass recovered its strength, his soul would dance upon the clouds and sail upon the winds.

This night the air was heavy, cloying and suffocating to Jakob. There were other voices upon the spirit winds, other presences that danced and flittered around him, just out of sight. In his mind's eye the skies blazed with fire and a sea of blood washed across the world. A great howling rent the air, and on the rocky steppes far below Jakob could see a great pack of hounds, thousands strong. They sat on their haunches and bayed into the night air, their eyes afire, their teeth glittering knives of steel.

Jakob knew what they waited for, though he had never seen them before. As a black sun pulsed against the blazing heavens, the chorus of howls grew louder and louder. Its intensity swept up over Jakob, buoying him further up into the skies, the energy flooding through him. The breath of the gods blew more strongly than before, a great gust of power from the north, and Kurt allowed himself to be carried along on the magical eddy. Far away to the north, just beyond the horizon, lay the Gate of the Gods. There, Jakob knew, the Sutenvulf was waiting, growing in power, biding his time. When his army was ready, when swords and axes unnumbered were raised in his honour, he would return and they would sweep south.

The thought of the war to come soothed Jakob. It calmed his fluttering spirit with its warmth, and he glided gently down towards the ground, swooping over the great mass of crying hounds.

Soon, Jakob realised. Soon he would come back. He must be ready for his return, the shaman thought. He and Vlamdir would travel to the west as quickly as they could, to meet the others. When all was prepared,

the Sutenvulf would come back, just as he had foreseen, and the hunting pack of the gods would be
unleashed.

THE MORNING WAS sunless and cold, the sky blanketed
with a thick layer of dark thunderheads. As the yellowing light of dawn bled across the heavens, Jakob
roused himself and stepped out of the tent. Smoke
curled lazily from the chimney holes of the tents,
bringing the scent of wood and cooking meat. A
young boy came running over from the direction of
Asdubar's tent and gestured for Jakob to follow, his
eyes fearful.

Jakob limped over the hard ground, every tap of his
staff sending a vibration running up through the
bones of his arm to his shoulder. He ignored his
aching joints and muscles, and looked ahead to where
a contingent of the Mendhir stood outside the chieftain's tent, Asdubar among them. The leader's face was
impassive as Jakob approached, and he nodded in
greeting.

'You have your decision?' asked Jakob, eschewing
any kind of formality. The visions of the night before
had filled him with a sense of urgency and he wanted
to waste no time, not even to banter words with the
chieftain of the Mendhir.

'I have one question before I make my choice,'
Asdubar said with a glance to his counsellors.

'Ask,' hissed Jakob, leaning on his staff.

'I require proof that what you claim is true,' said
Asdubar, his gaze now unwavering. 'Is it for the glory of
the gods or for your own glory that you wage this war?'

'Proof?' spat Jakob. He stopped and turned as he heard someone behind him. It was Vlamdir, yawning and stretching. 'What proof will convince you?'

'Show us this power you claim the gods have bestowed upon you,' blurted Sudai, earning himself a scowl from his uncle. 'Summon us a herald, so that we might know that this Sutenvulf sits beside the gods.'

'Summon a herald?' said Jakob, turning his unnatural gaze on the youth. 'Such things are not done lightly. Bargains must be made, oaths sworn. Are you ready for such an undertaking?'

'I am,' said Asdubar. Jakob turned his stare on the chieftain.

'I asked the boy,' the shaman snapped. 'He made the request, now he must answer.'

'I am ready,' Sudai said, crossing his arms defiantly.

'Then we will prepare for the ceremony of summoning,' said Jakob. Using his good hand to reach inside his ragged furs, he plucked one of the fist-sized runestones from his flesh. He handed it to Sudai, still smeared with the shaman's blood, who juggled it gingerly as if it were a live serpent.

He grabbed the boy by the arm and led him towards the open circle at the centre of the tent village, the others trailing behind. Tribesmen and women were emerging from their tents and word spread of the great conjuration about to occur. Here a great fire pit had been dug, filled with ash. He positioned the boy next to the pit and then Jakob stooped and rubbed a finger along a charred plank. With the soot, he drew a symbol on the boy's forehead, a swirling spiral cut across with a waving line.

Jakob then spat on his hand and lay it atop the rune-stone held in Sudai's outstretched palms. He began to chant, the words harsh and discordant, and he could feel the power of the runestone swelling, gathering in the breath of the gods from the air around. Closing his eyes, Jakob could feel the magic seeping up from the ground, passing through him into the stone and on into the youth. His chanting grew louder, more intricate. The first time he had tried such a spell, it had almost destroyed him. Now the words came easily, the power flowed smoothly from him into the other.

In the tainted vision of the golden orb in his eye socket, Jakob began to see the spell working. Invisible to the normal eye, a shape shimmered around the form of the boy, a pulsing window into another place. Starlight shone through the boy as the glowing portal enveloped him. With a final incantation, Jakob snarled the last words and the portal snapped apart, allowing the thing that dwelt beyond to come through.

There were gasps and shrieks from the Kurgan tribespeople, and Jakob opened his eye. Sudai was quivering madly, steam rising from the runestone in his grip. Jakob stepped back a little, one hand still on the runestone, and watched as the messenger unfolded itself into the mortal world.

Sudai's eyes were streaming with blood and his mouth was open in a silent scream. His flesh began to writhe and bubble with the presence of the daemon inside him. Crimson streamed from his mouth, his teeth elongated into fangs and his head began to crumble like a deflated wine skin. Oval, purple eyes ruptured the boy's face and bony protrusions jutted from his back, tearing his clothes from him.

The youth's legs twisted and folded, growing extra joints, bending unnaturally and lowering him. His arms stretched thinly, his elbows becoming vast knobbles of bone, his muscles wasting away. Light glowed inside his body, a pulsing visual heartbeat that shifted from pink to red to green in a kaleidoscope of colours.

The creature that remained was not at all human, its body formed from raw magic. Its torso sprouted mouths that shouted silently and then sealed again, its whole form in constant change. A tail lashed back and forth, tipped with grasping fingers that scraped at the ground and tossed stones and dust into the air.

With a screech, it tried to bound away from Jakob, but was stopped short. Its hands were stuck to the rune-stone, bound to the will of Jakob. It shrieked and leapt up and down, its body metamorphosing as it attempted to escape, but Jakob held it firm, turning on the spot as it threw itself left and right. The arms changed to legs and the creature tried to pull itself free, a new head sprouting from its tail, snapping with long fangs at Jakob, but he ignored it. The shaman spoke another word, the syllables drawn out in his harsh whisper, and the creature stopped its writhing, as if struck.

'What would you have me ask?' Jakob said, keeping his gaze firmly fixed on the messenger, which looked back at him with a shifting plethora of anger-filled purple eyes.

There was no reply, and Jakob asked again.

'I would know,' said Asdubar hesitantly, 'what has become of the Sutenvulf?'

The daemon's face drained sideways to look at the chieftain, fixing him with its baleful glare. A mouth split where its forehead should have been, and the words that it uttered were loud and shrill.

'He is gone,' the creature shrieked. 'He is beyond. He is and was, but no more. He is nowhere and everywhere.'

It slid its eyes back to Jakob.

'I have answered,' it howled. 'Release me! Set me free! I must dance upon the wind of change!'

'Another question first,' said Jakob.

The creature hissed and spat small sparks of blue energy.

'One question more,' it screeched.

'Sutenvulf was blessed by the gods in life,' said the shaman. 'Is he equally blessed now?'

'The gods do not grant their favours lightly,' the creature whined in its unnatural voice, its eyes sliding left and right as its face rearranged constantly. 'What is given may yet be taken away. Now release me!'

Jakob snarled another invocation and the creature whined with pain, its body rippling furiously as it tried to resist the shaman's dismissal. With a strange, sickly smell filling the air, it departed.

Sudai's bloodied, misshapen body fell to the ground, his limbs hanging limply in their sockets, his skin torn with gaping rents. Jakob stood over him, the runestone still held in his hand.

'Will the boy live?' Asdubar demanded, stepping forward. He stopped as Vlamdir also took a pace forward, his fingers on the handle of the axe at his belt.

'No,' said Jakob turning his head to look at the chieftain, motes of energy dancing around his unnatural eye. 'I can end his pain, if you wish.'

Asdubar nodded and Jakob turned away and crouched over the lad. With one long swing, he brought the runestone down onto the boy's skull, smashing it against the hard ground. The blood spattered from the wound across the runestone, and then soaked into it like water on dry sand.

Jakob pushed himself up, stranding as upright as he was able, and turned to face Asdubar and the others.

'The Pass of Kings,' the shaman said. 'There, you will find the truth.'

CHAPTER THREE
Signs
Wolfenburg. Late summer 1712

THE AUDIENCE HALL of Wolfenburg keep was silent, in contrast to the heated arguments that had raged for the past four days. Count Steinhardt glowered down the length of the table at Vapold, whose own stare was equally venomous. Between them, their aides and advisors sat stunned, avoiding each other's gazes, toying with the parchments and quills on the table in front of them.

Steinhardt stood slowly and leaned with his knuckles on the chipped polish of the long table, his stocky frame hunched forward. He moistened his lips with his tongue, his eyes not leaving the man at the other end of the table.

'I dare you to repeat that,' Steinhardt said, his voice low and deep.

Vapold looked back at him, swept a hand through his hair and assumed an air of indifference.

'A traitor once will be a traitor twice,' he repeated. 'The blood of my family stains your hands and no

assurances of yours can wash that away. I cannot coun-
tenance an alliance with an usurper.'

'Traitor?' Steiner said, his voice calm, his eyes betray-
ing the rage inside. 'Usurper? This from the man who
takes counsel from rebels?'

He pointed at Lord Bayard, who sat at Vapold's right
hand, and the knight stood up himself and returned
accusation.

'Your father swore the oath of the Osterknacht,'
Bayard shouted. 'His son has turned on us, betrayed
his own family and his comrades.'

'My forefather founded the Osterknacht,' replied
Steinhardt, 'when he was the count of Ostermark. Or
had you forgotten that? I am no usurper, to exert my
right to the station owed to me by my birth.'

'A claim that has not been made in a hundred years
since your grandfather ceded the title,' Vapold said. He
sighed heavily and waved for the two men to sit down.
'It appears that our positions are irreconcilable. For
four days we have made the same arguments back and
forth, with no resolution.'

'You realised that if we cannot agree this, a state of
war will still exist between us?' said Steinhardt, still
standing. 'Do you really wish that?'

'It would be you that is foolish if you wish to wage
war a hundred leagues from your capital,' said Bayard.
'Your threats are pointless.'

Steinhardt threw up his hands in despair and shook
his head.

'I did not want war,' he said, sitting down and
snatching a goblet from the table, spilling red wine
over its lip. He took a deep draught and then thudded

the goblet down. 'I simply want written assurances that the boy or his heirs will make no further claim to Ostermark. After that, you can do what you want with him.'

'And you think that when he is a man, he will be able to honour such a promise?' said Vapold. 'His brother's murderer sat on his throne in Mordheim, wielding the Runefang that should be his. No one would sign away his birthright, no one.'

'I did not murder the boy,' Steinhardt insisted through gritted teeth. 'He tried to attack me, I swear to Sigmar.'

'Be careful what you swear, my lord,' Ursula's voice cut across the room from where she was seated by the wall.

All turned towards her, having almost forgotten her presence in the heated debate. She stood and walked to the table, her cold gaze on Steinhardt.

'Do you really swear by Sigmar that the boy's death was unavoidable?' she asked.

'Yes I do!' replied Steinhardt. 'He snatched a sword from one of my men and charged at me. It was a reaction, nothing more. He would have carved open my gut if I hadn't stopped him.'

'Surely you cannot believe such a story,' said Bayard. 'The man's word is worthless.'

Ursula stared deep into Steinhardt's eyes, measuring him, judging him.

'I believe him,' she said eventually.

'You of all people must understand why I have done what I have done,' said Steinhardt, his voice almost pleading with Ursula. 'I make no secret of my ambition, but it is not for myself alone. If what you say is true, if there is indeed an army of the northmen on the verge of…'

'It is true,' Ursula interrupted him.

'Well then,' continued Steinhardt with only the briefest of pauses, 'you would agree that Ostermark must be strong. Count Emmereind was a mere boy, and more than half the knights and nobles had no faith in him or his regent. Ostermark was a land divided years before I took it upon myself to make her strong again. With Ostland and Talabecland, we stand against the northern borders. The invasion of the Iron-claw in the south has shown what can happen if our watch is not relentless, if our guard is not eternal. Ostermark was failing in its duty. A strong Ostermark is a strong Empire.'

'Spare us the speeches,' said Vapold. 'There has not been an Imperial election in two centuries. Ostland and Ostermark have been rivals in all that time.'

'And yet there was a time when they were not,' said Ursula, turning to Vapold. 'There was a time, like now, when the threat from the north waxed large. Your ancestor Count Urdin was here, sat in this very room, when news arrived from the Ostermark that the Blood-terror had crossed the Urskoy. Perhaps where you are seated right now, he wrote a letter to Count Vandel, pledging his army to the relief of Bechafen.'

She turned to Steinhardt.

'You know the tale,' she said, and the count nodded sombrely. 'That messenger dared the siege to bring hope to Vandel, your forefather, who held out against the savage attacks of the northmen for a month while

Urdin marched to his relief. Had he not known that another stood alongside him, would he have fought so hard? Had he believed himself alone, would he have walked the walls day and night with his Rune-fang bared, exhorting his men to fight against the tides of brutal warriors? Would he have had the courage to repel assault after assault if he had not believed there was hope?'

She looked along the table at all of the men gathered there, her hand straying to the hilt of Ulfshard. Her face was defiant, determined.

'Ask yourself this,' she said, pacing along the length of the table. 'Would we be sat here, would this castle have been built, would this city have existed if Sigmar and King Kurgan had allowed themselves to be divided? Would our great lord have been able to stand alone at Black Fire Pass?'

The counts and advisors shook their heads and stroked their chins, eyes fixed to Ursula as she rounded the end of the table and stood beside Vapold. She crossed her arms and glared at them.

'Men often scoff at legends,' she told them. 'The days of glory have passed, they tell themselves. They dismiss them as myths, or if true, then never to be repeated by mere mortals such as us. Every man contains within him the stuff of legend. You,' she pointed at one of the scribes, a wizened scholar with greying hair, his left arm quivering with palsy, 'would you have a part to play in creating a new legend?'

'My sword arm is not as strong as it used to be,' he chuckled, 'and I was never much of a fighter, but if you asked me, I would strap myself to a horse and do my best.'

'And yet, frail as you are, you have a part to play,' she said, standing behind him and plucking the quill from his hand. 'With this, you can record history. With strokes of this pen, you can draw up the alliance that will see Ostermark and Ostland united once again. You will be known down through the generations, and historians will know your name as the man who sat here while the great and the good forged their futures upon the anvil of battle. You will be the man who recorded their sagas so that in another hundred and fifty years, in times of worry, when doubt is strong, perhaps another man of power, another count of the Empire, might draw inspiration from the deeds that you will perform in honour of this agreement.'

Ursula fell silent for a moment, her audience entranced by her fiery passion, and placed the pen back into the old man's hand. She walked back down the table and gestured for Steinhardt to rise.

'Draw your Runefang,' she commanded, and the count of Ostermark did so without hesitation, laying the shining, rune-etched blade on the table, pommel held lightly in his grasp. Ursula turned to Vapold and pointed at him, and he did the same, though slightly more hesitantly. She then drew Ulfshard, bathing the faces of those present in the blue glow of the elven blade.

'Older still than your swords, I risked my life to reclaim the blade of Marbad,' she told them. 'It has taken me far, to dark and dangerous places, and yet I believe that I have honoured the privilege of being its

bearer with my deeds. I am not of noble birth. I am
not a baroness or a countess. I command no men
other than those who would willingly follow me. I
have no wealth, no coffers to hire an army. I wield no
power but this sword and my faith in our lord Sigmar.'

She paused then, looking at each of the counts to
ensure that her meaning was clear. She was relying
upon them both.

'Each of you carries a Runefang, your symbol of
power,' she continued. 'You did not earn them, they
were your birthright. They were forged seventeen centuries ago, and gifted to your forefathers by King
Kurgan, as he had gifted Ghal-maraz to almighty Sigmar. They swore oaths upon those blades, to uphold
the ideals of their first Emperor and to defend the
realm that he had created. They were forged to sym-
bolise the strength of the newborn Empire. Strong
leaders, brave warriors, united in their cause. When a
Runefang is raised against another, it is a joy to our
enemies, for in our division they can sense our weakness. Raise your swords not against each other, but
beside each other, and they shall know fear. Swear the
oaths that your ancestors swore seventeen hundred
years ago. Pledge yourselves to Sigmar and the Empire
once again. Do it not for ceremony, for rite of law or
tradition. Do it because you mean it. Do it because
you believe in Sigmar and what he bequeathed to us.'

Vapold and Steinhardt looked at each other, and then
looked at Ursula. She stood waiting patiently, looking
like a stern school matron if not for the shimmering
elven blade in her hand. They looked at each other again
and then, cautiously, raised their swords in the air.

'With this blade I pledge,' Ursula prompted them. 'You know the words.'

Indeed they both did, having uttered them at their investitures as electors of the Empire, though the position was now all but defunct. Though the words had subtly changed from the time of the first tribal leaders who had founded the Empire, their meaning was still clear.

'With this blade I pledge myself to Sigmar and his realm,' Steinhardt began and Vapold followed him, their words conjoining. 'I swear to uphold the honour of the Empire and my title as count. As it is my right to rule, so it is my duty to protect. I will wield this blade with righteous anger and ferocious courage against those who would despoil our lands. By our lord and Emperor, Sigmar Unberogen, I swear my allegiance to his eternal service. With the gods as my witness and my judges, this pledge to bind me until death and beyond.'

Silence once more descended on the hall as the two counts stood there, facing each other, their Runefangs held in salute. Steinhardt looked at Ursula and Vapold smiled wryly.

'My lords,' she said, pointing to the torn agreements and petitions scattered across the table, 'I thank you for your trust in me. Now you must put your trust in each other. In writing if you feel it necessary.'

THE TIN CUP trembled in Magnus's hand, splashing water over his robes. He swallowed the remaining contents and refilled it, draining this second fill in one long draught. The cup clattered out of his hand as he tried to put it down, and he left it lying on the floor and staggered to the window. Thrusting it open, he took in a deep breath of cool night air. Spots of rain dabbed his face but he did not notice them. He was too preoccupied with the sensations coursing through his body.

It had started in the audience chamber, where the counts still wrangled with each other. Ursula's impassioned speech had set Magnus's senses tingling, and when she had heard the pledges of the counts, her aura had grown even greater, feeding off the renewed hope and faith of everyone in the room. Even Magnus, who had been taught to manipulate such energies, and ward them away if necessary, had been touched by it.

It was not only that. The surge of thrilling power had been the beginning, but there was something else that now coursed through him on the winds of magic. To his hidden sense it was like a foul taste, an acrid smell. It was a foulness that hung in the air itself and seeped through the walls and ceiling.

Looking out over the lights of Wolfenburg, he could sense it even now, though it was much more dissipated than it had been in the lower levels of the castle. He could see it with his second sight, like a black cloud drifting down on the magical winds from the north, polluting everything that it rolled over.

Feeling its touch made his skin crawl, and he felt like retching. Holding back the contents of his stomach, he made his way back to the pitcher of water, half-clambering over the desks, using them to support himself. He drank straight from the jug, not caring that water spilled down his chest.

The taste, the rank smell would not leave him though. He floundered around the room for a moment, unsure what to do. Everything was steeped in the corrupting tide, lingering on the furniture, settling into the rugs beneath his feet. He could not concentrate, could not focus his mind enough to shape the ill forces sweeping around him.

He scrabbled at one desk, his cramped fingers fumbling with the catch to its secret drawer. He finally succeeded in opening it and snatched the book from inside. Staggering over to the bed, he collapsed, lying sideways, his vision swimming for a moment. Closing his eyes, he took another deep lungful of air and realised that he had been holding his breath. As if that would help him, he admonished himself.

Flicking open the book, he squinted at the small, neatly written words by the light of the single candle by the bedside. He hastily turned the pages, tearing one clumsily as he did so. Finding the page he wanted, he scanned the words and then began to read out loud.

As the words spilled from his lips, Magnus could feel the power flowing through him, shaping itself to his will. Like a bubble in water, the energy expanded around him, pushing back the mystical malaise that had overwhelmed him. As he finished the enchantment, the magic solidified into a protective barrier, cutting off all the energy.

Exhausted and sick, Magnus rolled to his back, the book flopping from his fingers onto the floor. Safe for the moment, he allowed unconsciousness to take him.

* * *

JOHANNES WAS CHATTERING happily as they walked down the street. He was in high spirits, and despite Ursula's short, often monosyllabic answers and Ruprecht's silence, he did a good job of keeping the one-sided conversation going.

Ruprecht drowned out the young man's idle musings on the weather, the state of the count's stables and other random subjects. He listened instead to the people around them. His eyes took in everything as they walked along the road winding around Wolfenburg. It was a technique he had learned while he had been an agent for Marius. Often he would travel to a place before the witch hunter, unknown and unobserved, and simply walk around the village or town, using his eyes and ears to pick up anything.

Thinking back to Marius, Ruprecht still felt a pang of regret. For years they had been companions, even friends. Though Marius had been claimed by a growing madness in the end, haunted by the death of his wife and determined to hunt down the son of her killer, he had not always been so obsessed. He had been a good man, and had saved the lives of many people from the dark forces that constantly threatened the Empire.

Marius had also taught Ruprecht much about the perils of the nameless foe, and the means by which it could be rooted out and destroyed. Those instincts now nagged at Ruprecht, and so he walked beside Ursula, filtering out the droning of Johannes, and instead observed the city.

There was tension in the air. He could hear arguments in the street and from open windows. As he

walked, he caught snippets of conversations, some of
them everyday topics, others with stranger subjects. He
heard a man discussing a dairy farm that had found all
its cows dead in the fields, their udders filled with
thick blood. From a merchant chatting to a stall
holder in one of the side alleys he learned of a snake
with two heads being found in the cellar of one of the
city's inns.

These and others pricked at Ruprecht's thoughts.
Strange occurrences, chance happenings, odd sight-
ings. He knew what they pointed to, these symptoms
of a much darker peril. It was witchcraft, drawing these
bizarre events to itself like a lodestone draws iron.
There was a warlock or witch in Wolfenburg, and
Ruprecht had a good idea who it might be.

He realised with a start that Ursula and Johannes
had stopped outside their destination and he had continued on several paces. They looked at him
quizzically as he turned and grinned.

'Head in the clouds, sorry,' he said, masking his worries.

They were outside a blacksmith's, a hammer and
small anvil hanging from a chain on the wall. The
building was open-fronted, its wide double doors
swung apart, hot air from the forge inside causing
sweat to prickle on Ruprecht's skin. He had no idea
why they were here, it had been Johannes's plan. He
had said something about a surprise for Ursula. Grinning like a child, Johannes led them into the ruddy
interior.

The smith, a heavily built young man, stood by the
furnace, throwing in faggots of wood. He turned at

Johannes's shout and waved. Tossing in a last piece of timber, he wiped his hands on his apron and strode over.

'Is it finished?' said Johannes.

'Finished it last night,' the smith replied with a smile. 'Wasn't too much bother in the end. Follow me.'

The smith turned and led them to a wooden door to one side of the smithy. He opened it and waved them through.

'Let me know if you need any adjustments,' he said, taking a step back but leaving the door open.

The room was cooler than the smithy, the walls lined with shelves and racks sporting swords and speartips, arrowheads and shields. Breastplates hung on pegs either side of the door, and in the middle of the room on a mannequin was an exquisitely crafted suit of armour.

Its polished plates gleamed in the light from the forge, chased with designs picked out in gold wire. It was small, and at first Ruprecht assumed it was for a teenager, until he noticed the overly rounded breastplate. It was very definitely designed for breasts, Ruprecht concluded. Ursula had come to the same realisation, and she stepped forward, running a hand over the armour, marvelling at the workmanship, drawing a finger along the gold beading of the vambraces.

'It's beautiful,' she said, turning and looking at Johannes. Her eyes shone with the same brightness as the armour. 'How?'

Johannes smiled and winked.

'A favour from the count,' he said. He glanced over at Ruprecht, who was glaring disapprovingly. 'No, really.

You can check with him. It was his armour when he was young, and he donated it to you. There had to be a few, well, adjustments, but hopefully it'll be a snug enough fit. He paid for those as well, before you ask.'

'It's magnificent,' Ursula said, smiling. For the first time it was a genuinely warm smile, and Ursula skipped across the room and kissed Johannes on the cheek. If he had smiled any wider, Johannes's face would have split.

'You should try it on,' Ruprecht said. 'In case it needs any tinkering with, if you know what I mean.'

Ursula nodded and gestured for Johannes to help her. As they began to untie the buckles and straps, Ruprecht heard an exclamation from the forge. He ducked his head through the door and saw the smith standing with his hands on his hips in front of the furnace.

'Everything sound?' Ruprecht asked, stepping through the doorway.

'Well, have you ever seen anything like that?' the smith replied. As he stepped back, Ruprecht saw that the flames in the forge were burning blue and green.

'Something about the wood, perhaps,' suggested Ruprecht to hide his sudden discomfort.

They stood for a while watching the flames, and after a short while they resumed their normal orange and yellow.

'Mayhap,' the smith said, and then his eyes widened as he looked past Ruprecht.

Alarmed, Ruprecht spun on his heel to confront whatever new strangeness had assailed the smithy. He relaxed when he saw that his cause for surprise was

Ursula. She was dressed in the armour, Ulfshard hanging in its scabbard at her belt. With her red hair and the gold of the armour, she looked stunning. Ruprecht realised his jaw was hanging slackly, as if he were some player in a comedy. Shutting his mouth, he swallowed hard.

'Fits then?' was all he could say.

WHEN THEY HAD returned to the castle, Ruprecht had sought out Magnus, determined to confront him. After inquiring of a servant, he was told that the counts were still negotiating their agreement. Johannes urged Ursula to go with Ruprecht, to show Vapold the results of his generosity. As the three walked along the winding corridors, Ruprecht was struck by the chill.

As a page opened the doors, Ruprecht looked around the room but could not see Magnus. He noticed servants hanging lanterns on the walls, and glanced up to see the sky was dark behind the high windows. He dismissed it as a summer storm coming in from the mountains and looked at the assembled people. The looks on the faces of the courtiers and scriptmasters was a picture as Ursula entered. One of the scribes, who Ursula had singled out during her speech of the previous day, clasped a hand across his mouth, and another dropped his goblet to the floor with a loud clatter. Vapold blinked heavily, while Steinhardt laughed and slapped his hand on the table.

'Well, it appears the maiden of Sigmar certainly looks the part now,' the count of Ostermark declared.

'I'm glad I never had it melted down.' Vapold said, standing up. 'I'm sure I never...'

He stopped as the sounds of shouting could be heard from outside the room. Frowning, the count strode down the hall, and Ruprecht turned as he heard the patter of running feet. Magnus came down the corridor at speed, the hem of his robe lifted above his knees to stop him tripping.

'My lords,' the astrologer gasped. 'Come quickly.'

'What is it?' snapped Steinhardt but Magnus had already turned and was hurrying back the way he had come.

Muttering to himself, Vapold set off at a jog after the astrologer, and the others followed close behind. Ruprecht could hear all manner of clamour through the walls of the castle: shouting, a cacophony of bells and the clatter of iron-shod boots on stone as soldiers ran to their posts.

They burst out into the courtyard, which was rapidly filling up with people, staring up into the sky, some ailing, others pointing or shielding their eyes. Ruprecht turned to look over the wall at the same time as the others.

'I think that's a sign,' said Magnus, gulping down panicked breaths.

'The hound will eat the sun,' said Ursula coldly, her hand resting on the pommel of Ulfshard.

'Oh shit,' muttered Ruprecht as a chill shadow fell over the world.

CHAPTER FOUR
Return
The High Pass, Late summer 1712

THE FREEZING WINDS of the pass had ceased to have any effect on Jakob's ravaged flesh. He stood on a ledge overlooking the valley below, and smiled to himself. The dark shapes of the assembled warriors sprawled across the landscape, the smoke from their cooking fires filling the pass.

Even here, high above the army, he could hear the bellowing of war beasts, the shouts of champions boasting to each other, the crackle of the fires. Undar had done well, better even than Jakob and Vlamdir. He had brought nearly ten thousand with him, most of them fierce Norse tribesmen, some of them Kurgan who he had encountered on his way south, and several hundred bestial, mutated warriors from the pine forests of the Norsca mountains. Other creatures had been brought south as well, lured by the scent of war, pushed on by the strengthening breath of the gods. From the east, Jakob had sent seven thousand, all of them skilled horsemen of the steppes.

Soon it would be time to march south, Jakob told himself. The breath of the gods seemed to get stronger with every day, building in intensity, ascending to the triumphant climax that would be Kurt's return.

Muttering words of power, Jakob sprouted shadowy bat wings and stepped from the ledge, floating down the side of the cliff on the currents of magic. He landed in the snow not far from the area that had been claimed by Undar and the others, their low tents erected in the lee of a large boulder. The other warbands were spread out in semicircles from this point, each tribe keeping to itself.

Undar saw Jakob and beckoned him over. He was sitting on a felled log outside his tent, using his knife to pare the flesh from a human head, his bulbous muscles flexing as he scraped off fat and skin.

'Another one?' said Jakob, shuffling up to the giant warrior. Undar turned and pointed to a polished skull sat at the end of the log.

'Two today,' he grunted. 'I let Bjordrin take the other one.'

Jakob chuckled and Undar frowned at him.

'I don't think it's funny,' Undar snapped. 'The war leaders are growing restless. With each one that speaks out against waiting, there are others who begin to doubt. I can't kill them all.'

'You have so far,' Jakob said, still grinning.

'What's so funny?' Undar asked, flicking away gobbets of flesh from the point of his long knife.

'I was just remembering, Kurt, before we set sail for Araby,' Jakob told the warrior. He sat down on the log and picked up the skull, looking at the fine silver wire that fixed the jaw in place. 'Bjordrin will remember it too. Twelve heads Kurt took in leadership challenges before he realised that they would never stop. That's when he decided to raid the Arabyans, to prove himself mightier than any other Chosen.'

'And look where that ended up,' said Undar. 'I still can't see the joke.'

'Oh, I'm laughing at the stupidity of people,' Jakob explained. 'Myself included. Once again, good men are losing their heads waiting for Kurt to prove himself. I had my doubts, my own ambitions. It is much clearer now. I am content.'

'I remember when I first saw him,' Undar recalled, now smiling himself. 'He was going to fight every champion in the army if he had too.'

'He would have won,' Jakob whispered, and Undar nodded.

'I believe he might have done,' the grotesquely large warrior replied. He dropped the skull into the snow at his feet and turned to Jakob, his thick arms resting on his thighs. 'Anyway, you must speak to the champions. You have to convince them to stop fighting amongst each other for the right to lead the army. Kurdar and his Raeslings left this morning to head out on their own, and Vindrigan and Leshen Dru are talking of banding together and heading towards Praag.'

'The Kislevites will find them and kill them,' Jakob said. 'It is of no concern, they are only a few hundred warriors.'

'And what makes you think that the Kislevites won't stop us?' asked Undar. 'A small force may escape detection and make it to the Empire. An army this size, it's obvious that we'll have to fight our way south.'

Jakob leaned forward and grabbed a handful of snow.

'Perhaps not,' the shaman said, letting the ice fall from his gnarled fingers. 'I have a feeling that winter will come early this year.'

'You're a cunning bastard,' said Undar with a grin, retrieving his skull from the ground. 'I always knew that.'

'Cunning enough to stall these fools,' Jakob replied, nodding his head towards a large group of men who were marching up the valley from the rest of the camp, some two dozen or more of the warbands' leaders.

THE DELEGATION HAD agreed to wait for two more days, no more. If the sign that Jakob had promised them had not come by then, they were agreed that Andar Kul would become leader and would take the army south.

Jakob was not worried. He knew that the gods would see Kurt returned to him before his army left. If there was no sign in the next two days, Jakob would create one himself. Or perhaps he would bring the snowstorms even earlier, trapping the army in the pass. Whatever happened, the horde would not be going anywhere until he was ready.

He had told them to spread the word to all the champions to come together at the meeting fire on the morning of the third day. There they would make their decision, and everyone present would abide by it or leave. That gave Jakob two days to prepare.

THE MEETING FIRE blazed high in the air, located at the highest point of the pass. On felled logs and rugs, the assembled champions and chieftains, over fifty of them, gathered to discuss what to do. In a larger version of the Norse freigattur, the Free Gathering where no man could raise arms against another for the agreed duration, the champions haggled and argued with each other over who should take command. Though many had pledged their support to Andar Kul two days ago, some had changed their minds now that it looked like becoming a reality.

Hors Skalding had risen as a strong contender, leader of nearly five hundred men, by far the largest warband in the army. The Norseman now walked around the fire, stating his claim to the assembled crowd, who booed and cheered depending on their predetermined preference or in judgement of his arguments. He was a tall, lean man, with white hair that hung to his waist, tied in heavy gold clasps shaped like skulls. His armour was of fine scale mail, the links that hung to his knees a ripple of iron as he walked. He wore a heavy fur cloak edged with the teeth of cave bears and his bare arms were covered with dark tattoos. Jakob, stood leaning on his staff behind the seated warriors, thought he looked quite impressive.

'Three summers ago, I led my warriors to victory against the southerners of the mountains, where we are headed,' Hors told them. 'I struck inland for many miles, leaving my ships on the shore. Twenty farms gave their bounty to me, and three towns. They sent soldiers against us and we slaughtered them and took their weapons.'

He reached under his cloak and brought forth a heavy pistol. He cocked the eagle head-shaped lock and raised his arm into the air. With a flare and sharp retort he fired the pistol, grinning broadly. There was clapping from some of the champions, but others hissed their displeasure, voicing their traditional dislike for ranged combat.

'Twenty barrels of their fire powder we took from one of their ships,' said Hors, thrusting the pistol back into his belt. 'With this we are the match of any of you here. Two years ago, I raided far to the south, in the lands of the horsemen. That too was a bountiful endeavour.'

He once again reached into his cloak and, with a flourish, produced a tall green bottle. He tossed it to the crowd, who pushed each other aside to have a look at the gift. The scarred veteran who ended up with the bottle broke the neck with his knife and poured some into his mouth. He turned to the others, red liquid dribbling into his greying beard, and raised the bottle above his head

'Booze!' Hors cried loudly, the cheers of the gathered men drowning out the words of the old chieftain. 'When I have brought you victory, I have enough drink for every man here and five of his most favoured fighters to share.'

'What about last year?' a voice called out.

'Last year?' Hors replied, his grin fading. His expression was one of exaggerated sadness. 'Last year I fell ill with a ravaging fever.'

There were hoots and cries of derision from the crowd, which did not quieten when he held up his hand.

'So I sent my son!' Hors shouted to be heard over the din of the gathered men, and they fell silent. 'He raided the coast of the Empire again, and like me the gods smiled upon his toil in their name.'

For a third time, Hors retrieved something concealed within his voluminous cloak. This time it was a small sack, about the size of a man's fist. He reached in and grabbed what was inside. The crowd were looking eagerly at him now, wondering what he would next produce. He stepped closer and lowered his voice. Those men at the back stood and leaned forward to hear him.

'South to Marbrig they sailed,' Hors whispered, voice barely audible above the crackling flames behind him. 'To the mouth of the great river, where the warships prowl and lie in wait. Under cover of night, they stole into the sound and there they boarded a ship moored on the river bank. The crew were taken without a fight, and now clean out my pig sty. And in the hold of that galleon, what do you think they found?'

'Gold!' one man shouted out.

'Gems!' suggested another.

'Fine women!' came another voice, to much laughter from the others as Hors looked at the small sack dubiously.

'The first man to swear to me receives the contents of this bag,' Hors promised, grinning.

There was sudden clamour as a dozen men rose to their feet, each trying to shout louder than the others.

Hors pointed at one, a young man with armour of rivet-studded black leather.

'Catch,' Hors called out, tossing the contents of the bag towards the champion.

The man scrambled over those in front of him with his arms outstretched. His fingers closed around the brown object, and something wet splattered over his face.

'Turnips,' said Hors with a shake of his head. 'Bloody turnips.'

The young champion snarled and threw the remnants of the rotten vegetable back at Hors, further fuelling the uproar of shouts and laughter that had erupted around him.

'My son still has much to learn,' Hors told them with his arms spread wide in apology. His face then grew serious. 'The gods favour me, that much is certain. In my twelve years as chieftain we have doubled the number of slaves we have. Our homes are built from the finest wood from the forests and are hung with gold and silver. We have feasted upon the sheep of the south well. I know nothing about the Sutenvulf, and care even less. I am the northern wolf, the real thing. Follow me and our glory is assured!'

Many in the crowd cheered and stamped their feet, and some stood with weapons drawn, waving them in the air. There were others though, mostly the darker-skinned Kurgan who favoured Kul, who shook their heads and waved their hands dismissively. Jakob sighed as Kul stood and strode towards the fire. This could last all day, he realised.

* * *

JAKOB HAD WANDERED away from the gathering, deep in thought. Doubts nagged at his mind. Whether it was Kul or Hors, it didn't matter to him. Neither was the true leader of the army. And yet there had been no sign. Jakob's proud proclamation in the howling wastes of the north seemed premature. He had tried his best, the gods knew, but he was at a loss now.

Had Kurt really survived? Jakob remembered the cryptic words of the daemon he had summoned for Asdubar Hunn. Perhaps it had meant that Kurt was dead. Where was a place that was no place, if not the realm where the souls of the slain were sent?

These thoughts and others assailed Jakob as he walked between the clusters of tents and fires, meandering between the conversations of the assembled marauders. He could feel their distrust as they saw him, their loathing. They had travelled far, risked their lives on his word, and now it seemed as if he had been wrong.

But it was not all bad, he considered. He had gathered the army. Perhaps he had been wrong, perhaps it was meant for another to lead the host of the gods. Kurt may have been spurned, or maybe he had failed in some other way?

And yet the simple truth was that Jakob believed. He believed, in that moment of insight the gods had granted him, when their storm had engulfed Kurt and swept him away. Had not Khar sent his hounds to guide Kurt?

But then again, the flesh hounds had left without him. Was that what had happened? Was Kurt still wandering those wastes, searching for the gate, lost and alone? Another doubt crept into Jakob's mind.

Had he been right for them to turn back, to leave Kurt to his fate?

He had felt so assured at the time, certain in the knowledge that it was by the will of the gods that Kurt had been taken from them. Or had it been his selfishness? He had achieved the power he craved, and perhaps part of him had wanted to return, to risk no more in those dread lands. Had he already betrayed the gods?

Each grim thought was followed by another as he dragged himself across the snow-covered ground, the staff fused to his hand leaving a furrow in his wake.

What would become of him once a new leader had been chosen? Would Hors or Kul continue to support him? They had no ties of loyalty to Jakob, and each had his own shamans to call upon. Would they view him as a threat?

This thought scared Jakob more than any other. For so many months he had been filled with purpose, with a destiny. It had made the long years of hardship he had endured seem like a distant memory. But really, what should he have expected, a mere bastard half-Norse who had tried to claim the power of the gods through Kurt's endeavours? Would he be scorned again, the fear and respect that he had enjoyed forgotten quickly as those around him recalled the great promises he had made but failed to deliver?

Jakob tried to hurry, but his crippled body would move no faster. He wanted to seek out Undar, and Orst and the others. They would protect him if things turned ill. If not, they would surely let him escape the clutches of the enemies that were even now choosing to usurp him. They had as much to lose, they had all spread the word of Kurt's triumphant return and the glorious conquest to come. Jakob stopped short, a new fear rising in his mind.

They had followed him. Undar, Bjordrin and the others had done what Jakob had asked of them, on the same promise. What if they too felt betrayed by his inability to bring about Kurt's return? Would they really offer him succour, or would they cast him to the wolves, or even worse?

I should flee, Jakob thought. I need to leave here before they come for me.

A commotion further down the valley cut through his paranoia. There were shouts of alarm and amazement echoing along the walls of the pass. Concentrating, Jakob could see men running to and fro, yelling to each other.

Broken from the cycle of self-doubts, Jakob now noticed something else, a change in the air, a different current carried on the breath of the gods. He could smell blood, hot blood. Gazing up into the sky, he could not locate the source, but it grew stronger with each passing second. As the sensation grew, so too did the cries of alarm. Looking down the valley again, Jakob's othersight detected something new, something ancient and dreadful.

He saw red shapes streaking across the snow, scattering the Norse and Kurgan in all directions as they ran in terror from the apparitions. There were eight of them, moving fast, coming directly up the pass. Jakob's heart leapt with joy and he gave a shout, raising his arms into the air.

'The hounds!' he shouted. 'The hounds are here!'

The warriors around him gave him bemused glances, but they turned to looks of fear and awe as they saw the bloodied creatures racing up the pass towards them. Jakob turned and began to shuffle back towards the gathering of champions and chieftains, wishing he could move faster.

He was halfway back when the hounds passed him, slavering and growling as they loped along on unnaturally swift limbs, their white eyes glowing with power. Ahead Jakob could see the crowd of war leaders jumping up from their seats, pointing down the hill towards him. Laughing, Jakob pushed himself onwards, and as he neared the fire, he felt a chill for the first time.

The hounds were sitting in a circle, each facing in towards the fire. The men of the steppes and Norsca had withdrawn a stone's throw away, eying the daemonic beasts warily. They looked at Jakob as he gasped and huffed his way into the circle. There were more gasps and amazed shouts. Seeing that they gazed into the sky, Jakob turned and looked upwards. The shock of what he saw made his legs weak and he collapsed to his backside, numbed.

Above the mountains a great shadow was rising, blotting out the light of the sun.

IT WAS THE errant moon, known in the Empire as Morrslieb, to many of the Norse as Tcharlit, in the east as Fung-Tzeng, and by a hundred other names besides. Irregular in shape and erratic in orbit, the green moon was seen by most as an ill omen, except in the north where it was regarded as the eye of the gods.

Now it rose up into the sky, fuller than Jakob had ever seen it. The breath of the gods blew even stronger around him, almost physically battering at the shaman. Slowly the shadow crept further and further up the pass, engulfing the army in darkness. There were bestial shouts from the wild creatures that had gathered in the pass, and cries of delight and dismay from the Norse and the Kurgan.

Slowly the moon swallowed up the lifegiving energies of the sun, swathing everything in twilight, the temperature dropping rapidly. Day became night and shadows as black as pitch swathed the pass.

Behind Jakob the hounds pulled back their heads and howled, a thunderous bass noise that made the ground tremble. The light of the gathering fire flickered and dimmed, and then died completely. An utter darkness descended upon the army, so complete that he could not see his hand an inch in front of his face. All that could be seen were the eight glowing pairs of eyes of Khorne's hounds.

Then the terror began.

The horses whinnied in the darkness and there were cries of utter dread. Jakob felt it grip his soul, a wrenching fear that was utter and eternal. He felt sick and rolled on to his stomach, his face buried in his hands, whimpering like a babe.

'As promised, I have returned.'

Jakob pulled his hands away as the terror subsided, and rolled over at the sound of the voice. It was strangely familiar, like something from a half-remembered dream. He looked up and could still see nothing but blackness.

Except for two more glittering orbs amongst the eyes of the hounds, burning with dark fire.

A ray of sun broke from behind the shrouding moon as it continued its ascent, and the darkness seemed to shatter. A pool of shadow remained for a moment longer, and then resolved itself into a more discernable form.

It stood three times the height of a man, large bat-like wings spread wide from its back. Its skin was crimson and shimmered with magical energy, oozing blood from its unnatural pores. Its face was narrow, heavily boned, and as it opened its fanged maw a long, forked tongue slithered over razor-sharp teeth. Its bestial face was framed by a mane of shaggy black hair that stretched down its back between its wings. It reached down towards Jakob, extending a clawed hand towards him.

A sense of overwhelming joy flooded though Jakob and he grasped the outstretched talon and was pulled gently to his feet.

'Kurt?' Jakob whispered, staring up into the massive face. The daemon prince's lips twisted into a smile.

'Kurt is no more. I am your master now. I am Suten-vulf Daemonkin.'

CHAPTER FIVE
Northwards to Battle
Wolfenburg, Late summer 1712

JOHANNES HAD A deep feeling of dread as he watched the sunlight fade, swathing the castle in darkness. He could hear screams from outside, in the city, and excited shouts from all around him. He paid them no attention, staring at the blot sweeping across the sky, his hand shielding his eyes from what little sunlight remained.

In a few more heartbeats, there was darkness.

The shouting was growing louder, closer and Johannes heard yells from the castle walls. Soldiers were running along the ramparts, pointing outside. Spurred into action, Johannes raced to the nearest steps, bounding up them two at a time. He ran to the edge of the wall and looked over.

From all around, people were converging in the wide plaza that surrounded the keep. The distraught inhabitants of Wolfenburg were converging on the castle and the air was filled with their cries of dread. The few guards outside fled from them and with a thud the gates were swung shut as the mob poured forwards.

Soon there were hundreds of people outside, as the sun began to show itself once more, the watery light cascading down onto the crowd below. Johannes looked around, seeking Count Vapold. He spied the noble in the courtyard still, standing transfixed, looking up at the sky.

The mob's fear was turning to anger, their shouted demands incoherent, and as others entered the plaza, they were forced forwards up to the castle walls itself. More and more of them came in, and Johannes could see that some were armed. Those by the gate were beating on it with fists and stones, demanding to see the count. Others were desperately pushing back against the human tide, trying to avoid being crushed against the merciless stone.

Johannes looked in horror as one woman fell into the living morass, trampled by the press of bodies behind her. Fighting broke out as a man tried to claw his way to reach her, but there was no space. Punches were thrown and as the man flailed to rescue his companion, others joined the fray. Back and forth the mass seethed, and soon the anger was again joined by shouts of terror.

Stones and sticks began to clatter against the wall as angry city folk lobbed the improvised missiles towards the guards who were standing on the walls, staring aghast and helpless at the chaos below.

Johannes ran to the inner edge of the parapet and gave a shout to attract attention.

'Lord!' he cried. 'Count Vapold!'

The ruler of Wolfenburg did not seem to hear and Johannes's desperation grew. Someone needed to speak to the people. Moving back to the battlements, Johannes looked out again, undecided as to what to do.

'Get back!' he called out, cupping his hands around his mouth.

A stone splintered on the parapet just below Johannes, causing him to flinch. He called out again, but the sea of people below was oblivious to his cries. And then, as he watched, he saw the mob quieting, and a stillness spread out as people realised that something was happening. The struggles and fights died down, until total stillness had descended across the mob. Johannes realised they were looking at the gate towers and he turned to see what had caught their attention. Johannes's breath caught short in his throat.

Ursula stood upon the battlements, her polished armour gleaming in the growing light. In her hand, Ulfshard blazed with its own fire. From the gates below, calm washed outwards over the desperate people, as they stared in fascination at the vision before them. Silence descended, broken by the wounded groaning of those who had been crushed or assaulted. Ursula said nothing, and simply stood there, her elven blade raised above her head. Slowly, she lowered the gleaming sword.

'Be at peace!' she shouted, her voice carrying clear and strong. 'Loyal people of Wolfenburg, listen to me!

I know you are afraid. I know that this is a terrible thing to behold. I understand your fear, your doubts, your questions. Yet be at peace. This is not the way to find your answers. Look at yourselves, and find the strength inside each of you. Do not give in to the weaknesses of dread and disbelief. Find courage within yourselves to face these terrible signs.

'I will not lie to you! This is a portent of foul things to come. You know that, and that is why you are here. But I beg you to resist the temptation of panic. I am here to show you that Sigmar sees your plight. Forget your desperation, and be comforted by his watchfulness. He yet protects you, as do I.

'You know me, I am the maiden of Sigmar. Have faith and we will overcome the woes that have befallen us. Look to yourselves for the strength to endure in the dark times ahead, and look to our lord Sigmar to grant you his strength in these troubling times. You have heard many things these past few months, and doubt and uncertainty have become the way of things. No more! Here, in front of you all, I make a solemn vow.

'I pledge upon my life and soul that while I still draw breath, I will let no harm come to you.'

A ripple of cheering began to spread through the crowd, growing in volume into a tumultuous roaring of approval. Hope had replaced fear, and the citizens of Wolfenburg vented their emotions loudly. Standing over the crowd, Ursula sheathed Ulfshard and raised her hands. Slowly, reluctantly, the clamour died down.

'Go back to your homes now,' she told the people. 'Speak to your families, your loved ones. Spread this

message across the city, across Ostland. War will soon
be upon us, but Sigmar will grant us victory! Prepare
yourselves for the fight ahead. Steel your souls against
the darkness, and embrace the light of faith. As long as
we stand with courage in our hearts and steel in our
hands, our foes will know the bitter taste of defeat.'

She turned stepped off the parapet as the shouting
and cheering rose up again, engulfing the castle. Inside
the keep soldiers were cheering also, waving their
weapons in the air. Having regained his composure,
Count Vapold waited at the bottom of the steps as
Ursula descended, clapping enthusiastically. He
stepped forward to speak to her but she did not break
her stride, walking straight past the count without
even a glance in his direction. Vapold frowned at her
back as Ursula walked across the courtyard and disappeared into the main hall.

A soldier passing Johannes slapped a hand to his
shoulder, grinning widely.

'With the maiden beside us, we can't lose,' he said,
his eyes filled with excitement.

'No,' said Johannes, nodding and smiling, one eye
still on Vapold who was standing in the courtyard calling for Captain Felsturm. 'No we can't.'

YET AGAIN THE audience chamber of Wolfenburg castle
was filled with activity. Officers from Vapold's army
and Count Steinhardt's aides came and went, carrying
sheaves of papers and armfuls of ledgers.

Since the eclipse, the leaders of the two provinces
had been deep in preparation for the coming war.
Steinhardt had already sent word back to his army at

Bechafen to make ready for another long march. His army would join Vapold's in northern Ostland and together they would stand against the horde about to be unleashed upon the Empire.

Riders were also sent further north, to Kislev, to warn about the encroaching threat. The messengers took with them missives to the Tsar, asking him to send out his scouts to trail the northmen, and to lend whatever aid he could. They also asked permission to cross into Kislevite lands, if it was necessary, so that the foe could be brought to battle at the most advantageous position. The riders were told to travel as swiftly as possible and return with the Tsar's reply with all speed.

If the build-up to the fight against Steinhardt had been industrious, the effort put into this new war was nothing short of miraculous. With the memory of the darkened sky still in their minds, and the countryside plagued with stories of beastmen and other creatures gathering in the forests in great numbers, the people of Wolfenburg and the surrounding town worked feverishly to ready the greatest army they could muster.

Supplies were brought in from all over the province as every mill that still stood worked day and night to grind the early harvest. The chimneys of the bakeries filled the sky with smoke as hardened loaves, the staple of any army's diet, were loaded in their thousands onto a steady train of wagons and carts that poured into and out of Wolfenburg. Whole herds were slaughtered to feed the growing army, warehouses were emptied and turned to salting houses to preserve the tons of meat.

Heralds of the count rode north, to warn the burgomeisters and mayors to prepare for the coming of the army, to load their storehouses with whatever provisions they had and to assemble every able-bodied man they could. The recruiters travelled back and forth across the province, accompanied by armed guards to protect the chests of silver they carried with them, the first wages of any man who would sign up for service to the count.

Ostland was bleeding itself dry, risking famine and starvation in the coming winter. There was no alternative, for even slow starvation was preferable to death or worse at the hands of the northmen.

As the war gathered momentum, the story tellers and minstrels plied their trade, earning their keep with old tales of the battles of the past. They horrified their listeners with epic poems about the deprivations of the Blood-terror and steeled their resolve with accounts of the great siege of Bechafen. They recalled the ancient times when Sigmar himself had walked these lands and, with his allies, waged war against the Norsii, driving them into the bleak north.

A vast training field was created outside the city, swathes of the forest cut down to make room for the growing encampment, the wood used to fuel the fires and forges burning constantly in the city. In their hundreds the newcomers made their way to the capital, some in twos and threes, daring the perils of the forests. Others arrived in large groups, the menfolk of whole villages setting off together, entrusting the safety of their loved ones to the gods.

During the hours of daytime, the training field was thronged with the recruits. As they arrived they were handed their uniforms, quickly woven on the looms of Wolfenburg and crudely dyed in faded black, and organised into new regiments. The field rang with swordplay and the shouts of men practising with halberds and spears. To the shouts of the sergeants, the newcomers, many of them youths barely fifteen and sixteen years old, learned to drill with handguns and crossbows. Hunters from the forests were formed up as archers, and would be tasked with continuing to supply the army once it was on the march.

The docks at Hoarsonburg were filled with ships and boats as agents of the count travelled to and from the south to trade with the merchants of Talabheim, who sensing that demand was high, raised their prices to extortionate levels. Messengers asking for support from the Count of Talabecland remained unanswered, and his silence was a source of concern to Vapold, as he voiced to his counsellors one day.

He feared that perhaps, seeing Ostland vulnerable, Talabecland would move against Vapold from the south. He was loath to spare any more men than were absolutely necessary to guard the river and the south-eastern border, knowing that he needed every able fighter to combat whatever force assailed them from the north.

Steinhardt had returned to Ostermark to marshal his own forces and speak to his nobles, agreeing to meet again with Vapold and his force in the northern forests of Ostland. Captain Felsturm had already been sent ahead with a vanguard of two thousand foot and a thousand cavalry. He was tasked with holding the road against any foe that dared to oppose him. If Ursula's predictions were true, and the northmen had amassed the sort of horde she had dreamt about, then this force could hope to do nothing more than delay their advance. However, Vapold was reluctant to move with his army until all was ready.

A week before the host was set to begin its long march northwards, three massive barges arrived at Hoarsonburg, flying the colours of Nuln. The bemused observers soon had their questions answered when the first barrel of a cannon was hoisted from the hold and lowered to the dock. The parts for its massive carriage were unloaded next, and crates filled with heavy shot. In all, six guns were transferred to heavy wagons pulled by twelve-strong horse teams and some three hundred cannonballs loaded onto a mile-long convoy of carts. With them came ten gun captains of Nuln, their expertise paid for out of the almost empty coffers of the count.

The Reiklanders were greeted as heroes as they arrived at the city, the people of Wolfenburg flocking out of the gates to cheer them as the wagons laden with the massive guns were formed up outside the city walls. They marvelled at the finely forged artillery pieces, larger even than the cannons on the wall of the keep, their black-painted barrels shaped into the muzzles of fierce wolves, griffons and dragons.

Ruprecht was among the throng as the cannons were slowly hoisted onto their carriages, a line of menacing metal that would put the fear of the gods into any man facing them. Count Vapold appeared with a small entourage, riding out of the gates and dismounting to inspect his new weapons. One of the gun captains, sporting a large red feather in his wide-brimmed hat, his black doublet decorated with the arms of Nuln in silver thread, climbed atop one of the guns and addressed the grateful crowd.

'My lord,' he began, and fell silent as another great cheer resounded from the gathered masses. 'My lord, fair people of Wolfenburg, it is with great honour that I present you with these fine pieces. Artefacts of the finest artisanship and craft, the best that the foundries of Nuln have to offer.'

He pointed to each of the cannons in turn, each receiving a cheer as he did so.

'First we have *Warwolf*, which first howled death at the siege of Altdorf,' he told the crowd. 'Her first shot slew a mighty wyvern. Next we have two veterans of the battles of Gunderbruche and Staghold, the venerable *Thunder of Sigmar*, and her sister *Storm of Justice*. On my right, pay attention to the wonderful craftsmanship of *Victory's Hammer* and the splendid magnificence of *Sigmar's Judgement*.'

He paused then and looked at the count.

'Your lord has spared you no expense in bringing you these five great cannons,' the gun captain said. He then crouched and patted the barrel of the cannon on which he was standing. 'This one, fresh from the forges no more than two months ago, is a gift to you all from Baron Vorst, patron of Nuln.'

'What is her name?' asked the count.

'That is for you to decide,' the captain replied with a smile. 'She is yours to call what you will. Choose wisely though, for if you honour her she will fight well for you, but a poor name will displease her.'

The count stood in thought, stroking his chin and looking at the crowd, who shouted helpful suggestions, and some not so helpful. The count walked over to the gun and patted a hand against its barrel, and then turned to the crowd.

'I have a name,' he called out to them, and they quietened, eagerly awaiting his proclamation. 'She shall be named *Maiden of Sigmar*, in honour of the greatest gift we have been given in the these dark times.'

The roar from the crowd was spontaneous and deafening, and Vapold was taken aback as the gathered people began to cheer his name as well. With a nod to the Reikland captain, he walked back to his horse, but before he could ride away, the crowd surged forward, surrounding him. Those at the front reached up and patted at his horse and the count's legs, and cries of blessing and thanked sounded out over the din. He reached down to grasp the proffered hands, sharing the moment with his people. As the cheers subsided and the throng withdrew, he raised his hand and stood in his stirrups. He looked out over the mass of humanity, eyes gleaming.

'There can be no better people than the folk of Ostland,' he said, the statement met with a cheer of gratitude. 'You do yourselves great service, and you have made me proud. Proud as a man, and proud as your lord. In five days we march forth to battle a foe as yet unknown to us in strength and malevolence. With your help and your prayers, there can be none that stand before us. With such strength and faith, we cannot fail. We will march to victory!'

Ruprecht felt himself swept up in the moment and his own bass cheers joined the yells and whistles of the throng as the count punched his hand into the air. In the days to come, Ruprecht would often think back on that moment. In the bleakest moments, when all hope had left him, he would cast his mind back to that sight, Vapold with one fist raised, a sea of grateful faces surrounding him. Of all the things he had witnessed in his life, and many of them had been truly remarkable, it was this one memory, this moment of honest hope and adoration and courage, that would give Ruprecht the strength he needed in the dire times to come.

THE ARMY WAS assembled as planned, and as the regiments mustered outside the east wall of the city, those who would remain behind gathered to see the soldiers depart. Wives and mothers cried to see husbands and sons going, perhaps never to return. Those too young, too old or too infirm to go with the brave men of Ostland stood and watched, some cheering, others saying prayers, many simply standing in sombre silence.

Rank after rank, regiment after regiment, nine thousand in all, the army lined up in blocks of two and three hundred men. The summer sun was waning and the first chill northern winds fluttered the forest of black and white banners upon their poles. Ahead, on the road, the cavalry waited, some three thousand knights and other horsemen, their mounts stamping their feet and trotting back and forth with brisk energy.

A clattering of hooves echoing in the gatehouse signalled the arrival of the Osterknacht, who had remained in Wolfenburg for the past months. Three wide, they galloped from the gateway, their armour polished to a gleaming sheen, long lance pennants streaming above them. At their fore, his face stern, rode Lord Bayard, sword held upright in front of his face in salute to the soldiers he passed.

Behind them came Count Vapold and his twenty-strong bodyguard, mounted on black stallions armoured in white-painted barding. Beside him rode Ursula, her golden armour easily visible amongst the lacquered black steel of the knights around her. Vapold appeared relaxed, as if he were merely riding out to his hunting lodge rather than embarking upon a war that might see him killed and his lands ravaged. Ursula's expression was one of serenity, her gaze taking in the massed soldiers of the Ostermark as she rode past them.

A blare of horns and trumpets signalled the start of the march, and with the heavy rhythm of drum beats resounding from the city walls, the gathered regiments wheeled out onto the road, following behind the knights. The tramp of booted feet resounded in time with the drumbeats, the ground beginning to tremble as more and more units fell into the column. For many minutes the infantry marched onto the road, forming a line that stretched for nearly two miles.

Axles grinding heavily over the rutted road, the count's six new cannons formed the beginning of the rear guard, long teams of horses straining at the traces to get the bulky artillery pieces moving. Behind them light cavalry formed up, a swift moving detachment that could quickly move forward if needed.

At the rear, another mile-long column assembled, formed by wagons and carts laden with the supplies needed to sustain the host. They carried farriers and smiths, carpenters and woodsmen, cooks and brew-masters, and many others besides including scribes and messengers who were no less essential to the smooth operation of any military effort.

With no river north of the Middle Mountains to bring them supplies, the army was forced to take all it needed on the winding forest road. It was this, more even than the mustering of the armed force, that had been so slow and ponderous and yet remarkably achieved. The baggage column was almost as numer-ous as the army itself, swelled by the wives and families of the soldiers who had been fortunate enough to bar-gain their way into the train, as well as those whose services were perhaps less noble and yet would sustain a man on a long march away from his loved ones.

For the whole morning the people who were to remain watched the army depart, and into the after-noon as the last carriages and drays disappeared along the road, moving beyond the fields and farms and out of sight into the dark forests beyond. Now, perhaps, would be the hardest time of all for those who were parted from friends and families. Now the waiting had begun, the long weeks without news, endless days spent fearing the worst and praying for the best. None knew how many of the thousands who had set out would return, if any.

* * *

FOR FIVE DAYS the army marched north and east, following the rutted, worn road that led to the Kislev port of Erengrad. Along the way they passed ruined farmsteads and towns, victims of the bestial hordes that were gathering in the depths of the forest. Sensing the carnage to come, made bold by the cold northern winds that heralded the coming storm of war, they raided from their lairs and camps, striking without warning and then disappearing back to their hidden retreats before reprisal.

A few hundred men further swelled the army as it advanced, joined by members of the militia and free companies of the towns and villages further east who had not travelled to the capital. They brought with them tales of dark shadows in the woods, of beastmen and mutants that lurked close at hand. Many were afraid, worried that their homes were defenceless, and as the risk of the count's course of action became more evident, there were those whose courage failed them. Alone or in small groups, deserters avoided the pickets and slipped away in the night, risking the predators of the woods to return to their homes.

On the sixth day, as afternoon began to darken to evening, the forests thinned and then petered out into the wind-swept plains of Kislev. A vast rolling expanse was spread out before the army, a cold tundra of rocky ground and small wooded thickets. They had left the boundaries of the Empire, many of the men having travelled much further from their homes than they had ever done before.

No longer protected against the growing autumnal winds by the trees, the camp of that night was cold and quiet. The good humour of the company faded further as dark clouds gathered in the skies, obscuring the moon and stars. Rain began to fall just before dawn, and the soldiers grumbled and swore as they paraded themselves in the early morning mist, the hundreds of campfires dull pools of light spread across a grey sea.

Armour dripping, clothes sodden, they marched north once more. As the sun eventually rose, burning off the morning mist, the scouts returned from ahead. With them came a force of riders, mounted upon sturdy horses, banners of feathers fluttering from their saddles. These were the winged lancers of Kislev, five hundred in all sent by the Tsar to aid his allies. With them came twice their number of horse archers, drawn from the nomadic tribes living in the tundra between the Urskoy and the Lynsk.

Archer and lancer alike were all veterans of the constant battles against the northmen. They brought news that another force had been sent to the north to seek out the foe. Riders from near the High Pass had come south earlier in the year, telling of a great horde of Norse and Kurgan gathering in the mountains. With them were beasts of the forests, twisted, monstrous creatures from the Troll Country and even mighty dragon ogres brought down from the highest mountain peaks by the lure of war.

Though he had feared as much, it was grim news for Vapold. The tribesmen reported that the army had been encamped in the pass for many weeks, growing larger every day. On the day of the Dark Sun, as the Kislevites referred to the eclipse, the horde had begun to advance out of the pass and they had fallen back before its endless numbers. No more news had been heard from the north in several days.

They also brought more welcome news. To the east, two days' ride away at Getzholm, Steinhardt waited with eight thousand men. Though he had not voiced his doubts to any of the others, Vapold had wondered whether the new Count of Ostermark would uphold his part of the pact they had signed. It seemed that, contrary to Vapold's impression of Steinhardt, he had stayed true to his word.

With Kislevite guides to lead them northwards, the army marched on for another day, and before dusk the glittering waters of the Lynsk could be seen in the distance. Here they would stand and face the storm to come. Here they would fight and if necessary die. In this cold bleak land, a hundred miles from their homes, the men of Ostland and the Ostermark would give their lives to protect their families.

CHAPTER SIX
The Storm Unleashed
Troll Country, Early autumn 1712

THE ARMY OF Sutenvulf Daemonkin spread across the tundra like a swarm, a swathe of men and beasts a mile across, moving further west and south with every passing day. A few miles ahead his Kurgan horsemen hunted the animals of the Troll Country, and pillaged the small communities that lay north of the Lynsk.

For now the tribes were as one, united under the daemon prince and their gods. Norsemen of the Raeslings marched beside their ancestral enemies, the Skeld. The dark-feathered banners of the Bloodravens were carried alongside the golden discs of the Sunhawks. Kul tribesmen on steppe ponies foraged with the tall, gaunt riders of the Saxin. Goat-headed beastmen and bull-headed minotaurs lurked on the edges of the mighty host, bickering and fighting amongst themselves. Their braying challenges to each other echoed across the frozen plains. Misshapen, shambling creatures like Orst, champions of the past that had been unable to resist the gods' gifts, slithered, bounded and crawled amongst the warbands, their hoots and lowing cries adding to the cacophony. From north and east they had all come together to wage war upon the south.

Sutenvulf himself strode at the head of the host, a dark, towering presence flanked by his eight flesh hounds. Jakob rode alongside him, grateful not to be walking the many miles every day. With them walked Undar, too large and heavy for any steed to carry, and Hors of the Skaldings, who had fallen to his knees and sworn oaths of fealty when Sutenvulf had manifested himself, as had every other champion in the pass. Bjordrin and Gird accompanied the daemon prince as well, his comrades who had journeyed with him into the far north and been his companions before his ascension. Their loyalty had been remembered, and each had been given command of a dozen warbands in the name of their daemonic general.

At dawn on the fourth day since they had journeyed out of the Pass of Kings, Jakob summoned the other shamans of the host to him. They were perhaps two days north of the Lynsk, and the Kurgan outriders had reported seeing Kislevite tribesmen in the distance, more of them in the last two days than before.

Sutenvulf would brook no distraction or delay, and had made it known to Jakob that he wished for no interference from the Kislevites. His goal was the Empire, and nothing would stand in his path.

The seven shamans gathered in a circle. Jakob stood at their centre within a smaller circle of his runestones, the ragged holes left in his flesh by their removal leaking thick blood into his furs. Around them the other marauders kept their distance, wary of the powers wielded by the wizards. Sutenvulf stood close at hand, watching intently. As the light of the sun could be seen through the clouds above the World's Edge Mountains to the east, Jakob closed his eye and raised his hands into the air.

He began to chant words of the Dark Tongue, the language of Chaos itself, magic given sound. Jakob could feel the closeness of the daemon prince, a fierce blaze of magical energy, draining the skies and ground of its power. He reached further afield, spreading his thoughts out beyond the presence of Sutenvulf, drawing in the breath of the gods. They were sluggish at first, but with gathering power they converged on Jakob, swirling in eddies around Sutenvulf, but drawn past his devouring incorporeal body by Jakob's spell. Around him the other shamans began their own chants, their voices raised discordantly against Jakob's. Their energy filled him, their power was passed into him as he stretched upwards, his soul carving up through the clouds above him.

From below he could feel the building vortex of magic, and as the mystical winds blew stronger, the air began to shift and turn at his command. The breeze grew in strength, building in ferocity until the army was engulfed by a raging gale. Men fought to hold their standards aloft, horses whinnied and bucked in fear, their owners holding tightly to their harnesses to stop them bolting.

Faster and faster the winds swirled, the clouds in the sky spiralling and darkening above the circle of shamans. The storm clouds began to grow and thicken, turning black and dangerous. A clap of thunder rolled across the tundra as Jakob concentrated his will, exerted his demands upon the raw elements. Lightning began to flicker, an occasional bolt at first, but growing in intensity until the heavens were alight with flashing bolts of energy, the sky shaking with a constant rolling thunder.

Rain began to fall, and within moments it pounded down across the plains, soaking the warriors of the Vangir, the Aster, the Baersonlings and all the other tribes besides, as they stood looking up at the magical storm. The wind grew chill, and soon the breath of the thousands of warriors was carving vaporous shapes in the icy air.

The rain turned to sleet and hail, and shields and cloaks were raised by the gathered warriors to protect them from the downpour of icy water. Then the first flakes of snow began to drift down, as small flurries at first, melting as they fell. Soon though, the snow began to settle, drifting over the men and land in a thin white veneer. On and on it came down, driven by the strong winds into covered faces, and men stood hugging their arms about themselves, stamping their feet in the frigid conditions.

With a shuddering gasp, Jakob collapsed to the ground, exhausted by the immense spell. He coughed blood into the snow layering onto the ground. Around him the ice hissed into steam where the runestones were placed, a fiery glow emanating from them.

Sutenvulf stepped forward and stooped to pick up Jakob's inert form. Snow steamed from his unnatural form, hissing and crackling. Cradling the unconscious shaman in one arm, the daemon prince pointed to the south.

'Onwards. Let nothing hinder you. Let my hunger for revenge drive you forward as it drives me. The Empire lies beyond the horizon, where war and glory await. Let the gods be your spur, so that we might fall swiftly upon the foe. We are the wolves of the north, and our hunger is without end. Onwards on swift limbs, to glory and death.'

SHROUDED BY THE snowstorm, the army continued south. Having been born and raised in the harsh climate of the north, the blizzard conditions were no hindrance to the marauders. With the wind at their backs, they walked and rode on stubbornly, mile after mile. As the day wore on into afternoon, riders returned from ahead, having found a small, ruined town a few miles to the west, with a bridge across the icy water. The army turned and as darkness fell it came to the river and they caught up with the Kurgan tribesmen, who had decided not to cross the river, not wishing to be separated from the main body of the horde.

Sutenvulf led them west, and as they entered the town night was falling. He commanded them to take what rest and shelter they could. Much of the town was little more than burned-out shells hidden in drifts of snow, but some twenty buildings still stood, surrounding a small square. There was much arguing and fighting between the warbands over possession of the precious respite from the storm that these offered, but there was one that none contested, claimed by Suten-vulf as his own. While his followers made what provision they could, his favoured few entered their shelter.

With them were Undar, Hors and Gird. In the dim light from the runestones fused into Jakob, the group could see that they were inside a tavern, the wide room filled with long tables and benches, a counter covered with dust stretching in front of one wall. Bjor-drin and Jakob exchanged glances, and the shaman began to laugh. They took off their packs and pushed them under the tables. As one they turned at a crashing noise from outside.

Wood and stone splintered as Sutenvulf ducked into the doorway, bent nearly double. Wings tightly folded against his back, he heaved himself through the small gap, ripping off the frame with his shoulders. Scattering the broken wood, he stepped forward, still crouched. He then stood, one arm raised above his head, and pushed through the ceiling above, splinters and shards of floor boards dropping around him. Tearing at the storey above, he cleared a space tall enough for him to stand, looking down at his companions through the ragged hole. He turned his head and looked at Jakob.

'Do you know where we are?'

The shaman nodded, still cackling.

'Tungask,' Bjordrin said, pacing around the room. He glanced at the benches and tables and then sat down at one. He chuckled and pointed at the bench opposite. 'I was sitting here, and you were there, when you called my brother a coward. You were Sutenmjar then.'

'Yes, the southern pup. I long thought it was here that my journey began, but I was wrong. It had already started fifteen years earlier, when the witch hunter murdered my family. Before then, since my birth, I have been walking this path, though I did not know it.'

'Your saga has grown long since that day,' said Jakob, sitting himself next to Bjordrin.

There was a hint of sadness in Sutenvulf's face when he next spoke, the fire in his eyes dimmed.

'My wife and son would have been proud.'

He raised his gaze to them and the flickering light within them grew bright again.

'We are close to my revenge. Four days south of here lies the Lynsk, a wide river that can only be crossed by bridge or ford. Our foes lie south of there. They will be waiting for you, you must be bold, but you must also be cunning.'

The daemon prince turned his fiery gaze upon Hors, who had lit a small fire in the grate at the far end of the room. The Norseman picked up a chair and smashed it against the hard flags of the floor. He tossed the wood into the fireplace and crouched down, warming his hands. Noticing the silence that had descended on the room he turned round to see Sutenvulf's burning eyes staring at him. Hors smiled weakly.

'I was listening,' he said. 'We must be cunning, you were saying.'

'You must find the foe, where he will make his stand. Will it be at the river, or on the plains? Is he gathered in one force, or is he divided? Count his warriors and plan. My warriors are brave and seek glory, but I demand more. I demand victory, and that requires patience and thought.'

'You speak as if you won't be there,' said Undar.

'I will leave you briefly but I will return. East of here lies the city of Praag. We passed far west of it, but when the Kislevites realise that we have avoided them, they will follow us. You must guard against attack from behind.'

'Where are you going?' asked Jakob. 'When will you be back?'

'Look for me when the sun is drenched in blood and I will be there. There is something that only I can do, a task that I must perform.'

Sutenvulf leaned forward and seemed to grow. Dread filled the room as he exerted his will.

'The girl is not to be killed. She is mine and mine alone to deal with. Once we have crushed her army and I have dealt with her, we go further south. The lands of the Empire are open and vulnerable to our desires. We shall wage a war upon the misguided fools such has not been seen since the time of your forefathers.'

Nobody replied, awed into silence by the aura of their inhuman master. As Sutenvulf shuffled to the door, they stood and followed. Squeezing himself back outside, the daemon prince opened his wings and leapt into the snow-filled night. Whorls carved in the snowstorm marked his progress as he climbed into the air, and a few moments later, he was gone. Lupine shapes moved in the darkness, and with barely a sound, Sutenvulf's hounds ran into the night after their master.

They returned to the benches, each quiet with his own thoughts for the time being. Hors pulled out his pack and rummaged through it, scattering the contents onto the table in front of him: a golden bracelet shaped like a snake eating its tail, a knife with a hilt carved in the likeness of a naked woman, a small wooden box covered in peeling in gold leaf. Eventually he pulled out a linen-wrapped package and unfolded it, revealing a leg of salted meat. He took a bite and then offered it to the others, who refused with shakes of their heads. Shrugging, Hors continued his meal.

'It's going to be difficult,' Gird said finally.

'What is?' asked Bjordrin.

'Trying to control this army will be like herding seals,' Gird told them. 'Sutenvulf can instil his will upon them, but they won't listen to us, or if they do they'll forget everything as soon as they catch sight of the enemy.'

'Good Norse tactics,' said Undar with a grunt.

'We need to break the army down,' Jakob said in his rattling whisper. 'Undar can command part of the warbands, Hors the other. We will give Kul the Kurgan to command. The beasts, well there's nothing we can do about them.'

'And what good will that do?' asked Gird. 'We don't know where we're going, so why divide our force and risk meeting the enemy without our full numbers?'

'As the master told us, we will find the foe,' Jakob said with a heavy sigh. 'I shall find them. We shall lure them onto a part of our army and then encircle and crush them.'

'You're going to find them?' said Undar. Jakob turned his golden eye towards the disfigured warrior. 'Oh, magic. Of course.'

As THE OTHERS snored in their sleep on the benches below, Jakob climbed the crumbling wooden steps to the first floor. Stepping around the gaping hole caused by Sutenvulf, the shaman made his way between the rooms. Opening a door, he let himself into one of the chambers, the same room where he had lain sleepless, waiting fearfully for the witch hunter to attack.

Things were very different now. Gone was the fear, the doubts, the cowardice. All that he had foreseen had come to pass. Back then, three years ago, he could not have dreamt of the power he now wielded. He had been scared to summon the bloodletters of Khorne, terrified of the possible consequences. Now he could do such a thing without such fears, though it was still not easy.

He pulled himself awkwardly onto the bed and lay on his back, closing his natural eye. Through the other, he watched the drifting currents of magic that played over him, taking pleasure in their random, erratic beauty. With a barely perceptible extension of power, he entered the coma-like state that allowed his spirit to slip from his body.

Tonight he would range far, further than he had spirit-travelled before. He drifted up through the rafters and roof of the tavern into the sky above ruined Tungask. He felt a shiver of excitement as the heavy snow continued to fall, passing through his incorporeal body.

Settling towards the ground Jakob skimmed from building to building, looking at the warriors huddled together, out of the biting wind. He veered away from the knots of dark shifting energies that signified the presence of the other shamans, and allowed himself to be carried on the magical current, floating out towards the bridge.

In one street, he paused for a moment, recognising it. Yes, it was here that he had soaked his runestones in blood and called upon Khorne to send his ferocious warriors across the void to aid him. Their touch lingered on still, after all this time, an after-image of gore and rage. Moving further on, he passed the spot where Kurt had finally achieved his vengeance against Marius van Diesl. Here the Chosen had learned of his true potential, the power that he could carry through himself and bend to his will.

Jakob's spirit accelerated up into the sky, heading southwards. Borne upon the wings of a dream, he raced beneath the dark clouds. It was not long before he had passed in front of the leading edge of the storm, and broke into a crisp, starlit sky. Slowing, Jakob revelled for a moment in the sensation, floating without effort amongst the firmament. He felt as if he could reach out and snatch a star.

Admonishing himself for this flight of fancy he focussed himself on the task at hand. Beneath him, stretching like a silver ribbon, the Urskoy ran to the Kislev coast. In the far distance, many miles to the west, he could see the lights of Erengrad, the port at the mouth of the river. They would want to stay clear of the city as much as possible, and so he turned eastwards, following the course of the river.

On both sides he could see pinpricks of light and swooped lower to investigate. They were campfires, gathered in small groups every few miles. They were the scouts of the southerners, sent ahead to watch for Sutenvulf's host. Here and there were larger concentrations of light, and Jakob saw that each was a larger party guarding a bridge, or where the river widened and became shallow enough to be forded. Further eastwards he travelled, and as he flew, a plan began to form in his mind.

Turning, he directed himself south again, seeking the army itself. It was not long until he spied the glow against the dark ground that spread across the earth. He was momentarily taken aback by the size of the army. Row after row after row of tents dotted the ground, stretching for over a mile in each direction.

Getting lower and lower, Jakob looked for other information that would be useful. At the centre of one square of tents was a wider open space and he moved towards it. He paused and hovered in the air above it. There sat six mighty cannons, wagons full of barrels and shot around them. They were larger than any gun Jakob had seen during his time in the Empire, and he realised that they would be able to hurl their shot a considerable distance. There was more than enough ammunition for them to sustain a constant barrage of fire.

Adding this to his thoughts, Jakob allowed himself to be buoyed upwards on the magical winds. The camp grew smaller beneath him until he could see it laid out like a map. A bright, painful glow to his right attracted his attention. He ventured as close as he could, which was not so very close he realised, before the burning in his golden eye was almost unbearable. It was the Sigmarite bitch, Ursula, he realised. It seemed as if Kurt was not the only one who wielded the power of the gods now, though her patron was weak compared to the mighty gods of the north.

Retreating from the stench of pure faith, Jakob turned to head north again, his mission complete. From his vantage point high above the ground, he could see the first rays of the sun creeping above the mountains in the east and knew that he had to return to his body soon. Just as he was about to speed away, something else caught his attention.

Amongst the swirling patterns of magic, the breath of the gods was carved into dreams and nightmares by the mortals below. There was one spot though where the waving currents became straight lines. He had not seen its like before, and Jakob was intrigued. He ghosted closer, following the lines of power, and as he drifted into them, he saw that the shifting energies were split, fragmented into ethereal ribbons of different hues.

He saw that the artificial lines were in fact radiating out from one point, like the spokes of a wheel. They coalesced into a single mass inside one of the tents, and Jakob flew forward to investigate.

The tent itself seemed no different to any of the others. Perhaps it was some magical artefact, he thought, allowing his spirit to pass through the fabric of the shelter. Inside a man sat in the middle of the tent on a rug, his legs crossed. In his lap he had a book open and he was whispering to himself. Jakob drifted lower until he was hovering just above the man's shoulder, and looked at the open page. The writing was meaningless to the illiterate shaman, but the diagrams of circles and angles looked familiar, like stylised versions of Norse runes.

The man hesitated in his incantation and stopped. He looked around the tent with a frown of confusion creasing his forehead, and as the man's face turned towards Jakob his eyes widened in surprise. Jakob realised that the man could see him, that he had the othersight.

Panic stabbed at the shaman's heart and in that moment of shock, he lost all control of the sorcerous powers sustaining his spirit so far from his body. In an instant the spell was shattered and the tug of his mortal flesh gripped him again. In a heartbeat he was back in his body, wracked with agony, screaming in pain and terror. Blood bubbled from around his runestones, his flesh burning and smoking at their touch.

There were heavy footsteps on the boards as Jakob rolled off the bed, clutching himself with his good arm, spitting with the pain that infused his being. Bjordrin rushed through the door and found Jakob on his knees. The shaman looked up at him, magical sparks dancing across the golden sphere of his magical eye.

'Get out!' Jakob snarled, motes of dark energy flaring from his mouth. Bjordrin needed no further prompting and fled the room.

* * *

THE SUN WAS close to dusk by the time Jakob recovered from his ordeal. During the day he had drifted in and out of the spirit world, his soul entangled between body and the winds of magic by a torn web of power.

Bjordrin and the others had sat in the bar room of the tavern, shuddering and exchanging worried glances as they listened to his hoarse screams and ago-nised ravings in the room above. Just after noon, Gird had ventured upstairs, but had stopped in the door-way of the room, horrified. Jakob had been splayed across the floor, his runestones pulsing with a sickly light. There were other presences in the room, half-seen, half-heard shadow creatures that flitted around the crippled shaman. One of them had brushed against Gird and its chill touch numbed his arm. He had retreated quickly, and had sat silently by the fire, refusing to reveal what he had witnessed, speaking only to warn the others not to repeat his folly.

Not long before dusk Jakob had fallen silent. It was Undar this time that braved the first floor, pulling his bulk along the narrow passageway to the bedchamber and peering inside. Jakob was lying on the floor still, but was calm, his chest rising and falling slowly. As Undar turned to move away, a floorboard creaked loudly and the shaman's eye fluttered open.

'Wait,' Jakob croaked, and Undar looked back. 'Help me up.'

Hesitantly, the gigantic warrior pushed through the doorway and stood beside Jakob. He waited for a moment, but as the shaman extended a withered hand, he instinctively grabbed hold of it and pulled Jakob to his feet. His touch was icy cold.

'You should rest,' Undar said as Jakob limped past him towards the door.

'No, no time,' the shaman replied with a shake of his head. 'Come with me, we have to prepare.'

Undar followed Jakob back along the landing and down the stairs. Hors rose from his seat and offered the shaman an arm to steady himself, but Jakob waved him away irritably.

'Do something useful,' he snarled, causing the Norseman to flinch. 'Go and fetch Andar Kul, he must be told what to do.'

Hors hesitated until the shaman hissed at him, baring his fangs. Glad to be away from Jakob's disturbing presence, he walked quickly out of the tavern. Jakob watched him leave and then turned to Gird.

'Fetch me water,' the shaman said, sitting down at one end of a long bench near to the fireplace.

Bjordrin sat opposite Jakob as Gird shuffled away. The glow from his runestones glittered over Bjordrin's metallic skin, dappling it with pools of yellow and green.

'What did you see?' Bjordrin asked.

'We will wait for Kul,' the shaman replied. 'I don't want to explain this twice.'

Gird returned with a waterskin clasped in his clawed hands, and passed it to Jakob. Unstoppering it with his teeth, the shaman upended the skin over his face, letting the cool water splash over him. It ran in rivulets down his gnarled skin and soaked into his dirty furs. With a snort, Jakob cleared his nose and tossed the empty waterskin onto the table before wiping his hand across his face.

'That's much better,' he said and he leaned forward, resting his arms on the table, the fused mess of his hand and staff held out in front of him. 'For a long while I didn't think I would make it back.'

'What went wrong?' Gird asked, seating himself awkwardly at the far end of the bench from Jakob.

'I was caught unawares,' Jakob admitted, shaking his head. 'I will not make the same mistake again.'

'Caught by what?' Bjordrin pressed for a fuller answer.

'There is one among them who has the sight,' Jakob told them, looking impatiently towards the tavern door. 'He has little power, but he can feel the breath of the gods. He untwined them with his spells, like a man who would use teased-out threads instead of rope. He is no threat.'

'Well, he seemed to have given you a fright,' said Gird, whose grin faded as the shaman turned an acidic stare in his direction.

The door banged open and Kul strode in, the stocky warlord advancing with a bow-legged gait gained from a life in the saddle.

'You asked for me?' he said, glaring at Jakob with narrow eyes.

'I sent for you,' Jakob replied, gesturing with a nod of his head for the Kurgan warrior to sit down. 'Listen carefully, I have instructions for you all.'

CHAPTER SEVEN
The Trap
Kislev, Early autumn 1712

'IT IS CERTAINLY not natural, my lord,' Magnus said as he stood next to Vapold watching the storm clouds skidding towards the encampment from the north.

'Really?' the count replied sarcastically.

'They are using the weather to shield their movements from our scouts, my lord,' the astrologer added.

'I thought you were paid to tell me things I did not already know,' said the count, shaking his head.

His mood had been foul ever since riders had come back to the camp during the night, bringing news of the blizzard bearing down across the Urskoy. They had lost sight of a large force of marauders heading east, probably towards the ford at Eskivaya some ten miles further along the river. To make matters worse, Ungol tribesmen, the horse archers of the Tsar, had reported a growing number of enemy horsemen moving westwards towards Erengrad. There were two crossings available to them between Vapold and the walled port, the bridges at Mursk and another ford at Gobri Danesk. Three places where the enemy could come at him, across a forty mile expanse.

Vapold knew he could not defend them all unless he split his forces, and to do that risked one part of his army meeting a much more numerous foe. The accursed blizzard the northerners had summoned to their aid made matters even worse, making it almost impossible to find the foe unless a scout almost literally ran into them.

Captain Felsturm was with them, a sheaf of papers in his hand. He scowled heavily at the dark clouds.

'Well, we can be pleased about one thing,' the captain said. 'Our Kislevite friends have done an admirable job keeping those damned Kurgan horsemen on the far side of the river. They're as blind to our position as we are.'

Felsturm's words sent a tremor of nervousness through Magnus as he recalled the apparition that had confronted him two nights before. The awful visage was etched on his mind, the fanged maw and glowing golden eye staring at him within arm's reach. He shuddered at the recollection.

Magnus alone knew the falsehood of Felsturm's words. The enemy knew exactly where they were, through arcane means. He had no way of warning the count though. He couldn't simply tell him that he had the ghostsight, could he? The lessons of his old master had been well learned and he was not about to betray his secret to these ignorant men.

But the knowledge burned at Magnus's thoughts like a hot iron. The enemy were trying to lead them around by the nose, and there was nothing he could do to stop them. Could he really let the count take his army into a trap to be annihilated? If only he knew what the enemy's true intentions were, he might somehow advise the count against making the wrong move, perhaps guide his decisions in the right direction.

'Did you hear me, Magnus?' Vapold's voice cut through Magnus's cogitation.

'I am sorry, my lord, I was lost in thought,' Magnus admitted. 'You were saying?'

'I asked if you would kindly send word for my council to be gathered at my pavilion within the hour,' the count said impatiently. 'We have to decide on what course of action to take.'

'Of course, my lord,' said Magnus with a bow of his head. 'I will attend to it immediately.'

As he walked back through the mud of the camp towards the tents and pavilions of the nobles, Magnus wracked his brain for an answer to his dilemma. Should he risk everything and admit what he knew? Did his loyalty to the count really run that deep? Or perhaps there was another person he could confide in, with more surety of secrecy. Ursula? He dismissed the idea as soon as it had occurred to him. Religious fanatics were the worst of them all, he told himself. Was it not the Grand Theogonist himself who sent his templars across the land, hunting and burning those who had the same extraordinary gifts as Magnus?

One by one he crossed names off a mental list as
being either too ignorant or too prejudiced for his
trust. So caught up in his own thoughts was Magnus,
he almost walked into a company of gunners marching between the tents. Quickly moving aside, he
tripped over a discarded barrel stave lying in the mud
and sprawled face first in the dirt. He could hear the
laughs of the soldiers behind him as he pushed himself to his knees, quickly silenced by the irate shouting
of their captain.

Someone loomed over him and crouched down,
offering him a gauntleted hand. At first he took it to be
a gauntlet, but then realised that it was not a glove at
all. Looking up he saw Ruprecht.

'Can I help?' he asked.

Magnus pushed himself to his feet, ineffectually
swiping at the mud on his robes.

'Thank you, but no,' Magnus replied turning away.
He then stopped and turned back. 'Actually, perhaps
you can.'

RUPRECHT ACCOMPANIED THE astrologer back to his tent
and followed him inside. Magnus had been silent
since asking if he had a little time to spare, and he did
not speak as he signalled for Ruprecht to take a seat.
He watched as the count's advisor rummaged in the
pile of scrolls and books beside his cot. Magnus
turned and without meeting Ruprecht's gaze, tossed a
slim volume into his lap. Ruprecht picked it up and
looked at it. The cover was vellum, unadorned with
any title. He opened it to the first page and read. It was
handwritten in small, neat letters, with alchemical and

mystical symbols penned along the edge. Not quite believing the evidence of his own eyes, he read it again.

'A spellbook?' he said, almost choking as he looked up at Magnus, eyes wide with surprise.

'My grimoire,' Magnus corrected him. 'Penned by my own hand from years of hard study.'

Ruprecht said nothing, shocked by Magnus's brazen revelation. He knew he shouldn't have been surprised, after all he had harboured suspicions about the man for several months now. But this admission of guilt was the last thing Ruprecht had expected.

'I need you to help me,' Magnus said, and Ruprecht realised that he could be even more surprised.

'You need my help?' he said slowly, eyes narrowing. 'I am sure you know about my past, and you are asking me for help?'

'It is precisely because of what you used to do that I am appealing to you,' Magnus said earnestly, stepping forward. Ruprecht stood up and backed away. 'You are the only man amongst these thousands who might perhaps understand what I have to tell you.'

'You're a warlock,' Ruprecht said flatly, as if finally stating it would make it seem more real. It didn't.

'I prefer the word seer,' Magnus said. 'Warlock is such a pejorative term, like witch, or sorcerer, or enchanter.'

'I knew a seer,' Ruprecht said shaking his head. 'Every month he was visited by priests, who prayed for him, and he wore protective holy icons to ward away evil influences. It didn't help, he was still possessed by a daemon in the end and tried to attack us. You are no seer.'

'A name does not change what I am,' Magnus said. 'It also does not change what I know. Listen to what I have to say. After that, I trust to your mercy and good judgement.'

'Mercy is something I have become short of lately,' warned Ruprecht. There was something sincere about Magnus's words, and his earnest admission of guilt had piqued Ruprecht's curiosity. He nodded. 'I make no promises though.'

'And I expect none,' Magnus replied. 'We do not have much time, the count will be devising his next stage of the campaign within the hour and we must act quickly. I need your help to cast an enchantment.'

Ruprecht spluttered and laughed loudly.

'Just when I thought this couldn't get any stranger,' he said.

'I cannot do this without you,' Magnus said, ignoring Ruprecht's reaction. 'And if I cannot do this, the army may be doomed.'

Ruprecht stopped laughing and stared at the warlock. He seemed serious. Magnus continued before he could say anything in reply.

'You have seen the sorcery that the northmen have unleashed,' he said. 'They have other magic at their disposal. Two nights ago I witnessed something terrible, a haggard apparition loitering in this very tent.'

Ruprecht cast his eyes around uneasily.

'An apparition?' he said.

'It was the spirit of one of the shamans,' Magnus replied. 'It was not of corporeal form, but created from the magic that surrounds us all. It was a spy, one of their foul shamans, watching our every move. They know exactly where we are, and what we are doing. The northmen are guiding us skilfully into a trap of their own devising.'

'How can you be sure of this?' asked Ruprecht. 'Those who dabble in the black arts are often plagued by supernatural occurrences. What makes this anything more significant?'

'I saw him again last night,' Magnus said, starting to pacing towards the bed and then turning and walking back again, head bowed in thought, 'Though he was very far away, I could feel his presence. I will never forget the disturbing sensation that rippled through me that first time.'

'And with that knowledge, they can anticipate what we are going to do next,' Ruprecht said, leaning forward with one elbow on his knee, his chin rested on his fist. 'Assuming I believe you, and don't turn you in out of hand, what do you expect of me? Why should I risk my soul dabbling in sorcery with you?'

'Because if we are successful, we might destroy this foe in one mighty battle,' Magnus said, his eyes gleaming with the thought. 'I am not an evil man, Ruprecht, you must believe me. Why else would I come to you, unless I wanted to avert the disaster that we are even now being lured into?'

'But I don't understand why you did come to me,' Ruprecht said, leaning back in the chair. He dropped the grimoire onto the rug beneath the chair and stood up. 'I know nothing of magic.'

'Your experiences with the witch hunter are unique, Ruprecht,' Magnus said. 'Surely he taught you prayers of protection, litanies of warding? The templars call

them blessings, granted by the gods, but prayers and
magic are not so dissimilar. Believe me, I have witnessed that very much lately. You learned some of the
secret symbols of my art, the better to notice them, did
you not?'

Ruprecht did not reply, afraid to admit the truth of
the warlock's words.

'There is one other thing, the most important of all,'
Magnus continued. 'Your experiences have hardened
you to the lure of the art, the deceptions it can weave
upon you. I trained for years with my old master to
harness the powers I was born with, but all men can
shape the energies that flow across the world, if they
but knew how and dedicated themselves to its practice. But it takes character, and strength of will, and
you have both in abundance. You will be in little danger, but your very loathing of magic will protect you
against even the small threat there is.'

'And you will submit yourself to my mercy when we
are done?' Ruprecht asked.

'I will,' said Magnus, stooping to retrieve the grimoire from the ground. 'Later, after the count's
council of war, we should meet again.'

'And this spell will stop the eyes of the enemy seeing
our every move?' Ruprecht sought more assurance,
still amazed at himself for having listened as long as
he had.

'Better than that,' Magnus replied with a cruel smile.
'Much better than that.'

MAGNUS SAT HALFWAY along the table set at the centre
of the count's pavilion, flanked by two scribes with

piles of parchment, ready to write the orders that were to be issued to the troops. To his left, at the end of the table, Count Vapold sat studying a cloth map, Lord Bayard to the count's right leaning over and running his finger along some feature shown on the chart. On the count's other side sat Ursula, her head bowed in thought, or perhaps in prayer. At the other end of the table, his mud-spattered riding cloak flung untidily over the back of his chair, sat Commander Iversson, recently arrived with messages from Count Steinhardt who waited with his army some fifteen miles to the east. Captain Felsturm sat next to the Ostermarker, flicking through the reports and letters the emissary had brought with him. Various other knights and officers of the army sat around the rest of the table, amongst them Felix Lothar, son of Bayard's predecessor who had been slain in the fighting in Bechafen when Steinhardt had claimed rulership of the Ostermark.

It had been a close-run thing, but after his meeting with Ruprecht, Magnus had scurried madly about the camp, sending messengers to assemble everyone who needed to be at the council of war. Only Boyar Streltzyn, leader of the winged lancers, had not arrived yet.

'We can't wait any more,' said Vapold, the conversations that had been buzzing around the table stopping quickly at the sound of his voice. 'We'll start without Streltzyn and if he deigns to turn up, he'll have to get up to speed on his own.'

Vapold stood and looked down the length of the table. The walls of the pavilion flapped noisily in the growing wind as the snowstorm unleashed by the northmen came ever closer. Vapold leaned forward onto the table.

'The enemy is close,' he began. 'They have been seen within thirty miles of the Urskoy, and I expect battle to be joined tomorrow, or the day after. They have displayed an unusual level of co-ordination and co-operation thus far, but it would be a false hope to assume that they will revert to their normal barbaric ways at this late stage. Their leader does not think like them; he was once one of our own.'

Vapold glanced at Bayard at this point and the knight's expression was dark.

'We cannot expect this horde to simply run at our guns,' Bayard picked up the thread of the count's words. 'The man who leads them was from the Empire, and fought in our armies. He knows the way we wage war, and we can expect him to have spent much time devising a strategy to outthink us. In this respect, we must do something unexpected, something unorthodox. This coming battle, or battles as it may turn out, might well be unlike anything you have encountered before.'

Bayard stopped and sternly regarded the other men around the table.

'We cannot afford to be dogmatic,' he warned. 'The plan we devise here must take the enemy by surprise, create a weakness that we can exploit, and then we must do so with ruthless aggression. We can afford no mistakes, for our foe is the very worst spawn of the world, a barbaric horde that will, if we fail, bring ruin and death to the lands we now stand guard before.

Your men must know this. You must assure them that whatever they face, whatever the horrors that confront them, they must stand against the enemy at all costs. We cannot have pity or mercy, for these savages will allow none for us.'

Vapold paused before speaking, to allow the lord's words to sink in, though he knew that every man at the table, and each and every soldier out in the camp were very aware of what was at stake. He cleared his throat and took a sip of wine to compose his thoughts.

'Now is not the time to question the wisdom of our strategy,' the count said. 'All doubts must be put aside. The questions of whether we should have stayed and defended our homes rather than march to meet the enemy in open battle must be put aside. It is this stand, this positive response, that has granted us the opportunity to crush this hideous foe before our home and loved ones are in danger.'

'We understand,' said Commander Iversson. 'Perhaps we should move on to the business of how we might achieve this crushing victory? My count awaits your recommendations.'

'Then let us begin in earnest,' said Vapold, sitting down. 'Captain Felsturm?'

The Ostland officer stacked the papers he was holding in a neat pile and stroked a finger down across his moustache, gathering his thoughts. He nodded to one of his subordinates who stood and walked around the table handing out a crudely drawn map to each of the council members. Magnus glanced at his, noting that it covered only the most basic features and terrain within a few miles of each bank of the Urskoy.

'We know that the enemy have divided into two forces,' he told them. 'A large number of cavalry have been sighted heading to the west, possibly to take the ford at Gobri Danesk or to cross the Urskoy at Mursk. Gobri Danesk is too far from our current position, but does lie within twenty miles of Erengrad. It is not beyond the realms of hope that our Kislevite comrades can guard the crossing against attack, and so we should discount it from our plans. This leaves us with a possible attack at Mursk.'

Felsturm stopped and took the top leaf from his pile of notes and set it to one side before continuing.

'We have another confirmed sighting of the horde far to our east, but heading west towards our position,' he told them. 'It would be reasonable to believe that they intend to ford the river at Eskivaya, thus having a force both to our right and our left.'

'So if we move as one force to intercept either, we run the risk of the other either slipping by without a fight, or turning our flank,' said Iversson.

'That is correct,' Felsturm said, removing the next page of notes and placing it on the first. 'However, there is no reason to believe that the enemy are aware of Count Steinhardt's forces at Getzholm.'

'So one of us holds Mursk and the other Eskivaya?' suggested Iversson. 'They are less than twenty miles apart, half a day's hard marching. Our force would be more than capable of holding up these thugs at Eskivaya until you arrive to wipe them out.'

'And what if they do not cross at Eskivaya, but instead continue onwards to Mursk?' asked Bayard. 'That is ten miles to the west, twenty-five from Eskivaya. To defend the town, we would have to split this army, leaving some in reserve to reinforce either crossing depending on where the enemy attack fell.'

'If they're coming from the east, they'll have to march right past us,' said Iversson. 'We could cross and follow them.'

Vapold gave a snort and stood. He walked down the length of the table to the door flaps of the pavilion. He untied the laces and opened one of the flaps, the cold wind gusting through the opening, scattering the papers on the table. Felsturm shook his head angrily as he tried to retrieve his windswept notes. Outside, a thin layer of snow was beginning to form, more flakes drifting down quickly. Vapold let the flap fall back and Felsturm gave a nod to one of his men sat next to Bayard to go and re-tie the straps.

'Why do you think this gods-cursed storm is upon us?' Vapold asked as he stalked back to his chair. 'With the coming blizzard to shield them, they could very well march straight past you and you'd not notice a damn thing.'

The man at the door gave a shout of surprise as a figure appeared outside and barged in, knocking him aside. Another gust of wind accompanied the man's entrance, scattering Felsturm's notes once more. The captain shot a pleading look to the heavens.

Boyar Streltzyn was a short, wiry man, much like most Kislevites, but was marked by a jagged scar that ran the length of the right side of his face. His right eye was milky white, blinded by the injury, though he didn't wear an eye patch to cover the disfigurement, instead displaying the scar as proudly as a medal.

'I sorry for my lateness,' the boyar said with a perfunctory bow towards the count.

He took off his horsehair-plumed helmet and strode to the empty chair that had been vacated by the officer. Dropping the helmet onto the table he sat down and brought up his muddied riding boots beside it, rocking the chair onto its back legs.

'I have important news,' he said, crossing his arms. 'I late because I speak to the men who bring it directly.'

They waited for the lancer commander to continue, but nothing more was forthcoming. He leaned forward and picked up the half full goblet of wine from in front of Lord Bayard.

'Would you like to share it with us?' Bayard suggested with a frown.

Streltzyn took a long draught of wine and placed it back on the table with a wide grin, revealing his uneven, yellowing teeth.

'The glorious lancers and horse archers of the Tsar of Kislev have engaged the enemy,' he declared with a laugh. 'And were victorious! Even now, our brave cavalry are pursuing the Kurgan scum back to the north, driving them from the regions of Erengrad.'

Bayard sat in stunned silence, while Vapold joined the boyar's laughter, slapping the table.

'The west is secure?' Felsturm asked, and the boyar took his feet of the table and the chair fell forward. Leaning across the table, Streltzyn nodded, still grinning. Felsturm took two pages of his notes and neatly tore them in half, letting the pieces flutter to the floor.

'Perhaps we should devise a new plan,' the captain suggested.

THE SUMMER DAYS were not so long here in Kislev, and the snow clouds obscured the light of the dying sun. The storm had begun to slow, though the snow was still constant, the winds were dying down and the flurries of ice came less often. The campfires hissed and steamed, fighting against the snow. Magnus navigated his way through the maze of guy ropes by their flickering light, fervently hoping that he had not been delayed too long by the interminable council of war. As soon as Vapold had dismissed him, Magnus had sent one of the count's servants to Ruprecht, asking him to come to his tent.

As he walked, Magnus began to visualise the spell he would need to cast. It was something he had never attempted before, but was a variation on well-practiced skills and he was confident of success. Ruprecht would have to play his part well, but he had only to play it for a short time.

Clambering through the flap of his tent, Magnus fumbled in the darkness for the tinderbox and flints he kept close to the opening, and after several unsuccessful attempts managed to strike a spark into the oil lamp. Placing the bubbled glass of the cover over the burning wick, he picked up the lantern and carried it to the table beside his cot.

From under his pillow, he pulled forth his small grimoire and the leaf of parchment onto which he had earlier copied the incantation for Ruprecht. From beneath the bed he produced a small box, and opening the lid took out a small phial of gold-flecked liquid. Dragon's tears it was called, though he knew it was nothing quite so mythic, but rather an alchemical solution that any scholar with the knowledge and patience could create in an alembic over a hot fire.

Magnus pulled off his snow-moistened robe and stained boots and lay down on the bed, naked except for his undergarments. He pulled the stopper from the phial, revealing a thin nail imbedded in its bottom. Tipping the bottle slightly, he dipped the nail into the dragon's tears and with smooth, swift strokes, scratched a pattern of triangles and five-pointed stars into the skin of his chest. He had not finished when he heard someone outside. Turning his head, he saw Ruprecht ducking into the tent. He stopped halfway in, eying Magnus with suspicion.

'Come in and shut out that damnable cold air,' Magnus said.

Ruprecht hesitated for a moment and then complied, pulling tight the drawstrings on the tent flaps and knotting it securely. Magnus nodded to the parchment on the table beside him.

'Read that, and tell me if there is anything you cannot decipher,' Magnus told Ruprecht.

'I'm not reading anything until you tell me what it is,' he replied.

'It's a spell of warding,' said Magnus, finishing with the dragon's tears and pushing the stopper back into the phial. 'It's not couched in any religious nonsense, so it's a bit more potent, but it's nothing that you haven't done before, I assure you.'

Ruprecht's doubt showed on his face, but he stepped forward and lifted the parchment, scanning down the few lines.

'It's meaningless,' he said. 'It's just random syllables.'

'It's not random at all,' snapped Magnus. 'That's the art in written form. Read it out for me so I can check your pronunciation.'

Ruprecht had the look of a man fighting with his conscience, or rather a boy who knew that he was about to do something forbidden, but was now too afraid to back down.

'Ak'sha, falara, ten'she,' Ruprecht intoned slowly, 'Amial, phantos, ak'sha, falara, ten'she, adon.'

'That should be amila,' said Magnus with a frown.

Ruprecht looked at the parchment again.

'My mistake,' he said. 'Your handwriting is very small, you know. Amila.'

'Yes, amila,' said Magnus, with a sudden sense of regret. Perhaps this was not the most intelligent course of action after all.

'And why do you need an enchantment of protection?' Ruprecht said, sitting down in the chair beside the bed.

'The shaman will return tonight,' Magnus explained. 'I need to confront him to weave my own hex. Your spell will protect me from his powers, for long enough at least.'

'So what else do I need to do?' Ruprecht asked, more comfortable than before.

'Just keep up the incantation, a bit faster than before, but not too quickly,' Magnus told him.

'How about this?' Ruprecht said, holding up the parchment again. 'Ak'sha falara, ten'she amila, phantos Ak'sha, falara ten'she, adon.'

'Yes, that was pretty much perfect,' Magnus said, laying his hands on his protruding belly.

'The same cadence as a prayer of warding,' Ruprecht replied. 'Just like you said it was.'

'You begin,' said Magnus.

'When do I stop?' asked Ruprecht.

'It'll be very obvious, I suspect,' Magnus said, closing his eyes. 'Start now.'

Magnus allowed Ruprecht's deep voice to soothe him, listening to the rhythm of his chanting. Feeling relaxed, he began to murmur his own spell, whispering it, his lips barely moving.

The warlock felt the same jolt he always did when his soul made the transition from his body during a ghostwalk. He pushed himself upward, glancing back just before he left the tent. Ruprecht was still chanting, looking intently at Magnus's inert form.

Magnus allowed himself to float upwards. Spinning gently, he looked across the skies, seeking his foe. Magnus allowed himself a smile as he spied the tortured, tangled knot of seething power that betrayed his adversary's location. He rose upwards towards it, gaining speed.

The shaman turned towards him, surrounded by a black cloud of magic, his golden eye blazing brightly. The Chaos sorcerer allowed Magnus to come closer, and he could see a twisted smile on the other spellcaster's face. Magnus brought himself to a halt not far from the shaman, and floated with his arms crossed.

'So you know some tricks,' the shaman said, in a language that was not translated into words, but was pure thought.

'Some,' Magnus replied.

'And what do you hope to do?' sneered the shaman. 'You are pitifully weak, I could crush you without effort.'

'Perhaps,' conceded Magnus. 'Perhaps not.'

'You doubt I have the power?' the shaman said angrily. 'Perhaps you are not as clever as I thought.'

'It is not always about power,' Magnus said, smiling.

'It's always about power,' the shaman spat back, baring his fangs. The was an inrushing of energy towards the sorcerer, and immense gathering of mystical force.

This was what Magnus had hoped for. He had been slow in realising it, but listening to the stories of how the northmen could hurls bolts of devastating energy, Ursula's accounts of plague being spread upon the winds and Ruprecht's tales of devastating earthquakes brought about by the dread Chaos worshippers had helped Magnus understand the source of their power.

He could never hope to match the full ferocity of the raw energy they could channel. But the shamans were crude and inefficient compared to the delicate art that Magnus had been taught by his old master. They had no subtlety, and it was this that he was about to use.

Unleashing his fury, the shaman thrust an ethereal hand out towards Magnus and a dark stream of energy erupted from his clawed fingertips. As the sorcerous bolt struck Magnus it encountered the ward provided by Ruprecht far below them, and a bright blue light engulfed both of them.

The protection would last only a matter of heart-beats, but it gave Magnus the time he needed. In that moment of connection as Magnus's soul was joined to the shaman's by the dark lighting, he unleashed the hex he had been preparing. It was small, unnoticed amongst the surging energy of the shaman's assault, gliding instantly along the merest thread of magic into Magnus's opponent. It was almost nothing, just a thought, an image, that Magnus had been preparing in his mind all the while he had sat and listened to the deliberations of the war council.

The protective shield melted away almost instantly and the dark flames of the shaman's attack engulfed Magnus. His soul searing with unholy pain, Magnus plummeted back towards his body.

RUPRECHT FALTERED IN his chant as he saw smoke begin to rise from Magnus's body. The spell wasn't working, he realised. Panicked, he began again, but it was too late: already the warlock's skin was beginning to blister and split. The stench of charring flesh filled Ruprecht's nostrils and he gagged.

Magnus's eyes fluttered open and he cried out hoarsely. Ruprecht leaned over him, and Magnus flopped a burnt arm around his shoulders. Tears of pain rolled down the warlock's seared cheeks. His cracked lips turned into a smile.

'It worked?' asked Ruprecht and Magnus nodded, wincing with the effort. He pulled Ruprecht closer.

'The pain is harsh, but I will survive,' he whispered.

'I know,' said Ruprecht.

'Now I am at your mercy,' croaked Magnus. 'You have fulfilled your end of the bargain.'

'Yes I have,' Ruprecht answered quietly. 'I will tell no one of what has happened tonight.'

Magnus laughed, a cracked, tortured sound.

'I knew that I could trust you,' he said. 'But in any case you have no other option. Your involvement implicates you. You have willingly participated in the conjuration of magic, for which there can be no excuse. You would be signing your own death warrant.'

'Your secret dies with me,' said Ruprecht with a smile.

He pulled Magnus's arm from his shoulder and sat up. Slowly, almost gently, Ruprecht placed a meaty hand across the smouldering face of the warlock. Magnus tried to struggle, but in his weakened state he was no match for the heavy warrior. Ruprecht kept his grip over Magnus's nose and mouth for several minutes, long after he had ceased struggling. Standing, he folded the dead man's arms over his chest and then wiped the smear of blood and charred skin from his palms on the blanket. He picked up the oil lantern as he stepped away, tossing the glass case to the floor. With his free hand he pulled the slipknot he had tied earlier, and darted a glance into the darkness. There was no one to see him.

Ducking out of the tent, Ruprecht tossed the lamp onto the rug, spilling boiling oil everywhere. As Ruprecht hurried away into the night, the fire took hold, engulfing the tent in a small inferno.

'And my secret dies with you,' he muttered to himself as shouts of alarm began to echo across the camp.

CHAPTER EIGHT
Battle Joined
Mursk, Early autumn 1712

JAKOB WAS FEELING pleased with himself. Everything was unfolding as he had planned, and when Sutenvulf returned the southerners would be trapped like rabbits in a snare. The storm was dissipating quickly now, its fury spent, but it no longer mattered, it had served its purpose well.

He had loitered above the camp of the Empire soldiers until daybreak, to be sure that they had fallen for his ploy. As he had guessed they would, they had marched to the ford, believing that their Kislevite allies had secured the west and thinking that Sutenvulf's marauders were crossing at the ford.

Sutenvulf's forces were even now closing for the kill on the Empire army at Eskivaya, and Mursk would not hold for longer against the nine thousand battle-hungry warriors under the command of Hors Skalding. From here, joined from the west by Kul's horsemen, they would sweep along the Urskoy and attack the army waylaid by Undar's three thousand men and beasts.

Yes, today was indeed going to be a fine day.

KIRIS KUL BID farewell to his father and turned his horse around. The snows were definitely thinning and he wanted to get as far north as possible before the stupid Kislevites realised their mistake. As his father led the three thousand horsemen still under his command to the east, to turn south again later, Kiris joined the two hundred riders that had been given to him to lead. With a shout, he set them riding north. Moving at a trot, the Kurgan tribesmen wove their horses in and around each other, their hooves kicking up swathes of snow that heaped upon each other, leaving obvious tracks that could be followed, but would not give away their numbers. It was a tactic the Kul had employed often when travelling across the steppes in a rival's territory, but normally to hide their strength rather than mask their lack of numbers.

They stopped at irregular intervals and rode in circles, marking time until they again saw the dark silhouettes of the pursuing Kislevites in the distance, obscured by the lightening snow. Kiris would wait just long enough to ensure that the troops following them could see them, giving his foes the hope that they might yet catch their elusive prey. He would then order the march to begin again, quickly moving out of sight so that the enemy would never see their true numbers.

It was not as glorious as the battle that his father was riding towards, but Kiris had felt honoured when his father had entrusted him with this important task. The snow was no longer so heavy that it made riding unpleasant, and Kiris was enjoying his game of wolf and hare with the lancers that trailed him.

He made a wager with Entai, his cousin, that he could keep the Kislevites following for two whole days.

DRUMBEATS FILLED THE air as the warriors of Hors Skalding marched upon Mursk. Holding aloft standards of skulls and bones, banners daubed with runes and symbols of their Dark Gods flapping the breeze, the northmen surged across the snowy plains in a tide of fury.

Amongst them larger shapes moved, the hunched and tortured shapes of the Gifted. Dwarfing even these were three monstrous beasts at the forefront of the host, their lower portions four-legged and heavily scaled like a reptile, their more humanoid upper bodies broad and muscular. These were the dragon ogres that had ventured down from the mountain tops to investigate the large army that disturbed their slumber and had decided to join the war.

Horned and furred figures were spread in loose groups amongst the tribesmen. From the mountains and the forests, the beastmen had come forth, feeling the breath of the gods strong in the air, answering the call of their divine masters. They barked and brayed constantly to one another, squabbling amongst themselves, even more unruly than the marauders.

At the centre of the army marched the toughest of the fighters, heavily armoured warriors and champions of the gods who had learned the art of war battling constantly against each other in the Northern Wastes. Amongst them, Jakob was mounted on a sturdy steppe horse, riding alongside Hors. The Norse warlord was in high spirits, joking with his companions and boasting about how much loot he would take from the Kislevite town.

Mursk itself could be seen in the distance, straddling the glittering waters of the Urskoy. It was surrounded by a high wall of thick wooden stakes, and beyond, the roofs of the houses could be seen, interspersed with the occasional golden dome of a temple.

'Look, more gold for the Skaldings,' said Hors with a laugh, pointing towards the minarets glimmering in the sunlight that was now breaking through gaps in the thinning cloud.

'And how do you suppose to loot a temple dome?' asked Jakob, sharing the Norseman's enthusiasm. 'Will you carry it away on your back?'

'If I have to,' Hors replied. 'I'll find a way, I always do.'

'Do you think they'll surrender?' asked one of the other warriors in the group, a tall, blond-haired man with a plaited beard.

'I hope so,' Hors said, clapping his hands and rubbing them together. 'My wives are complaining that their slaves are too lazy, and I need some new ones.'

'More slaves or more wives?' Jakob said.

'Both!' said Hors with a wink.

'Kislevites don't surrender,' another of the warriors remarked. 'They're stubborn bastards, usually have to kill every last one of them.'

'They don't surrender, but I wouldn't be surprised if they're already heading south,' Hors said. 'Look at this fine army!

The drumbeats were joined by discordant, blaring horns as the warbands announced themselves to the enemy in the town, now less than half a mile away. Figures could be made out on the wall, gathering in groups to look at the approaching horde.

Battle cries were shouted out over the clamour, and chants of praise to the gods could be heard. Some of the warbands clattered their weapons on their shields, trying to discomfort the foe with the rhythmic beating.

A bell could be heard tolling in the distance, resounding out over the walls of Mursk, warning of the nearness of the foe. To Hors it sounded like sweet music, a ringing declaration of the defenders' fears. Many times over the years he had heard similar alarms as his longship had glided along the coast of the Empire. To his ears, it was the sound of victory.

NEAR THE FRONT of the army, Vlamdir walked alongside Orst, who growled and snorted in anticipation. Vlamdir's own excitement was rising as they neared the town. He could sense the eyes of his bloodthirsty god upon him, willing him on to the coming slaughter.

He pulled a stitched bladder from his belt and with his sharp teeth tore a hole in it. Horse's blood, from the mare Vlamdir had sacrificed the night before, poured through the gash and over his face.

It cascaded down his chin and chest, gathering in the cracks of his skin-armour, seeping into his body in a luxurious wash of crimson. The scent was strong in Vlamdir's nostrils and he began to feel the battle-frenzy rising up within him.

They were now less than a quarter of a mile from the walled town, and Vlamdir began to shake with excitement. He dragged his sword from its scabbard and swung it above his head, flinging droplets of blood across the snow and Orst's pale fur.

'The head harvest begins!' he screamed, breaking into a run. Orst gave a roar and bounded forward, keeping pace with the young Kurgan tribesman.

Around him other warriors succumbed to their battle lust as well and they charged forward yelling and screaming, followed by the brutish beastmen uttering their bestial cries and brandishing crude, looted weapons.

Vlamdir saw the first volley of arrows arc over the parapet of the wall in a ragged cloud. They soared high into the air and then dropped down, plunging into the ground and warriors alike. A few of the possessed berserkers fell, others that were struck ignored their wounds and continued their sprint.

Vlamdir's heart pounded in his chest as he charged forward, energy pulsing through his body, driving him onwards. His vision was blurring as the blood dripped into his eyes and he could taste it on his tongue. Licking his lips he cried out again.

'Skulls for the skull lord!' he screamed.

He could hardly see now, but it didn't matter, the wall was barely a hundred yards away. He could feel the ground trembling underfoot as the army thundered forward behind him, their hoarse shouts and the cry of horns growing ever louder.

Vlamdir could dimly see more dark shapes on the walls above as more arrows sailed past him. Great Kharneth would keep him safe from their cowardly weapons. He felt as if his legs were strong enough for him to leap to the top of the wall in one great bound. He laughed as he ran.

There was a thunderous detonation from ahead and a moment later something round and metallic slammed into Vlamdir's chest, punching through his fused armour and exploding out of his back, shattering his spine. His legs gave way beneath him and he fell head first into the snowy ground. As his lifeblood ebbed away, he barely registered the claws and hooves and boots of the warriors sweeping forward over him.

JAKOB SAT UP with a start as the black and white uniformed troops appeared at the walls, handguns ready. In a single ragged salvo they fired, a ripple of fire and smoke engulfing the parapet. At such short range the volley was lethal, cutting down a swathe of warriors. Behind them the marauders and beastmen began to falter.

Hors was swearing, staring at the shaman with angry eyes.

'You told me that the town would be barely defended!' he growled.

Jakob could not understand it. In the morning he had seen the army marching to the east, obviously headed for Eskivaya. And now the Ostlanders were here, at Mursk. He shook his head in confusion.

'They shouldn't be here…' he muttered but Hors was not listening. He pressed forward, bellowing at his warriors to press home the attack.

More flashes caught Jakob's attention, this time from a hill to the right, on the far side of the river, half a mile from the town. He counted six blossoms of fire and realised what it meant.

The cannonballs screamed into the packed mass of warriors as they closed ranks to assault the walls. The spinning balls of hot iron smashed men apart, flung ragged corpses into the air and tore off limbs, spraying blood and snow in their wake.

Hors and his hardened champions drove forward, pushing the tribesmen ahead into the attack. A constant stream of arrows now descended from the walls, cutting down even more of the men around Jakob.

With sickening realisation, the shaman thought back to the night before, and the encounter with the weakling sorcerer. Jakob cursed himself for his arrogance, and then cursed the other man for the illusion he had placed in Jakob's mind.

Jakob dismissed the worrisome thoughts easily. It did not matter that the town was defended. This left the ford at Eskivaya free for Undar and his men to cross without opposition. When combined with the Kul and other Kurgans who were even now closing from the west, these two forces were enough to crush the Empire army like an egg in a vice.

Another volley of musket fire tore through the attackers, sending them reeling backwards. Though he knew that victory was assured, casualties were mounting rapidly. Sutenvulf would not thank Jakob for getting half his army slaughtered.

Jakob dismounted awkwardly and slapped his horse on the rump to send it away. He ignored the warriors pouring past him towards the town and focussed his mind. As he had done so many times before, he allowed the breath of the gods to sweep into him, building a reserve of power.

He held the energy longer than he had ever done before, the magic crackling from the runestones in his body, earthing itself in bursts of purple lightning. The pressure was growing almost intolerable and Jakob fought to control the magic coursing through his body. His anger at the deception that he had accepted gave him renewed strength and he pulled at the magical winds, twisting them together, fusing them into a densely packed mass of raw Chaos.

He was surrounded by a visible corona of energy now, a churning sphere of coloured flames that sparked and hissed. With a shout, Jakob released his grip on the magic, hurling it forwards with the power of his mind.

The gigantic magical fireball roared towards the town wall, tearing through the men in front of Jakob, igniting hair and hurling charred corpses in all directions. It impacted on the wall with an explosion that flung shattered logs and flaming bodies a hundred feet into the air, ripping a breach a dozen yards wide.

As flaming debris fell to the ground, the forces of Sutenvulf charged once again towards the stunned defenders, their battle cries louder than ever. At the forefront were Hors and his chosen warriors.

THE BREACH WAS choked with bodies and burning wood, and through the smoke Hors could see the defenders gathering again. Limbs protruded from the ragged mess, and the groans of those unfortunate enough to have survived Jakob's spell mixed with the crackle of flames.

'Come on you dogs!' Hors bellowed, gripping his axe in both hands and running forward.

A stuttering roar of cannon fire heralded another artillery salvo. As Hors jumped over the bodies scattered on the melted snow, dozens of men behind him were bludgeoned to gory masses and crushed beneath the weight of iron falling upon them.

Arrows and bullets from the men still on the remaining parts of the wall whirred past Hors as he advanced, and he heard the grunts and cries of those behind him as the missiles found their marks. Unperturbed, he rushed towards the smoking gap.

Bounding up onto the pile of debris and corpses, Hors was confronted by a wall of spear points. He lashed out with his axe, the blade smashing through the shafts of the soldiers' weapons.

On either side of him, his chosen warriors ran up, hurling themselves towards the enemy. Many died on the spears of the Empire soldiers, heads and chests transfixed by the iron-tipped demi-pikes, while others cannoned into the mass, their thick armour brushing aside the defenders' attacks.

Hors fended off a thrust towards his stomach and threw himself forwards, burying the head of his axe into the shoulder of the frightened young man at the other end of the spear. Wrenching his weapon clear, Hors swung to the right, the axe chopping through the armour of another man.

The clatter of steel and wood surrounded him as he pressed forwards, hewing left and right, his foes unable to use their long weapons at such close quarters. Their screams and howls echoed in his ears.

'Die, you sons of whores,' he spat between gritted teeth, decapitating a grey-haired veteran with one sweep. 'May the worms enjoy your flesh!'

The spearmen held firm against the charge, the shouts of their sergeants urging them forwards again when they began to falter. As more and more warriors from both sides pressed into the breach it became a matter of brute strength.

With no more room to swing his axe, Hors let go of it, leaving the weapon buried in the back of the last man to have felt its bite. He smashed his large fists into the faces of those around him, breaking jaws and noses. He grabbed one soldier by the throat and squeezed hard, crushing his windpipe. As he let go of the body, kept upright by the weight of people around it, he drove his forehead into the face of a man trying to wrap his arm around the Norseman's throat.

Hors felt someone grabbing at his face from behind and he snatched the arm in his strong grip and twisted. There was a scream and Hors pulled hard, the limb coming away in a spray of blood. Ignoring the punches raining onto his back and shoulders, he turned to face the man who had attacked him. He was gibbering madly, staring at the ragged stump of his shoulder.

'This is yours,' snarled Hors, smashing the severed limb into the man's face, breaking his neck with the blow.

The Norseman rammed his elbow into the throat of another soldier, and then drove his fist into his chest, buckling his thin breastplate. Choking, the man staggered back, giving Hors enough time to pull a knife from his belt. He rammed it point first into the injured man's eyeball.

Gouging and slashing, Hors drove ever deeper into the spearmen, leaving a trail of dismembered dead and injured in his wake.

The brutal, unrelenting assault of the Chaos warriors proved too much for them in the end, and the spearmen turned to flee. Hors snatched up one of their fallen weapons and drove its point into the back of one southerner as he tried to run. With inhuman strength he lifted the flailing man into the air and then flung him after his routed comrades. Spear in one hand, knife in the other, Hors led his men onwards into the town.

The buildings were built mostly from wood, with stone foundations. They had high sloping roofs of dark slate and narrow windows, and as Hors advanced more archers and musketeers appeared on the vantage points, firing into the streets below.

A bullet smashed off a wall next to Hors, filling his face with wooden shards. As blood dribbled down his cheek, the warlord spat and turned to his warriors behind him.

'Bring fire,' he shouted at them. 'We'll burn them out!'

The army spread out through the streets in their hundreds, fighting building by building, pouring into the beleaguered town in a ferocious wave. Burning torches brought from the shattered ruins of the wall were used to set fire to houses and shops and soon a dark pall of smoke hung over Mursk, blotting out the light of the sun.

Choking on the fumes from the fires below, defenders in the buildings were forced to climb from the windows and haul themselves up to the roofs. They looked on aghast as flames and smoke crept up the walls towards them. Where they could, they retreated along the rooftops, jumping over the narrow gaps between some of them when necessary.

All the while that the warriors of Chaos advanced, they were met by a hail of crossbow bolts, shot and arrows. Their dead littered the streets, marking the routes of their attacks. Hors stopped half a mile from the wall and allowed his howling fighters to advance past him.

He was covered with blood and soot, his face cut and punctured, his hair a tangled mess. Reaching into his cloak he pulled out a small silver mirror and opened it. With his knife clenched between his teeth he began to wipe the grime from his face and pick the pieces of wood and gore from his long locks. Turning his head to each side to check the results, he snapped the mirror shut with satisfaction and placed it back in its pouch.

He was firmly of the belief that no god would ever favour a man who did not take pride in his appearance. Contented that all was well with the way he looked, he took his dagger from his mouth and advanced again.

As he rejoined the hundreds of warriors battling through the street fighting from house to house, he realised that they were near the river. Along the street ahead he could see a long stone bridge arcing up into view.

Knowing that this was where they had the best chance of keeping the attackers at bay, the soldiers of the Empire had formed up resolutely on the banks of the river, over a thousand fighting men. Amongst them were some of the most battle-hardened soldiers in the army, including such regiments as the Wolfenburg Heavy Spear, the Forest of Shadows Patrol and van Bronckhurst's Swords.

The veteran warriors stood shoulder to shoulder, their faces grim, as the warriors of the Dark Gods advanced down the streets towards them. To the steady barked shouts of their sergeants and captains, the veterans readied their weapons and raised their shields. Their banners fluttered in the smoke, their many battle honours embroidered around designs of griffons and dragons.

At their centre, defending the bridge itself, the Gold Company waited, their plate armour tarnished from the fires, their two-handed swords reflecting the firelight from the burning buildings. A trumpet sounded a single long note and they raised their swords to the guard position. In the middle of their front rank, two of the veteran soldiers stepped aside to allow someone through.

Hors almost laughed as he saw the diminutive figure in silver and gold armour step forward and take up position. His laughter died in his throat as he strode closer, seeing her long red hair in a plait that hung down across her breast. The woman drew her sword, and Hors saw blue flames flickering along the edges of the blade.

Hors slowed and called to his men to halt. They did so reluctantly, darting questioning looks towards him. The Norse warlord needed time to think.

How in the all the names of the gods was he supposed to take the town without harming Sutenvulf's woman?

THE STORM HAD passed and cool wind whipped at Andar Kul's face as he rode eastwards along the south bank of the Urskoy. The crossing at Gobri Danesk had been held by only a few hundred Kislevites, a rearguard of the army that chased his own so far across the tundra. His three thousand warriors had swept them aside easily, though they had valiantly tried to hold against the overwhelming force that had descended upon them with the rising sun and the abatement of the storm. They had been good enemies, and as a sign of respect Kul had taken the head of their leader and it now hung from his saddlecloth so that others might see it and know the face of great warrior.

His horsemen moved at a fast walk, covering the ground quickly enough but without tiring their mounts. In this way, they passed mile after mile as the sun rose in the air, always the icy waters of the river a few hundred yards to their left.

By mid-morning Kul could see a column of smoke in the distance, a black cloud that rose high into the air. It could only be Mursk, he knew, but Hors was supposed to take the bridge and then move on to the true battlefield further to the east.

The Kurgan chieftain thought that perhaps the ignorant Norseman had stopped anyway for some looting and fun. Well, Kul thought, if Hors missed the battle at Eskivaya Sutenvulf would have him tortured to death. The thought pleased the steppesman, and he imagined what pain he might inflict on his rival if his master invited him to do the honours.

As he rode nearer the town, Kul could sense that something was wrong. There were dark shapes on a hill not far ahead, and a shadow covered the ground along the northern approaches. Flames snaked into the air above the wooden palisade surrounding Mursk and there were sounds of battle. Surely the Norseman wasn't having difficulty overrunning a poorly defended Kislevite hovel?

Bright lights flared from the hill, blossoming against the lightening sky. Kul was not sure what this signified until he heard the rolling booms and saw the black streaks hurtling towards him. There were shouts from the others around him and he kicked his horse into a canter.

The shots from the cannons wrought as much havoc and death amongst the Kurgan riders as they had the infantry. Massive gaps were torn into the mounted horde, filled with the tangled remains of riders and horses.

Following the lead of Andar Kul, the Kurgan picked up the pace, now moving at some speed towards the hill. Riding at the front of the irregular column, Kul drew his sword, a wickedly curved blade, and raised it above his head. Bringing it down with a sweeping motion he signalled the charge and dug in his heels.

The ground trembled under the thousands of hoof-beats as the Kurgan charged the Empire guns. A forest of spears and swords held above their heads, they swept up the hill towards the Imperial position, mud and snow flying from the hooves of their horses, the plaited manes and tails of their steeds streaming in the wind.

Kul gave a piercing battle cry that could be heard over the thunder of hooves and rushing wind, a chilling ululation from the depths of his throat. The cry was echoed by the others of his tribe, and joined by shouts and whistles from the other riders, until the whole force was a screaming mass.

They were almost upon the cannons now and Kul could see the smoke-stained faces of the crews looking at him. A man stood by each of the six guns with a burning taper in his hand. Now only fifty yards away and still moving fast, Kul directed the point of his sword at the cowardly southerners.

At a shouted order from their captain, the gunners put their matches to the touch holes of their weapons and a moment later the hill erupted with flame and smoke. One of the cannons misfired, sending red-hot shards of metal scything through its crew as its barrel split, but the others discharged their lethal loads at point blank range into the charging Kurgan.

A storm of lead pellets filled the air as the grapeshot chewed through the riders, ripping men from their saddles, tearing the flesh from horses, breaking bones and smashing apart skulls. The devastation wrought by the volley was horrendous, hundreds lying scattered over the hillside, but it was not enough to stop the charge.

Miraculously unscathed except for a slight scratch on his arm, Kul was the first to reach the gunners. He swept out his sword without slowing and its razor edge slashed across the face of one man. Turning his horse with his thighs, he rode straight over another, who fell beneath the hooves of his sturdy mount.

It was over in a matter of moments, the Kurgan reining in their mounts as the last of the gunners fell beneath the storm of blades and spears that had descended like the vengeance of the gods upon the Empire soldiers. From the hill, Kul could see into the town and marvelled at the burning buildings.

He was wondering what to do next when a horn blast from the south caught his attention.

CHAPTER NINE
Retreat
Mursk, Early autumn 1712

LORD BAYARD HAD held his knights back from the town, knowing that his men would be wasted fighting amongst the tight streets. Instead, he had promised Count Vapold that the Osterknacht would act as a reserve, ready to move forwards and cover a retreat to the position on the hill.

When he had first seen the shadow on the horizon to the west he thought it was the victorious Kislevites marching to their aid. As the horde had become easier to see he had realised with horror that it was not the Kislevites at all, but instead their supposedly defeated foes, the barbaric Kurgan.

He had argued against leaving the cannons unprotected on the hill, but the count had said that every man would be needed to hold the bridge. Vapold had reasoned that, sited on the far bank from the assault, if the artillery were ever under threat it meant the battle was probably already lost.

Now the foe had appeared from an unexpected quarter, and there was nothing that Bayard could do about it. He had watched in admiration as the gun crews wheeled their war machines around to face this new threat, refusing to flee in the face of the overwhelming force coming towards them. They had calmly loaded their guns and fired, then loaded grapeshot and waited for the final, devastating onslaught. They had died as brave men, manning their guns to the last.

With the attention of the Kurgan focussed on the cannons, Bayard had given the order to form up and advance. In neat files ten wide, the three hundred had trotted northwards, towards the hill. Bayard had been less than half a mile away at the front of the column when the final charge had hit amidst the thunder and fire of the cannons' final shots.

The Kurgan were disorganised, their opponents so easily overwhelmed that they had continued on over the far side of the hill a little way. They milled around the summit waiting for their leaders to regain control.

Bayard signalled to his hornblower, Lothar, and the youth raised his instrument to his lips and blew a clear, long note. As the sound died away Bayard kicked his horse into a run, the knights behind him keeping pace.

From the south the hill was not so steep and as the Kurgan hurriedly turned towards their new foes, Bayard urged his horse on faster. At a speedy run, the Osterknacht drove up the hill towards the Kurgan.

Though they lacked the speed of their foes, the impact of their charge was even more impressive. Having not broken into a full gallop they had retained their solid formation. With lances at full tilt, the Osterknacht literally smashed into the steppe riders.

Bayard picked out a target and aimed his lance at the savage, scalp-locked warrior. The point struck the rider high in the left shoulder, almost tearing his arm off, and Bayard ripped the lance free as his horse carried him past. He was in the thick of the foe now, the impetus of his warhorse carrying him forwards, shoving aside the smaller, lighter steeds of the Kurgan.

Their hasty sword blows and thrusting spears clanged harmlessly from the steel plates of Bayard's armour, scratching gouges in the dark enamel but otherwise having no effect. Another thrust of his lance spitted the gut of a bare-chested Kurgan with dark red warpaint across his face. The man kicked and struggled for a moment as he was dragged from his horse, tearing the lance out of Bayard's grip.

He drew his sword and set about the enemy around him, using high sweeps and cuts to slash at faces and necks. The impetus of their charge had hardly faltered, and though outnumbered almost ten to one, the Osterknacht cleaved into the Kurgan horde like a sword through bare flesh.

Caught almost unawares by the attack, unsure of how many foes assailed them in the chaos of the mêlée, those Kurgan who could kicked their horses in the flanks and fled back down the hill.

The Osterknacht's momentum carried them through the splintering mass of riders, scattering their enemies

in all directions. Bayard signalled to the left and
Lothar gave two short blasts of his horn. As precisely
as if they were on a parade ground and not a corpse-
strewn hill, the Osterknacht wheeled after the fleeing
marauders, chasing them down onto the plains.

Though not as quick over short distances, the Kurgan's mounts carried them clear of the pursuing
knights and Bayard signalled for the company to halt,
not wishing to unnecessarily tire the knights' mounts.
Redressing their ranks, the Osterknacht watched the
Kurgan bolting back to the west. Free from immediate
harm the steppes nomads gathered and stopped their
rout some half a mile away, and there they stayed,
watching the knights warily.

Bayard stood in his stirrups and looked back over
his men. He saw no more than a dozen holes in the
ranks. In contrast, nearly five hundred Kurgan dead
and wounded lay upon the bloodied snow and mud
of the hill.

'WHAT ARE THEY waiting for?' asked Gunther Fletzen
quietly, turning to the spearman to his left.

'It's the maiden,' Paulus Greid whispered back out of
the side of his mouth, his stare fixed on the mass of
warriors that were gathering in the streets ahead.

The horde of the north filled the spaces between the
buildings with a mass of dark armour, fur and tattooed flesh. A tall warrior with long blond plaits stood
at their front, regarding the Empire line coolly. No
more than fifty yards separated the two armies, and yet
the wide street that ran alongside the river was deathly
quiet.

'What do you mean?' said Gunther.

'She's the maiden of Sigmar, in't she,' replied Paulus. 'Her holiness is like poison to 'em.'

'I never knew that,' said Gunther.

There were barks and howls from their right and dozens of beast-headed mutants burst forth from the ranks, rushing towards the Imperial soldiers.

'Hold,' the deep voice of Sergeant Tilven told them.

There were shouts and the sound of weapons clashing from further along the line and Gunther had to muster all of his willpower to resist the urge to step forward and see what was happening.

Instead Gunther kept his gaze on the blond-haired warlord. As the spearman watched, it looked like the tall warrior shrugged and then with a howling battle cry launched himself into a run, spear raised above his head. Behind him the dark horde gave a roar and poured forwards.

'Shit,' muttered Paulus. 'Here they come.'

'Poison eh?' snapped Gunther.

'Brace!' shouted Sergeant Tilven, and as one the Third Wolfenburg Company of Pike snapped their weapons into position.

Gunther stepped up with his left foot and leaned forward, spear held with his right hand halfway down the shaft, his left hand a little further up, its butt braced against his right foot. The wide shield on his left arm covered his chest. His heart pounded as he watched the onrushing line of savage warriors.

He could see the hate in their eyes as they charged, and smell the stench of their unwashed bodies.

'Strike!' the sergeant bellowed when the first of the warriors were almost on top of the spearmen. Over Gunther's shoulder, Leburg thrust his pike forward, driving the hardened iron tip clean through the helmet of the Chaos warrior in front of him.

With a small movement, Gunther guided the tip of his own weapon towards the chest of a fur-clad savage who was howling as he charged towards Paulus. The northman's own momentum carried him on to the sharpened point, the force of the impact snapping the spear shaft as his breastbone was carved open.

Gunther reached for his short sword, but it was only halfway out of its scabbard when a snarling barbarian leapt upon him, smashing a heavy club into his helmet. Gunther's ears rang and he stumbled. The Norse's next blow smashed Gunther's jaw into his brain and he fell.

IT WAS A SLAUGHTER, which was just the way that Count Steinhardt liked to wage war. From the vantage point of his horse's back, he watched as the enemy floundered through the freezing waters of the ford, the river swelled by the recent snow, his archers and crossbowmen loosing a steady torrent of steel-tipped death into the northerners.

'How many do you think so far?' he asked, turning to Iversson.

'A thousand at least,' the commander replied. 'Probably more.'

The count watched impassively as the bodies in the water began to pile up, further hindering those behind. Corpses floated downstream, spinning slowly in the swirling current pierced by bolts and arrows.

The marauders gamely continued to come on though, ignoring their losses, urged on by the bellows of the obscenely muscled warrior on the far bank. Through sheer weight of numbers, the northmen were making ground, some crawling onto the bank, their furs sodden, panting for breath.

As hard as they tried, the missile troops simply could not keep up a sufficient rate of fire to take down every foe. Steinhardt was also worried about ammunition. They had been shooting steadily for several minutes now.

There were now dozens of enemy clawing their way up the bank, only a hundred yards away. One brute of a man was wading across now as well, an axe in each hand. Steinhardt watched as a crossbow quarrel punched into the warlord's exposed chest. He barely even noticed it. Other bolts and arrows studded his warped body by the time he reached the near bank.

'The cavalry, my lord?' asked Iversson. Steinhardt nodded, not taking his gaze from the monstrous northman now clambering up through the snow towards him.

A trumpeter sounded the signal for the missile troops to fall back and they did so in good order, breaking to the left and right before retreating, leaving a clear run for the knights who were standing behind them.

The disfigured northman raised his axes above his head in defiance and bellowed in his crude tongue, no doubt some cutting insult.

'Now, my lord?' asked Iversson.

'No, let some more come across first,' the count replied. 'We'll only have to waste time chasing down the survivors.'

Within a few minutes there were several hundred warriors on the closest shore. With their leader at the front, they began to advance.

'Now, I think,' Steinhardt said to Iversson. A couple of seconds later the trumpet called for the cavalry to charge.

Bolstered by the two thousand knights sent to him this morning by Vapold, Steinhardt's cavalry careened forward with lances poised. As the count had expected, the cavalry crashed into the enemy with brutal efficiency.

Everywhere except near the misshapen giant, that was.

With a speed that should have been impossible for his bulk, the bestial man was cleaving men and horses with his double-bladed axes, their heads whirling in impossible arcs around him.

He leapt aside from a spear point and with a backhand blow from his left-hand axe detached the head of the knight's horse, a split second later his other axe cleaving the rider in the chest.

Limbs were severed and heads lopped off as the northman strode up the bank towards Steinhardt. Like the sea breaking against a headland, the knights were pushed to either side of him, decapitated and dismembered if they strayed too close.

He was now only thirty yards away, and showed no sign of tiring. Beyond him the knights were now in the ford, sweeping across the river and riding down the

Norse as they struggled against the current. On the near bank, however, the northern warlord showed no sign of relenting in his attack. Step by step, corpse by corpse, he advanced slowly. Fortunately, the press of knights heading into the ford barred his way, otherwise he would have already been upon Steinhardt.

'He's getting rather close,' said Iversson, shifting nervously in his saddle. 'Perhaps we ought to retreat a little ways?'

'Ridiculous,' Steinhardt snapped. 'There are at least fifty more men between him and us.'

The fifty become forty, and then thirty, and then twenty. At fifteen, Steinhardt pulled his pistols free from his saddlebags and cocked them. With only ten men left, the fighting now only five yards away, the count could see his adversary more clearly.

His skin was awash with blood from dozens of cuts and gashes, some of them quite deep. One of his fingers hung by a thread of skin from his hand, and more blood poured from his ruined nose. His muscles bulged and swelled with a life of their own, in a way not at all related to his movements. He was at least as broad across the chest as a horse and his shoulders were almost as wide as a man is tall. The veins in his arms stood out like thick cords, his upper arms thicker than both thighs of a normal man combined.

Steinhardt took aim, the pistols aimed directly at the marauder's face. As the last man between the warlord and the count was struck down, the chieftain looked up.

'Good effort,' said Steinhardt, pulling the triggers.

The twin impacts of the bullets smashed apart the man's head, sending shards of bone and a flurry of

blood in all direction. His headless corpse was thrown
backwards, crashing into the snow and mud. Beyond
the decapitated body the rampant knights were running down the surviving warriors of his army.

'Come on,' Steinhardt said, looking over his shoulder at Iversson, who sat on his horse as rigid as a post.
'Vapold won't be able to wait all day for us.'

THE FIGHTING IN Mursk was bitter and intense, as the
battle fractured into a series of running clashes in the
twisting streets. The Imperial line had held against the
initial impact of the Chaos force, but in the close fighting, unsupported by their guns, the soldiers of
Ostland fared poorly. Though they fought with disci-
pline and bravery, they could not match the strength
and ferocity of their foes.

Ruprecht fought close to the bridge, the head of his
hammer slicked with blood as he smashed it into the
helmet of an armoured warrior, crushing his adversary's head. The din of battle rang off the buildings
that lined the Urskoy, the crackle of flames from the
burning town drowned out by hoarse shouts and the
screams of the dying, the ringing of metal on metal
and the bellowing of titanic beasts.

Despite the efforts of the soldiers around him,
Ruprecht could feel the Empire army being pushed
back towards the icy waters behind them. While it had
seemed sensible to defend the bridge at all costs, it was
now clear that the river would likely become their
grave. To his right, Ruprecht heard cries of terror and
saw the towering shapes of the dragon ogres looming
over the spearmen who were embattled on the very

edge of the river not far away. The large blades of the Chaos beasts carved bloodily through the ranks of the spearmen, felling a dozen men, and the survivors turned to flee. Some were driven into the freezing waters of the river itself, the others running into their comrades as they broke towards the bridge.

Blocking an axe blade with his hammer, Ruprecht drove his fist into the face of a marauder with a shaven head and red, flame-shaped tattoos across his face. The tide of twisted warriors seemed almost endless. Over the clamour of the fighting, a trumpet sounded out, three short bursts. It was the signal for retreat.

Ruprecht battled his way back towards the bridge, almost tripping over the armoured bodies of the Gold Company that littered the muddy street. A small knot of the greatsword-armed veterans held back a snarling horde of beastmen, their long blades chopping through fur and flesh. Her golden armour splashed with dark, foul blood, Ursula fought with them.

The retreat was enacted with a careful precision, regiments pulling back from the line in a pre-arranged plan, their comrades to either side, closing the gap. It took several minutes for the thousands of soldiers to collapse back towards the bridge, the officers and sergeants bellowing orders, instilling their will on their men to avoid the retreat becoming a rout.

Ruprecht stood with the remnants of the Gold Company now, not far from Ursula. During brief breaks in the fighting Ruprecht threw hurried glances towards Ursula. She appeared unharmed, and in fact as Ruprecht watched, protected for a moment by two swordsmen who were in front of him battling against a tall, bull-headed mutant, he realised that none of the enemy's attacks were directed against her. Trailing blue flames, Ulfshard cut through the enemy in Ursula's hands, but her foes backed away from her or attacked those who stood beside her.

The Gold Company and the Wolfenburg Heavy Spear had been designated as the rearguard, and they held on grimly against the beasts and northmen that threw themselves against the town's defenders. Before the battle, they had received the blessings of the priests of Morr, their souls already consecrated to the god of death. They knew they were going to die on the banks of the Urskoy, and fought to sell their lives dearly.

Ruprecht had other plans, and pushed his way through the swordsmen and called to Ursula, but she either did not hear her or chose to ignore him. Pushing his hammer into his belt, he plunged into the melee and grabbed the woman, wrapping an arm around her waist and pulling her back from the fighting. She struggled, smashing an elbow into his face.

'Easy!' he shouted, dropping Ursula to her feet.

'What are you doing?' she snarled. 'My place is here, with the fighting! I'm needed here.'

She turned and took a stride back towards the clashing weapons and shouts of the dying but Ruprecht pointed across bridge towards the regiments marching back through the town.

'Your place is with your people,' he told her, dragging her towards the bridge. 'They need you! This battle is just beginning, not ending.'

'I have to fight!' she screeched, ripping her arm free.

'If you die, this army will fall apart!' Ruprecht roared at her, stopping her short.

Ursula looked up into his face and then back to the fighting. He could see her pain in her expression. Slowly, reluctantly, she walked backwards across the bridge, watching as the last few dozen men held the crossing, buying time for the army to reorganise at its rally point.

COUNT VAPOLD HAD suspected that the bridge would fall and had drawn up plans for the army to retreat to the hill on which the guns were stationed. He silently thanked the gods and the Osterknacht that the defensive position was still in Imperial hands. The knights had charged forwards again as the Chaos forces had poured out of the town gates, covering the retreat of the last regiments who were still marching up the hill.

Both armies were significantly smaller than they had been when the fighting had begun, their dead choking the streets and alleys of Mursk. Now as the northmen and their bestial allies advanced up the hill, Vapold looked longingly to the east. He prayed that Steinhardt had been victorious and would arrive in time, otherwise this hill would become his grave.

JAKOB WATCHED THE fighting dispassionately. The Empire soldiers had fought valiantly, but their resistance was in vain. Soon Undar would be here with his warriors, and with their extra numbers the outcome was inevitable. That was if he arrived before Sutenvulf returned, Jakob thought. If Undar delayed, he might miss the fighting altogether.

The sound of hoof beats trembled along the ground and Jakob looked along the line of embattled fighters. The Imperial knights had smashed a hole through Hors's marauders, and swung around the back of the Chaos army. If they were not stopped, they could charge into the rear of Sutenvulf's men.

Jakob began to summon the energy of the gods again, preparing to unleash a storm of devastating power against the knights. The knights wheeled along the hill, coming straight towards him. As the breath of the gods swirled around him, Jakob could see a gold-armoured figure at their head. Barking words of power, Jakob unleashed the power of the gods towards the knights.

Nothing happened, the magic dissipated harmlessly back to the mystical winds. The knights were coming straight for Jakob and fear gripped his heart. He turned and tried to hobble away, but the swift-moving cavalry were quickly upon him. He felt something hard strike him in the back and he toppled forward, his head smashing into a rock, stunning him.

Awkwardly rolling to his back, he saw the gold-armoured figure dismounting as the knights thundered onwards towards Hors's battle-line. The shaman could feel a trickle of blood running down his knobbled forehead.

He looked up into the face of the Imperial warrior and saw that it was Ursula. She had changed, not physically, but in her demeanour. Her hard eyes bored into the shaman as his smiled cruelly.

'It's been a long time,' Jakob said, his Reikspiel heavily accented.

'Where's Kurt?' she demanded, drawing a blazing sword, its point directed at Jakob's throat. The light of the blade hurt Jakob's eye.

'Where is he?' she asked again, grabbing Jakob's furs and pulling him forward, the sword tip hovering inches from his throat.

It was a good question, Jakob thought. Where was the Sutenvulf?

A reflection in Ursula's silvered armour caught his attention. It was his magical eye, a golden disc, looking like a shimmering sun against the blue steel of the armour. In the reflection, blood trickled down across it, and Jakob began to laugh.

'He'll be here soon enough,' he sneered. 'He'll be here soon enough.'

Ursula pushed him back to the ground and plunged the magical sword into his chest. Pain flared through Jakob at the touch of the enchanted blade, but he did not mind. As his blood bubbled away, he watched Ursula mount her horse and turn back to the fight. The vision of the reflection hovered in Jakob's mind as the last of his life force seeped from his twisted form, and Sutenvulf's words came back to him.

'Look for me when the sun is drenched in blood and I will be there.'

CHAPTER TEN
Ostland

URSULA GALLOPED UP the hill, Ulfshard in hand. She rode across the corpse-strewn ground in the wake of the Osterknacht, who had discarded their lances and were fighting their way through the minions of the Chaos gods with swords, maces, axes and warhammers. Ursula joined the attack, sweeping off the head of a savage marauder with a sweep of Ulfshard.

From the back of her horse, Ursula could see a group of two dozen or so halberdiers. They had been cut off from the main battle-line and were surrounded by a constricting ring of Kul horsemen, their scalplocks waving as they circled in for the kill. Beside the halberdiers' standard bearer Ursula spied a flash of white and saw Brother Helgurd, one of the warrior priests that accompanied the army. The halberdiers were hopelessly outmatched by their mounted foes, who darted close and hurled throwing spears into their ranks.

With a shout, Ursula dug her heels into the flanks of her mount, swinging Ulfshard left and right. With half a dozen blows she had cut her way clear of the mêlée and was heading towards the priest and his guards. Even as she closed, the Kul drew their swords and charged towards the bristling blades of the soldiers. Unaware of the warrior woman bearing down on him, the first horseman fell from his saddle without a sound, his back opened to the ribs by Ursula's magical blade.

Seeing his kinsman fall, another of the riders turned, just in time to catch the point of Ulfshard in the face. Screaming, he fell from the saddle, trampled by the hooves of Ursula's horse as she urged it on, swinging Ulfshard in wide arcs around her head.

She broke through just as Brother Helgurd fell, a Kurgan spear puncturing his shoulder. The halberdiers closed in around the wounded priest, protecting him from further attack. They parted to let Ursula pass into the centre of their formation.

'We're done for, but get him out of here!' the sergeant yelled to her, helping the warrior priest clamber belly down on to the horse behind Ursula. Sheathing Ulfshard, Ursula held him in place with her right hand and gripped the reins with the left. The halberdiers gave a shout and pushed forwards, opening a gap for Ursula to rid through. As the raced free from the Kul, one of them turned his horse and set after her. Laden with two people, her steed could not match the steppe warrior's mount for pace. He overhauled

Ursula and swung his mount across the nose of her steed and Ursula swayed back, the edge of the Kurgan's sword slicing past barely inches for her face.

'Here,' Helgurd yelled through gritted teeth, thrusting his hammer towards Ursula. Releasing her grip of the priest's robes she snatched the weapon from him and swung it at the horseman's head.

The Kurgan was a more skilled rider than Ursula and veered his horse away, slashing at the hamstrings of her steed as he rode past. Whinnying shrilly her horse fell to one side, its gashed leg twitching, throwing Ursula and Helgurd into the snowy ground. Helgurd struggled to his feet and was thrown back a moment later as the steppe marauder twisted his mount quickly and slashed the tip of his sword across the priest's throat. Helgurd's blood spattered across her face, Ursula screamed and launched herself at the rider, the hammer smashing into his thigh, crushing bone.

Knocked sideways by the attack, the Kul warrior struggled to maintain his balance and Ursula grabbed hold of his tattered cloak, pulling him from his horse. She kicked him in the face as he tried to rise and brought the hammer down onto his shaved scalp, cracking his skull and driving the back of his head into the sodden earth.

The dead Kurgan's horse stood close by and Ursula walked over and climbed up onto its chequered saddlecloth. As she turned the horse's head towards the Imperial army it gave a terrified whinny and tried to bolt.

A moment later Ursula felt the ground tremble. Overhead the sky darkened and the air became thick and oppressive. The clouds began to spin, spiralling down towards the ground in a whirlwind of crackling energy. Fell voices screamed on the rushing wind and shapes moved amongst the seething energy – dark shapes, seen only in nightmares.

With a thunderous crash the portal opened, a gaping maw of energy tearing though into the world of mortals from the Realm of Chaos. A tide of daemonic warriors and creatures burst forth, a wave of magical malevolence sweeping over the Ostland army. Inside the vortex titanic energies crashed and men began to turn and run, crying in fear, whispering prayers to the gods. Ursula forced the horse into a gallop, swinging around the flank of the battle.

'Do not run!' she cried, and the fleeing men, now numbering in the hundreds and growing with every moment, slowed and turned to her. 'If you run now, then you must run for the rest of your lives. You may survive the day, but the threat of Chaos is never defeated by retreat! Only by staying and fighting can you ever defeat these foes. They are fell and unnatural, but they are not undefeatable.

'Faith and steel, my brave warriors! Faith and steel will turn this misfortune to our glory. The Dark Gods shall rue the day they pitted themselves against the men of Ostland!'

The heartened soldiers began to return to their units, and Ursula turned to watch the gibbering, baying, howling morass of nightmarish creatures charging towards the Empire soldiers. From the portal a winged shadow emerged, larger than even the dragon ogres. It swept across the sky and circled once before landing behind the daemonic legion.

Ursula felt a sense of horror drain her strength as she looked at the daemon prince and recalled Jakob's dying words. Her momentary despair was soon replaced with anger. Dismounting, she walked among the frightened troops.

'Men of the Empire!' She shouted, raising the hammer of the dead priest above her head. 'Let your deaths not be in vain! Strike down these abominations with happiness in your heart, and if you should fall be content that the gods have seen your sacrifice! Destroy them all! For the Empire! For Sigmar!'

THE BODIES OF the dead littered the snow-covered ground. In half a day of bitter fighting, twenty thousand already lay dead or wounded and still the battle raged. Sutenvulf Daemonkin surveyed the carnage with a smile twisting his inhuman lips. The daemon prince stretched out his leathery wings, and leapt into the air, his mighty pinions beating slowly, carrying him down the slope on which he had been standing. All around was the din of war, a pleasing melody of battle cries and screams, the ring of metal on metal, his unnatural ears delighting to the sound of axe blade in flesh and sword through bone. The battle had ebbed and flowed for seven hours now, and as the cold northern sun dipped over the eastern mountains, the daemonic general felt it was time to finish off the upstart warriors from the Empire of the south.

He looked with great pride over the army that he had gathered. Warbands of the gods' champions fought side by side with legions of daemons he had brought forth with his own powerful magic, alongside the savage, undisciplined beastmen, bull-headed minotaurs, scaled dragon ogres and other monsters of the Chaos Wastes. This was his all-conquering force, and when the incursion of the foolish mortals was dealt with, he would sweep further south, sacking and burning, offering up thousands in sacrifice to the Dark Gods who had granted him such power and his immortality.

Looking with his daemonsight, Sutenvulf could sense the emotions that swirled across the bloodied glacier: the rage of the champions of Khorne; the fear of the Imperial knights as he swept towards them; the loathing of the weakling Sigmarite priest who hid behind the armour-clad horsemen; the ferocious, instinctual bloodthirst of the beastmen who hacked and slashed at the halberdiers protecting the Imperial clergyman.

The daemon prince savoured it all, landing in front of the knights with a great bellow. Opening up his immaterial form to the magical winds that poured from the north, Sutenvulf pulled the power of raw Chaos into himself, feeling invigorated and strengthened. He drew his sword, longer than a man was tall and forged with runes in the Dark Tongue, which twisted in on themselves when seen by mortal eyes, and held it above his head. Exerting some of the energy that coursed through his unnatural form, he pushed his power outwards, causing the blade of his daemon weapon to explode with flame. It seemed such a petty trick now, requiring the minutest amount of his power, but the thrill of dread that flowed from the knights and the surge of exaltation from his followers was justification enough for the simple parlour trick.

The knights spurred their horses forward, lances levelled, their steeds whinnying in terror yet hurtling at him under the unkind urging of their riders. Growling, Sutenvulf pivoted slightly on the ball of his right foot, balancing himself like the practiced swordsman he once was, his wings furling behind him out of harm's way. He raised his sword to the guard position in a mock salute of the knights thundering towards him, then leapt forward with a gargantuan stride, his clawed feet churning up red-stained snow. Lances shattered on his black-scaled hide, failing to pierce his immortal flesh, and with the speed of a lightning bolt, the daemon prince struck back, a snarl of satisfaction issuing from his throat.

The flaming blade carved off the head of the first knight, whose horse buckled and fell, passed through the upraised arm and then the chest of the next, the magical flames cauterising the wounds instantly, the sweet aroma of charred flesh filling the daemon prince's nostrils. The backhand sweep sliced a horse in half from shoulder to spine, its head and forelegs spinning into the air, the rider's thigh cleaved in two by the blow, his armour no defence against Sutenvulf's daemonblade.

Sword cuts and mace blows glanced harmlessly from the daemon's arms and torso, failing to cause even the lightest of wounds on his magical flesh. Two dozen more knights were carved to pieces by his fell sword, parts of them flung yards into the air, to topple amongst their comrades, panicking the knights and their warhorses.

Feeling their panic building, Sutenvulf extended his will once more, pushing out a wave of pure malevolence and hatred that washed over the Imperial soldiers in a tide of terror, causing them to falter. One leapt from his horse screaming, clawing at his visored face. Another was crushed as his horse reared and fell backwards, while the man next to him slipped from his saddle to his knees and began gibbering a prayer to his upstart god, Sigmar.

The knights routed en masse, fleeing before the daemon prince, whose guttural laughs echoed after them. The daemon turned his fiery gaze to the halberdiers and the priest who was mounted upon a fine white horse in their midst. He pointed his sword at the priest and uttered a command in the Dark Tongue. Either side of him, the animal-headed beastmen renewed their attacks, hurling themselves forward in a flurry of wild axe blows, flailing maces, gouging horns and biting fangs.

Then something stirred on the edge of Sutenvulf's daemon vision, drawing his attention away from the hapless priest and his bodyguard. The stench of impure faith was rank in the air as he looked about the battlefield, locating a white glow from which it emanated. Here was their champion, the Sigmarite lapdog who dared to defy the will of the Northern Gods. He would rip the upstart's head from his shoulder's with his bare hands and crush his skull with taloned fingers made strong by the power of the Chaos gods. He would teach the soft-bellied southerners what gods rule the lands, and what manner of warriors fought for them.

With spiteful glee in his heart, Sutenvulf once more took the skies on black-skinned wings and drifted on the waves of hate and fear, swiftly gliding over the mounds of the fallen. The Empire soldiers and their fawning Kislevite allies fled before his wrath, but the glowing figure of the Sigmarite champion remained. Anger flared through Sutenvulf's being at the audacity of the mortal, and he plunged down through the air, his sword ready for the killing blow.

Throwing up fountains of earth, ice and blood, the daemon prince landed before the Imperial leader and snarled a curse in the Chaos tongue; words that lashed the soul to the core. Yet the shining figure that confronted him remained unafflicted, standing resolutely, a two-handed hammer in their grasp. The daemon prince towered above his foe, fully three times taller, and spread his wings with a noise like the clap of thunder. He once more exerted his immortal power in a pulse of terror-inspiring magic, but still the figure remained motionless. Sutenvulf was intrigued, wanting to know more about this courageous mortal who glowed with unholy light. Leaving behind his gift of daemonsight, Sutenvulf looked upon his foe with mortal eyes. Looking at the pale, determined faced that regarded him coolly, there was a flicker of remembrance.

URSULA!

The maiden of Sigmar threw herself at the daemon prince, the hammer swinging through the air towards its chest. Contemptuously, Sutenvulf brought his flaming sword down, chopping the hammer in two and spraying droplets of molten metal into the air. Ursula threw the molten remnants of the weapon at the daemon prince's face and drew her sword.

'This is Ulfshard,' she snarled as Sutenvulf flinched from its holy light. 'It was created to destroy your kind.'

'You have lost none of your charm.'

With a hate-filled snarl, Ursula lunged forwards, Ulfshard spearing toward the daemon prince. Sutenvulf leapt into the air, wings beating, and hovered above Ursula.

'Coward!' she shouted, and the daemon prince laughed.

'Your efforts to resist are endearing, but futile. You cannot win.'

'Come down here and I'll prove you wrong,' spat Ursula.

'I do not mean whether you can defeat me. I mean your pointless resistance to my masters. You cannot defeat them, you cannot destroy them. They are as eternal as the universe. Why do you fight that which cannot be fought?'

'All evil can be overcome,' Ursula said.

Sutenvulf landed a few yards away.

'Chaos is not evil, it is elemental, it is everything. You might just as well declare war on the wind or the ocean. When you are long dead and your bones are not even dust, Chaos will still rule this world.'

'I don't believe you,' Ursula said. 'Faith is eternal.'

'You are wrong. I have seen the future, and it is Chaos. The fleeting lives of mortals are but flickering candles in the night sky. It is of no concern to my gods whether you fight or not. My death is inconsequential.'

'It is important to me to fight,' Ursula told him as the two began to circle each other. 'I have a choice, to fight or to surrender. You gave up. You lacked the strength and courage, and is the weak such as you who allow Chaos to endure.'

'Is it weakness to accept the desire of the gods? I am strong, revered, immortal. Who has lost? I did not surrender, I embraced my true destiny. You fight against the very thing that will make you great.'

'I am also strong, and revered,' she said. 'I have no need of immortality, for my actions will live in legend. When I slay you, your memory will be forgotten, your deeds worthless.'

Trumpet blasts sounded from the gates of Mursk and a long column of knights rode forth. The standards that flittered above them were embroidered in the colours of the Ostland and the Ostermark. Steinhardt had arrived. Five thousand cavalry charged into the remnants of Sutenvulf's army and the daemonic horde, carving a swathe half a mile wide with their lances and swords.

'Your army is defeated,' said Ursula. 'You have lost.'

'There are always other battles, other armies. Men die fast but they breed quickly. I have seen the end of the world, the coming of the Realm of Chaos, the End Times. The fragile cities of men and dwarfs and elves cannot stand against the power of Chaos. You cannot slay me. Ten, a hundred, a thousand lifetimes from now I will still exist. If you strike me down I will return.'

'And I will ensure that there will be someone like me to send you back to your masters,' snarled Ursula, racing forwards.

Sutenvulf's wings folded as he leapt aside from her overhead cut, laughing.

'You forget that I taught you to fight. You should thank me for keeping you alive all these years.'

'Get away from her!' a voice shouted.

Ursula saw Johannes galloping across the hill towards them. His armour was battered and blood-stained and his leg was heavily bandaged, his horse lathered with sweat.

'I can feel his love for you, it is very strong. Perhaps you should have cared more for him while you had the chance.'

'No!' screamed Ursula as Sutenvulf turned and snapped his wings open, gliding easily across the body-strewn snow towards Johannes. The would-be knight snatched something from his belt and threw it at the daemon prince, who instinctively slashed at it with his clawed hand. As the tattered remnants of the waterskin fluttered into the air, clear liquid splashed across Sutenvulf's arm and wing, burning like acid. He gave a roar of pain as his wing snapped and folded, sending him towards the blood-slicked ground.

'The waters of Taal, you bastard!' shouted Johannes triumphantly as Sutenvulf crashed into the piles of corpses, carving a furrow in the snow and rock. Johannes lowered his lance and charged, but the daemon prince reacted quickly, bringing his flaming sword around in a wide arc.

The flaming ruins of Johannes and his steed dropped smoking to the snows, sending up small wisps of steam. Pulling himself to his feet Sutenvulf bit back the pain that seared through him.

Ursula was running down the hill towards Sutenvulf, Ulfshard trailing blue fire behind her. Grabbing the sword in both hands, she swung at the half-crippled daemon prince, who brought his sword around to block the attack. Magical fire and sparks erupted where their blades clashed together.

'Why do you not accept that you cannot win, and give yourself over to the power that I know you can have?'

'Because I would rather die free,' said Ursula, thrusting Ulfshard forward. Again Sutenvulf parried, knocking Ursula to one knee. The daemon prince towered over her, sword raised. 'You are nothing more than a slave to darkness,'

'I am a willing servant; it is you who are the slave.'

'You exist for nothing more than to fight for your Dark Gods, to battle for their amusement,' said Ursula, rising to her feet.

The daemon smiled cruelly and brought his sword down. Ursula reacted just in time, throwing herself to one side. Rolling she swung with Ulfshard, all her faith and hatred directed through the sword.

Ulfshard carved into the immaterial flesh of Sutenvulf's chest, opening him up like a ripe fruit. Energy spilled from the shell of his body, like blood from the wound of a mortal. He did not cry out, or bellow in pain. His eyes seemed strangely calm as he fell to one knee, his flaming sword dropping from his grip. His face was level with Ursula's, eye to eye.

'And yet these past three years, it is you who that amused them the most.'

EPILOGUE
Osterreim, Spring 1713

THE ARMY WAS bedraggled, and pitifully small, their tattered black and white banners hanging limply in the drizzle that had turned the battlefield into a mire. Seated astride his warhorse, Count Vapold of Ostland watched the dreary scene with a sense of foreboding.

The winter had been harsh, Ostland's stores had been emptied for the march north. The joy of victory had been short-lived as his people had begun to count the cost. The army was all but shattered, barely a third of the men that had marched into Kislev returning to their homes. Starvation and disease had taken their toll, and against such foes all the power of Wolfenburg was for nought.

The Battle of Mursk had not ended the war, and heavily armed patrols had been left at the Kislev border as the scattered remnants of the Chaos host had continued south where they could, still intent upon exacting revenge for the raids against their people.

When spring had come, Vapold hoped that the new year would bring new hope, but it was not to be. As he had feared, the Ottila of Talabecland had moved against Ostland, sending armed bands foraying across the Talabec into Vapold's lands.

Sensing Ostland's weakness, Talabheim had then moved in force, capturing several villages and castles not far from the river dividing the two states. Vapold had been forced once again to muster the army and march to war, and here, at Osterreim, the two forces now met. He had sent messengers to Mordheim to request Steinhardt's assistance, and had gone to great lengths to explain to the Ostermark count the threat he was under should Talabecland seize power in Ostland, for surely the Ottila's gaze would turn eastwards before the year was out. As yet he had heard no reply, and so Ostland battled bravely on.

Vapold would be damned before he let Talabecland reach Wolfenburg, for surely such a retreat would only serve to fuel the Ottila's ambitions. He would make his rival retreat back to the Talabec or die in the attempt. He even hoped that the Count of Hochland, a long time vacillator trapped between the great powers of Ostland, Talabecland and Middenland, would send aid, even if he refused to break his convenient neutrality by sending troops.

The battle was desultory, almost embarrassing, as soldiers struggled through the muddle, the fizz of misfiring black powder filled the air and the regiments of the two forces were reduced to brawling in the sodden conditions.

Felsturm rode up, his heavy cloak damp and hanging tightly over the flanks of his horse. The captain guided his steed so that he was beside his count. He pointed to the south-east, where the road from Oster-reim wound between the dark forests. There were men, arrayed for battle, marching along the road. Above them flew standards of purple and yellow, the colours of the Ostermark.

'Bless Steinhardt!' said Vapold with the first happiness he had felt for many months.

They watched as the army spread out through the fields, climbing over walls and moving through gates to array their battle-line. As they marched, the regiments of Steinhardt turned to the north-west, towards Vapold and his army.

'He seems to be lining up beside the Talabeclanders,' Vapold said slowly, not quite believing what he saw.

'I believe we are undone, my lord,' said Felsturm, and Vapold noticed that it was not rain upon the captain's cheeks, but tears. 'We are betrayed.'

Northern Steppes, Summer 1714

THE SUN WAS shining bright, a great yellow eye in the face of the cloudless sky. The wind was cold, from the north, but the chill only served to invigorate Asdubar Hunn even further. The swaying grass of the steppes swept past as he rode on, the shouts of his warriors behind him.

The last year and a half had been good to him and his Hunn. After escaping the slaughter at Mursk, they had ridden north, looting a few villages on the way back to the Pass of Kings. His sons, now come of age, had started calling the campaign south the Golden Path of Asdubar. The hunting last summer had been particularly fine, for beasts and slaves. Few of the western tribes had returned from the south, and the Hunn had little competition for the prized elk herds. Those tribes that had returned had suffered badly, firstly during the battle and then from the vengeful pursuit of the shamed Kislevites.

They had been even easier pickings than the elk, and the slaves Asdubar had captured had numbered many times over the number of warriors he commanded. The stunted firemasters of the bleak lands to the south had been pleased and exchanged many fine swords and suits of armour for the slaves.

Now another rival had arisen. Upstart easterners, the slant-eyed Hung, had come, hearing that the west was theirs for the taking. Not here though, not on Asdubar's chosen ground.

Ahead, the Khannin riders formed up around their totem, a great net of golden wire attached to a standard pole, hung with the heads of the chieftains they had slain. For many days they had swept westwards, putting to the sword all that refused to bend their knee to their new chieftain, Hagrin. But they had made a fatal error crossing into Hunn lands, Asdubar thought.

He raised his spear above his head and kicked his heels into the flanks of his horse, urging it into a gallop. In his left hand he carried a shield marked with an eagle, a prized trophy from one of the Empire horsemen he had slain in the battle at Mursk. It was a good shield and had saved his life on more than one occasion.

'Let's show these Khannin dogs what manner of men follow Asdubar!' he cried.

'Asdubar!' his hundred warriors in response.

'These cowards do not know the brave deeds of the Hunn!' he shouted with a grin.

'The Hunn!' came the bellowed reply, heard clearly over the thunder of hoofbeats.

'From the steppes of our birth, to the towers of the Gospodar scum, we shall ever taste victory!' Asdubar yelled.

'Victory!'

Marienburg, Early spring 1715

THE THUNDER OF cannon fire reverberated along the hull causing the planks of the deck to shudder as the greatship fired a full broadside. To starboard, the Arabyan corsair disintegrated as the weight of iron crashed into her. Her lateen-rigged sail plummeted into the waves as her mast snapped. Gaping holes just above her waterline began to ship in the sea, causing her to sink fast.

'Secure guns!' Master Verhoen called out, satisfied that any further firing would simply be a waste of powder and shot.

'Bloody superb!' crowed Leerdamme from beside Verhoen on the quarterdeck. 'That'll teach those squint-eyed bastards!'

He showed little sign of the fatigue and weariness that had marked him when he had been released from the count's gaol two months ago. For two years he had resisted Luiten's demands, putting up with the potential for disease, the rank food and the loss of freedom to protect his principles.

Finally he had given in, a wandering soul trapped in a ten foot square cell, slowly going mad. He had needed to feel salt air on his face and feel a deck rising and falling beneath his feet.

He could have rotted away in prison, and none would have been the wiser. All this for helping Ursula escape with Ulfshard. It hadn't seemed such a bad idea at the time, but as the days became a week, the weeks became a month, and the month became a year, Leerdamme had suffered doubts.

His will had finally been broken by the rat. It had been a small rat, skinny in comparison to the beasts that inhabit a ship's hold. It had come into his cell each morning and Leerdamme thought he had befriended it with his crumbs of stale bread. Alas, the rat had better things to do and it had stopped visiting after a few weeks.

For some reason this had struck Edouard Leerdamme hard and he had finally relented. He had signed his name to a commission in the Marienburg navy and now flew the colours on his masthead. Perhaps the most galling, the most unprincipled concession had been the renaming of his ship. It had been this, more than anything else, which he had been loath to do, but in the end the count had even forced this out of Leerdamme.

Still a ship's a ship, he told himself. Better to be on the waves hunting these foreign devils than inside a room barely large enough to pace in. He was in high spirits as he walked to the lee side of the quarterdeck and stood watching the Arabyan coaster sinking stern first. Brightly coloured spots could be seen in the water where her crew had jumped overboard. Even now, Verhoen was ordering the longboat out to capture any survivors. Better to go down with the ship, Leerdamme thought, than hang by your neck.

Yes, any pirate would rue the day he ran into the Count Luiten...

Talagaad, Winter 1715

'FIFTY?' EXCLAIMED RUPRECHT, amazed at the man's audacity. 'It's worth five hundred if it's worth a shilling!'

'Then it's worth a shilling, 'cos I ain't got five hundred,' the pawnbroker replied. 'Go find someone else if'n yer lookin' fer that kinda money. I ain't got it.'

Ruprecht sighed.

'Two fifty?' he said. The pawnbroker laughed.

'The Shallya mission's two streets over if'n yer lookin' fer charity,' the pawnbroker said with a grimace. 'Alright, I'll gi' you seventy-five, last offer.'

'Look at it!' said Ruprecht. 'That's quality dwarf craftsmanship. That's the finest artisans around, you know. This isn't some tin knock-off from Marienburg, but quality blue steel from Karak Norn. Rune work, even.'

'It's rusted and squeaks,' said the pawnbroker, holding up the mechanical hand in his palm. He flexed a finger and the delicate gears inside turned stiffly. 'You ain't looked after it.'

'Try being a bloody boatman, out in all kinds of weather, and looking after a metal hand,' Ruprecht snapped back.

'Boatman, eh?' said the pawnbroker, and his expression genuinely softened. 'Bad business that storm, bad business. I hear near half of all them boats and lighters was sunk, can fair walk from one side of the river to the other on the wreckage.'

'Well, my bloody boat was one of them,' said Ruprecht. 'And it was a bad business, though not bad for business in your case, as I can see.'

'Seventy-five, or go somewhere else,' the pawnbroker said, placing the hand on the counter and crossing his arms.

'A hundred and fifty,' said Ruprecht. 'Come on, man, this is my livelihood we're talking about here. I need a new boat, and it's a bloody seller's market isn't it?'

'I need to make a livin' too, y'know,' the pawnbroker replied. 'Look, yer breakin' me heart with yer story of bravery and poverty, so I'll do you a favour and cut the hagglin'. You got hunnerd and ten for it, okay?'

'Hundred and ten crowns?' said Ruprecht with a grin.

'Good offer, take it or leave it,' said the pawnbroker, opening a drawer in the counter. He picked up the hand and waved it in Ruprecht's face. 'Sure you ain't gonna need it? Seems a shame to part with such a valuable 'eirloom.'

'It doesn't mean anything,' said Ruprecht, unconsciously rubbing the stump of his left arm. 'A hook'll be just as useful.'

The pawnbroker counted out the coins, a hundred and ten in all, and Ruprecht swept them off the counter into a small sack.

'Good doing business with you,' he said. 'Now all I need is to find a new boat.'

Skaldinghold, Winter 1721

THE FALLING SNOW did little to quench the excitement of the gathered tribesmen. They were dressed in their finest clothes, their mail shirts polished, their hair and beards ornately braided. They were dressed in brightly patterned leggings and heavy fur cloaks trimmed with gilded animal fangs and claws.

The warriors formed two lines facing each other, their swords, axes and spears raised to form an arch, along which the sons and grandsons of Hors Skalding carried his body upon a bier of woven leather. Over the wind the sound of a horn sounded along the fjord, echoing from the steep mountainsides across the waves.

The funeral possession passed beneath the raised weapons of Hors's kinsmen and arrived at his long-ship. It was stacked with piles of wood doused in oil and fat, and they swiftly carried the body along the gangplank and placed it at the foot of the mast.

The sun was just beginning to rise and the morning tide began to pull the waves from the shoreline. The funeral host returned their weapons to belts and sheaths and ran forwards to take their places around the ship. With a shout from Jurd, Hors's eldest son, they pushed as one, heaving the longship into the water, its keel cutting a furrow in the shale shore. As the longship began to float away, Jurd tossed a burning torch on to the deck, the flames quickly spreading to the sail and mast. He waded ashore in the wake of the others.

Wet from the surf, they assembled again on the shale beach in a line facing towards the burning ship. Jurd Skalding, new chieftain of the tribe, pulled his sword from its scabbard and raised it above his head. The tribe set up a great clamour, bellowing and roaring, clapping their hands and stamping their feet. Jurd shouted above the noise.

'Beware!' he cried. 'Beware those who live beyond the edge of the sea in the lands of the birthing sun. Hors Skalding comes to you, greatest of the Norse. In this, his thirty-second summer, he has lain down his soul for the gods to judge. And they shall judge him well. Great wealth has he brought his tribe. With his strong sword-arm and his wolfish cunning, he brought terror and desolation to his foes. The coffers of the southerners were his for the plundering, and he drew deeply of their generosity.

'Beware, souls upon the fiery waves in the realms of the gods, that Hors Skalding slew many foes. Chosen as champion to the great Sutenvulf, he led the armies of the gods at the Battle of a Thousand Winters. Though the gods did not grant us victory, a score of enemies fell to his blade as he escaped from their wrath.

'Beware those brave warriors who fell in brave battle, that Hors Scalding has long reigned over the seas, and his longship has brought dread across the known world. Hear now as we raise up our voices and cheer him into the land of the gods, where he shall sail forever, most blessed of our people, most favoured of our gods!'

The weak light of the sun broke over the fjord, glowing from the waters, which seemed aflame with reflections. In one last final salute, the men of the Skaldings drew their knives across their open palms and let their blood drip into the receding waters, a tribute to the gods so that they would welcome Hors Skalding into their eternal realm.

Mordheim, Early winter 1771

'THE NOVICES AND sisters train in the shrine itself,' said Magda Hauptstrecht, Matriarch of the Sisters of Sigmar.

She was with a young girl, less than ten years old, in Sigmar's Rock, a forbidding fortress-convent raised upon an island in the River Stir. She held the hand of her newest acolyte and led her across the tiled floor of the shrine, towards the statue of Sigmar at the far end. It was a wide open space where the sisters would stand in prayer and during hymnals, and where for much of the day they would practise the art of fighting, with whip and hammer and sword. It was empty now as the sisters of the order spread through the city of Mordheim performing their other duties of tending to the poor and the infirm.

From an archway to their right, a frail figure appeared, dressed in the white and red robes of an augur. She was old, ancient even, but she walked with her back straight and her head high, though her skin was heavily wrinkled, her head almost bald, her eyes rheumy. Magda stopped, reluctant to intrude upon the peace of the venerable sister.

'Who is she?' the little girl whispered. Magda crouched down next to her.

'I do not know, little one,' replied Magda. 'She was old when I was your age, and the matriarch who took me under her wing did not know her either. She has been here a very long time, perhaps even since the founding of Sigmar's Rock. She never speaks, and I think she is very sad.'

They watched in silence as the aged augur knelt before the statue of Sigmar and bowed her head in prayer. After a few minutes she rose and walked to the effigy and laid something over the hammer extended towards the centre of the shrine.

As she walked away, they could see that it was a small circlet of flowers from the gardens.

ABOUT THE AUTHOR

Gav Thorpe works as the Lead Background Designer of the Key Design team at Games Workshop, and so is one of the people responsible for the development of the Warhammer and Warhammer 40,000 universes. Dennis the mechanical hamster, having been scorned by his new lady, has now returned to the fold, but is still sulking.

More Warhammer from the Black Library

WILD KINGDOMS
by Robert Earl

A WEEK LATER and the pain from the fight had been replaced by the pain in Florin's backside. It had been a long time since he'd ridden a horse, but even then, it had been with the aid of a decent, well tanned saddle. Compared to the supple leatherwork he was used to, this one felt as though it had been carved from a block of teak.

But even if he'd been a trained cavalryman, riding along with the best saddle in the world, the pace that Domnu Chervez set would have been gruelling.

It started every day in the first grey light of dawn. Before the sun had even risen, the Strigany's women and the merchant's servants would crawl reluctantly from their wagons, coughing and a grumbling loud enough to drown out the birdsong. Huddled in ragged blankets they'd stumble about the camp, drawing water or shivering as they blew life back into their cooking fires.

Meanwhile, whilst the acrid smell of wood smoke mingled with that of honeyed porridge in the cold dawn air, the men would harness their oxen back to their wagons, whispering to them with a tenderness that their families could only dream of.

Then, with the sun still little more than a rumour beyond the black silhouettes of the mountains beyond, the day's journey would begin. The beat of the march was slow, but it was constant. The remorseless tread of the oxen stopped for nothing but a black thread that Domnu Chervez kept wound around his wrist. When the sky was so dark that this thread could no longer be seen against it, the caravan would stop.

Then, and only then.

And yet the trail oxen that pulled the wagons seemed perfectly content to grind along for hour after hour, day after day. Not only that, but so did the caravan's outriders. There were perhaps a dozen of them, two-man patrols that flitted around the caravan like bees around a hive.

It was only a matter of time before Florin and Lorenzo, both well-armed and mounted, were asked to join them.

'How about it?' the Domnu had asked them one night as they sat around his camp fire. 'We're coming up to the foothills now, which is where things start to get interesting.'

'Of course,' Florin had replied. 'We'd be glad to.'

And in fact, he had been glad to. Although picking his way through the wilderness was harder than just plodding along behind the caravan, it was also a lot more enjoyable. Even Lorenzo stopped grumbling, the better to study this land.

Although empty of human life, the rolling country-side was rich and bountiful. Fields of wild corn gave way to lush green meadows. Glades of autumn-ripened pear trees, their leaves alive with the buzz of insects, lay unguarded. Their fruit was left to rot where it fell, or was picked through by flocks of stringy looking hens.

Occasionally, they would come across the remains of abandoned villages. The stubborn angles of their walls remained standing and, despite the wisteria that softened their edges, defiant. There was no telling how long the derelict buildings had stood thus. Perhaps decades. Perhaps centuries.

Either way, the two friends hurried through them. Accidental shrines to a population long since washed away by bloody tides of war or plague, they seemed best left undisturbed.

And all the while, the mountains loomed larger in the east. Despite the clear skies and bright sunlight they remained black, as though permanently overcast by a shadow of their own making. Only their highest crests shone, white tips of ice scattered amongst the hazy clouds like pearls amongst wool.

As the weeks passed the mountains drew nearer. The ravines that splintered their craggy hides could be seen with the naked eye, as deep as the wrinkles of a crone's frown. Florin, frowning himself from saddle soreness and sunburn, was staring at them when they came across the ambush.

It was their horses who saved them. They'd been trotting along a shaded deer path, the passing tree trunks rippling the sunlight into zebra patterns on their coats, when they'd reared up in a sudden stop.

There seemed neither warning nor reason for the halt, and it came so unexpectedly that Florin was flung over his mare's neck.

He landed on his shoulder and rolled, cursing to himself as he tumbled through the undergrowth. The thorns scratched, but at least they broke his fall, and a moment later he was scrambling back to his feet. He turned to see that Lorenzo had seized his horse's bridle, catching her before she bolted.

'She's smelled something,' the older man said, keeping his voice calm as the horses shifted beneath him. Florin saw that he was right. Nelly's ears were laid back, her eyes white and rolling, her nostrils quivering as she sniffed at the breeze; he could almost see the fear rising off her.

'Wolves?' Florin suggested, matching Lorenzo's gentle tones as he went back to stroke her. Nelly whinnied and turned her muzzle into his hand, her ears lifting a little.

'Maybe.'

'The wind is coming from over that ridge,' Florin said, gesturing towards a rocky outcrop that cut across the path ahead. 'Tell you what, you hold on to Nelly here and I'll go and have a look.'

Lorenzo sucked his front tooth and looked doubtful.

'Maybe we should both go. It could be wolves. Then again, it could be anything. It could a dragon.'

'A dragon!' Florin scoffed uneasily, his voice lowering to a whisper.

'Who knows?' Lorenzo shrugged. 'Might as well say dragon as wolf. Why do you think all the villages hereabouts are empty? Do you think a few mangy old wolves would scare farmers away from land this good?'

Florin frowned, and looked again at the ridge. It looked a little like a dragon itself: a long, low shape that stretched through the forest. Then he sighed and turned back to Lorenzo.

'Probably not. But what can we do? We're supposed to be on patrol. We can't just go back because one of the horses jumped. No, I'll look. Just hold the horses ready. I want to sneak up on whatever they've smelled.'

'And if it sneaks up on you first?'

'Then we'll see if this still works,' Florin winked, and drew his pistol.

He'd bought it in Bordeleaux before setting out. It was expensive, ornately decorated, and heavy. It was also frighteningly inaccurate. Despite hours of practice Florin still couldn't hit anything farther away than twenty feet, unless the target happened to be a barn door. But even though he'd known of all these disadvantages when he'd bought it, the lure of blackpowder technology had been too much.

Besides, he thought, as he checked the firing pan and pulled back the wheel lock, it's powerful. The bullets could punch through steel plate as easily like it was rusted tin.

At least, they could if they hit it.

Returning the gun to its holster he padded quietly off through the leafy ground, his eyes already searching for handholds on the stone outcrop ahead. It wouldn't be a difficult climb, he could see that much. The surfaces were sloping and uneven, almost stepped, and creepers as thick as his wrist trailed across it like a tangle of ropes.

Slowing his pace, Florin began to slide his feet through the detritus of the forest floor, pushing it gently out of the way before stepping down so as to avoid crunching fallen twigs. Not that he believed in Lorenzo's dragon, he told himself, as he slowed his breathing.

Not at all.

He was just being cautious.

By the time he reached the outcrop his passage through the forest had become almost perfectly silent.

The stone was hot beneath his fingers, sun-baked despite the sweet scented breeze that blew across it. Florin crawled up it, pulling himself up ledge to ledge, his palms sticky as a chameleon's as he worked his way towards the top, damp with warmth and the effort of moving quietly.

The breeze whispered in the trees behind him, the sound as soothing as the stone was warm. As Florin climbed up to the last ledge he wondered if they should rest here. They could eat the frugal bread and water meal the Domnu had provided them with whilst arguing about imaginary dragons.

Then he crested the top of the outcrop, and suddenly he was no longer thinking of bread and water.

He was thinking of pork.

The sleeping herd below were surely wild boar, he decided. They certainly smelled wild enough. It was no wonder the horses had stopped; this close even Florin's nose wrinkled at the musk that rose up from their snoring bodies.

Cautiously flattening himself against the rock, he licked his lips and gazed down upon the animals. Their fur, as orange as the rusty bristles of a wire brush, was coarse and ungroomed, and their tusks were jagged.

Still, there was no reason to suppose that the flesh within it was inedible.

Florin, visions of pork chops sizzling in his imagination, counted twenty-three of the slumbering animals. As he did so he thought back to the last time he'd seen their like. That had been on the other side of the world, and in much less happy circumstances. Then, he had been the hunted, not the hunter.

Shuddering at the memory, he drew his pistol and, biting his lip with the effort of maintaining his silence, he slowly readied it. The single mechanical click of the wheel lock was lost beneath the grunting and snoring of the herd. Florin inched the hexagonal barrel forward, resting it along one arm as he wondered about which one to take.

A young one, he thought, but not too young. We want meat that's tender, but we want quite a lot of it.

It really was a shame that he only had one shot. If he shot the grizzled old tusker which was lying nearest to him, sprawled out as if already dead, the younger ones would run. But if he shot one of them, would they provide enough meat?

Torn between one target and the next, he hesitated. And in this moment of hesitation, the boars' owners appeared.

They loped into the clearing with a clumsy grace, rolling along like sailors on a pitching deck. The gait set their shoulders rising and falling, and their trailing knuckles swung back and forth like drummer's fists. Although man-tall they were heavier than humans; their blunt heads misshapen with mastiff jaws and their mottled green hides bulged with a deformed strength.

Some of the rags the creatures had stretched between their scraps of armour may well have been made for humans. Indeed, one of them was even wearing what could once have been the jacket from an Imperial soldier's uniform, the fine gold braid now as grubby as the strings of a mop.

But there was no mistaking these vile creatures for anything other than what they were. Not even for a moment. Even Florin, who'd never seen a live one before, knew orcs when he saw them.

He pressed his racing heart closer to the rock as more of them bundled into the clearing, and unhooked his finger from the trigger. Firing suddenly seemed like a very, very bad idea. In fact, perched above a clearing full of such beasts, even his breath seemed too loud.

The orcs were too intent on their business to hear him, though, or even to look up. As they dispersed amongst the herd, each seeking its own animal, the boars began to wake. And their mood, upon being woken up, wasn't sweet.

They squealed and snarled. They slashed their tusks at the legs of the orcs and at each other. One, a cunning old boar with a face that reminded Florin of Lorenzo, kept its eyes closed in feigned sleep, snoring away as the riders approached. It waited for one of the smaller orcs to wander within reach and then, when he was no more than a foot away, it struck.

The blunt daggers of its teeth tore a piece of flesh out of the rider's leg, a fist-sized chunk of green meat followed by a gout of dark blood. The orc howled with pain and staggered backwards, dancing about to the raucous laughter of his companions. The boar chewed contentedly as its victim stumbled away, its blood darkening the ground.

But a moment later, the wounded orc had recovered. Florin winced as he watched it grind a handful of dirt into its wound, carelessly staunching the bleeding before resuming the search for its boar.

By now, most of the orcs had found their mounts. Whatever savage bargain the beasts had struck amongst themselves, it was obviously an individualistic one. It also seemed to be strangely democratic: the boars allowed their chosen riders to roll up onto their massive shoulders because it was their will, not because they were in any way cowed or broken in.

Florin, his sweat dampening the stone, watched the chaos below gradually resolve itself. Once they were mounted, the orcs, each armed with a thick stabbing spear, milled restlessly about. Florin was seized with a terrible suspicion that they were going to round the outcrop upon which he was hiding and head towards Lorenzo and the horses.

But even as he wondered whether or not to make a run for it, the leader, its skin as dark as ivy beneath its rusted plate mail, bellowed an order. Before it had time to finish the call, his mount decided to leave. With an impatient grunt the boar turned and trotted off towards the north. The mob followed, a ragged stampede that crashed through the undergrowth in a graceless avalanche of snarling boars and cursing orcs.

Florin remained frozen as the noise of their progress faded. When it was no louder than the frightened chatter of the swallows that wheeled overhead, he turned and slithered back down to the forest floor.

'What was it?' Lorenzo asked as he hastened back to the horses.

'Trouble,' Florin said, wiping his palms before swinging back up into his saddle. 'Orcs. Dozens of 'em.'

'Ah,' Lorenzo nodded wisely. 'Orcs. I thought so.'

Ignoring Florin's raised eyebrow he turned and started to canter his horse back towards the caravan.

KROM HAD NO illusions about the men he was with. After only a couple of months in their lands, the ogre had no illusions about men at all. They were all weak, and most of them were cowards. He'd been shocked to see that even the most powerful amongst them, Mordicio, allowed a mere female to disrespect him.

And the fragility of their bodies... well, it would shame a gnoblar. The bruises that had covered Florin after his pathetically bloodless fight with the Strigany had lasted for more than a week.

Still, despite this healthy contempt, Krom wasn't fool enough to underestimate his travelling companions to the extent that they underestimated him. Humans, he knew, were intelligent. It was a strange, overly complicated sort of intelligence, and was just as likely to tangle up their planning as to facilitate it. But it was to be respected, just the same.

Take Domnu Chervez, Krom thought, turning back on the ox he was riding to study the Strigany. He was weaker than most with age, but he had more power in his head than many ogres did in their fists. He seemed oddly immune to the human disease of fear, too.

When he'd heard of the orcs that were gathering in the hills ahead, he'd just smiled.

Krom's face became blank with thoughtfulness as he remembered the scene. It had been evening when Florin and Lorenzo, their faces flushed and their horses winded, had brought news of the orcs. Within minutes, the entire caravan had gathered around them, the merchants fluttering about like a gaggle of frightened geese.

Chervez had waited for the fluttering to die down. Then, as confidently as if they were discussing something that had already happened, he'd told them exactly how they were going to deal with the orcs.

It was a good plan too, Krom reflected. So good that he'd seen no reason to open his mouth. Especially when every other traveller on the caravan had been doing just that.

Now, as morning drifted into afternoon, the ogre could see the place the Domnu had mentioned in his plan. It lay no more than half a mile ahead: a gap where the hills closed in on the trail like the posts of a cemetery gate. Oak trees, their foliage as thick as the hairs on his ox's back, covered the slopes of these hills, hiding the ambushers who waited there.

The leaves couldn't disguise their smell, though. To Krom's flattened nose, it was as sharp as an outhouse in high summer. He knew it for what it was too.

It was orcs. Full-grown orcs, and lots of them.

Some sort of animals seemed to be waiting with them, but he couldn't quite decide what they were. Goats, perhaps.

The sun sailed over the caravan towards the safety of the west, lengthening the shadows of the fifteen wagons and two horsemen who were following the ogre. The hills closed in towards them, as slow and eager as a pack of wolves surrounding a flock of sheep.

The smell of orcs became stronger.

Krom could already see where Chervez had guessed the attack would come. Up ahead, the trail wound through a meadow that was barely an acre across. On either side, the forested hills loomed as close as they could, the shadows they cast darkening the clearing.

As the caravan rolled into the clearing, Krom turned again to see that the wagons were keeping up and keeping close.

He knew that it was their fear, not their bravery, which kept the men following him into this trap. They knew they'd be safer facing the orcs this way than trying to outrun them. Even so, Krom half expected them to panic and flee.

Humans, he thought contemptuously, and lifted one leg to break wind.

A moment later, as though in answer to the obscene gesture, a harsh, discordant horn sounded out of the woods to their right. Krom stopped and squinted towards the treeline. Although the horn still rang out, the sound of it was lost in a sudden commotion. A noise of splintering branches, rumbling hooves, angry porcine squeals and fleeing deer.

But what it was mostly composed of was a terrifying chorus of inhuman warcries.

The noise of the boar riders' charge grew even louder as they crashed into the meadow. A terrible joy entered the orcs' voices as they caught sight of the caravan. It twisted their mouths up into snarls of glee, and the yellow slashes of their eyes narrowed with an unholy excitement.

Krom noted how the front-runners of this ragged charge leaned forward, lantern jaws hanging between the flapping sails of their mounts' ears as they closed in. The same bloodthirsty eagerness set them to swinging their short spears about in wild arcs, as if the weapons themselves were eager for battle.

Some of the spear tips were already bloodied, wet from accidental blows the riders had struck against their comrades. Two of the orcs were locked in combat after one such incident, the caravan forgotten as they tried to strangle each other beneath their boars' disgusted gaze.

But for the most part, the charge continued despite such distractions, the weapons continuing to whirl.

Krom swung to the ground, hefted his axe, and spared a single look down the line of wagons. The snapshot glance was filled with the blur of crossbow bolts and the sudden gleam of unsheathed steal. Contented, Krom turned all of his attention back to the task in hand.

And the task in hand was now. Despite their ungainly appearance, and despite the weight they were carrying, the boars had crossed the meadow with a frightening speed. Barely a minute had passed since their horn had sounded, yet already Krom found the anticipation of combat becoming reality.

With a bone-shaking roar he threw himself forward to embrace it.

If the nearest orc was surprised at this response it gave no sign. Instead it lowered its spear towards

Krom's belly, the tip of the weapon weaving back and forth as it hurled itself towards the ogre.

Krom waited, holding himself in perfect stillness until the steel was a second away from spitting him. Only then did he move, spinning his bulk to one side and seizing the spear in one fist.

The boar continued in its charge, snarling as it barreled through the space where the ogre had been. Its rider, however, instinctively refusing to let go of his weapon, was hoisted from its back and thrown up into the air.

Its warcry became a howl of surprise as it rocketed upwards, legs windmilling. Krom waited for it to begin to fall before he struck, swinging his axe in a one-handed blow that sent the falling orc's arm and its head tumbling into the grass.

The ogre grunted with the satisfaction of a job well done. Then he slapped his free hand onto the haft of his axe and turned towards the enraged squeal of his victim's boar.

There was no subtlety in the animal's attack. No strategy at all. It just barreled forward, tusks jutting up from the battering ram of its lowered head as it thundered towards the ogre.

Again, Krom made himself wait. Time stretched around him, a single second trickling past as slowly as a minute. At the end of it the boar was close enough to taste the cloth of the ogre's breeches. It bit down hungrily, but even as the muscles in its jaws were bunching Krom was moving, swinging away and cutting down in a single, liquid movement.

The axe blade rose and fell as easily as if it had been wielded by a servant splitting wood. As easily and as successfully. With a deep crunch the razored edge bit down through fur and skin, muscle and bone. Then it cleaved through the boar's skull, splitting its brain as neatly as a ripe apple.

The animal's squeal faded into a death rattle. Krom, with a wary glance around him, struggled to free his blade from the animal's carcass. But no matter which way he pulled it it remained stuck, trapped within the solid bone of the boar's skull. Even in death, it seemed, the foul-tempered beast was too stubborn to relent.

Krom felt a flicker of admiration for it as he abandoned his axe and picked up the orc's spear instead.

With a lick of his lips he searched for his next opponent, sniffing as eagerly as a hunting dog on the scent of its quarry. And there was plenty of quarry here, Krom thought contentedly, turning to select one. Most of them had made straight for the wagon train and were circling around the wagons, whooping with the joy of battle as the blood flowed.

Initially the high wooden sides of their carts had provided the travellers with some protection from the orcs' charge. Even now, most of the men remained perched on top of them, slashing down at the cavorting green figures.

Not all of the wagons remained, though. A couple of them, their oxen maddened with fear, had broken from the line and were now being dragged towards the opposite patch of forest, orcs in pursuit.

Another had been overturned. One of the barrels of wine it had carried had smashed open to bleed into the dust of the track. A boar was wallowing in the liquor, drinking greedily as its rider kicked at it and cursed.

Krom was about to go and put that particular orc out of its misery when, with a flash of movement, Domnu Chervez leapt into his line of sight. The Strigany hurled an empty crossbow at one of the attackers, then rushed forward to slash a cutlass across the nose of its mount.

It would have been a good tactic against a horse. The slash of pain across its muzzle would have been enough to send it rearing up in panic, probably throwing its rider down into a heap of broken bones. But against a boar the manoeuvre almost proved to be fatal. Far from frightening it, the pain just inflamed its temper.

With an almost human roar of anger, the animal lunged forward, its rider thrown off its back by the unexpected movement. Chervez leapt away from its first bite and scrambled back onto his wagon, losing the heel of his boot to the boar's snapping teeth.

The fallen orc, meanwhile, had scrambled back to its feet. Leaving its mount to distract the Strigany, it ducked under the wagon and popped up to attack the Strigany from the rear.

Krom saw its cleaver raise to strike, and threw his spear in a perfect, thoughtless reaction. The weapon hissed gleefully through the air. There was a meaty thump and the barbed tip punched through the orc's back and into the planking of the wagon. It scrabbled around as helplessly as a cockroach on a pin, howling in sudden terror as the ogre rushed forwards, drawing his belt knife.

Chervez felt the wagon shaking beneath him and looked up to see Krom's looming shape. The boar did the same. But it was a second too late; its teeth snapped on empty air as the ogre seized the wiry scruff of its neck and stabbed down between the first two vertebrae of its spine.

'Thanks,' the pale-faced Strigany shouted above the noise of the battle.

Krom, his own misshapen features now freckled with sprayed blood, dazzled him with a grin full of quartz.

Chervez was glad to see it. As gruesome as it was, he couldn't think of another face he'd rather see.

Then their smiles faded as, just as another wagon fell crashing onto its side, the forest burst asunder with a fresh tide of attackers.

What dangers lie ahead for Florin and Lorenzo in the mysterious and savage lands of the Ogre Kingdoms?
Find out in:
WILD KINGDOMS
by Robert Earl

Coming soon from
THE BLACK LIBRARY